Fourth Planet from the Sun

Previous anthologies from *F&SF*

Edited by Anthony Boucher and J. Francis McComas

The Best from Fantasy & Science Fiction (1952)
The Best from Fantasy & Science Fiction: Second Series (1953)
The Best from Fantasy & Science Fiction: Third Series (1954)

Edited by Anthony Boucher

The Best from Fantasy & Science Fiction: Fourth Series (1955)
The Best from Fantasy & Science Fiction: Fifth Series (1956)
The Best from Fantasy & Science Fiction: Sixth Series (1957)
The Best from Fantasy & Science Fiction: Seventh Series (1958)
The Best from Fantasy & Science Fiction: Eighth Series (1959)

Edited by Robert P. Mills

The Best from Fantasy & Science Fiction: Ninth Series (1960)
A Decade of Fantasy and Science Fiction (1960)
The Best from Fantasy & Science Fiction: Tenth Series (1961)
The Best from Fantasy & Science Fiction: Eleventh Series (1962)

Edited by Avram Davidson

The Best from Fantasy & Science Fiction: Twelfth Series (1963)
The Best from Fantasy & Science Fiction: Thirteenth Series (1964)
The Best from Fantasy & Science Fiction: Fourteenth Series (1965)

Edited by Edward L. Ferman

The Best from Fantasy & Science Fiction: Fifteenth Series (1966)
The Best from Fantasy & Science Fiction: Sixteenth Series (1967)
The Best from Fantasy & Science Fiction: Seventeenth Series (1968)
Once and Future Tales from The Magazine of Fantasy and Science Fiction (1968)
The Best from Fantasy & Science Fiction: Eighteenth Series (1969)
The Best from Fantasy & Science Fiction: Nineteenth Series (1971)
The Best from Fantasy & Science Fiction: 20th Series (1973)
The Best from Fantasy & Science Fiction: 22nd Series (1977)
The Best from Fantasy & Science Fiction: 23rd Series (1980)
The Best from Fantasy & Science Fiction: A 30 Year Retrospective (1980)
The Best from Fantasy & Science Fiction: 24th Series (1982)
The Best Fantasy Stories from The Magazine of Fantasy & Science Fiction (1986)
The Best from Fantasy & Science Fiction: A 40th Anniversary Anthology (1989)
Oi, Robot: Competitions and Cartoons from The Best from Fantasy & Science Fiction (1995)

Edited by Edward L. Ferman and Robert P. Mills

Twenty Years of The Magazine of Fantasy & Science Fiction (1970)

Edited by Edward L. Ferman and Anne Devereaux Jordan

The Best Horror Stories from The Magazine of Fantasy & Science Fiction (1988)

Edited by Edward L. Ferman and Kristine Kathryn Rusch

The Best from Fantasy & Science Fiction: A 45th Anniversary Anthology (1994)

Edited by Edward L. Ferman and Gordon Van Gelder

The Best from Fantasy & Science Fiction: The 50th Anniversary Anthology (1999)

Edited by Gordon Van Gelder

One Lamp: Alternate History Stories from Fantasy & Science Fiction (2003)
In Lands That Never Were: Tales of Swords and Sorcery from The Magazine of Fantasy & Science Fiction (2004)

Fourth Planet from the Sun

Tales of Mars from
The Magazine of
Fantasy&ScienceFiction

Edited by Gordon Van Gelder

THUNDER'S MOUTH PRESS
NEW YORK

Fourth Planet from the Sun

Tales of Mars from The Magazine of Fantasy and Science Fiction

Published by
Thunder's Mouth Press
An Imprint of Avalon Publishing Group, Inc.
245 West 17th St., 11th Floor
New York, NY 10011

AVALON
publishing group incorporated

ISBN 0-7394-5190-1

Book design by Jamie McNeely
Printed in the United States of America

This book is for Scott and Kevin Thomas—

if either of you gets to Mars, send me a postcard

Contents

Acknowledgments

A BIG THANK-YOU for this book goes to John Joseph Adams, whose contributions have been invaluable. Thanks also to Lisa Rogers, Cristina Concepcion, Russell Galen, Eleanor Wood, Christine Cohen, Barry N. Malzberg, Kay McCauley, Michael O'Connor, Betsy Steve, Kim Stanley Robinson, Byron Abrams, and the Chums on Fictionmags.

What we learn by sending astronauts into space is how humans can survive there. Let's be honest: We send humans into space for the adventure of it, not for science.

—Lawrence Krauss, Wired, *December 2003*

Introduction

Everyone knows that the reason we can observe planet Mars is because sunlight reflects off of it.

My premise for this book was going to be that in the same way the planet reflects sunlight, it reflects humanity back at itself. I had the book sketched out in my head:

From 1908 through the 1940s, Mars reflected dying empires back at us in the form of planetary romances—Edgar Rice Burroughs's Mars stories and their ilk.

In the 1940s and 1950s, Ray Bradbury reflected Mars back at us like a vision of life in the Midwest United States.

In the mid-1960s, the tradition of planetary romances died out as explorations of inner space took precedence, typified by Philip K. Dick's contribution to this volume.

Then in the later 1960s and in the '70s, as the *Mariner* and *Viking* flybys brought new scientific information about Mars, our whole concept of the planet was reshaped, with stories of stranded astronauts (like John Varley's "In the Hall of the Martian Kings") becoming dominant.

Then in the 1990s, stories about Mars became even more reflective as they concentrated on terraforming Mars—on literally trying to make that planet look more like our own. Kim Stanley Robinson's *Red Mars* trilogy is obviously the prime example of this trend.

And here in the new century, the stories seem to have shifted again to focus on celebrity and the media.

Well, guess what. As theories go, it's not a bad one, but when you look at the data closely, the picture is much more complicated. And with Mars back in the news again, thanks to *Spirit* and *Opportunity,* the two Mars Exploration Rovers that landed in January of 2004, the time seems right to collect these various stories and let you see for yourself how our perceptions and images of Mars have changed over the past fifty years.

For this book, I stuck with stories that go *to* Mars—there are no stories here about Martians invading Earth, nor even stories about making contact with Martians. Those stories, particularly the ones descended from H. G. Wells's *War of the Worlds,* strike me as belonging to a somewhat different tradition and deserve a book of their own. (In fact, Kevin J. Anderson edited just such a book in 1996: *War of the Worlds: Global Dispatches.*) This book's an outward bound volume, it's about us going there and not about them coming here. I think it's filled with adventure, romance, and a lot of great reading. I hope you agree.

The Wilderness

Ray Bradbury

"For years Mr. Bradbury has been writing about Mars, until his readers know that planet as well as the devotees of Sinclair Lewis know Zenith." Thus wrote our magazine's founding editors, Anthony Boucher and J. Francis McComas, in the second issue of F&SF. *Here is a bit more of their perceptive remarks from the header notes to one of Mr. B's stories:*

> It is difficult to classify the work of Ray Bradbury. There can be no question of his pre-eminence among our younger short story writers. He's thc "young" master and that's that. But no two Bradbury fans (ourselves included) can agree on just what type of story Mr. Bradbury tells best. . . . he does *everything* well.

Simply put, Ray Bradbury's Mars stories set the standard for many years—they were lyrical prose poems about humanity's first efforts to colonize the red planet and about the shape-changing Martians they encountered there. The stories were vivid and imaginative; they left an indelible mark on countless readers. Christopher Isherwood said of them that they have "the profound psychological realism of a good fairy story," and perhaps it's best now to view them in that manner, rather than by the standard of scientific realism. But remember that fifty years ago, our concepts of Mars were still shaped by Giovanni Schiaparelli's canals and by Percival Lowell's strident vision of Mars as a celestial Sahara. For readers who had grown accustomed to Edgar Rice Burroughs's tales of a heroic earthman dueling green Tharks and wooing the princess of another world, readers who never believed a human would set foot on the Moon, Mr. Bradbury's Martian tales were far more immediate. This story dates from 1952.

OH, THE GOOD *Time has come at last—*

It was twilight and Janice and Leonora packed steadily in their summer house, singing songs, eating little, and holding to each other when necessary. But they never glanced at the window where the night gathered deep and the stars came out bright and cold.

"Listen!" said Janice.

A sound like a steamboat down the river, but it was a rocket in the sky. And beyond that—banjos playing? No, only the summer night crickets in this year 2003. Ten thousand sounds breathed through the town and the weather. Janice, head bent, listened. Long, long ago, 1849, this very street had breathed the voices of ventriloquists, preachers, fortune-tellers, fools, scholars, gamblers, gathered at this selfsame Independence, Missouri. Waiting for the moist earth to bake and the great tidal grasses to come up heavy enough to hold the weight of their carts, their wagons, their indiscriminate destinies, and their dreams.

Oh, the Good Time has come at last,
To Mars we are a-going, Sir,
Five Thousand Women in the sky,
That's quite a springtime sowing, Sir!

"That's an old Wyoming song," said Leonora. "Change the words and it's fine for 2003."

Janice lifted a matchbox of food pills, calculating the totals of things carried in those high-axled, tall-bedded wagons. For each man, each woman, incredible tonnages! Hams, bacon slabs, sugar, salt, flour, dried fruits, pilot bread, citric acid, water, ginger, pepper—a list as big as the land! Yet here, today, pills that fit a wristwatch fed you not from Fort Laramie to Hangtown, but all across a wilderness of stars.

Janice threw wide the closet door and almost screamed.

Darkness and night and all the spaces between the stars looked out at her.

Long years ago two things had happened. Her sister had locked her, shrieking, in a closet. And, at a party, playing hide-and-seek, she had run through the kitchen and into a long dark hall. But it wasn't a hall. It was an unlit stair-well, a swallowing blackness. She had run out upon empty air. She had pedaled her feet, screamed, and fallen! Fallen in midnight blackness. Into the cellar. It took a long while, a heart-beat, to fall and she had smothered in that closet a long, long time without daylight, without friends, no one to hear her screamings. Away from everything, locked in darkness. Falling in darkness. Shrieking!

The two memories.

Now, with the closet door wide, with darkness like a velvet shroud hung before her to be stroked by a trembling hand, with the darkness like a black panther breathing there, looking at her with unlit eyes, the two memories rushed out. Space and a falling. Space and being locked away, screaming. She and Leonora working steadily, packing, being careful not to glance out the window at the frightening Milky Way and the vast emptiness. Only to have the long-familiar closet, with its private night, remind them at last of their destiny.

This was how it would be, out there, sliding toward the stars, in the night, in the great hideous black closet, screaming, but no one to hear. Falling forever among meteor clouds and godless comets.

Down the elevator shaft. Down the nightmare coal-chute into nothingness.

She screamed. None of it came out of her mouth. It collided upon itself in her chest and head. She screamed. She slammed the closet door! She lay against it! She felt the darkness breathe and yammer at the door and she held it tight, eyes watering. She stood there a long time, until the trembling vanished, watching Leonora work. And the hysteria, thus ignored, drained away and away, and at last was gone. A wristwatch ticked, with a clean sound of normality, in the room.

"Sixty *million* miles." She moved at last to the window as if it were a deep well. "I can't believe that men on Mars, tonight, are building towns, waiting for us."

"The only thing to believe is catching our Rocket tomorrow."

Janice raised a white gown like a ghost in the room.

"Strange, strange. To marry—on another world."

"Let's get to bed."

"No! The call comes at midnight. I couldn't sleep, thinking how to tell Will I've decided to take the Mars Rocket. Oh, Leonora, think of it, my voice traveling 60,000,000 miles on the light-phone to him. I changed my mind so quick—I'm scared!"

"Our *last* night on Earth."

Now they really knew and accepted it, now the knowledge had found them out. They were going away, and they might never come back. They were leaving the town of Independence in the state of Missouri on the continent of North America, surrounded by one ocean which was the Atlantic and another the Pacific, none of which could be put in their traveling cases. They had shrunk from this final knowledge. Now it was facing them. And they were struck numb.

"Our children, they won't be Americans, or Earth people at all. We'll all be Martians, the rest of our lives."

"I don't want to go!" cried Janice, suddenly.

The panic rose in her, with ice and fire.

"I'm afraid! The space, the darkness, the rocket, the meteors! *Everything* gone! Why should I go out there!"

Leonora took hold of her shoulders and held her close, rocking her. "It's a New World. It's like the old days. The men first and the women following."

"Why, why should I go, tell me!"

"Because," said Leonora, at last, quietly, seating her on the bed, "Will is up there."

His name was good to hear. Janice quieted.

"These men make it so hard," said Leonora. "Used to be if a woman ran 200 miles after a man, it was something. Then they made it a thousand miles. And now they put a whole universe between us. But that can't stop us, can it?"

"I'm afraid I'll be a fool on the Rocket."

"I'll be a fool with you." Leonora got up. "Now, let's walk around town, let's see everything one last time."

Janice stared out at the town. "Tomorrow night, this'll all be here, but we won't. People'll wake up, eat, work, sleep, wake again, but we won't know it, and they'll never miss us."

Leonora and Janice moved around each other as if they couldn't find the door.

"Come on."

They opened the door, switched off the lights, stepped out, and shut the door behind them.

In the sky there was a great coming-in and coming-in. Vast flowering motions, huge whistlings and whirlings, snowstorms falling. Helicopters, white flakes, dropping quietly. From west and east and north and south the women were arriving, arriving, their hearts neatly tissue-papered in their suitcases. Through all of the night sky you saw helicopters blizzard down. The hotels were full, private homes were making accommodations, tent cities rose in meadows and pastures like strange, ugly flowers, and the town and the country were warm with more than summer tonight. Warm with women's pink faces and the sunburnt faces of new men watching the sky. Beyond the hills rockets tried their fire, and a sound like a giant organ pressed upon all its keys at once, shuddered every crystal window and every hidden bone. You felt it in your jaw, your toes, your fingers, a shivering.

Leonora and Janice sat in the drugstore among strange women.

"You ladies look pretty, but you sure look sad," said the soda-fountain man.

"Two chocolate malteds." Leonora smiled for both of them, as if Janice were mute.

They gazed at the chocolate drink as if it was a rare museum painting. Malts would be scarce, for many years, on Mars.

Janice fussed in her purse and took out an envelope, reluctantly, and laid it on the marble counter.

"This is from Will to me. It came in the rocket mail two days ago. It was this that made up my mind for me, made me decide to go. I didn't tell you. I want you to see it now. Go ahead, read the note."

Leonora shook the note out of the envelope and read it aloud:

" 'Dear Janice: This is *our* house if you decide to come to Mars. Will.' "

Leonora tapped the envelope again and a color photograph dropped out, glistening, on the counter. It was a picture of a house, a dark, mossy, ancient, caramel-brown, comfortable house with red flowers and green cool ferns bordering it, and a disreputably hairy ivy on the porch.

"But, Janice!"

"What?"

"This is a picture of *your* house, here on Earth, here on Elm Street!"

"No. Look close."

And they looked again, together, and on both sides of the comfortable dark house and behind it was scenery that was not Earth scenery. The soil was a strange color of violet, and the grass was the faintest bit red, and the sky glowed like a gray diamond, and a strange crooked tree grew to one side, looking like an old woman with crystals in her white hair.

"That's the house Will's built for me," said Janice, "on Mars. It helps to look at it. All yesterday, when I had the chance, alone, and was most afraid and panicky, I took out this picture and looked at it."

They both gazed at the dark comfortable house 60,000,000 miles away, familiar but unfamiliar, old but new, a yellow light shining in the right front parlor window.

"That man Will," said Leonora, nodding her head, "knows just what he's doing."

They finished their drinks. Outside, a vast warm crowd of strangers wandered by and the "snow" fell steadily in the summer sky.

They bought many silly things to take with them, bags of lemon candy, glossy women's magazines, fragile perfumes (let the take-off weighers worry later about what constitutes "essential load"); and then they walked out into the town and not minding the expense, rented two belted jackets—two small machines that refused gravity and imitated the butterfly—and touched the delicate controls and felt themselves whispered like white blossom petals over the town.

"Anywhere," said Leonora, "anywhere at all."

They let the wind blow them where it would, they let the wind take them through the night of summer apple trees and the night of warm preparation, over the lovely town, over the houses of childhood and other days, over schools and avenues, over creeks and meadows and farms so familiar that each grain of wheat was a golden coin. They blew as leaves must blow before the threat of a fire-wind, with warning whispers and summer lightning crackling among the folded hills. They saw the milk-dust country roads where not so long ago they had drifted in moonlit helicopters in great whorls of sound spiraling down to touch beside cool night streams with the young men who were now gone.

They floated in an immense sigh above a town already made remote by the little space between themselves and the earth, a town receding behind them in a black river and coming up in a tidal wave of lights and color ahead, untouchable and a dream now, already smeared in their eyes with nostalgia, with a panic of memory that began before the thing was gone.

Blown quietly, eddying, they gazed secretly at a hundred faces of dear friends they were leaving behind, the lamplit people held and framed by windows which slid by on the wind, it seemed; all of Time breathing them along. There was no tree they did not examine for old confessions of love carved and whittled there, no sidewalk they did not skim across as over fields of mica-snow. For the first time they knew that their town was beautiful and the lonely lights and the ancient bricks beautiful, and they both felt their eyes grow large with the beauty of this feast they were giving themselves. All floated upon an evening carousel, with fitful drifts of music wafting up here and there, and voices calling and murmuring from houses that were whitely haunted by television.

The two women passed like needles, sewing one tree to the next with their perfume. Their eyes were too full, and yet they kept putting away each detail, each shadow, each solitary oak and elm, each passing car upon the small snaking streets below, until not only their eyes but their heads and then their hearts were too full.

I feel like I'm dead, thought Janice, and in the graveyard on a spring night and everything alive but me and everyone moving and ready to go on with life without me. It's like I felt each spring when I was very young, passing the graveyard and weeping for them because they were dead and it didn't seem fair, on nights as soft as that, that I was alive. I was guilty of living. And now, here, tonight, I feel they have taken me from the graveyard and let me go above the town just once more to see what it is like to be living, to be a town and a people, before they slam the black door on me again.

Softly, softly, like two white paper lanterns on a night wind, the women moved over their lifetime and their past, and over the meadows where the tent cities glowed and the highways where supply trucks would be clustered and running until dawn. They hovered above it all for a long time.

The courthouse clock was booming 11:45 when they came like spiderwebs floating from the stars, touching on the moonlit pavement before Janice's old house. The city was asleep, and Janice's house waited for them to come in searching for *their* sleep, which was not there.

"Is this *us,* here?" asked Janice. "Janice Smith and Leonora Holmes, in the year 2003?"

"Yes."

Janice licked her lips and stood straight. "I wish it was some other year."

"1492? 1612?" Leonora sighed and the wind in the trees sighed with her, moving away. "It's always Columbus Day or Plymouth Rock Day, and I'll be darned if I know what we women can do about it."

"Be old maids."

"Or, do just what we're doing."

They opened the door of the warm night house, the sounds of the town dying slowly in their ears. As they shut the door, the phone began to ring.

"The call!" cried Janice, running.

Leonora came into the bedroom after her and already Janice had the receiver up and was saying, "Hello, hello!" And the operator in a far city was readying the immense apparatus which would tie two worlds together, and the two women waited, one sitting and pale, the other standing but just as pale, bent toward her.

There was a long pause, full of stars and time, a waiting pause not unlike the last three years for all of them. And now the moment had arrived, and it was Janice's turn to phone through millions upon millions of miles of meteors and comets, running away from the yellow sun which might boil or burn her words or scorch the meaning from them, her voice like a silver needle through everything, in stitches of talking, across the big night, reverberating from the moons of Mars and rushing on. And then her voice found its way to a man in a room in a city there on another world, five minutes by radio away. And her message was this:

"Hello, Will. This is Janice!"

She swallowed.

"They say I haven't much time. A minute."

She closed her eyes.

"I want to talk slow but they say talk fast and get it all in. So, I want to say—I've decided. I *will* come up there. I'll go on the Rocket tomorrow. I will come up there to you, after all. And I love you. I hope you can hear me. I love you. It's been so long . . ."

Her voice motioned on its way to that unseen world. Now, with the message sent, the words said, she wanted to call them back, to censor, to rearrange them, to make a prettier sentence, a fairer explanation of her soul. But already the words were hung between planets and if, by some cosmic radiation, they could have been illuminated, caught fire in vaporous wonder there, her love would have lit a dozen worlds and startled the night side of Earth into a premature dawn, she thought. Now the words were not hers at all, they belonged to space, they belonged to no one until they arrived, and they were traveling at 186,000 miles a second to their target.

What will he say to me? What will he say back in his minute of time? she wondered. She fussed with and twisted the watch on her wrist, and the light-phone receiver on her ear crackled and space talked to her with electrical jigs and dances and audible auroras.

"Has he replied?" whispered Leonora.

"Shhh!" said Janice, bending, as if sick.

Then the voice came through space from him.

"I hear him!" cried Janice.

"What does he say?"

The voice called out from Mars and took itself through the places where there was no sunrise or sunset, but always the night with a sun in the middle of the blackness. And somewhere between Mars and Earth everything of the message was lost, perhaps in a sweep of electrical gravity rushing by on the flood tides of a meteor, or interfered with by a rain of silver meteors. In any event, the small words and the unimportant words of the message were washed away. And his voice came through saying only one word:

". . . love . . ."

After that, there was the huge night again and the sound of stars turning and suns whispering to themselves and the sound of her heart, like another world in space, filling her earphones.

"Did you *hear* him?" asked Leonora.

Janice could only nod.

"What did he say, what did he say?" cried Leonora.

But Janice could not tell anyone, it was much too good to tell. She sat, listening to that one word again and again, as her memory played it back to her. She sat listening, while Leonora took the phone away from her without her knowing it, and put it back upon its hook.

Then they were in bed and the lights out and the night wind blowing through the rooms a smell of the long journey in darkness and stars, and their voices talking of tomorrow, and the days after tomorrow which would not be days at all, but day-nights of timeless time; their voices faded away into sleep or wakeful thinking, and Janice lay alone in her bed.

Is this how it was over a century ago, she wondered, when the women, the night before, lay ready for sleep, or not ready, in the small towns of the East, and heard the sound of horses in the night and the creak of the Conestoga wagons ready to go, and the brooding of oxen under the trees, and the cry of children already lonely before their time? All the sounds of arrivals and departures into the deep forests and fields, the blacksmiths working in their own red hells through midnight? And the smell of bacons and hams ready for the journeying, and the heavy feel of the wagons like ships foundering with goods, with water in the wooden kegs to tilt and slop across prairies, and the chickens hysterical in their slung-beneath-the-wagon crates, and the dogs running out to the wilderness ahead and, fearful, running back with a look of empty space in their eyes? Is this then how it was so long ago? On the rim of the precipice, on the edge of the cliff of stars. In their time the smell of buffalo, and in our time the smell of the Rocket. Is this then how it was?

And she decided, as sleep assumed the dreaming for her, that yes, yes indeed, very much so, irrevocably, this was as it had always been and would forever continue to be.

Mars Is Ours

Alfred Coppel

Here's one of those stories that throws off my great overarching theory of how stories about Mars have evolved—a vision of the red planet that owes nothing to the scientific romances of Burroughs and everything to Mars, the god of war.

Alfredo José de Marini y Coppel, Jr. was a fighter pilot during World War II and published his first story in 1947. Over the years, he wrote two dozen novels, including thrillers such as Show Me a Hero *and* Thirty-Four East, *and science-fiction novels such as* Dark December. *His most recent books are the three in the "Glory" series:* Glory, Glory's War, *and* Glory's People. *He lived in California until his death in 2004 at the age of eighty-three.*

THE RED DUNES woke to the morning sun. The stars dimmed, but did not fade before the dawn. Light touched the mare's tails of high ice clouds and turned them pink against the great cobalt sky. To the far west, the eroded hills along the edge of Syrtis came alive with brilliant yellows and sere browns.

The long column of armored vehicles, insectlike in the vast emptiness, inched northward. The sound of their engines faded quickly in the thin, cold air and the drifting iron sands swiftly covered the tracks of the steel cleats.

Marrane woke from fitful slumber in his tank. The tiny reading light was still on and the book of plays lay open across his chest. He glanced at the clock in the footing of the tank and wondered if he had slept at all.

He rubbed a hand across his stubbled face and fought down the familiar clamoring terror of waking. He forced himself to lie back and relax, letting the undulating movement of the Weasel soothe him.

—this is real, he thought. Steel and rivets and the steady chugchugchug of the air compressor. Forget the nightmare of sticky, fear-ridden plains stretching out and out forever. *And lay off the luminol.*

He felt sodden with the residue of the drug, thick in the mouth and eyes with it. Corday would have to give him something else. He was building up a tolerance for luminol, and it wasn't driving away the nightmares. Corday would have to come up with something different. Something out of a bottle to buy a few hours' rest and sleep without dreams. He couldn't lead men into battle feeling this kicked out inside—

The communicator light flashed. "What is it, Sergeant?" he asked heavily.

"0600 hours, Major." Grubich's voice sounded tinny through the grille. "We're starting to climb the shelf. You asked me to call you."

"Very well, Sergeant."

—out of the coffin, he thought. Out of the coffin and back to life. For God's sake *why?* Another endless day crawling across the endless, featureless desert. He thought of blue lakes and the sea again. How long had it been? Years now. Not that it mattered.

He slipped on his respirator and decompressed the tank. The latches didn't stick, thank God. He had a horror of that happening.

The interior of the Weasel was icy and Marrane shivered naked on the pitching deck. He wondered about shaving and decided against it. What water there was would be frozen, and he had no decent blades left. The power shaver had been ruined by the sand months ago crossing Syrtis. All supplies were getting short—like sand running out in a glass. They'd have to make contact soon or the Task Group would fall apart of its own dry decay. *All hail the conquerors—*

Grubich stuck his cropped head around a bulkhead and asked: "Did you say something to me, Major?"

"No," he said sharply. "Carry on."

Grubich's head vanished with a muttered yes, *sir.*

Marrane dressed slowly. Each movement seemed an effort. He wondered whether it was the dry cold and the low pressure and the canned air. Or was it himself?

—I'm thirty, he thought. Not old. But I feel old. Tired and sticky, somehow, and when I look out at the desert, I feel very small.

He thought of the play he had been reading last night. One of the proscribed authors, but it didn't seem to matter much up here. Graylist, Blacklist. The Loyalty Boards. They all seemed far-off and unreal across the gulf of night. But the play had troubled him. Steinbeck, or some such name. And the title so apt as the line of Weasels crawled their way across the Martian plain through the star-shot darkness. *The Moon Is Down.* About invaders in a war that was forgotten now in a place he'd never heard of. Yet there was a frightening phrase in the play. One that brought on the nightmare again in spite of the luminol. Perhaps it had been wise to keep such a book out of the hands of civilians.

He shook his head wearily. It showed the way discipline was breaking down in the Task Group when an officer could lend a Graylist book to his commander without a twinge of conscience or fear. But my God, he wondered, what else can be expected after ten months on this desert looking for a Cominform Base that might not even exist. He told himself that he must remember to thank Hallerock for lending him the book.

From the galley came the smell of burning synthetic proteins. The stoves never had worked properly here under seven pounds air pressure. Nor had the engines—gasping for breath in spite of all the huffing and puffing of the superchargers. Nothing worked properly. Nothing but the guns. And there was nothing to shoot at.

—all hail the conquerors, he thought again, sardonically. Mars is ours. Marzizarz. It made just as much sense that way and it had the sound of officialese. He found himself smiling idiotically at the thought, Marzizarz.

"Crest ahead, Major," Grubich called.

Marrane stopped smiling and finished dressing hurriedly. His heart was pounding when he took a grip on himself.

—I'm going sand-happy, he thought, and so is every other man in the Task Group. Something basic was wrong with all this—the military vehicles trekking endlessly across the face of a world that had been quiet and dead and at peace for ten times ten million years. We should have come here for some *other* reason, he thought.

He stumbled onto the bridge and stood behind Grubich and the driver.

Behind the lumbering 200-foot machine, he could see the rest of the group strung out behind, following blindly across an endless wasteland of iron sands, radar antennae rotating with idiot military precision, searching for an enemy where none but the bitter frozen land could be seen.

He checked the course and climbed to the navigation deck, his boots gritting on the sand that drifted everywhere in the Weasel. He checked the guns as he went by, making sure they were muzzled and protected against the abrasive rusty filth.

At the chart table he checked the column's position with young Hallerock, a gaunt and skeletal caricature of the trim officer who had left Mars Base almost a year ago.

—this patrol has to end soon, Marrane thought, the men can't last much longer.

"Sparks got the radio fixed last night, Major," Hallerock said.

Marrane's eyes widened. He felt an illogical stab of anger. "Why wasn't I told?" he asked.

Hallerock refused to meet his eyes. "We couldn't raise Mars Base, sir. And Captain Corday said you shouldn't be disturbed until we could."

"I see."

Hallerock looked oddly at him. "Do you, sir?"

"They can't be guarding our channel all the time," Marrane said. And even as he said it, he knew it wasn't so.

"We've had no contact for three months, Major," Hallerock said unsteadily.

"And what does that mean, Mister?" Marrane asked, frowning.

Hallerock didn't answer. In the stillness, the thrumming beat of the engines was all that lived.

—no, Marrane thought, don't say it. Don't even think it. They'd not leave us here. And then: If they hadn't been so damned frugal with the equipment, it might have been different. It was insanity to send a column out on patrol with only the lead Weasel equipped to contact Base. But equipment cost money. And all the money went into the pounds of plutonium and lithium hydride that rested quiescent in the once shiny now rusty shells waiting to be fed to the guns. The killing matériel was ample; it was only the saving stuff that was in short supply.

"How far have we come, Mister Hallerock?" Marrane asked brusquely.

Hallerock tapped his charts. "Nine thousand miles, sir. We've quartered almost all of Syrtis and a good bit of Solis, too."

Marrane's mouth felt dry. "How far are we from Mars Base now?

"Eight hundred miles, Major," Hallerock said, and then added: "Within easy radio range."

"Has Sparks picked up the beacon?"

Marrane fought back the clamoring fear. "They are probably keeping radio silence. Things may have worsened back home."

"Yes, sir. It might be that."

The commander turned from the gaunt face to look out at the iron sands. The Task Group was approaching a line of low hillocks, windworn rock outcroppings covered with lichens. Reefs of a long-ago sea.

—old he thought. Empty. And alone. The end was getting near. Another 800 miles and Mars Base. They had to be there waiting. The thin spire of the ship pointing at blue lakes and the sea. Just 800 more miles of silence and desert and silted, dead canals. And an end to the hostility of the silent land. They couldn't have deserted us, Marrane thought. They *couldn't* have done a thing like that.

He turned away toward the bridge and stopped suddenly. "Thanks for the book, Evan," he said.

"You read it, sir?"

"I read it."

"We're flies, aren't we?"

Marrane frowned at the drawn face. "You'd better see Corday," he said.

Hallerock laughed. The sound was eerie though the filter of his respirator. "We've conquered the flypaper. Remember *The Moon Is Down?* You did read it?"

"I read it, Mister," Marrane said. "We haven't conquered anything. Not yet."

Hallerock rose unsteadily, rocking on the balls of his feet. There were tears running down his cheeks and he shook with unholy mirth, but he wasn't making a sound. Marrane stood looking at him, numb with shock, knowing his navigator was mad.

They were standing so when the battle alarm shrieked through the steel labyrinth of the Weasel.

"Get to your station, Mister," Marrane shouted at the navigator. Hallerock sat down again and started sobbing.

"Major Marrane!" It was Grubich calling from the bridge. "A contact, sir! Russkis just over the hill! We've found the nest of them!"

"Stay put, Evan," Marrane ordered and ran down the companionway, his steel-shod boots ringing on the deck.

The gunners were unlimbering the guns and Marrane slipped into the conning tower, buckling on his headset.

"Plan B. Weasel Able to Group. Plan B."

Grubich was at his side, binoculars extended. "They're just over the ridge, Major. We almost stumbled into them."

Marrane cursed the thin air of Mars that wouldn't support aircraft. The Cominform Base was in defilade and the Group would have to spread out along the ridge to bring the enemy under fire. An armored attack against fortified positions without air support was always deadly.

—nothing can go wrong now, he thought bitterly. Not here, so close to home. And then the torturing doubt began eating at him. Was there still a Mars Base? Maybe the Russkis had wiped it out. Raw hate was tearing at his insides, but he felt alive for the first time in almost a year.

The Weasel crawled up the ridge and stopped just short of the top. "Scouts out," Marrane ordered. "Team Six."

A squad of Marines tumbled out of the last Weasel in the column of six and started over the crest in a skirmish line.

The squad leader's walkie-talkie cut through the static in Marrane's headset. "No hostile action, Major. I see a group of prefabs and a few light tanks. There's quite a bit of milling about. I think we have them cold."

The memory of years of soldiering rose up inside Marrane to clamor a warning. One couldn't be sure. Intelligence was always faulty. The evidence of one's own eyes could be a lie. Maybe there was a Russki tank column just under the hillcrest to the north. Waiting. This could be an ambush.

"Let's see," he muttered. "Have the forward elements move up. Weasel Charlie to load fissionables. Dog and Baker into line abreast on the ridge."

Am I being too cautious, he wondered. Have all these endless weeks of sand and stillness drained the marrow out of my bones? We can strike quickly and win. He felt a sudden hysteric laughter bubbling just under the surface of his mind. The Cominform Base was under their guns. Grouped like a field problem around the blackened field where the Russki rocket towered over the shabby buildings. Ground zero. Epicenter. The terms from the field manuals were so inexpressive, he thought vaguely. What did ground zero have to do with a fireball at a million or two degrees centigrade? Maybe the zero part made sense. Zero for the Russki and it would be ended. Marzizarz marzizarz—*stop it!*

He dug his hands into the pockets of his parka, clenching his fists, letting the pain of his fingernails on the palms steady him. He could see the people pouring out of the prefabs to look at the line of Weasels that had materialized out of the dark morning on the ridge.

—they're helpless, Marrane thought.

He could hear his orders being relayed to the Task Group. Weasel Charlie was complaining of some trouble with its fission bomb. Marrane fought down his irritation and let Charlie finish the report.

"How long to clear your trouble?" he asked.

The radio crackled with static.

"How long, God damn it?"

"Ten minutes, sir."

Ten minutes. What were ten minutes in ten years—twenty? He could give them ten minutes of life, he thought, looking down at the frightened figures on the sandy plain. Odd, he thought. They look almost human. Strange to see something so familiar in this endless, whispering desolation.

The Marines were spaced out along the ridge in a skirmish line, digging themselves into the sand as though expecting an attack by infantry. We go by the book, Marrane thought. We always go by the book. And the men who wrote the book went by the book, too—and so on, down the endless mirrored halls of time back to Cain killing Abel and even beyond that to the ancestral memory of grisly delight as stone axe crushed blood and bones into the slime. "Tank moving up, Major," the squad leader called.

—time, Marrane thought. Ten minutes and we'll be done with this. "Track it," Marrane said to the gunpointer. "Weasel Charlie—how are you coming?"

"Getting it cleared now, sir."

He wondered briefly if he should have assigned Dog or Baker to fire the fission shell—but no, this playing with time was oddly appealing. And if there were a Russki column coming up, it would give them time to arrive and share in the warmth of the fireball. Risky, very risky. Not according to the book. Blacklist, Graylist, Marzizarz. God, how tired I am, Marrane thought.

"White flag, sir," said Grubich.

"Stay on them," Marrane said to the gunpointer. "Able to Group. Lay your guns on the camp, but hold your fire until we see what's happening here. If anyone makes a move toward that rocket, blast them. Able to Charlie. How much longer?"

"Five minutes or less, Major."

He stood indecisively, weighing life or death. Why the white flag? Bargaining for their lives? With what? He had them cold. The book said kill them wherever you find them.

He glanced at Grubich. The sergeant's eyes were intent on him. How would this hesitancy look to a Loyalty Board? Bad—very bad.

"Fire when ready, Charlie," he said slowly.

"Yes, sir."

"The book always wins, Grubich," he said. "Did you doubt that?"

"I'm afraid I don't understand the major," Grubich said.

Life or death, Marrane thought. I can still play God. I could change my mind.

No one moved in the camp. The tank rumbled up the slope, red sand streaming from its cleat tracks. Its long gun was pointed at the ground, and a white steamer fluttered in the thin air. It reached the skirmishers and two heavily padded figures dismounted.

"Bring them in," Marrane ordered.

Somewhere, up on the navigation deck, he imagined he could hear Hallerock still sobbing. Flies conquering flypaper—

The two Russkis, masked against the cold and clumsy in quilted uniforms, clambered through the hatch. Marrane saw the smaller of the two wore the collar tabs of a colonel. The colonel's companion was a sergeant, armed.

"Get that burp gun," Marrane snapped.

Grubich snatched the weapon away and pushed the Russki into a corner of the bridge.

"Get my tank ready, Grubich," Marrane said. "We'll talk inside."

"Recorder, too, Major?"

"Yes, get it all down." Since there was room only for two in the sleeping tank, it wouldn't do not to have a permanent record of everything said that could be run off for the Loyalty Boards back home.

—home, Marrane thought. Blue lakes, the tossing green of the open ocean.

He gave fire control to Wilson in Weasel Dog and led the way to the tank. Grubich stuck the muzzle of the burp gun hard into the Russki sergeant's middle. "You stay put, you red bastard."

The colonel seemed about to protest, but apparently thought better of it and followed Marrane into the tank. Marrane started the compressor. When the pressure stood at eleven pounds, he removed his mask and indicated the Russki should do the same. He watched the operation, letting his hand rest on the icy grip of his automatic. Suspicion, he thought. The book says they're treacherous. One move and I'll blow a hole in the bastard's head.

The mask came away and Marrane sat looking at a woman of about thirty. A thin face, with high cheekbones and hollows under them. A tired face, with reddish, sandy grime worn into the skin, pale eyes and prematurely gray hair.

"I surprise you, Major?" She spoke English with only a faint accent.

"Not really."

"No," she said. "There are few taboos left on our side of the line."

"Very enlightening," he said. "Are we here to compare political systems?"

She shook her head slowly. "Why are we here?"

—I can't answer that, Marrane thought. There's the recorder to think of. And even if there were not—what could I tell her? That war is part of the intercourse of the human race? Should I quote Clausewitz to her? Here? Thirty million miles from lakes and rivers, from home—?

"Your base is under my guns," he said.

—that's according to the book, he thought. Formal. Stern. And a hundred yards away, the rusty shell casing would be in the lift, its blunt nose seeking the breech of Charlie's rifle, caressing the lands and grooves, tasting them voluptuously with its fuse, feeling the eager grains of powder behind it as the breech lock slammed shut and the gunpointer spun his oily wheels and the muzzle came up searchingly, ready to spit the fireball at a mass of flies trapped on an endless plain of blood-colored flypaper—

He glanced at his watch. Two minutes. Certainly not more. She caught his meaning and bit her lip. "You can't," she said. "Surely you can't. We are surrendering."

—but the Task Group wasn't equipped to take a surrender, Marrane thought. It was equipped only to destroy. To carry out its Directive. Blast the Cominform Base.

"Give the order not to fire. Tell your men we are their prisoners," the colonel said hoarsely.

"I cannot accept a surrender," Marrane said. It was as though a voice other than his own had spoken. Astonished, he felt his hand tighten on the grip of his pistol.

She looked down at the weapon. "But no, you would kill me? Why, in God's name? I came to you under a white flag to surrender my command? Is there no way I can touch you?"

"You can try. I haven't seen a woman in almost a year—"

—time, one minute now. Or less.

She pulled off her helmet and unbuttoned her tunic. She was a handsome woman in spite of the weariness and the grime.

"It won't do any good," he said.

Her hands dropped wearily into her lap. She seemed drained of life. Her eyes opened again and she saw the book of plays on the still-rumpled bed. "Steinbeck—an angry man," she said.

"He seemed to be," Marrane said. "He hated anything that destroyed human dignity."

She began to laugh, soundlessly, as though the spasms were painful.

"We've come so far."

"Far?"

"Yes, far. Far enough to forget what it was that we were sent here to do." She was shaken by a sudden shudder, as though she had looked into the face of chaos. "I wish I had forgotten it sooner. Oh, God, how I wish I had forgotten it sooner!"

—either she is mad, or I am, Marrane thought.

"We came here so full of hate," she said. "But what does it matter? We are only men and women against the bitter land. Can you forgive what I have done? Can I, I wonder?"

—this is all wrong, Marrane thought, I shouldn't have these doubts. But maybe it was more than just doubt. Maybe war had no place here on this silent, empty, world. We should have come here to do something better than kill. But we are in a cul-de-sac, trapped by what we are.

They sat close together in the tiny tank, listening to the chugging of the air compressor.

"Give the order," she whispered. "While there is still time."

—yes, he thought. Yes. I'll give the order because she's worn and as sick of this icy loneliness as I am.

She moved closer to him.

"Major—Major!"

He scarcely heard Grubich's voice, frantic in the speaker grill.

"Don't listen," she said softly.

"*Major!* We've picked up radioactivity. The stinking bastards have hit our Base! Major!"

The thought tumbled crazily through Marrane's mind. How long ago? It could have been days, or minutes. Terror and revulsion came throbbing up into his throat and he pushed the woman away.

"Three days ago," she said, her face suddenly shut tight.

Marrane was on his feet, strapping his respirator into place. He flung open the hatch of the tank, filled with a corroding, acid hatred. He flung the woman out into the subzero cold ahead of him, watching the agony on her face as she gasped for breath. "Slut," he breathed. "Rotten red slut—"

He left her crumpled against a bulkhead and clattered across the steel deck. He could hear her faint voice, barely more than a whisper. "I—had—to—do—it—" And then it faded to less than a sigh and was heard no more.

—yes, she had to do it. Just as he must watch while the ground rumbled and the white-hot fireball blossomed in the camp, consuming it, vaporizing it.

The shock wave hit the Weasel and he braced himself against it. Grubich was shouting: "*We got the filthy muckers—every last rotten soul of 'em! Die, you bastards!*"

The rumbling died with surprising quickness. The dust cloud fell in the thin air. The silence came again. For what seemed a long while, Marrane stood staring at the spot where the Russki rocket had been. The last link with home? But how could he know?

—how could he ever know?

In a dull, muffled voice he gave the orders and the Task Group wheeled and took up its search formation again.

Marrane thought:—Hallerock. He might have the answer. Only a madman could give meaning to this ugliness that so briefly disfigured the icy quiet peace of this frozen land.

He opened the hatch to the navigating deck and stood rocking in the doorway. He had his answer.

Hallerock's feet hung a few inches above the deck. He swung gently to and fro with the undulating movements of the Weasel. Back and forth, to and fro, east and west—

Marrane began to laugh. Here it is at last, he thought. We've done it. Mars is ours. The flies have conquered the flypaper. The flies, oh, God—

His shoulders shook helplessly and tears streaked his cheeks. The sound of his laughter penetrated the steel flanks of the Weasel, filtered through the dust of its passing. It drifted out into the thin dry air. Past the dead of the camp, and out across the yellow-red dunes until it was silenced and lost in the thin wind that blew endlessly and forever across the face of the bitter land.

Crime on Mars

Arthur C. Clarke

Thus far, the stories haven't been all that light in tone. Mars was a forbidding and fearsome place. But here we have a less somber tale, a criminal caper story set on a lightly colonized Mars. This story actually first appeared in Ellery Queen's Mystery Magazine, *back when* F&SF *and* EQMM *were published by the same publisher.*

Arthur C. Clarke is one of the three best-known science-fiction writers of the twentieth century (along with Isaac Asimov and Robert A. Heinlein). Perhaps best known for his work with director Stanley Kubrick in writing 2001: A Space Odyssey, *he is also the author of dozens of novels, stories, and works of nonfiction, including* The Fountains of Paradise, Rendezvous with Rama, *and* Childhood's End. *His most recent novel is* Time's Eye, *written in collaboration with Stephen Baxter. His second novel,* The Sands of Mars *(1951), was one of the first attempts to show a realistic (by current standards) exploration of Mars. He lives in Sri Lanka nowadays.*

"WE DON'T HAVE much crime on Mars," said Detective-Inspector Rawlings, a little sadly. "In fact, that's the chief reason I'm going back to the Yard. If I stayed here much longer, I'd get completely out of practice."

We were sitting in the main observation lounge of the Phobos Spaceport, looking out across the jagged sun-drenched crags of the tiny moon. The ferry rocket that had brought us up from Mars had left ten minutes ago and was now beginning the long fall back to the ochre-tinted globe hanging there against the stars. In half an hour we would be boarding the liner for Earth—a world on which most of the passengers had never set foot, but still called "home."

"At the same time," continued the Inspector, "now and then there's a case that makes life interesting. You're an art dealer, Mr. Maccar; I'm sure you heard about that spot of bother at Meridian City a couple of months ago."

"I don't think so," replied the plump, olive-skinned little man I'd taken for just another returning tourist. Presumably the Inspector had already checked through the passenger list; I wondered how much he knew about me, and tried to reassure myself that my conscience was—well, reasonably clear. After all, everybody took *something* out through Martian customs—

"It's been rather well hushed up," said the Inspector, "but you can't keep these things quiet for long. Anyway, a jewel thief from Earth tried to steal Meridian Museum's greatest treasure—the Siren Goddess."

"But that's absurd!" I objected. "It's priceless, of course—but it's only a lump of sandstone. You might just as well steal the *Mona Lisa*."

The Inspector grinned, rather mirthlessly. "*That's* happened too," he said. "Maybe the motive was the same. There are collectors who would give a fortune for such an object, even if they could only look at it themselves. Don't you agree, Mr. Maccar?"

"That's perfectly true," said the art dealer. "In my business you meet all sorts of crazy people."

"Well, this chappie—name's Danny Weaver—had been well paid

by one of them. And if it hadn't been for a piece of fantastically bad luck, he might have brought it off."

The Spaceport P.A. system apologized for a further slight delay owing to final fuel checks, and asked a number of passengers to report to Information. While we were waiting for the announcement to finish, I recalled what little I knew about the Siren Goddess. Although I'd never seen the original, like most other departing tourists I had a replica in my baggage. It bore the certificate of the Mars Bureau of Antiquities, guaranteeing that "this full-scale reproduction is an exact copy of the so-called Siren Goddess, discovered in the Mare Sirenium by the Third Expedition, A.D. 2012 (A.M. 23)."

It's quite a tiny thing to have caused so much controversy. Only eight or nine inches high—you wouldn't look at it twice if you saw it in a museum on Earth. The head of a young woman, with slightly oriental features, elongated earlobes, hair curled in tight ringlets close to the scalp, lips half parted in an expression of pleasure or surprise—and that's all.

But it's an enigma so baffling that it has inspired a hundred religious sects, and driven quite a few archaeologists out of their minds. For a perfectly human head has no right whatsoever to be found on Mars, whose only intelligent inhabitants were crustaceans—"educated lobsters," as the newspapers are fond of calling them. The aboriginal Martians never came near to achieving spaceflight, and in any event their civilization died before men existed on Earth.

No wonder the Goddess is the Solar System's number-one mystery. I don't suppose we'll find the answer in my lifetime—if we ever do.

"Danny's plan was beautifully simple," continued the Inspector. "You know how absolutely dead a Martian city gets on Sunday, when everything closes down and the colonists stay home to watch the TV from Earth. Danny was counting on this when he checked into the hotel in Meridian West, late Friday afternoon. He'd have Saturday for reconnoitering the Museum, an undisturbed Sunday for the job itself, and on Monday morning he'd be just another tourist leaving town. . . .

"Early Saturday he strolled through the little park and crossed over into Meridian East, where the Museum stands. In case you don't know, the city gets its name because it's exactly on longitude 180 degrees; there's a big stone slab in the park with the Prime Meridian engraved on it, so that visitors can get themselves photographed standing in two hemispheres at once. Amazing what simple things amuse some people.

"Danny spent the day going over the Museum, exactly like any other tourist determined to get his money's worth. But at closing time he didn't leave; he'd holed up in one of the galleries not open to the public, where the museum had been arranging a Late Canal Period reconstruction but had run out of money before the job could be finished. He stayed there until about midnight, just in case there were any enthusiastic researchers still in the building. Then he emerged and got to work."

"Just a minute," I interrupted. "What about the night watchman?"

"My dear chap! They don't have such luxuries on Mars. There weren't even any burglar alarms, for who would bother to steal lumps of stone? True, the Goddess was sealed up neatly in a strong glass and metal cabinet, just in case some souvenir hunter took a fancy to her. But even if she were stolen, there was nowhere the thief could hide, and of course all outgoing traffic would be searched as soon as the statue was missed."

That was true enough. I'd been thinking in terms of Earth, forgetting that every city on Mars is a closed little world of its own beneath the force field that protects it from the freezing near-vacuum. Beyond those electronic shields is the utterly hostile emptiness of the Martian Outback, where a man will die in seconds without protection. That makes law enforcement very easy.

"Danny had a beautiful set of tools, as specialized as a watchmaker's.

The main item was a microsaw no bigger than a soldering iron; it had a wafer-thin blade, driven at a million cycles a second by an ultrasonic power-pack. It would go through glass or metal like butter—and leave a cut only about as thick as a hair. Which was very important for Danny, as he could not leave any traces of his handiwork.

"I suppose you've guessed how he intended to operate. He was going to cut through the base of the cabinet and substitute one of those souvenir replicas for the genuine Goddess. It might be a couple of years before some inquisitive expert discovered the awful truth, and long before then the original would have taken to Earth, perfectly disguised as a copy of itself, with a genuine certificate of authenticity. Pretty neat, eh?

"It must have been a weird business, working in that darkened gallery with all those million-year-old carvings and unexplainable artifacts around him. A museum on Earth is bad enough at night, but at least it's—well, *human*. And Gallery Three, which houses the Goddess, is particularly unsettling. It's full of bas-reliefs showing quite incredible animals fighting each other; they look rather like giant beetles, and most paleontologists flatly deny that they could ever have existed. But imaginary or not, they belonged to this world, and they didn't disturb Danny as much as the Goddess, staring at him across the ages and defying him to explain her presence here. She gave him the creeps. How do I know? He told me.

"Danny set to work on that cabinet as carefully as any diamond cutter preparing to cleave a gem. It took most of the night to slice out the trapdoor, and it was nearly dawn when he relaxed and put down the saw. There was still a lot of work to do, but the hardest part was over. Putting the replica into the case, checking its appearance against the photos he'd thoughtfully brought with him, and covering up his traces might take a good part of Sunday, but that didn't worry him in the least. He had another twenty-four hours, and would welcome Monday's first visitors so that he could mingle with them and make his exit.

"It was a perfectly horrible shock to his nervous system, therefore, when the main doors were noisily unbarred at eight-thirty and the Museum staff—all six of them—started to open up for the day. Danny bolted for the emergency exit, leaving everything behind—tools, Goddesses, the lot.

"He had another big surprise when he found himself in the street: it should have been completely deserted at this time of day, with everyone at home reading the Sunday papers. But here were the citizens of Meridian East, as large as life, heading for plant or office on what was obviously a normal working day.

"By the time poor Danny got back to his hotel, we were waiting for him. We couldn't claim much credit for deducing that only a visitor from Earth—and a very recent one at that—could have overlooked Meridian City's chief claim to fame. And I presume you know what *that* is."

"Frankly, I don't," I answered. "You can't see much of Mars in six weeks, and I never went east of the Syrtis Major."

"Well, it's absurdly simple, but we shouldn't be too hard on Danny—even the locals occasionally fall into the same trap. It's something that doesn't bother us on Earth, where we've been able to dump the problem in the Pacific Ocean. But Mars, of course, is all dry land; and that means that *somebody* is forced to live with the International Date Line. . . .

"Danny, you see, had planned the job from Meridian West. It was Sunday over there all right—and it was still Sunday there when we picked him up at the hotel. But over in Meridian East, half a mile away, it was only Saturday. That little trip across the park had made all the difference! I told you it was rotten luck."

There was a long moment of silent sympathy, then I asked, "What did he get?"

"Three years," said Inspector Rawlings.

"That doesn't seem very much."

"Mars years—that makes it almost six of ours. And a whopping fine which, by an odd coincidence, came to exactly the refund value of his return ticket to Earth. He isn't in jail, of course—Mars can't afford that kind of nonproductive luxury. Danny has to work for a living, under discreet surveillance. I told you that the Meridian Museum couldn't afford a night watchman. Well, it has one now. Guess who?"

"All passengers prepare to board in ten minutes! Please collect your hand baggage!" ordered the loudspeakers.

As we started to move toward the airlock, I couldn't help asking one more question.

"What about the people who put Danny up to it? There must have been a lot of money behind him. Did you get them?"

"Not yet; they'd covered their tracks pretty thoroughly, and I believe Danny was telling the truth when he said he couldn't give us a lead. Still, it's not my case. As I told you, I'm going back to my old job at the Yard. But a policeman always keeps his eyes open—like an art dealer, eh, Mr. Maccar? Why, you look a bit green about the gills. Have one of my space-sickness tablets."

"No thank you," answered Mr. Maccar, "I'm quite all right."

His tone was distinctly unfriendly; the social temperature seemed to have dropped below zero in the last few minutes. I looked at Mr. Maccar, and I looked at the Inspector. And suddenly I realized that we were going to have a very interesting trip.

Purple Priestess of the Mad Moon

Leigh Brackett

Born in 1915, Leigh Brackett grew up in California, a self-described tomboy who was strongly influenced by Edgar Rice Burroughs's adventure stories. She published her first story in 1940 and quickly established herself as one of the leading contributors to the pulp magazines of the time, particularly to Planet Stories. *Her stories blended swords-and-sorcery adventure with fantastic science-fictional settings into a mixture known nowadays as the planetary romance. In 1955, Anthony Boucher described her as "the acknowledged mistress of the flamboyant interplanetary adventure" and joked, "No one can rival her in telling such a story as, say, 'Purple Priestess of the Mad Moon' so skillfully and even artistically that readers normally allergic to such extravaganzas are astonished to find themselves enjoying it." The title "Purple Priestess" was mistaken for a real publication of hers, and for nearly a decade fans hounded her about the story, until she finally wrote this story to fill out the spot in her bibliography. It's not quite her finest work, but to my mind, it's one of two endcaps on the planetary adventure; after it and Roger Zelazny's "A Rose for Ecclesiastes," that sort of story needed a different form. (In fact, when Leigh Brackett revived her character*

Eric John Stark for more stories in the 1970s, she moved the setting for the stories out of our solar system.)

Ms. Brackett was a versatile writer who also wrote several crime novels, one western, and a lot of movie scripts. Her last script was for a film by the name of The Empire Strikes Back, *for which she received a Hugo Award after her death in 1978. Much of her best short work was collected recently in* Martian Quest: The Early Brackett.

IN THE OBSERVATION bubble of the TSS *Goddard*, Harvey Selden watched the tawny face of the planet grow. He could make out rose-red deserts where tiny sandstorms blew, and dark areas of vegetation like textured silk. Once or twice he caught the bright flash of water from one of the canals. He sat motionless, rapt and delighted. He had been afraid that this confrontation would offer very little to his emotions; he had since childhood witnessed innumerable identical approaches on the tri-di screen, which was almost the same as being there one's self. But the actuality had a flavor and imminence that he found immensely thrilling.

After all, an alien planet . . .

After all, *Mars* . . .

He was almost angry when he realized that Bentham had come into the bubble. Bentham was Third Officer and at his age this was an admission of failure. The reason for it, Selden thought, was stamped quite clearly on his face, and he felt sorry for Bentham as he felt sorry for anyone afflicted with alcoholism. Still, the man was friendly and he had seemed much impressed by Selden's knowledge of Mars. So Selden smiled and nodded.

"Quite a thrill," he said.

Bentham glanced at the onrushing planet. "It always is. You know anybody down there?"

"No. But after I check in with the Bureau . . ."

"When will you do that?"

"Tomorrow. I mean, counting from after we land, of course . . . a little confusing, isn't it, this time thing?" He knew they did three or four complete orbits on a descending spiral, which meant three or four days and nights.

Bentham said, "But in the meantime, you don't know anybody."

Selden shook his head.

"Well," said Bentham, "I'm having dinner with some Martian friends. Why don't you come along? You might find it interesting."

"Oh," said Selden eagerly, "that would be . . . But are you sure your friends won't mind? I mean, an unexpected guest dragged in at the last minute . . ."

"They won't mind," Bentham said. "I'll give them plenty of warning. Where are you staying?"

"The Kahora-Hilton."

"Of course," said Bentham. "I'll pick you up around seven." He smiled. "Kahora time."

He went out, leaving Selden with some lingering qualms of doubt. Bentham was perhaps not quite the person he would have chosen to introduce him to Martian society. Still, he was an officer and could be presumed to be a gentleman. And he had been on the Mars run for a long time. Of course he would have friends, and what an unlooked-for and wonderful chance this was to go actually into a Martian home and visit with a Martian family. He was ashamed of his momentary uneasiness, and was able to analyze it quite quickly as being based in his own sense of insecurity, which of course arose from being faced with a totally unfamiliar environment. Once he had brought this negative attitude into the open, it was easy to correct it. After a quarter of an hour of positive therapy, he found himself hardly able to wait for the evening.

Kahora had grown in half a century. Originally, Selden knew, it had been founded as a Trade City under the infamous old Umbrella

Treaty, so-called because it could be manipulated to cover anything, which had been concluded between the then World Government of Terra and the impoverished Martian Federation of City-States. At that time the city was housed under a single dome, climate-conditioned for the comfort of the outworld traders and politicians who frequented it and who were unused to the rigors of cold and thin-aired Mars. In addition to the climate, various other luxuries were installed in the Trade Cities, so that they had been compared with certain Biblical locales, and crimes of many different sorts, even murder, had been known to occur in them.

But all of that, or nearly all of that, was in the bad old days of *laissez-faire,* and now Kahora was the administrative capital of Mars, sheltered under a complex of eight shining domes. From the spaceport fifteen miles away, Selden saw the city as a pale shimmer of gossamer bubbles touched by the low sun. As the spaceport skimmer flew him across the intervening miles of red sand and dark green moss-grass, he saw the lights come on in the quick dusk and the buildings underneath the domes rose and took shape, clean and graceful and clothed in radiance. He thought that he had never seen anything so beautiful. From the landing stage inside one of the domes, a silent battery-powered cab took him to his hotel along gracious streets, where the lights glowed and people of many races walked leisurely. The whole trip, from debarkation to hotel lobby, was accomplished in completely air-conditioned comfort, and Selden was not sorry. The landscape looked awfully bleak, and one needed only to glance at it to know that it was damnably cold. Just before the skimmer entered the airlock it crossed the Kahora canal, and the water looked like black ice. He knew that he might have to cope with all this presently, but he was not in any hurry.

Selden's room was pleasantly homelike and the view of the city was superb. He showered and shaved, dressed in his best dark silk, and then sat for a while on his small balcony overlooking the Triangle with the Three Worlds represented at its apices. The air he breathed was warm and faintly scented. The city sounds that rose to him were pleasantly subdued. He began to run over in his mind the rules he had learned for proper behavior in a Martian house, the ceremonial phrases and gestures. He wondered whether Bentham's friends would speak High or Low Martian. Low, probably, since that was most commonly in use with outsiders. He hoped his accent was not too barbarous. On the whole he felt adequate. He leaned back in his comfortable chair and found himself looking at the sky.

There were two moons in it, racing high above the glow and distortion of the dome. And for some reason, although he knew perfectly well that Mars had two moons, this bit of alienage had a powerful effect on him. For the first time he realized, not merely with his intellect but with his heart and bowels, that he was on a strange world a long, long way from home.

He went down to the bar to wait for Bentham.

The man arrived in good time, freshly turned out in civilian silks and, Selden was glad to see, perfectly sober. He bought him a drink and then followed him into a cab, which bore them quietly from the central dome into one of the outer ones.

"The original one," Bentham said. "It's chiefly residential now. The buildings are older, but very comfortable." They were halted at a concourse waiting for a flow of cross traffic to pass and Bentham pointed at the dome roof. "Have you seen the moons? They're both in the sky now. That's the thing people seem to notice the most when they first land."

"Yes," Selden said. "I've seen them. It is . . . uh . . . striking."

"The one we call Deimos . . . that one there . . . the Martian name is Vashna, of course . . . that's the one that in certain phases was called the Mad Moon."

"Oh, no," Selden said. "That was Phobos. Denderon."

Bentham gave him a look and he reddened a bit. "I mean, I think it was." He knew damn well it was, but after all . . . "Of course you've been here many times, and I could be mistaken . . ."

Bentham shrugged. "Easy enough to settle it. We'll ask Mak."

"Who?"

"Firsa Mak. Our host."

"Oh," said Selden, "I wouldn't . . ."

But the cab sped on then and Bentham was pointing out some other thing of interest and the subject passed.

Almost against the outer curve of the dome there was a building of pale gold and the cab stopped there. A few minutes later Selden was being introduced to Firsa Mak.

He had met Martians before, but only rarely and never *in situ*. He saw a dark, small, lean, catlike man with the most astonishing yellow eyes. The man wore the traditional white tunic of the Trade Cities, exotic and very graceful. A gold earring that Selden recognized as a priceless antique hung from his left earlobe. He was not at all like the rather round and soft Martians Selden had met on Terra. He flinched before those eyes, and the carefully mustered words of greeting stuck in his throat. Then there was no need for them as Firsa Mak shook his hand and said, "Hello. Welcome to Mars. Come on in."

A wiry brown hand propelled him in the most friendly fashion into a large low room with a glass wall that looked out through the dome at the moon-washed desert. The furniture was simple modern stuff and very comfortable, with here and there a bit of sculpture or a wall-plaque as fine as, but no better than, the Martian handcrafts obtainable at the good specialty shops in New York. On one of the couches a very long-legged, gaunt and white-haired Earthman sat drinking in a cloud of smoke. He was introduced as Altman. He had a face like old leather left too long in the sun, and he looked at Selden as from a great height and a far distance. Curled up beside him was a dark girl, or woman. . . . Selden could not decide which because of the smoothness of her face and the too-great wisdom of her eyes, which were as yellow and unwinking as Firsa Mak's.

"My sister," Firsa Mak said. "Mrs. Altman. And this is Lella."

He did not say exactly who Lella was, and Selden did not at the moment care. She had just come in from the kitchen bearing a tray of something or other, and she wore a costume that Selden had read about but never seen. A length of brilliant silk, something between red and burnt orange, was wrapped about her hips and caught at the waist by a broad girdle. Below the skirt her slim brown ankles showed, with anklets of tiny golden bells that chimed faintly as she walked. Above the skirt her body was bare and splendidly made. A necklace of gold plaques intricately pierced and hammered circled her throat, and more of the tiny bells hung from her ears. Her hair was long and deeply black and her eyes were green, with the most enchanting tilt. She smiled at Selden, and moved away with her elfin music, and he stood stupidly staring after her, hardly aware that he had taken a glass of dark liquor from her proffered tray.

Presently Selden was sitting on some cushions between the Altmans and Firsa Mak, with Bentham opposite. Lella kept moving distractingly in and out, keeping their glasses filled with the peculiar smoky-tasting hellfire.

"Bentham tells me you're with the Bureau of Interworld Cultural Relations," Firsa Mak said.

"Yes," said Selden. Altman was looking at him with that strange remote glare, making him feel acutely uncomfortable.

"Ah. And what is your particular field?"

"Handcrafts. Metalwork. Uh . . . the ancient type of thing, like that . . ." He indicated Lella's necklace, and she smiled.

"It is old," she said, and her voice was sweet as the chiming bells. "I would not even guess how old."

"The pierced pattern," Selden said, "is characteristic of the Seventeenth Dynasty of the Khalide Kings of Jekkara, which lasted for approximately two thousand years at the period when Jekkara was declining from her position as a maritime power. The sea was receding significantly then, say between fourteen and sixteen thousand years ago."

"So old?" Lella said, and fingered the necklace wonderingly.

"That depends," said Bentham. "Is it genuine, Lella, or is it a copy?" Lella dropped to her knees beside Selden. "You will say."

They all waited. Selden began to sweat. He had studied hundreds of necklaces, but never *in situ*. Suddenly he was not sure at all whether the damned thing was genuine, and he was just as suddenly positive that they did know and were needling him. The plaques rose and fell gently to the lift of Lella's breathing. A faint dry, spicy fragrance reached his nostrils. He touched the gold, lifted one of the plaques, and felt of it, warm from her flesh, and yearned for a nice uncomplicated textbook that had diagrams and illustrations and nothing more to take your mind off your subject. He was tempted to tell them to go to hell. They were just waiting for him to make a mistake. Then he got madder and bolder and he put his whole hand under the collar, lifting it away from her neck and testing the weight of it. It was worn thin and light as tissue paper and the under surface was still pocked by the ancient hammer strokes in the particular fashion of the Khalide artificers.

It was a terribly crude test, but his blood was up. He looked into the tilted green eyes and said authoritatively, "It's genuine."

"How wonderful that you know!" She caught his hand between hers and pressed it and laughed aloud with pleasure. "You have studied very long?"

"Very long." He felt good now. He hadn't let them get him down. The hellfire had worked its way up into his head, where it was buzzing gently, and Lella's attention was even more pleasantly intoxicating.

"What will you do now with this knowledge?" she asked.

"Well," he said, "as you know, so many of the ancient skills have been lost, and your people are looking for ways to expand their economy, so the Bureau is hoping to start a program to reeducate metalworkers in places like Jekkara and Valkis . . ."

Altman said in a remote and very quiet voice, "Oh good God Albloodymighty."

Selden said, “I beg your pardon?”

“Nothing,” Altman said. “Nothing.”

Bentham turned to Firsa Mak. “By the way, Selden and I had a difference of opinion on the way here. He’s probably right, but I said I’d ask you . . .”

Selden said hastily, “Oh, let’s forget it, Bentham.” But Bentham was obtuse and insistent.

“The Mad Moon, Firsa Mak. I say Vashna, he says Denderon.”

“Denderon, of course,” said Firsa Mak, and looked at Selden. “So you know all about that, too.”

“Oh,” said Selden, embarrassed and annoyed with Bentham for bringing it up, “please, we thoroughly understand that that was all a mistake.”

Altman leaned forward. “A mistake?”

“Certainly. The early accounts”—he looked first at Firsa Mak and his sister and Lella and they all seemed to be waiting for him to go on, so he did, uncomfortably—”I mean, they resulted from distortions of folklore, misinterpretation of local customs, pure ignorance . . . in some cases, they were downright lies.” He waved his hand deprecatingly. “We don’t believe in the Rites of the Purple Priestess and all that nonsense. That is to say, we don’t believe they ever *occurred,* really.”

He hoped that would close the subject, but Bentham was determined to hang to it. “I’ve read eyewitness accounts, Selden.”

“Fabrications. Traveller’s tales. After all, the Earthmen who first came to Mars were strictly the piratical exploiter type and were hardly either qualified or reliable observers . . .”

“They don’t need us anymore,” said Altman softly, staring at Selden but not seeming to see him. “They don’t need us at all.” And he muttered something about winged pigs and the gods of the marketplace. Selden had a sudden horrid certainty that Altman was himself one of those early piratical exploiters and that he had irreparably insulted him. And then Firsa Mak said with honest curiosity, “Why is it that all you young Earthmen are so ready to cry down the things your own people have done?"

Selden felt Altman's eyes upon him, but he was into this now and there was no backing down. He said with quiet dignity, "Because we feel that if our people have made mistakes, we should be honest enough to admit them."

"A truly noble attitude," said Firsa Mak. "But about the Purple Priestess . . ."

"I assure you," said Selden hastily, "that old canard is long forgotten. The men who did the serious research, the anthropologists and sociologists who came after the . . . uh . . . the adventurers, were far better qualified to evaluate the data. They completely demolished the idea that the rites involved human sacrifice, and of course the monstrous Dark Lord the priestess was supposed to serve was merely the memory of an extremely ancient earth-god—mars-god, I should say—but you know what I mean, a primitive nature thing, like the sky or the wind."

Firsa Mak said gently, "But there was a rite . . ."

"Well, yes," said Selden, "undoubtedly. But the experts proved that it was purely vestigial, like . . . well, like our own children dancing around the Maypole."

"The Low-Canallers," said Altman, "never danced around any Maypoles." He rose slowly and Selden watched him stretch higher and higher above him. He must have stood a good six inches over six feet, and even from that height his eyes pierced Selden. "How many of your qualified observers went into the hills above Jekkara?"

Selden began to bristle a bit. The feeling that for some reason he was being baited grew stronger. "You must know that until very recently the Low-Canal towns were closed to Earthmen . . ."

"Except for a few adventurers."

"Who left highly dubious memoirs! And even yet you have to have a diplomatic passport involving miles of red tape, and you're allowed very little freedom of movement when you get there. But it *is* a beginning, and we hope, we hope very greatly, that we can persuade the Low-Canallers to accept our friendship and assistance. It's a pity that their own secretiveness fostered such a bad image. For decades the only ideas we had of the Low-Canal towns came from the lurid accounts of the early travelers, and the extremely biased . . . as we learned later . . . attitude of the City-States. We used to think of Jekkara and Valkis as, well, perfect sinks of iniquity. . . ."

Altman was smiling at him. "But my dear boy," he said. "They are. They are."

Selden tried to disengage his hand from Lella's. He found that he could not, and it was about then that he began to be just the least little bit frightened.

"I don't understand," he said plaintively. "Did you get me here just to bait me? If you did, I don't think it's very . . . Bentham?"

Bentham was at the door. The door now seemed to be much farther away than Selden remembered and there was a kind of mist between him and it so that Bentham's figure was indistinct. Nevertheless he saw it raise a hand and heard it say, "Goodbye." Then it was gone, and Selden, feeling infinitely forlorn, turned to look into Lella's eyes. "I don't understand," he said. "I don't understand." Her eyes were green and enormous and deep without limit. He felt himself topple and fall giddily into the abyss, and then of course it was far too late to be afraid.

Hearing returned to him first, with the steady roar of jets, and then there was the bodily sensation of being borne through air that was shaken occasionally by large turbulences. He opened his eyes, in wild alarm. It was several minutes before he could see anything but a thick fog. The fog cleared gradually and he found himself staring at Lella's gold necklace and remembering with great clarity the information concerning it that he had rattled off so glibly and with such modest pride. A simple and obvious truth came to him.

"You're from Jekkara," he said, and only then did he realize that there was a gag in his mouth. Lella started and looked down at him.

"He's awake."

Firsa Mak rose and bent over Selden, examining the gag and a set of antique manacles that bound his wrists. Again Selden flinched from those fierce and brilliant eyes. Firsa Mak seemed to hesitate, on the verge of removing the gag, and Selden mustered his voice and courage to demand explanations. A buzzer sounded in the cabin, apparently a signal from the pilot, and at the same time the motion of the copter altered. Firsa Mak shook his head.

"Later, Selden. I have to leave you this way because I can't trust you, and all our lives are in danger, not just yours . . . though yours most of all." He leaned forward. "This is necessary, Selden. Believe me."

"Not necessary," Altman said, appearing stooped under the cabin ceiling. "Vital. You'll understand that, later."

Lella said harshly, "I wonder if he will."

"If he doesn't," Altman said, "God help them all, because no one else can."

Mrs. Altman came with a load of heavy cloaks. They had all changed their clothes since Selden had last seen them, except Lella, who had merely added an upper garment of native wool. Mrs. Altman now wore the Low-Canal garb, and Firsa Mak had a crimson tunic held with a wide belt around his hips. Altman looked somehow incredibly right in the leather of a desert tribesman; he was too tall, Selden guessed, to pass for a Jekkaran. He wore the desert harness easily, as though he had worn it many times. They made Selden stand while they wrapped a cloak around him, and he saw that he had been stripped of his own clothing and dressed in a tunic of ochre-yellow, and where his limbs showed they had been stained dark. Then they strapped him into his seat again and waited while the copter slowed and dropped toward a landing.

Selden sat rigid, numb with fear and shock, going over and over in his mind the steps by which he had come here and trying to make sense out of them. He could not. One thing was certain; Bentham had deliberately led him into a trap. But why? *Why?* Where were they taking him, what did they mean to do with him? He tried to do positive therapy, but it was difficult to remember all the wisdom that that had sounded so infinitely wise when he had heard it, and his eyes kept straying to the faces of Altman and Firsa Mak.

There was a quality about them both, something strange that he had never seen before. He tried to analyze what it was. Their flesh appeared to be harder and drier and tougher than normal, their muscles more fibrous and prominent, and there was something about the way they used and carried themselves that reminded him of the large carnivores he had seen in the zoo parks. There was, even more striking, an expression about the eyes and mouth, and Selden realized that these were violent men, men who could strike and tear and perhaps even kill. He was afraid of them. And at the same time he felt superior. He at least was above all that.

The sky had paled. Selden could see desert racing past below. They settled onto it with a great spuming of dust and sand. Altman and Firsa Mak between them half-carried him out of the copter. Their strength was appalling. They moved away from the copter and the backwash of the rotors beat them as it took off. Selden was stricken by the thin air and bitter cold. His bones felt brittle and his lungs were full of knives. The others did not seem to mind. He pulled his cloak tight around him as well as he could with his bound hands, and felt his teeth chattering into the gag. Abruptly Lella reached out and pulled the hood completely down over his face. It had two eyeholes so that it could be used as a mask during sandstorms, but it stifled him and it smelled strangely. He had never felt so utterly miserable.

Dawn was turning the desert to a rusty red. A chain of time-eaten mountains, barren as the fossil vertebrae of some forgotten monster, curved across the northern horizon. Close at hand was a tumbled mass of rocky outcrops, carved to fantastic shapes by wind and sand. From among these rocks there came a caravan.

Selden heard the bells and the padding of broad splayed hoofs. The beasts were familiar to him from pictures. Seen in their actual scaly reality, moving across the red sand in that wild daybreak with their burdens and their hooded riders, they were apparitions from some older and uglier time. They came close and stopped, hissing and stamping and rolling their cold bright eyes at Selden, not liking the smell of him in spite of the Martian clothing he wore. They did not seem to mind Altman. Perhaps he had lived with the Martians so long that there was no difference now.

Firsa Mak spoke briefly with the leader of the caravan. The meeting had obviously been arranged, for led animals were brought. The women mounted easily. Selden's stomach turned over at the idea of actually riding one of these creatures. Still, at the moment, he was even more afraid of being left behind, so he made no protest when Firsa Mak and Altman heaved him up onto the saddle pad. One of them rode on each side of him, holding a lead rein. The caravan moved on again, northward toward the mountains.

Within an hour Selden was suffering acutely from cold, thirst, and the unaccustomed exercise. By noon, when they halted to rest, he was almost unconscious. Altman and Firsa Mak helped him down and then carried him around into some rocks where they took the gag out of his mouth and gave him water. The sun was high now, piercing the thin atmosphere like a burning lance. It scalded Selden's cheeks but at least he was warm, or almost warm. He wanted to stay where he was and die.

Altman was quite brutal about it. "You wanted to go to Jekkara," he said. "Well, you're going . . . just a little bit earlier than you planned, that's all. What the hell, boy, did you think it was all like Kahora?"

And he heaved Selden onto his mount again and they went on.

In mid-afternoon the wind got up. It never really seemed to stop blowing, but in a tired sort of way, wandering across the sand, picking up a bit of dust and dropping it again, chafing the upthrust rocks a little deeper, stroking the ripple-patterns into a different design. Now it seemed impatient with everything it had done and determined to wipe it out and start fresh. It gathered itself and rushed screaming across the land, and it seemed to Selden that the whole desert took up and went flying in a red and strangling cloud. The sun went out. He lost sight of Altman and Firsa Mak at either end of his reins. He hung in abject terror to his saddle pad, watching for the small segment of rein he could see to go slack, when he would know that he was irretrievably lost. Then as abruptly as it had risen the wind dropped and the sand resumed its quiet, eternal rolling.

A little while after that, in the long red light from the west, they dipped down to a line of dark water strung glittering through the desolation, banded with strips of green along its sides. There was a smell of wetness and growing things, and an ancient bridge, and beyond the canal was a city, with the barren hills behind it.

Selden knew that he was looking at Jekkara. And he was struck with awe. Even at this late day, few Earthmen had seen it. He stared through the eyeholes of his hood, seeing at first only the larger masses of rose-red rock, and then as the sun sank lower and the shadows shifted, making out the individual shapes of buildings that melted more and more gently into the parent rock the higher they were on the sloping cliffs. At one place he saw the ruins of a great walled castle that he knew had once housed those selfsame Khalide Kings and lord knew how many dynasties before them in the days when this desert was the bottom of a blue sea, and there was a lighthouse still standing above the basin of a dry harbor halfway up the cliffs. He shivered, feeling the enormous weight of a history in which he and his had no part whatever, and it came to him that he had perhaps been just the tiniest bit presumptuous in his desire to teach these people.

That feeling lasted him halfway across the bridge. By that time the western light had gone and the torches were flaring in the streets of Jekkara, shaken by the dry wind from the desert. His focus of interest shifted from the then to the now, and once more he shivered, but for a different reason. The upper town was dead. The lower town was not, and there was a quality to the sight and sound and smell of it that petrified him. Because it was exactly as the early adventurers in their dubious memoirs had described it.

The caravan reached the broad square that fronted the canal, the beasts picking their way protestingly over the sunken, tilted paving stones. People came to meet them. Without his noticing it, Altman and Firsa Mak had maneuvered Selden to the end of the line, and now he found himself being detached and quietly led away up a narrow street between low stone buildings with deep doorways and small window-places, all their corners worn round and smooth as streambed rocks by time and the rubbing of countless hands and shoulders. There was something going on in the town, he thought, because he could hear the voices of many people from somewhere beyond, as though they were gathering in a central place. The air smelled of cold and dust, and unfamiliar spices, and less-identifiable things.

Altman and Firsa Mak lifted Selden down and held him until his legs regained some feeling. Firsa Mak kept glancing at the sky. Altman leaned close to Selden and whispered, "Do exactly as we tell you, or you won't last the night."

"Nor will we," muttered Firsa Mak, and he tested Selden's gag and made sure his cowl was pulled down to hide his face. "It's almost time."

They led Selden quickly along another winding street. This one was busy and populous. There were sounds and sweet pungent odors and strange-colored lights, and there were glimpses into wickednesses of such fantastic array and imaginative genius that Selden's eyes bulged behind his cowl and he remembered his Seminars in Martian Culture with a species of hysteria. Then they came out into a broad square.

It was full of people, cloaked against the night wind and standing quietly, their dark faces still in the shaking light of the torches. They seemed to be watching the sky. Altman and Firsa Mak, with Selden held firmly between them, melted into the edges of the crowd. They waited. From time to time, more people came from the surrounding streets, making no sound except for the soft slurring of sandaled feet and the faint elfin chiming of tiny bells beneath the cloaks of the women. Selden found himself watching the sky, though he did not understand why. The crowd seemed to grow more silent, to hold all breath and stirring, and then suddenly over the eastern roofs came the swift moon Denderon, low and red.

The crowd said, "Ah-h-h!" a long musical cry of pure despair that shook Selden's heart, and in the same moment harpers who had been concealed in the shadow of a timeworn portico struck their double-banked harps and the cry became a chant, half a lament and half a proud statement of undying hate. The crowd began to move, with the harpers leading and other men carrying torches to light the way. And Selden went with them, up into the hills behind Jekkara.

It was a long, cold way under the fleeting light of Denderon. Selden felt the dust of millennia grate and crunch beneath his sandals and the ghosts of cities passed him to the right and left, ruined walls and empty marketplaces and the broken quays where the ships of the Sea-Kings docked. The wild, fierce music of the harps sustained and finally dazed him. The long chanting line of people strung out, moving steadily, and there was something odd about the measured rhythm of their pace. It was like a march to the gallows.

The remnants of the works of man were left behind. The barren hills bulked against the stars, splashed with the feeble moonlight that now seemed to Selden to be inexpressibly evil. He wondered why he was no longer frightened. He thought perhaps he had reached the point of complete emotional exhaustion. At any rate, he saw things clearly but with no personal involvement.

Even when he saw that the harpers and the torchbearers were passing into the mouth of a cavern, he was not afraid.

The cavern was broad enough for the people to continue marching ten abreast. The harps were muffled now, and the chanting took on a deep and hollow tone. Selden felt that he was going downward. A strange and rather terrible eagerness began to stir in him, and this he could not explain at all. The marchers seemed to feel it, too, for the pace quickened just a little to the underlying of the harpstrings. And suddenly the rock walls vanished out of sight and they were in a vast cold space that was completely black beyond the pinprick glaring of the torches.

The chanting ceased. The people filed on both sides into a semicircle and stood still, with the harpers at the center and a little group of people in front of them, somehow alone and separate.

One of these people took off the concealing cloak and Selden saw that it was a woman dressed all in purple. For some obscure reason, he was sure it was Lella, though the woman's face in the torchlight showed only the smooth gleaming of a silver mask, a very ancient thing with a subtle look of cruel compassion. She took in her hands a pale globed lamp and raised it, and the harpers struck their strings once. The other persons, six in number, laid aside their cloaks. They were three men and three women, all naked and smiling, and now the harps began a tune that was almost merry and the woman in purple swayed her body in time to it. The naked people began to dance, their eyes blank and joyous with some powerful drug, and she led them dancing into the darkness, and as she led them she sang, a long, sweet fluting call.

The harps fell silent. Only the woman's voice sounded, and her lamp shone like a dim star, far away.

Beyond the lamp, an eye opened and looked and was aware.

Selden saw the people, the priestess and the six dancing ones, limned momentarily against that orb as seven people might be limned against a risen moon. Then something in him gave way and he fell, clutching oblivion to him like a saving armor.

* * *

They spent the remainder of that night and the following day in Firsa Mak's house by the dark canal, and there were sounds of terrible revelry in the streets. Selden sat staring straight ahead, his body shaken by small periodic tremors.

"It isn't true," he said, again and again. "It isn't true."

"It may not be true," Altman said, "but it's a fact. And it's the facts that kill you. Do you understand now why we brought you?"

"You want me to tell the Bureau about . . . about *that.*"

"The Bureau and anyone that will listen."

"But why me? Why not somebody really important, like one of the diplomats?"

"We tried that. Remember Loughlin Herbert?"

"But he died of a heart . . . Oh."

"When Bentham told us about you," Firsa Mak said, "you seemed young and strong enough to stand the shock. We've done all we can now, Selden. For years Altman and I have been trying . . ."

"They won't listen to us," Altman said. "They will not listen. And if they keep sending people in, nice well-meaning children and their meddling nannies, not knowing . . . I simply will not be responsible for the consequences." He looked down at Selden from his gaunt and weathered height.

Firsa Mak said softly, "This is a burden. We have borne it, Selden. We even take pride in bearing it." He nodded toward the unseen hills. "*That* has the power of destruction. Jekkara certainly, and Valkis probably, and Barrakesh, and all the people who depend on this canal for their existence. It can destroy. We know. This is a Martian affair, and most of us do not wish to have outsiders brought into it. But Altman is my brother, and I must have some care for his people, and I tell you that the Priestess prefers to choose her offerings from among strangers . . ."

Selden whispered, "How often?"

"Twice a year, when the Mad Moon rises. In between, it sleeps."

"It sleeps," said Altman. "But if it should be roused, and frightened, or made angry . . . For God's sake, Selden, tell them, so that at least they'll *know* what they're getting into."

Selden said wildly, "How can you live here, with that . . ."

Firsa Mak looked at him, surprised that he should ask. "Why, because we always have."

Selden stared, and thought, and did not sleep, and once he screamed when Lella came softly into the room.

On the second night they slipped out of Jekkara and went back across the desert to the place of rocks, where the copter was waiting. Only Altman returned with Selden. They sat silently in the cabin, and Selden thought, and from time to time he saw Altman watching him, and already in his eyes there was the understanding of defeat.

The glowing domes of Kahora swam out of the dusk, and Denderon was in the sky.

"You're not going to tell them," Altman said.

"I don't know," whispered Selden. "I don't know."

Altman left him at the landing stage. Selden did not see him again. He took a cab to his hotel and went directly to his room and locked himself in.

The familiar, normal surroundings aided a return to sanity. He was able to marshall his thoughts more calmly.

If he believed that what he had seen was real, he would have to tell about it, even if no one would listen to him. Even if his superiors, his teachers, his sponsors, the men he venerated and whose approval he yearned for, should be shocked, and look at him with scorn, and shake their heads, and forever close their doors to him. Even if he should be condemned to the outer darkness inhabited by people like Altman and Firsa Mak. Even if.

But if he did not believe that it was real, if he believed instead that it was illusion, hallucination induced by drugs and heaven knew what antique Martian chicanery . . . He had been drugged, that was certain. And Lella *had* practiced some sort of hypnotic technique upon him . . .

If he did *not* believe . . .

Oh God, how wonderful not to believe, to be free again, to be secure in the body of truth!

He thought, in the quiet and comforting confines of his room, and the longer he thought, the more positive his thinking became, the more free of subjectivity, the deeper and calmer in understanding. By the morning he was wan and haggard but healed.

He went to the Bureau and told them that he had been taken ill immediately upon landing, which was why he had not reported. He also told them that he had had urgent word from home and would have to return there at once. They were very sorry to lose him, but most sympathetic, and they booked him onto the first available flight.

A few scars remained on Selden's psyche. He could not bear the sound of a harp nor the sight of a woman wearing purple. These phobias he could have put up with, but the nightmares were just too much. Back on Earth, he went at once to his analyst. He was quite honest with him, and the analyst was able to show him exactly what had happened. The whole affair had been a sex fantasy induced by drugs, with the Priestess as mother-image. The Eye which had looked at him then and which still peered unwinking out of his recurring dreams was symbolic of the female generative principle, and the feeling of horror it aroused in him was due to the guilt complex he had because he was a latent homosexual. Selden was enormously comforted.

The analyst assured him that now that things were healthily out in the open, the secondary effects would fade away. And they might have done so, except for the letter.

It arrived just six Martian months after his unfortunate dinner date with Bentham. It was not signed. It said, *"Lella waits for you at moonrise."* And it bore the sketch, very accurately and quite unmistakably done, of a single monstrous eye.

A Rose for Ecclesiastes

Roger Zelazny

> Thus, not only do the observations we have scanned lead us to the conclusion that Mars at this moment is inhabited, but they land us at the further one that these denizens are of an order whose acquaintance was worth making. . . . A sadder interest attaches to such existence: that it is, cosmically speaking, soon to pass away. To our eventual descendants life on Mars will no longer be something to scan and interpret. It will have lapsed beyond the hope of study or recall.

So wrote Percival Lowell in 1908, and thus did generations of writers follow in the conceit that if there is life on Mars, it must be that of a dying civilization, one whose once-great canals have all dried up. This conceit was as prevalent in its day as the current Hollywood notion that if we encounter aliens, they will be humans in makeup and prosthetics.

But with Mariner 4 *due to fly past Mars in 1965, Roger Zelazny knew that the traditional planetary romance would soon be supplanted by updates in scientific knowledge, so he spun out two stories that served as capstones on the genre. Here you have the first of them, from 1963; the other, "The Doors of His Face, the Lamps of*

His Mouth," was set on Venus and was published in 1965. These two stories helped establish Roger Zelazny as one of the preeminent writers of his generation, a position he held until his untimely death from cancer in 1995. Among his many other works are Lord of Light, Jack of Shadows, Damnation Alley, *and the classic fantasy novels in the "Amber" series, starting with* Nine Princes in Amber.

I

I was busy translating one of my *Madrigals Macabre* into Martian on the morning I was found acceptable. The intercom had buzzed briefly, and I dropped my pencil and flipped on the toggle in a single motion.

"Mister G," piped Morton's youthful contralto, "the old man says I should 'get hold of that damned conceited rhymer' right away, and send him to his cabin.—Since there's only one damned conceited rhymer . . ."

"Let not ambition mock thy useful toil." I cut him off.

So, the Martians had finally made up their minds! I knocked an inch and a half of ash from a smoldering butt, and took my first drag since I had lit it. The entire month's anticipation tried hard to crowd itself into the moment, but could not quite make it. I was frightened to walk those forty feet and hear Emory say the words I already knew he would say; and that feeling elbowed the other one into the background.

So I finished the stanza I was translating before I got up.

It took only a moment to reach Emory's door. I knocked twice and opened it, just as he growled, "Come in."

"You wanted to see me?" I sat down quickly to save him the trouble of offering me a seat.

"That was fast. What did you do, run?"

I regarded his paternal discontent:

Little fatty flecks beneath pale eyes, thinning hair, and an Irish nose; a voice a decibel louder than anyone else's . . .

Hamlet to Claudius: "I was working."

"Hah!" he snorted. "Come off it. No one's ever seen you do any of that stuff."

I shrugged my shoulders and started to rise.

"If that's what you called me down here—"

"Sit down!"

He stood up. He walked around his desk. He hovered above me and glared down. (A hard trick, even when I'm in a low chair.)

"You are undoubtedly the most antagonistic bastard I've ever had to work with!" he bellowed, like a belly-stung buffalo. "Why the hell don't you act like a human being sometime and surprise everybody? I'm willing to admit you're smart, maybe even a genius, but—oh, Hell!" He made a heaving gesture with both hands and walked back to his chair.

"Betty has finally talked them into letting you go in." His voice was normal again. "They'll receive you this afternoon. Draw one of the jeepsters after lunch, and get down there."

"Okay," I said.

"That's all, then."

I nodded, got to my feet. My hand was on the doorknob when he said:

"I don't have to tell you how important this is. Don't treat them the way you treat us."

I closed the door behind me.

I don't remember what I had for lunch. I was nervous, but I knew instinctively that I wouldn't muff it. My Boston publishers expected a Martian Idyll, or at least a Saint-Exupéry job on spaceflight. The National Science Association wanted a complete report on the Rise and Fall of the Martian Empire.

They would both be pleased. I knew.

That's the reason everyone is jealous—why they hate me. I always come through, and I can come through better than anyone else.

I shoveled in a final anthill of slop, and made my way to our car barn. I drew one jeepster and headed it toward Tirellian.

Flames of sand, lousy with iron oxide, set fire to the buggy. They swarmed over the open top and bit through my scarf; they set to work pitting my goggles.

The jeepster, swaying and panting like a little donkey I once rode through the Himalayas, kept kicking me in the seat of the pants. The Mountains of Tirellian shuffled their feet and moved toward me at a cockeyed angle.

Suddenly I was heading uphill, and I shifted gears to accommodate the engine's braying. Not like Gobi, not like the Great Southwestern Desert, I mused. Just red, just dead . . . without even a cactus.

I reached the crest of the hill, but I had raised too much dust to see what was ahead. It didn't matter, though, I have a head full of maps. I bore to the left and downhill, adjusting the throttle. A crosswind and solid ground beat down the fires. I felt like Ulysses in Malebolge—with a terza-rima speech in one hand and an eye out for Dante.

I rounded a rock pagoda and arrived.

Betty waved as I crunched to a halt, then jumped down.

"Hi," I choked, unwinding my scarf and shaking out a pound and a half of grit. "Like, where do I go and who do I see?"

She permitted herself a brief Germanic giggle—more at my starting a sentence with "like" than at my discomfort—then she started talking. (She is a top linguist, so a word from the Village Idiom still tickles her!)

I appreciate her precise, furry talk; informational, and all that. I had enough in the way of social pleasantries before me to last at least the rest of my life. I looked at her chocolate-bar eyes and perfect teeth, at her sun-bleached hair, close-cropped to the head (I hate blondes!), and decided that she was in love with me.

"Mr. Gallinger, the Matriarch is waiting inside to be introduced. She has consented to open the Temple records for your study." She paused here to pat her hair and squirm a little. Did my gaze make her nervous?

"They are religious documents, as well as their only history," she continued, "sort of like the *Mahabharata*. She expects you to observe certain rituals in handling them, like repeating the sacred words when you turn the pages—she will teach you the system."

I nodded quickly, several times.

"Fine, let's go in."

"Uh—" she paused. "Do not forget their Eleven Forms of Politeness and Degree. They take matters of form quite seriously—and do not get into any discussions over the equality of the sexes—"

"I know all about their taboos," I broke in. "Don't worry. I've lived in the Orient, remember?"

She dropped her eyes and seized my hand. I almost jerked it away.

"It will look better if I enter leading you."

I swallowed my comments and followed her, like Samson in Gaza.

Inside, my last thought met with a strange correspondence. The Matriarch's quarters were a rather abstract version of what I imagine the tents of the tribes of Israel to have been like. Abstract, I say, because it was all frescoed brick, peaked like a huge tent, with animal-skin representations like gray-blue scars, that looked as if they had been laid on the walls with a palette knife.

The Matriarch, M'Cwyie, was short, white-haired, fiftyish, and dressed like a Gypsy queen. With her rainbow of voluminous skirts she looked like an inverted punch bowl set atop a cushion.

Accepting my obeisances, she regarded me as an owl might a rabbit. The lids of those black, black eyes jumped upward as she discovered my perfect accent.—The tape recorder Betty had carried on her interviews had done its part, and I knew the language reports from the first two expeditions, verbatim. I'm all hell when it comes to picking up accents.

"You are the poet?"

"Yes," I replied.

"Recite one of your poems, please."

"I'm sorry, but nothing short of a thorough translating job would do justice to your language and my poetry, and I don't know enough of your language yet."

"Oh?"

"But I've been making such translations for my own amusement, as an exercise in grammar," I continued. "I'd be honored to bring a few of them along one of the times that I come here."

"Yes. Do so."

Score one for me!

She turned to Betty.

"You may go now."

Betty muttered the parting formalities, gave me a strange sidewise look, and was gone. She apparently had expected to stay and "assist" me. She wanted a piece of the glory, like everyone else. But I was the Schliemann at this Troy, and there would be only one name on the Association report!

M'Cwyie rose, and I noticed that she gained very little height by standing. But then I'm six-six and look like a poplar in October: thin, bright red on top, and towering above everyone else.

"Our records are very, very old," she began. "Betty says that your word for their age is 'millennia.' "

I nodded appreciatively.

"I'm very eager to see them."

"They are not here. We will have to go to the Temple—they may not be removed."

I was suddenly wary.

"You have no objections to my copying them, do you?"

"No. I see that you respect them, or your desire would not be so great."

"Excellent."

She seemed amused. I asked her what was funny.

"The High Tongue may not be so easy for a foreigner to learn."

It came through fast.

No one on the first expedition had gotten this close. I had had no way of knowing that this was a double-language deal—a classical as well as a vulgar. I knew some of their Prakrit, now I had to learn all their Sanskrit.

"Ouch! and damn!"

"Pardon, please?"

"It's nontranslatable, M'Cwyie. But imagine yourself having to learn the High Tongue in a hurry, and you can guess at the sentiment."

She seemed amused again, and told me to remove my shoes.

She guided me through an alcove . . .

. . . and into a burst of Byzantine brilliance!

No Earthman had ever been in this room before, or I would have heard about it. Carter, the first expedition's linguist, with the help of one Mary Allen, M.D., had learned all the grammar and vocabulary that I knew while sitting cross-legged in the antechamber.

We had no idea this existed. Greedily, I cast my eyes about. A highly sophisticated system of aesthetics lay behind the decor. We would have to revise our entire estimation of Martian culture.

For one thing, the ceiling was vaulted and corbeled; for another, there were side-columns with reverse flutings; for another—oh, hell! The place was big. Posh. You could never have guessed it from the shaggy outsides.

I bent forward to study the gilt filigree on a ceremonial table. M'Cwyie seemed a bit smug at my intentness, but I'd still have hated to play poker with her.

The table was loaded with books.

With my toe, I traced a mosaic on the floor.

"Is your entire city within this one building?"

"Yes, it goes far back into the mountain."

"I see," I said, seeing nothing.

I couldn't ask her for a conducted tour, yet.

She moved to a small stool by the table.

"Shall we begin your friendship with the High Tongue?"

I was trying to photograph the hall with my eyes, knowing I would have to get a camera in here, somehow, sooner or later. I tore my gaze from a statuette and nodded, hard.

"Yes, introduce me."

I sat down.

For the next three weeks, alphabet-bugs chased each other behind my eyelids whenever I tried to sleep. The sky was an unclouded pool of turquoise that rippled calligraphies whenever I swept my eyes across it. I drank quarts of coffee while I worked and mixed cocktails of Benzedrine and champagne for my coffee breaks.

M'Cwyie tutored me two hours every morning, and occasionally for another two in the evening. I spent an additional fourteen hours a day on my own, once I had gotten up sufficient momentum to go ahead alone.

And at night the elevator of time dropped me to its bottom floors. . . .

I was six again, learning my Hebrew, Greek, Latin, and Aramaic. I was ten, sneaking peeks at the *Iliad*. When Daddy wasn't spreading hellfire, brimstone, and brotherly love, he was teaching me to dig the Word, like in the original.

Lord! There are so many originals and so *many* words! When I was twelve I started pointing out the little differences between what he was preaching and what I was reading.

The fundamentalist vigor of his reply brooked no debate. It was worse than any beating. I kept my mouth shut after that and learned to appreciate Old Testament poetry.

—Lord, I am sorry! Daddy—Sir—I am sorry!—It couldn't be! It couldn't be . . .

On the day the boy graduated from high school, with the French, German, Spanish, and Latin awards, Dad Gallinger had told his fourteen-year-old, six-foot scarecrow of a son that he wanted him to enter the ministry. I remember how his son was evasive:

"Sir," he had said, "I'd sort of like to study on my own for a year or so, and then take pre-theology courses at some liberal-arts university. I feel I'm still sort of young to try a seminary, straight off."

The Voice of God: "But you have the gift of tongues, my son. You can preach the Gospel in all the lands of Babel. You were born to be a missionary. You say you are young, but time is rushing by you like a whirlwind. Start early, and you will enjoy added years of service."

The added years of service were so many added tails to the cat repeatedly laid on my back. I can't see his face now; I never can. Maybe it is because I was always afraid to look at it then.

And years later, when he was dead, and laid out, in black, amidst bouquets, amidst weeping congregationalists, amidst prayers, red faces, handkerchiefs, hands patting your shoulders, solemn-faced comforters . . . I looked at him and did not recognize him.

We had met nine months before my birth, this stranger and I. He had never been cruel—stern, demanding, with contempt for everyone's shortcomings—but never cruel. He was also all that I had had of a mother. And brothers. And sisters. He had tolerated my three years at St. John's, possibly because of its name, never knowing how liberal and delightful a place it really was.

But I never knew him, and the man atop the catafalque demanded nothing now; I was free not to preach the Word.

But now I wanted to, in a different way. I wanted to preach a word that I could never have voiced while he lived.

I did not return for my senior year in the fall. I had a small inheritance coming, and a bit of trouble getting control of it, since I was still under eighteen. But I managed.

It was Greenwich Village I finally settled upon.

Not telling any well-meaning parishioners my new address, I entered into a daily routine of writing poetry and teaching myself Japanese and Hindustani. I grew a fiery beard, drank espresso, and learned to play chess. I wanted to try a couple of the other paths to salvation.

After that, it was two years in India with the Old Peace Corps—which broke me of my Buddhism, and gave me my *Pipes of Krishna* lyrics and the Pulitzer they deserved.

Then back to the States for my degree, grad work in linguistics, and more prizes.

Then one day a ship went to Mars. The vessel settling in its New Mexico nest of fires contained a new language.—It was fantastic, exotic, and aesthetically overpowering. After I had learned all there was to know about it, and written my book, I was famous in new circles:

"Go, Gallinger. Dip your bucket in the well, and bring us a drink of Mars. Go, learn another world—but remain aloof, rail at it gently like Auden—and hand us its soul in iambics."

And I came to the land where the sun is a tarnished penny, where the wind is a whip, where two moons play at hot-rod games, and a hell of sand gives you the incendiary itches whenever you look at it.

I rose from my twistings on the bunk and crossed the darkened cabin to a port. The desert was a carpet of endless orange, bulging from the sweepings of centuries beneath it.

"I a stranger, unafraid—This is the land—I've got it made!"

I laughed.

I had the High Tongue by the tail already—the roots, if you want your puns anatomical, as well as correct.

The High and Low Tongues were not so dissimilar as they had first seemed. I had enough of the one to get me through the murkier parts of the other. I had the grammar and all the commoner irregular verbs down cold; the dictionary I was constructing grew by the day, like a tulip, and would bloom shortly. Every time I played the tapes, the stem lengthened.

Now was the time to tax my ingenuity, to really drive the lessons home. I had purposely refrained from plunging into the major texts until I could do justice to them. I had been reading minor commentaries, bits of verse, fragments of history. And one thing had impressed me strongly in all that I read.

They wrote about concrete things: rocks, sand, water, winds; and the tenor couched within these elemental symbols was fiercely pessimistic. It reminded me of some Buddhist texts, but even more so, I realized from my recent *recherches*, it was like parts of the Old Testament. Specifically, it reminded me of the Book of Ecclesiastes.

That, then, would be it. The sentiment, as well as the vocabulary, was so similar that it would be a perfect exercise. Like putting Poe into French. I would never be a convert to the Way of Malann, but I would show them that an Earthman had once thought the same thoughts, felt similarly.

I switched on my desk lamp and sought King James amidst my books.

Vanity of vanities, saith the Preacher, vanity of vanities; all is vanity. What profit hath a man . . .

My progress seemed to startle M'Cwyie. She peered at me, like Sartre's Other, across the tabletop. I ran through a chapter in the Book of Locar. I didn't look up, but I could feel the tight net her eyes were working about my head, shoulders, and rapid hands. I turned another page.

Was she weighing the net, judging the size of the catch? And what for? The books said nothing of fishers on Mars. Especially of men. They said that some god named Malann had spat, or had done something disgusting (depending on the version you read), and that life had gotten under way as a disease in inorganic matter. They said that movement was its first law, its first law, and that the dance was the only legitimate reply to the inorganic . . . the dance's quality its justification,—fication . . . and love is a disease in organic matter—Inorganic matter?

I shook my head. I had almost been asleep.

"M'narra."

I stood and stretched. Her eyes outlined me greedily now. So I met them, and they dropped.

"I grow tired. I want to rest awhile. I didn't sleep much last night."

She nodded, Earth's shorthand for "yes," as she had learned from me.

"You wish to relax, and see the explicitness of the doctrine of Locar in its fullness?"

"Pardon me?"

"You wish to see a Dance of Locar?"

"Oh." Their damned circuits of forms and periphrasis here ran worse than the Korean! "Yes. Surely. Anytime it's going to be done, I'd be happy to watch.

I continued, "In the meantime, I've been meaning to ask you whether I might take some pictures—"

"Now is the time. Sit down. Rest. I will call the musicians."

She bustled out through a door I had never been past.

Well, now, the dance was the highest art, according to Locar, not to mention Havelock Ellis, and I was about to see how their centuries-dead philosopher felt it should be conducted. I rubbed my eyes and snapped over, touching my toes a few times.

The blood began pounding in my head, and I sucked in a couple of deep breaths. I bent again and there was a flurry of motion at the door.

To the trio who entered with M'Cwyie, I must have looked as if I were searching for the marbles I had just lost, bent over like that.

I grinned weakly and straightened up, my face red from more than exertion. I hadn't expected them *that* quickly.

Suddenly I thought of Havelock Ellis again in his area of greatest popularity.

The little redheaded doll, wearing, sari-like, a diaphanous piece of the Martian sky, looked up in wonder—as a child at some colorful flag on a high pole.

"Hello," I said, or its equivalent.

She bowed before replying. Evidently I had been promoted in status.

"I shall dance," said the red wound in that pale, pale cameo, her face. Eyes, the color of dream and her dress, pulled away from mine.

She drifted to the center of the room.

Standing there, like a figure in an Etruscan frieze, she was either meditating or regarding the design on the floor.

Was the mosaic symbolic of something? I studied it. If it was, it eluded me; it would make an attractive bathroom floor or patio, but I couldn't see much in it beyond that.

The other two were paint-spattered sparrows like M'Cwyie, in their middle years. One settled to the floor with a triple-stringed instrument faintly resembling a *samisen.* The other held a simple woodblock and two drumsticks.

M'Cwyie disdained her stool and was seated upon the floor before I realized it. I followed suit.

The *samisen* player was still tuning up, so I leaned toward M'Cwyie.

"What is the dancer's name?"

"Braxa," she replied, without looking at me, and raised her left hand, slowly, which meant yes, and go ahead, and let it begin.

The stringed-thing throbbed like a toothache, and a tick-tocking, like ghosts of all the clocks they had never invented, sprang from the block.

Braxa was a statue, both hands raised to her face, elbows high and outspread.

The music became a metaphor for fire.

Crackle, purr, snap . . .

She did not move.

The hissing altered to splashes. The cadence slowed. It was water now, the most precious thing in the world, gurgling clear then green over mossy rocks.

Still she did not move.

Glissandos. A pause.

Then, so faint I could hardly be sure at first, the tremble of the winds began. Softly, gently, sighing and halting, uncertain. A pause, a sob, then a repetition of the first statement, only louder.

Were my eyes completely bugged from my reading, or was Braxa actually trembling, all over, head to foot?

She was.

She began a microscopic swaying. A fraction of an inch right, then left. Her fingers opened like the petals of a flower, and I could see that her eyes were closed.

Her eyes opened. They were distant, glassy, looking through me and the walls. Her swaying became more pronounced, merged with the beat.

The wind was sweeping in from the desert now, falling against Tirellian like waves on a dike. Her fingers moved, they were the gusts. Her arms, slow pendulums, descended, began a countermovement.

The gale was coming now. She began an axial movement and her hands caught up with the rest of her body, only now her shoulders commenced to writhe out a figure eight.

The wind! The wind, I say. O wild, enigmatic! O muse of Saint-John Perse!

The cyclone was twisting round those eyes, its still center. Her head was thrown back, but I knew there was no ceiling between her gaze, passive as Buddha's, and the unchanging skies. Only the two moons, perhaps, interrupted their slumber in that elemental Nirvana of uninhabited turquoise.

Years ago, I had seen the Devadasis in India, the street dancers, spinning their colorful webs, drawing in the male insect. But Braxa was more than this: she was a Ramadjany, like those votaries of Rama, incarnation of Vishnu, who had given the dance to man: the sacred dancers.

The clicking was monotonously steady now; the whine of the strings made me think of the stinging rays of the sun, their heat stolen by the wind's halations; the blue was Sarasvati and Mary, and a girl named Laura. I heard a sitar from somewhere, watched this statue come to life, and inhaled a divine afflatus.

I was again Rimbaud with his hashish, Baudelaire with his laudanum, Poe, De Quincy, Wilde, Mallarmé, and Aleister Crowley. I was, for a fleeting second, my father in his dark pulpit and darker suit, the hymns and the organ's wheeze transmuted to bright wind.

She was a spun weather vane, a feathered crucifix hovering in the air, a clothesline holding one bright garment lashed parallel to the ground. Her shoulder was bare now, and her right breast moved up and down like a moon in the sky, its red nipple appearing momently above a fold and vanishing again. The music was as formal as Job's argument with God. Her dance was God's reply.

The music slowed, settled; it had been met, matched, answered. Her garment, as if alive, crept back into the more sedate folds it originally held.

She dropped low, lower, to the floor. Her head fell upon her raised knees. She did not move.

There was silence.

I realized, from the ache across my shoulders, how tensely I had been sitting. My armpits were wet. Rivulets had been running down my sides. What did one do now? Applaud?

I sought M'Cwyie from the corner of my eye. She raised her right hand.

As if by telepathy, the girl shuddered all over and stood. The musicians also rose. So did M'Cwyie.

I got to my feet, with a charley horse in my left leg, and said, "It was beautiful," inane as that sounds.

I received three different High Forms of "thank you."

There was a flurry of color and I was alone again with M'Cwyie.

"That is the one hundred-seventeenth of the two thousand, two-hundred-twenty-four dances of Locar."

I looked down at her.

"Whether Locar was right or wrong, he worked out a fine reply to the inorganic."

She smiled.

"Are the dances of your world like this?"

"Some of them are similar. I was reminded of them as I watched Braxa—but I've never seen anything exactly like hers."

"She is good," M'Cwyie said, "she knows all the dances."

A hint of her earlier expression which had troubled me . . .

It was gone in an instant.

"I must tend my duties now." She moved to the table and closed the books. "M'narra."

"Good-bye." I slipped into my boots.

"Good-bye, Gallinger."

I walked out the door, mounted the jeepster, and roared across the evening into night, my wings of risen desert flapping slowly behind me.

II

I had just closed the door behind Betty, after a brief grammar session, when I heard the voices in the hall. My vent was opened a fraction, so I stood there and eavesdropped:

Morton's fruity treble: "Guess what? He said 'hello' to me a while ago."

"Hummph!" Emory's elephant lungs exploded. "Either he's slipping, or you were standing in his way and he wanted you to move."

"Probably didn't recognize me. I don't think he sleeps anymore, now he has that language to play with. I had night watch last week, and every night I passed his door at 0300—I always heard that recorder going. At 0500, when I got off, he was still at it."

"The guy *is* working hard," Emory admitted, grudgingly. "In fact, I think he's taking some kind of dope to keep awake. He looks sort of glassy-eyed these days. Maybe that's natural for a poet, though."

Betty had been standing there, because she broke in then:

"Regardless of what you think of him, it's going to take me at least a year to learn what he's picked up in three weeks. And I'm just a linguist, not a poet."

Morton must have been nursing a crush on her bovine charms. It's the only reason I can think of for his dropping his guns to say what he did.

"I took a course in modern poetry when I was back at the university," he began. "We read six authors—Yeats, Pound, Eliot, Crane, Stevens, and Gallinger—and on the last day of the semester, when the prof was feeling a little rhetorical, he said, 'These six names are written on the century, and all the gates of criticism and Hell shall not prevail against them.' "

"Myself," he continued, "I thought his *Pipes of Krishna* and his *Madrigals* were great. I was honored to be chosen for an expedition he was going on.

"I think he's spoken two dozen words to me since I met him," he finished.

The Defense: "Did it ever occur to you," Betty said, "that he might be tremendously self-conscious about his appearance? He was also a precocious child, and probably never even had school friends. He's sensitive and very introverted."

"Sensitive? Self-conscious?" Emory choked and gagged. "The man is as proud as Lucifer, and he's a walking insult machine. You press a button like 'Hello' or 'Nice day' and he thumbs his nose at you. He's got it down to a reflex."

They muttered a few other pleasantries and drifted away.

Well bless you, Morton boy. You little pimple-faced, Ivy-bred connoisseur! I've never taken a course in my poetry, but I'm glad someone said that. The Gates of Hell. Well, now! Maybe Daddy's prayers got heard somewhere, and I am a missionary, after all!

Only . . .

. . . Only a missionary needs something to convert people *to*. I have my private system of esthetics, and I suppose it oozes an ethical by-product somewhere. But if I ever had anything to preach, really, even in my poems, I wouldn't care to preach it to such lowlifes as you. If you think I'm a slob, I'm also a snob, and there's no room for you in my Heaven—it's a private place, where Swift, Shaw, and Petronius Arbiter come to dinner.

And oh, the feasts we have! The Trimalchios, the Emorys we dissect!

We finish you with the soup, Morton!

I turned and settled at my desk. I wanted to write something. Ecclesiastes could take a night off. I wanted to write a poem, a poem about the one hundred-seventeenth dance of Locar; about a rose following the light, traced by the wind, sick, like Blake's rose, dying . . .

I found a pencil and began.

When I had finished I was pleased. It wasn't great—at least, it was no greater than it needed to be—High Martian not being my strongest tongue. I groped, and put it into English, with partial rhymes. Maybe I'd stick it in my next book. I called it *Braxa:*

> In a land of wind and red,
> where the icy evening of Time
> freezes milk in the breasts of Life,
> as two moons overhead—
> cat and dog in alleyways of dream—

scratch and scramble agelessly my flight . . .
This final flower turns a burning head.

I put it away and found some phenobarbital. I was suddenly tired.

When I showed my poem to M'Cwyie the next day, she read it through several times, very slowly.

"It is lovely," she said. "But you used three words from your own language. 'Cat' and 'dog,' I assume, are two small animals with a hereditary hatred for one another. But what is 'flower'?"

"Oh," I said. "I've never come across your word for 'flower,' but I was actually thinking of an Earth-flower, the rose."

"What is it like?"

"Well, its petals are generally bright red. That's what I meant, on one level, by 'burning head.' I also wanted it to imply fever, though, and red hair, and the fire of life. The rose, itself, has a thorny stem, green leaves, and a distinct, pleasant aroma."

"I wish I could see one."

"I suppose it could be arranged. I'll check."

"Do it, please. You are a—" She used the word for "prophet," or religious poet, like Isaiah or Locar. "—and your poem is inspired. I shall tell Braxa of it."

I declined the nomination, but felt flattered.

This, then, I decided, was the strategic day, the day on which to ask whether I might bring in the microfilm machine and the camera. I wanted to copy all their texts, I explained, and I couldn't write fast enough to do it.

She surprised me by agreeing immediately. But she bowled me over with her invitation.

"Would you like to come and stay here while you do this thing? Then you can work night and day, anytime you want—except when the Temple is being used, of course."

I bowed.

"I should be honored."

"Good. Bring your machines when you want, and I will show you a room."

"Will this afternoon be all right?"

"Certainly."

"Then I will go now and get things ready. Until this afternoon . . ."

"Good-bye."

I anticipated a little trouble from Emory, but not much. Everyone back at the ship was anxious to see the Martians, talk with the Martians, poke needles in the Martians, ask them about Martian climate, diseases, soil chemistry, politics, and mushrooms (our botanist was a fungus nut, but a reasonably good guy)—and only four or five had actually gotten to see them. The crew had been spending most of its time excavating dead cities and their acropolises. We played the game by strict rules, and the natives were as fiercely insular as the nineteenth-century Japanese. I figured I would meet with little resistance, and I figured right.

In fact, I got the distinct impression that everyone was happy to see me move out.

I stopped in the hydroponics room to speak with our mushroom-master.

"Hi, Kane. Grow any toadstools in the sand yet?"

He sniffed. He always sniffs. Maybe he's allergic to plants.

"Hello, Gallinger. No, I haven't had any success with toadstools, but look behind the car barn next time you're out there. I've got a few cacti going."

"Great," I observed. Doc Kane was about my only friend on board, not counting Betty.

"Say, I came down to ask you a favor."

"Name it."

"I want a rose."

"A what?"

"A rose. You know, a nice red American Beauty job—thorns, pretty smelling—"

"I don't think it will take in this soil. *Sniff, sniff.*"

"No, you don't understand. I don't want to plant it, I just want the flowers."

"I'd have to use the tanks." He scratched his hairless dome. "It would take at least three months to get you flowers, even under forced growth."

"Will you do it?"

"Sure, if you don't mind the wait."

"Not at all. In fact, three months will just make it before we leave." I looked about at the pools of crawling slime, at the trays of shoots. "—I'm moving up to Tirellian today, but I'll be in and out all the time. I'll be here when it blooms."

"Moving up there, eh? Moore said they're an in-group."

"I guess I'm 'in' then."

"Looks that way—I still don't see how you learned their language, though. Of course, I had trouble with French and German for my Ph.D., but last week I heard Betty demonstrate it at lunch. It sounds like a lot of weird noises. She says speaking it is like working a *Times* crossword and trying to imitate birdcalls at the same time."

I laughed, and took the cigarette he offered me.

"It's complicated," I acknowledged. "But, well, it's as if you suddenly came across a whole new class of *Mycetae* here—you'd dream about it at night."

His eyes were gleaming.

"Wouldn't that be something! I might, yet, you know."

"Maybe you will."

He chuckled as we walked to the door.

"I'll start your roses tonight. Take it easy down there."

"You bet. Thanks."

Like I said, a fungus nut, but a fairly good guy.

* * *

My quarters in the Citadel of Tirellian were directly adjacent to the Temple, on the inward side and slightly to the left. They were a considerable improvement over my cramped cabin, and I was pleased that Martian culture had progressed sufficiently to discover the desirability of the mattress over the pallet. Also, the bed was long enough to accommodate me, which *was* surprising.

So I unpacked and took sixteen 35-mm shots of the Temple, before starting on the books.

I took 'stats until I was sick of turning pages without knowing what they said. So I started translating a work of history.

"Lo. In the thirty-seventh year of the Process of Cillen the rains came, which gave rise to rejoicing, for it was a rare and untoward occurrence, and commonly construed a blessing.

"But it was not the life-giving semen of Malann which fell from the heavens. It was the blood of the universe, spurting from an artery. And the last days were upon us. The final dance was to begin.

"The rains brought the plague that does not kill, and the last passes of Locar began with their drumming . . ."

I asked myself what the hell Tamur meant, for he was a historian and supposedly committed to fact. This was not their Apocalypse.

Unless they could be one and the same . . . ?

Why not? I mused. Tirellian's handful of people were the remnant of what had obviously once been a highly developed culture. They had had wars, but no holocausts; science, but little technology. A plague, a plague that did not kill . . . ? Could that have done it? How, if it wasn't fatal?

I read on, but the nature of the plague was not discussed. I turned pages, skipped ahead, and drew a blank.

M'Cwyie! M'Cwyie! When I want to question you most, you are not around!

Would it be a *faux pas* to go looking for her? Yes, I decided. I was restricted to the rooms I had been shown, that had been an implicit understanding. I would have to wait to find out.

So I cursed long and loud, in many languages, doubtless burning Malann's sacred ears, there in his Temple.

He did not see fit to strike me dead, so I decided to call it a day and hit the sack.

I must have been asleep for several hours when Braxa entered my room with a tiny lamp. She dragged me awake by tugging at my pajama sleeve.

I said hello. Thinking back, there is not much else I could have said.

"Hello."

"I have come," she said, "to hear the poem."

"What poem?"

"Yours."

"Oh."

I yawned, sat up, and did things people usually do when awakened in the middle of the night to read poetry.

"That is very kind of you, but isn't the hour a trifle awkward?"

"I don't mind," she said.

Someday I am going to write an article for the *Journal of Semantics,* called "Tone of Voice: An Insufficient Vehicle for Irony."

However, I was awake, so I grabbed my robe.

"What sort of animal is that?" she asked, pointing at the silk dragon on my lapel.

"Mythical," I replied. "Now look, it's late. I am tired. I have much to do in the morning. And M'Cwyie just might get the wrong idea if she learns you were here."

"Wrong idea?"

"You know damned well what I mean!" It was the first time I had had an opportunity to use Martian profanity, and it failed.

"No," she said, "I do not know."

She seemed frightened, like a puppy being scolded without knowing what it has done wrong.

I softened. Her red cloak matched her hair and lips so perfectly, and those lips were trembling.

"Here now, I didn't mean to upset you. On my world there are certain uh, mores, concerning people of different sex alone together in bedrooms, and not allied by marriage. . . . Um, I mean, you see what I mean?"

"No."

They were jade, her eyes.

"Well, it's sort of . . . Well, it's sex, that's what it is."

A light was switched on in those jade lamps.

"Oh, you mean having children!"

"Yes. That's it! Exactly."

She laughed. It was the first time I had heard laughter in Tirellian. It sounded like a violinist striking his high strings with the bow, in short little chops. It was not an altogether pleasant thing to hear, especially because she laughed too long.

When she had finished she moved closer.

"I remember, now," she said. "We used to have such rules. Half a Process ago, when I was a child, we had such rules. But"—she looked as if she were ready to laugh again—"there is no need for them now."

My mind moved like a tape recorder played at triple speed.

Half a Process! HalfaProcessa-ProcessaProcess! No! Yes!

Half a Process was two hundred-forty-three years, roughly speaking!

—Time enough to learn the 2,224 dances of Locar.

—Time enough to grow old, if you were human.

—Earth-style human, I mean.

I looked at her again, pale as the white queen in an ivory chess set.

She was human, I'd stake my soul—alive, normal, healthy, I'd stake my life—woman, my body . . .

But she was two and a half centuries old, which made M'Cwyie

Methuselah's grandma. It flattered me to think of their repeated complementing of my skills, as linguist, as poet. These superior beings!

But what did she mean "there is no such need for them now"? Why the near-hysteria? Why all those funny looks I'd been getting from M'Cwyie?

I suddenly knew I was close to something important, besides a beautiful girl.

"Tell me," I said, in my Casual Voice, "did it have anything to do with 'the plague that does not kill,' of which Tamur wrote?"

"Yes," she replied, "the children born after the Rains could have no children of their own, and—"

"And what?" I was leaning forward, memory set at "record."

"—and the men had no desire to get any."

I sagged backward against the bedpost. Racial sterility, masculine impotence, following phenomenal weather. Had some vagabond cloud of radioactive junk from God knows where penetrated their weak atmosphere one day? One day long before Schiaparelli saw the canals, mythical as my dragon, before those "canals" had given rise to some correct guesses for all the wrong reasons, had Braxa been alive, dancing, here—damned in the womb since blind Milton had written of another paradise, equally lost?

I found a cigarette. Good thing I had thought to bring ashtrays. Mars had never had a tobacco industry either. Or booze. The ascetics I had met in India had been Dionysiac compared to this.

"What is that tube of fire?"

"A cigarette. Want one?"

"Yes, please."

She sat beside me, and I lighted it for her.

"It irritates the nose."

"Yes. Draw some into your lungs, hold it there, and exhale."

A moment passed.

"Ooh," she said.

A pause, then, "Is it sacred?"

"No, it's nicotine," I answered, "a very *ersatz* form of divinity."

Another pause.

"Please don't ask me to translate '*ersatz.*' "

"I won't. I get this feeling sometimes when I dance."

"It will pass in a moment."

"Tell me your poem now."

An idea hit me.

"Wait a minute," I said. "I may have something better."

I got up and rummaged through my notebooks, then I returned and sat beside her.

"These are the first three chapters of the Book of Ecclesiastes," I explained. "It is very similar to your own sacred books."

I started reading.

I got through eleven verses before she cried out, "Please don't read that! Tell me one of yours!"

I stopped and tossed the notebook onto a nearby table. She was shaking, not as she had quivered that day she danced as the wind, but with the jitter of unshed tears. She held her cigarette awkwardly, like a pencil. Clumsily, I put my arm about her shoulders.

"He is so sad," she said, "like all the others."

So I twisted my mind like a bright ribbon, folded it, and tied the crazy Christmas knots I love so well. From German to Martian, with love, I did an impromptu paraphrasal of a poem about a Spanish dancer. I thought it would please her. I was right.

"Ooh," she said again. "Did you write that?"

"No, it's by a better man than I."

"I don't believe you. You wrote it."

"No, a man named Rilke did."

"But you brought it across to my language.—Light another match, so I can see how she danced."

I did.

" 'The fires of forever,' " she mused, "and she stamped them out, 'with small, firm feet.' I wish I could dance like that."

"You're better than any Gypsy," I laughed, blowing it out.

"No, I'm not. I couldn't do that."

Her cigarette was burning down, so I removed it from her fingers and put it out, along with my own.

"Do you want me to dance for you?"

"No," I said. "Go to bed."

She smiled, and before I realized it, had unclasped the fold of red at her shoulder.

And everything fell away.

And I swallowed, with some difficulty.

"All right," she said.

So I kissed her, as the breath of fallen cloth extinguished the lamp.

III

The days were like Shelley's leaves: yellow, red, brown, whipped in bright gusts by the west wind. They swirled past me with the rattle of microfilm. Almost all the books were recorded now. It would take scholars years to get through them, to properly assess their value. Mars was locked in my desk.

Ecclesiastes, abandoned and returned to a dozen times, was almost ready to speak in the High Tongue.

I whistled when I wasn't in the Temple. I wrote reams of poetry I would have been ashamed of before. Evenings I would walk with Braxa, across the dunes or up into the mountains. Sometimes she would dance for me; and I would read something long, and in dactylic hexameter. She still thought I was Rilke, and I almost kidded myself into believing it. Here I was, staying at the Castle Duino, writing his *Elegies*.

> . . . It is strange to inhabit the Earth no more,
> to use no longer customs scarce acquired,
> nor interpret roses . . .

No! Never interpret roses! Don't. Smell them, (sniff, Kane!), pick them, enjoy them. Live in the moment. Hold to it tightly. But charge not the gods to explain. So fast the leaves go by, are blown . . .

And no one ever noticed us. Or cared.

Laura. Laura and Braxa. They rhyme, you know, with a bit of a clash. Tall, cool, and blond was she (I hate blondes!), and Daddy had turned me inside out, like a pocket, and I thought she could fill me again. But the big, beat word-slinger, with Judas-beard and dog-trust in his eyes, oh, he had been a fine decoration at her parties. And that was all.

How the machine cursed me in the Temple! It blasphemed Malann and Gallinger. And the wild west wind went by and something was not far behind.

The last days were upon us.

A day went by and I did not see Braxa, and a night.

And a second. A third.

I was half-mad. I hadn't realized how close we had become, how important she had been. With the dumb assurance of presence, I had fought against questioning roses.

I had to ask. I didn't want to, but I had no choice.

"Where is she, M'Cwyie? Where is Braxa?"

"She is gone," she said.

"Where?"

"I do not know."

I looked at those devil-bird eyes. Anathema maranatha rose to my lips.

"I must know."

She looked through me.

"She has left us. She is gone. Up into the hills, I suppose. Or the desert. It does not matter. What does anything matter? The dance draws to a close. The Temple will soon be empty."

"Why? Why did she leave?"

"I do not know."

"I must see her again. We lift off in a matter of days."

"I am sorry, Gallinger."

"So am I," I said, and slammed shut a book without saying "m'narra."

I stood up.

"I will find her."

I left the Temple. M'Cwyie was a seated statue. My boots were still where I had left them.

All day I roared up and down the dunes, going nowhere. To the crew of the *Aspic* I must have looked like a sandstorm, all by myself. Finally, I had to return for more fuel.

Emory came stalking out.

"Okay, make it good. You look like the abominable dustman. Why the rodeo?"

"Why, I, uh, lost something."

"In the middle of the desert? Was it one of your sonnets? They're the only thing I can think of that you'd make such a fuss over."

"No, dammit! It was something personal."

George had finished filling the tank. I started to mount the jeepster again.

"Hold on there!" He grabbed my arm.

"You're not going back until you tell me what this is all about."

I could have broken his grip, but then he could order me dragged back by the heels, and quite a few people would enjoy doing the dragging. So I forced myself to speak slowly, softly:

"It's simply that I lost my watch. My mother gave it to me and it's a family heirloom. I want to find it before we leave."

"You sure it's not in your cabin, or down in Tirellian?"

"I've already checked."

"Maybe somebody hid it to irritate you. You know you're not the most popular guy around."

I shook my head.

"I thought of that. But I always carry it in my right pocket. I think it might have bounced out going over the dunes."

He narrowed his eyes.

"I remember reading on a book jacket that your mother died when you were born."

"That's right," I said, biting my tongue. "The watch belonged to her father and she wanted me to have it. My father kept it for me."

"Hmph!" He snorted. "That's a pretty strange way to look for a watch, riding up and down in a jeepster."

"I could see the light shining off it that way," I offered, lamely.

"Well, it's starting to get dark," he observed. "No sense looking any more today."

"Throw a dust sheet over the jeepster," he directed a mechanic.

He patted my arm.

"Come on in and get a shower, and something to eat. You look as if you could use both."

Little fatty flecks beneath pale eyes, thinning hair, and an Irish nose; a voice a decibel louder than anyone else's . . .

His only qualifications for leadership!

I stood there, hating him. Claudius! If only this were the fifth act!

But suddenly the idea of a shower, and food, came through to me. I could use both badly. If I insisted on hurrying back immediately, I might arouse more suspicion.

So I brushed some sand from my sleeve.

"You're right. That sounds like a good idea."

"Come on, we'll eat in my cabin."

The shower was a blessing, clean khakis were the grace of God, and the food smelled like Heaven.

"Smells pretty good," I said.

We hacked up our steaks in silence. When we got to the dessert and coffee, he suggested:

"Why don't you take the night off? Stay here and get some sleep."

I shook my head.

"I'm pretty busy. Finishing up. There's not much time left."

"A couple days ago you said you were almost finished."

"Almost, but not quite."

"You also said they'll be holding a service in the Temple tonight."

"That's right. I'm going to work in my room."

He shrugged his shoulders.

Finally, he said, "Gallinger," and I looked up because my name means trouble.

"It shouldn't be any of my business," he said, "but it is. Betty says you have a girl down there."

There was no question mark. It was a statement hanging in the air. Waiting.

—Betty, you're a bitch. You're a cow and a bitch. And a jealous one, at that. Why didn't you keep your nose where it belonged, shut your eyes? Your mouth?

"So?" I said, a statement with a question mark.

"So," he answered it, "it is my duty, as head of this expedition, to see that relations with the natives are carried on in a friendly, and diplomatic, manner."

"You speak of them," I said, "as though they are aborigines. Nothing could be further from the truth."

I rose.

"When my papers are published, everyone on Earth will know that truth. I'll tell them things Dr. Moore never even guessed at. I'll tell the tragedy of a doomed race, waiting for death, resigned and disinterested. I'll tell why, and it will break hard, scholarly hearts. I'll write about it, and they will give me more prizes, and this time I won't want them.

"My God!" I exclaimed. "They had a culture when our ancestors were clubbing the saber-tooth and finding out how fire works!"

"*Do* you have a girl down there?"

"Yes!" I said. *Yes, Claudius! Yes, Daddy! Yes, Emory!* "I do. But

I'm going to let you in on a scholarly scoop now. They're already dead. They're sterile. In one more generation there won't be any Martians."

I paused, then added, "Except in my papers, except on a few pieces of microfilm and tape. And in some poems, about a girl who did give a damn and could only bitch about the unfairness of it all by dancing."

"Oh," he said.

After a while:

"You *have* been behaving differently these past couple months. You've even been downright civil, on occasion, you know. I couldn't help wondering what was happening. I didn't know anything mattered that strongly to you."

I bowed my head.

"Is she the reason you were racing around the desert?"

I nodded.

"Why?"

I looked up.

"Because she's out there, somewhere. I don't know where, or why. And I've got to find her before we go."

"Oh," he said again.

Then he leaned back, opened a drawer, and took out something wrapped in a towel. He unwound it. A framed photo of a woman lay on the table.

"My wife," he said.

It was an attractive face, with big, almond eyes.

"I'm a Navy man, you know," he began. "Young officer once. Met her in Japan.

"Where I come from, it wasn't considered right to marry into another race, so we never did. But she was my wife. When she died, I was on the other side of the world. They took my children, and I've never seen them since. I couldn't learn what orphanage, what home, they were put into. That was long ago. Very few people know about it."

"I'm sorry," I said.

"Don't be. Forget it. But," he shifted in his chair and looked at me, "if you do want to take her back with you—do it. It'll mean my neck, but I'm too old to ever head another expedition like this one. So go ahead."

He gulped his cold coffee.

"Get your jeepster."

He swiveled the chair around.

I tried to say "thank you" twice, but I couldn't. So I got up and walked out.

"Sayonara, and all that," he muttered behind me.

"Here it is, Gallinger!" I heard a shout.

I turned on my heel and looked back up the ramp.

"Kane!"

He was limned in the port, shadow against light, but I had heard him sniff.

I returned the few steps.

"Here is what?"

"Your rose."

He produced a plastic container, divided internally. The lower half was filled with liquid. The stem ran down into it. The other half, a glass of claret in this horrible night, was a large, newly opened rose.

"Thank you," I said, tucking it into my jacket.

"Going back to Tirellian, eh?"

"Yes."

"I saw you come aboard, so I got it ready. Just missed you at the Captain's cabin. He was busy. Hollered out that I could catch you at the barns."

"Thanks again."

"It's chemically treated. It will stay in bloom for weeks."

I nodded. I was gone.

* * *

Up into the mountains now. Far. Far. The sky was a bucket of ice in which no moons floated. The going became steeper, and the little donkey protested. I whipped him with the throttle and went on. Up. Up. I spotted a green, unwinking star, and felt a lump in my throat. The encased rose beat against my chest like an extra heart. The donkey brayed, long and loudly, then began to cough. I lashed him some more and he died.

I threw the emergency brake on and got out. I began to walk.

So cold, so cold it grows. Up here. At night? Why? Why did she do it? Why flee the campfire when night comes on?

And I was up, down around, and through every chasm, gorge, and pass, with my long-legged strides and an ease of movement never known on Earth.

Barely two days remain, my love, and thou hast forsaken me. Why?

I crawled under overhangs. I leapt over ridges. I scraped my knees, and elbow. I heard my jacket tear.

No answer, Malann? Do you really hate your people this much? Then I'll try someone else. Vishnu, you're the Preserver. Preserve her, please! Let me find her.

Jehovah?

Adonis? Osiris? Thammuz? Manitou? Legba? Where is she?

I ranged far and high, and I slipped.

Stones ground underfoot and I dangled over an edge. My fingers so cold. It was hard to grip the rock.

I looked down.

Twelve feet or so. I let go and dropped, landed rolling.

Then I heard her scream.

I lay there, not moving, looking up. Against the night, above, she called.

"Gallinger!"

I lay still.

"Gallinger!"

And she was gone.

I heard stones rattle and knew she was coming down some path to the right of me.

I jumped up and ducked into the shadow of a boulder.

She rounded a cutoff, and picked her way, uncertainly, through the stones.

"Gallinger?"

I stepped out and seized her shoulders.

"Braxa."

She screamed again, then began to cry, crowding against me. It was the first time I had ever heard her cry.

"Why?" I asked. "Why?"

But she only clung to me and sobbed.

Finally, "I thought you had killed yourself."

"Maybe I would have," I said. "Why did you leave Tirellian? And me?"

"Didn't M'Cwyie tell you? Didn't you guess?"

"I didn't guess, and M'Cwyie said she didn't know."

"Then she lied. She knows."

"What? What is it she knows?"

She shook all over, then was silent for a long time. I realized suddenly that she was wearing only her flimsy dancer's costume. I pushed her from me, took off my jacket, and put it about her shoulders.

"Great Malann!" I cried. "You'll freeze to death!"

"No," she said, "I won't."

I was transferring the rose-case to my pocket.

"What is that?" she asked.

"A rose," I answered. "You can't make it out much in the dark. I once compared you to one. Remember?"

"Y-Yes. May I carry it?"

"Sure." I stuck it in the jacket pocket.

"Well? I'm still waiting for an explanation."

"You really do not know?" she asked.

"No!"

"When the Rains came," she said, "apparently only our men were affected, which was enough . . . Because I—wasn't—affected—apparently—"

"Oh," I said. "Oh."

We stood there, and I thought.

"Well, why did you run? What's wrong with being pregnant on Mars? Tamur was mistaken. Your people can live again."

She laughed, again that wild violin played by a Paganini gone mad. I stopped her before it went too far.

"How?" she finally asked, rubbing her cheek.

"Your people live longer than ours. If our child is normal, it will mean our races can intermarry. There must still be other fertile women of your race. Why not?"

"You have read the Book of Locar," she said, "and yet you ask me that? Death was decided, voted upon, and passed, shortly after it appeared in this form. But long before, the followers of Locar knew. They decided it long ago. 'We have done all things,' they said, 'we have seen all things, we have heard and felt all things. The dance was good. Now let it end.' "

"You can't believe that."

"What I believe does not matter," she replied. "M'Cwyie and the Mothers have decided we must die. Their very title is now a mockery, but their decisions will be upheld. There is only one prophecy left, and it is mistaken. We will die."

"No," I said.

"What, then?"

"Come back with me, to Earth."

"No."

"All right, then. Come with me now."

"Where?"

"Back to Tirellian. I'm going to talk to the Mothers."

"You can't! There is a Ceremony tonight!"

I laughed.

"A ceremony for a god who knocks you down, and then kicks you in the teeth?"

"He is still Malann," she answered. "We are still his people."

"You and my father would have gotten along fine," I snarled. "But I am going, and you are coming with me, even if I have to carry you—and I'm bigger than you are."

"But you are not bigger than Ontro."

"Who the hell is Ontro?"

"He will stop you, Gallinger. He is the Fist of Malann."

IV

I scudded the jeepster to a halt in front of the only entrance I knew, M'Cwyie's. Braxa, who had seen the rose in a headlamp, now cradled it in her lap, like our child, and said nothing. There was a passive, lovely look on her face.

"Are they in the Temple now?" I wanted to know.

The Madonna-expression did not change. I repeated the question. She stirred.

"Yes," she said, from a distance, "but you cannot go in."

"We'll see."

I circled and helped her down.

I led her by the hand, and she moved as if in a trance. In the light of the new-risen moon, her eyes looked as they had the day I met her, when she had danced. I snapped my fingers. Nothing happened.

So I pushed the door open and led her in. The room was half-lighted.

And she screamed for the third time that evening:

"Do not harm him, Ontro! It is Gallinger!"

I had never seen a Martian man before, only women. So I had no way of knowing whether he was a freak, though I suspected it strongly.

I looked up at him.

His half-naked body was covered with moles and swellings. Gland trouble, I guessed.

I had thought I was the tallest man on the planet, but he was seven feet tall and overweight. Now I knew where my giant bed had come from!

"Go back," he said. "She may enter. You may not."

"I must get my books and things."

He raised a huge left arm. I followed it. All my belongings lay neatly stacked in the corner.

"I must go in. I must talk with M'Cwyie and the Mothers."

"You may not."

"The lives of your people depend on it."

"Go back," he boomed. "Go home to *your* people, Gallinger. Leave *us!*"

My name sounded so different on his lips, like someone else's. How old was he? I wondered. Three hundred? Four? Had he been a Temple guardian all his life? Why? Who was there to guard against? I didn't like the way he moved. I had seen men who moved like that before.

"Go back," he repeated.

If they had refined their martial arts as far as they had their dances, or, worse yet, if their fighting arts were a part of the dance, I was in for trouble.

"Go on in," I said to Braxa. "Give the rose to M'Cwyie. Tell her that I sent it. Tell her I'll be there shortly."

"I will do as you ask. Remember me on Earth, Gallinger. Good-bye."

I did not answer her, and she walked past Ontro and into the next room, bearing her rose.

"Now will you leave?" he asked. "If you like, I will tell her that we fought and you almost beat me, but I knocked you unconscious and carried you back to your ship."

"No," I said, "either I go around you or go over you, but I am going through."

He dropped into a crouch, arms extended.

"It is a sin to lay hands on a holy man," he rumbled, "but I will stop you, Gallinger."

My memory was a fogged window, suddenly exposed to fresh air. Things cleared. I looked back six years.

I was a student of Oriental Languages at the University of Tokyo. It was my twice-weekly night of recreation. I stood in a thirty-foot circle in the Kodokan, the *judogi* lashed about my hips by a brown belt. I was *Ik-kyu,* one notch below the lowest degree of expert. A brown diamond above my right breast said "Jiu-Jitsu" in Japanese, and it meant *atemiwaza,* really, because of the one striking-technique I had worked out, found unbelievably suitable to my size, and won matches with.

But I had never used it on a man, and it was five years since I had practiced. I was out of shape, I knew, but I tried hard to force my mind *tsuki no kokoro,* like the moon, reflecting the all of Ontro.

Somewhere, out of the past, a voice said, "*Hajime,* let it begin."

I snapped into my *neko-ashidachi* cat-stance, and his eyes burned strangely. He hurried to correct his own position—and I threw it at him!

My one trick!

My long left leg lashed up like a broken spring. Seven feet off the ground, my foot connected with his jaw as he tried to leap backward.

His head snapped back and he fell. A soft moan escaped his lips. *That's all there is to it,* I thought. *Sorry, old fellow.*

And as I stepped over him, somehow, groggily, he tripped me, and I fell across his body. I couldn't believe he had strength enough to remain conscious after that blow, let alone move. I hated to punish him any more.

But he found my throat and slipped a forearm across it before I realized there was a purpose to his action.

No! Don't let it end like this!

It was a bar of steel across my windpipe, my carotids. Then I realized that he was still unconscious, and that this was a reflex instilled by countless years of training. I had seen it happen once, in *shiai*. The man had died because he had been choked unconscious and still fought on, and his opponent thought he had not been applying the choke properly. He tried harder.

But it was rare, so very rare!

I jammed my elbows into his ribs and threw my head back in his face. The grip eased, but not enough. I hated to do it, but I reached up and broke his little finger.

The arm went loose and I twisted free.

He lay there panting, face contorted. My heart went out to the fallen giant, defending his people, his religion, following his orders. I cursed myself as I had never cursed before, for walking over him, instead of around.

I staggered across the room to my little heap of possessions. I sat on the projector case and lit a cigarette.

I couldn't go inside the Temple until I got my breath back, until I thought of something to say?

How do you talk a race out of killing itself?

Suddenly—

—Could it happen? Would it work that way? If I read them the Book of Ecclesiastes—if I read them a greater piece of literature than any Locar ever wrote—and as somber—and as pessimistic—and showed them that our race had gone on despite one man's condemning all of life in the highest poetry—showed them that the vanity he had mocked had borne us to the Heavens—would they believe it?—would they change their minds?

I ground out my cigarette on the beautiful floor, and found my notebook. A strange fury rose within me as I stood.

And I walked into the Temple to preach the Black Gospel according to Gallinger, from the Book of Life.

There was silence all about me.

M'Cwyie had been reading Locar, the rose set at her right hand, target of all eyes.

Until I entered.

Hundreds of people were seated on the floor, barefoot. The few men were as small as the women, I noted.

I had my boots on.

Go all the way, I figured. *You either lose or you win—everything!*

A dozen crones sat in a semi-circle behind M'Cwyie. The Mothers.

The barren earth, the dry wombs, the fire-touched.

I moved to the table.

"Dying yourselves, you would condemn your people," I addressed them, "that they may not know the life you have known—the joys, the sorrows, the fullness.—But it is not true that you all must die." I addressed the multitude now. "Those who say this lie, Braxa knows, for she will bear a child—"

They sat there, like rows of Buddhas. M'Cwyie drew back into the semicircle.

"—my child!" I continued, wondering what my father would have thought of this sermon.

". . . And all the women young enough may bear children. It is only your men who are sterile.—And if you permit the doctors of the next expedition to examine you, perhaps even the men may be helped. But if they cannot, you can mate with the men of Earth.

"And ours is not an insignificant people, an insignificant place," I went on. "Thousands of years ago, the Locar of our world wrote a book saying that it was. He spoke as Locar did, but we did not lie down, despite plagues, wars, and famines. We did not die. One by one we beat down the diseases, we fed the hungry, we fought the wars and, recently, have gone a long time without them. We may finally have conquered them. I do not know.

"But we have crossed millions of miles of nothingness. We have visited another world. And our Locar had said, 'Why bother? What is the worth of it? It is all vanity, anyhow.'

"And the secret is"—I lowered my voice, as at a poetry reading—"he was right! It *is* vanity, it *is* pride! It is the hubris of rationalism to always attack the prophet, the mystic, the god. It is our blasphemy which has made us great, and will sustain us, and which the gods secretly admire in us.—All the truly sacred names of God are blasphemous things to speak!"

I was working up a sweat. I paused dizzily.

"Here is the Book of Ecclesiastes," I announced, and began:

" 'Vanity of vanities, saith the Preacher, vanity of vanities; all is vanity. What profit hath a man . . .' "

I spotted Braxa in the back, mute, rapt.

I wondered what she was thinking.

And I wound the hours of night about me, like black thread on a spool.

Oh it was late! I had spoken till day came, and still I spoke. I finished Ecclesiastes and continued Gallinger.

And when I finished there was still only a silence.

The Buddhas, all in a row, had not stirred through the night. And after a long while, M'Cwyie raised her right hand. One by one, the Mothers did the same.

And I knew what that meant.

It meant no, do not, cease, and stop.

It meant that I had failed.

I walked slowly from the room and slumped beside my baggage.

Ontro was gone. Good that I had not killed him . . .

After a thousand years, M'Cwyie entered.

She said, "Your job is finished."

I did not move.

"The prophecy is fulfilled," she said. "My people are rejoicing. You have won, holy man. Now leave us quickly."

My mind was a deflated balloon. I pumped a little air back into it.

"I'm not a holy man," I said, "just a second-rate poet with a bad case of hubris."

I lit my last cigarette.

Finally, "All right, what prophecy?"

"The Promise of Locar," she replied, as though the explaining were unnecessary, "that a holy man would come from the heavens to save us in our last hours, if all the dances of Locar were completed. He would defeat the Fist of Malann and bring us life."

"How?"

"As with Braxa, and as the example in the Temple."

"Example?"

"You read us his words, as great as Locar's. You read to us how there is 'nothing new under the sun.' And you mocked his words as you read them—showing us a new thing.

"There has never been a flower on Mars," she said, "but we will learn to grow them.

"You are the Sacred Scoffer," she finished. "He-Who-Must-Mock-in-the-Temple—you go shod on holy ground."

"But you voted 'no,' " I said.

"I voted not to carry out our original plan, and to let Braxa's child live instead."

"Oh." The cigarette fell from my fingers. How close it had been! How little I had known!

"And Braxa?"

"She was chosen half a Process ago to do the dances—to wait for you."

"But she said that Ontro would stop me."

M'Cwyie stood there for a long time.

"She had never believed the prophecy herself. Things are not well with her now. She ran away, fearing it was true. When you completed and we voted, she knew."

"Then she does not love me? Never did?"

"I am sorry, Gallinger. It was the one part of her duty she never managed."

"Duty," I said flatly . . . Dutydutyduty! Tra-la!

"She has said good-bye, she does not wish to see you again.

". . . and we will never forget your teachings," she added.

"Don't," I said, automatically, suddenly knowing the great paradox which lies at the heart of all miracles. I did not believe a word of my own gospel, never had.

I stood, like a drunken man, and muttered, "M'narra."

I went outside, into my last day on Mars.

I have conquered thee, Malann—and the victory is thine! Rest easy on thy starry bed. God damned!

I left the jeepster there and walked back to the *Aspic,* leaving the burden of life so many footsteps behind me. I went to my cabin, locked the door, and took forty-four sleeping pills.

But when I awakened I was in the dispensary, and alive.

I felt the throb of engines as I slowly stood up and somehow made it to the port.

Blurred Mars hung like a swollen belly above me, until it dissolved, brimmed over, and streamed down my face.

We Can Remember It for You Wholesale

✦

Philip K. Dick

Science fiction changed a lot in the 1960s. Social, cultural, artistic, and scientific tides of change brought on the New Wave of the '60s, which washed away many of science fiction's older traditions. One effect of the New Wave was to shift focus from outer space to inner space, and one writer who responded well to these new influences was Philip K. Dick. Always an imaginative writer, Dick was extremely creative and prolific through the 1960s, publishing nineteen novels and a score of stories over the course of the decade, including such classics as The Man in the High Castle, A Maze of Death, Martian Time-Slip, *and* Do Androids Dream of Electric Sheep?

"We Can Remember It for You Wholesale" was adapted into the film Total Recall, *and it's somewhat different in tone from a lot of this book. Where most of the stories included here are fairly exacting in the mechanics of getting from Earth to Mars, Philip K. Dick gives us a story in which the protagonist cannot even know if he has gone to Mars or not!*

HE AWOKE—AND wanted Mars. The valleys, he thought. What would it be like to trudge among them? Great and greater yet: the dream grew as he became fully conscious, the dream and the yearning. He could almost feel the enveloping presence of the other world, which only Government agents and high officials had seen. A clerk like himself? Not likely.

"Are you getting up or not?" his wife Kirsten asked drowsily, with her usual hint of fierce crossness. "If you are, push the hot-coffee button on the darn stove."

"Okay," Douglas Quail said, and made his way barefoot from the bedroom of their conapt to the kitchen. There, having dutifully pressed the hot coffee button, he seated himself at the kitchen table, brought out a yellow, small tin of fine Dean Swift snuff. He inhaled briskly, and the Beau Nash mixture stung his nose, burned the roof of his mouth. But still he inhaled; it woke him up and allowed his dreams, his nocturnal desires and random wishes, to condense into a semblance of rationality.

I will go, he said to himself. Before I die, I'll see Mars.

It was, of course, impossible, and he knew this even as he dreamed. But the daylight, the mundane noise of his wife now brushing her hair before the bedroom mirror—everything conspired to remind him of what he was. A miserable little salaried employee, he said to himself with bitterness. Kirsten reminded him of this at least once a day and he did not blame her; it was a wife's job to bring her husband down to Earth. Down to Earth, he thought, and laughed. The figure of speech in this was literally apt.

"What are you sniggering about?" his wife asked as she swept into the kitchen, her long busy-pink robe wagging after her. "A dream, I bet. You're always full of them."

"Yes," he said, and gazed out the kitchen window at the hover-cars and traffic runnels, and all the little energetic people hurrying to work. In a little while he would be among them. As always.

"I'll bet it has to do with some woman," Kirsten said witheringly.

"No," he said. "A god. The god of war. He has wonderful craters with every kind of plant-life growing deep down in them."

"Listen." Kirsten crouched down beside him and spoke earnestly, the harsh quality momentarily gone from her voice. "The bottom of the ocean—*our* ocean is much more, an infinity of times more beautiful. You know that; everyone knows that. Rent an artificial gill-outfit for both of us, take a week off from work, and we can descend and live down there at one of those year-round aquatic resorts. And in addition—" She broke off. "You're not listening. You should be. Here is something a lot better than that compulsion, that obsession you have about Mars, and you don't even listen!" Her voice rose piercingly. "God in heaven, you're doomed, Doug! What's going to become of you?"

"I'm going to work," he said, rising to his feet, his breakfast forgotten. "That's what's going to become of me."

She eyed him. "You're getting worse. More fanatical every day. Where's it going to lead?"

"To Mars," he said, and opened the door to the closet to get down a fresh shirt to wear to work.

Having descended from the taxi, Douglas Quail slowly walked across three densely populated foot runnels and to the modern, attractively inviting doorway. There he halted, impeding midmorning traffic, and with caution read the shifting-color neon sign. He had, in the past, scrutinized this sign before . . . but never had he come so close. This was very different; what he did now was something else. Something which sooner or later had to happen.

REKAL, INCORPORATED.

Was this the answer? After all, an illusion, no matter how convincing, remained nothing more than an illusion. At least objectively. But subjectively—quite the opposite entirely.

And anyhow, he had an appointment. Within the next five minutes.

* * *

Taking a deep breath of mildly smog-infested Chicago air, he walked through the dazzlingly polychromatic shimmer of the doorway and up to the receptionist's counter.

The nicely articulated blonde at the counter, bare-bosomed and tidy, said pleasantly, "Good morning, Mr. Quail."

"Yes," he said. "I'm here to see about a Rekal course. As I guess you know."

"Not 'rekal' but '*re*call,' " the receptionist corrected him. She picked up the receiver of the vid-phone by her smooth elbow and said into it, "Mr. Douglas Quail is here, Mr. McClane. May he come inside, now? Or is it too soon?"

"Giz wetwa wum-wum wamp," the phone mumbled.

"Yes, Mr. Quail," she said. "You may go in; Mr McClane is expecting you." As he started off uncertainly, she called after him, "Room D, Mr. Quail. To your right."

After a frustrating but brief moment of being lost he found the proper room. The door hung open and inside, at a big genuine walnut desk, sat a genial-looking man, middle-aged, wearing the latest Martian frog-pelt gray suit; his attire alone would have told Quail that he had come to the right person.

"Sit down, Douglas," McClane said, waving his plump hand toward a chair which faced the desk. "So you want to have gone to Mars. Very good."

Quail seated himself, feeling tense. "I'm not so sure this is worth the fee," he said. "It costs a lot, and as far as I can see, I really get nothing." Costs almost as much as going, he thought.

"You get tangible proof of your trip," McClane disagreed emphatically. "All the proof you'll need. Here; I'll show you." He dug within a drawer of his impressive desk. "Ticket stub." Reaching into a manila folder, he produced a small square of embossed cardboard. "It proves you went—and returned. Postcards." He laid out four franked picture 3-D full-color postcards in a neatly arranged row on the desk for Quail to see. "Film. Shots you took of local sights on Mars with a rented movie camera." To Quail he displayed those, too. "Plus the names of people you met, two hundred poscreds' worth of souvenirs, which will arrive—from Mars—within the following month. And passport, certificates listing the shots you received. And more." He glanced up keenly at Quail. "You'll know you went, all right," he said. "You won't remember us, won't remember me or ever having been here. It'll be a real trip in your mind; we guarantee that. A full two weeks of recall; every last piddling detail. Remember this: If at any time you doubt that you really took an extensive trip to Mars, you can return here and get a full refund. You see?"

"But I didn't go," Quail said. "I won't have gone, no matter what proofs you provide me with." He took a deep, unsteady breath. "And I never was a secret agent with Interplan." It seemed impossible to him that Rekal, Incorporated's extra-factual memory implant would do its job—despite what he had heard people say.

"Mr. Quail," McClane said patiently. "As you explained in your letter to us, you have no chance, no possibility in the slightest, of ever actually getting to Mars; you can't afford it, and what is much more important, you could never qualify as an undercover agent for Interplan or anybody else. This is the only way you can achieve your, ahem, lifelong dream; am I not correct, sir? You can't be this; you can't actually do this." He chuckled. "But you can *have been* and *have done*. We see to that. And our fee is reasonable; no hidden charges." He smiled encouragingly.

"Is an extra-factual memory that convincing?" Quail asked.

"More than the real thing, sir. Had you really gone to Mars as an Interplan agent, you would by now have forgotten a great deal; our analysis of true-mem systems—authentic recollections of major events in a person's life—shows that a variety of details are very quickly lost to the person. Forever. Part of the package we offer you is such deep implantation of recall that nothing is forgotten. The packet which is fed to you while you're comatose is the creation of trained experts, men who have spent years on Mars; in every case we verify details down to the last iota. And you've picked a rather easy extra-factual system; had you picked Pluto or wanted to be Emperor of the Inner Planet Alliance we'd have much more difficulty . . . and the charges would be considerably greater."

Reaching into his coat for his wallet, Quail said, "Okay. It's been my lifelong ambition, and I can see I'll never really do it. So I guess I'll have to settle for this."

"Don't think of it that way," McClane said severely. "You're not accepting second best. The actual memory, with all its vagueness, omissions and ellipses, not to say distortions—that's second best." He accepted the money and pressed a button on his desk. "All right, Mr. Quail," he said, as the door of his office opened and two burly men swiftly entered. "You're on your way to Mars as a secret agent." He rose, came over to shake Quail's nervous, moist hand. "Or rather, you have been on your way. This afternoon at four-thirty you will, um, arrive back here on Terra; a cab will leave you off at your conapt, and as I say, you will never remember seeing me or coming here; you won't, in fact, even remember having heard of our existence."

His mouth dry with nervousness, Quail followed the two technicians from the office; what happened next depended on them.

Will I actually believe I've been on Mars? he wondered. That I managed to fulfill my lifetime ambition? He had a strange, lingering intuition that something would go wrong. But just what—he did not know.

He would have to wait to find out.

The intercom on McClane's desk, which connected him with the work area of the firm, buzzed and a voice said, "Mr. Quail is under sedation now, sir. Do you want to supervise this one, or shall we go ahead?"

"It's routine," McClane observed. "You may go ahead, Lowe; I don't think you'll run into any trouble." Programming an artificial memory of a trip to another planet—with or without the added fillip of being a secret agent—showed up on the firm's work-schedule with monotonous regularity. In one month, he calculated wryly, we must do twenty of these . . . ersatz interplanetary travel has become our bread and butter.

"Whatever you say, Mr. McClane," Lowe's voice came, and thereupon the intercom shut off.

Going to the vault section in the chamber behind his office, McClane searched about for a Three packet—trip to Mars—and a Sixty-two packet: secret Interplan spy. Finding the two packets, he returned with them to his desk, seated himself comfortably, poured out the contents—merchandise which would be planted in Quail's conapt while the lab technicians busied themselves installing the false memory.

A one-poscred sneaky-pete sidearm, McClane reflected; that's the largest item. Sets us back financially the most. Then a pellet-sized transmitter, which could be swallowed if the agent were caught. Codebook that astonishingly resembled the real thing . . . the firm's models were highly accurate: based, whenever possible, on actual U.S. military issue. Odd bits which made no intrinsic sense but which would be woven into the warp and woof of Quail's imaginary trip, would coincide with his memory: half an ancient silver fifty-cent piece, several quotations from John Donne's sermons written incorrectly, each on a separate piece of transparent tissue-thin paper, several match folders from bars on Mars, a stainless-steel spoon engraved PROPERTY OF DOME-MARS NATIONAL KIBBUZIM, a wiretapping coil which—

The intercom buzzed. "Mr. McClane, I'm sorry to bother you, but something rather ominous has come up. Maybe it would be better if you were in here after all. Quail is already under sedation; he reacted well to the narkidrine; he's completely unconscious and receptive. But—"

"I'll be in." Sensing trouble, McClane left his office; a moment later he emerged into the work area.

On a hygienic bed lay Douglas Quail, breathing slowly and regularly, his eyes virtually shut; he seemed dimly—but only dimly—aware of the two technicians and now McClane himself.

"There's no space to insert the false memory-patterns?" McClane felt irritation. "Merely drop out two work weeks; he's employed as a clerk at the West Coast Emigration Bureau, which is a government agency, so he undoubtedly has or had two weeks' vacation within the last year. That ought to do it." Petty details annoyed him. And always would.

"Our problem," Lowe said sharply, "is something quite different." He bent over the bed, said to Quail, "Tell Mr. McClane what you told us." To McClane he said, "Listen closely."

The gray-green eyes of the man lying supine in the bed focused on McClane's face. The eyes, he observed uneasily, had become hard; they had a polished, inorganic quality, like semiprecious tumbled stones. He was not sure that he liked what he saw; the brilliance was too cold. "What do you want now?" Quail said harshly. "You've broken my cover. Get out of here before I take you all apart." He studied McClane. "Especially you," he continued. "You're in charge of this counteroperation."

Lowe said, "How long were you on Mars?"

"One month," Quail said gratingly.

"And your purpose there?" Lowe demanded.

The meager lips twisted; Quail eyed him and did not speak. At last, drawling the words out so that they dripped with hostility, he said, "Agent for Interplan. As I already told you. Don't you record everything that's said? Play your vid-aud tape back for your boss and leave me alone." He shut his eyes, then; the hard brilliance ceased. McClane felt, instantly, a rushing splurge of relief.

Lowe said quietly, "This is a tough man, Mr. McClane."

"He won't be," McClane said, "after we arrange for him to lose his memory-chain again. He'll be as meek as before." To Quail he said, "So *this* is why you wanted to go to Mars so terribly badly."

Without opening his eyes Quail said, "I never wanted to go to Mars. I was assigned it—they handed it to me and there I was: stuck. Oh yeah, I admit I was curious about it; who wouldn't be?" Again he opened his eyes and surveyed the three of them, McClane in particular. "Quite a truth drug you've got here; it brought up things I had absolutely no memory of." He pondered. "I wonder about Kirsten," he said, half to himself. "Could she be in on it? An Interplan contact keeping an eye on me . . . to be certain I didn't regain my memory? No wonder she's been so derisive about my wanting to go there." Faintly, he smiled; the smile—one of understanding—disappeared almost at once.

McClane said, "Please believe me, Mr. Quail; we stumbled onto this entirely by accident. In the work we do—"

"I believe you," Quail said. He seemed tired, now; the drug was continuing to pull him under, deeper and deeper. "Where did I say I'd been?" he murmured. "Mars? Hard to remember—I know I'd like to see it; so would everybody else. But me—" His voice trailed off. "Just a clerk, a nothing clerk."

Straightening up, Lowe said to his superior, "He wants a false memory implanted that corresponds to a trip he actually took. And a false reason which is the real reason. He's telling the truth; he's a long way down in the narkidrine. The trip is very vivid in his mind—at least under sedation. But apparently he doesn't recall it otherwise. Someone, probably at a government military-sciences lab, erased his conscious memories; all he knew was that going to Mars meant something special to him, and so did being a secret agent. They couldn't erase that: It's not a memory, but a desire, undoubtedly the same one that motivated him to volunteer for the assignment in the first place."

The other technician, Keeler, said to McClane, "What do we do? Graft a false memory-pattern over the real memory? There's no telling what the results would be; he might remember some of the genuine trip, and the confusion might bring on a psychotic interlude. He'd have to hold two opposite premises in his mind simultaneously: that he went to Mars and that he didn't. That he's a genuine agent for Interplan and he's not, that it's spurious. I think we ought to revive him without any false memory implantation and send him out of here; this is hot."

"Agreed," McClane said. A thought came to him. "Can you predict what he'll remember when he comes out of sedation?"

"Impossible to tell," Lowe said. "He probably will have some dim, diffuse memory of his actual trip, now. And he'd probably be in grave doubt as to its validity; he'd probably decide our programming slipped a gear-tooth. And he'd remember coming here; that wouldn't be erased—unless you want it erased."

"The less we mess with this man," McClane said, "the better I like it. This is nothing for us to fool around with; we've been foolish enough to—or unlucky enough to—uncover a genuine Interplan spy who has a cover so perfect that up to now even he didn't know what he was—or rather *is.*" The sooner they washed their hands of the man calling himself Douglas Quail the better.

"Are you going to plant packets Three and Sixty-two at his conapt?" Lowe said.

"No," McClane said. "And we're going to return half his fee."

" 'Half!' Why half?"

McClane said lamely, "It seems to be a good compromise."

As the cab carried him back to his conapt at the residential end of Chicago, Douglas Quail said to himself, It's sure good to be back on Terra.

Already the month-long period on Mars had begun to waver in his memory; he had only an image of profound gaping craters, an ever-present ancient erosion of hills, of vitality, of motion itself. A world of dust where little happened, where a good part of the day was spent checking and rechecking one's portable oxygen source. And then the life forms, the unassuming and modest gray-brown cacti and maw-worms.

As a matter of fact, he had brought back several moribund examples of Martian fauna; he had smuggled them through customs. After all, they posed no menace; they couldn't survive in Earth's heavy atmosphere.

Reaching into his coat pocket, he rummaged for the container of Martian maw-worms—

And found an envelope instead.

Lifting it out he discovered, to his perplexity, that it contained five hundred and seventy poscreds, in cred bills of low denomination.

Where'd I get this? he asked himself. Didn't I spend every 'cred I had on my trip?"

With the money came a slip of paper marked: *one-half fee ret'd. By McClane.* And then the date. Today's date.

"Recall," he said aloud.

"Recall what, sir or madam?" the robot driver of the cab inquired respectfully.

"Do you have a phone book?" Quail demanded.

"Certainly, sir or madam." A slot opened; from it slid a microtape phone book for Cook County.

"It's spelled oddly," Quail said as he leafed through the pages of the yellow section. He felt fear, then; abiding fear. "Here it is," he said. "Take me there, to Rekal, Incorporated. I've changed my mind; I don't want to go home."

"Yes, sir, or madam, as the case may be," the driver said. A moment later the cab was zipping back in the opposite direction.

"May I make use of your phone?" he asked.

"Be my guest," the robot driver said. And presented a shiny new emperor 3-D color phone to him.

He dialed his own conapt. And after a pause found himself

confronted by a miniature but chillingly realistic image of Kirsten on the small screen. "I've been to Mars," he said to her.

"You're drunk." Her lips writhed scornfully. "Or worse."

" 'S god's truth."

"When?" she demanded.

"I don't know." He felt confused. "A simulated trip, I think. By means of one of those artificial or extra-factual or whatever-it-is memory places. It didn't take."

Kirsten said witheringly, "You are drunk." And broke the connection at her end. He hung up, then, feeling his face flush. Always the same tone, he said hotly to himself. Always the retort, as if she knows everything and I know nothing. What a marriage, Keerist, he thought dismally.

A moment later the cab stopped at the curb before a modern, very attractive little pink building, over which a shifting, polychromatic neon sign read: REKAL, INCORPORATED.

The receptionist, chic and bare from the waist up, started in surprise, then gained masterful control of herself. "Oh hello, Mr. Quail," she said nervously. "H-how are you? Did you forget something?"

"The rest of my fee back," he said.

More composed now the receptionist said, "Fee? I think you are mistaken, Mr. Quail. You were here discussing the feasibility of an extra-factual trip for you, but—" She shrugged her smooth pale shoulders. "As I understand it, no trip was taken."

Quail said, "I remember everything, miss. My letter to Rekal, Incorporated, which started this whole business off. I remember my arrival here, my visit with Mr. McClane. Then the two lab technicians taking me in tow and administering a drug to put me out." No wonder the firm had returned half his fee. The false memory of his "trip to Mars" hadn't taken—at least not entirely, not as he had been assured.

"Mr. Quail," the girl said, "although you are a minor clerk, you are a good-looking man and it spoils your features to become angry. If it would make you feel any better, I might, ahem, let you take me out . . ."

He felt furious, then. "I remember you," he said savagely. "For instance the fact that your breasts are sprayed blue; that stuck in my mind. And I remember Mr. McClane's promise that if I remembered my visit to Rekal, Incorporated, I'd receive my money back in full. Where is Mr. McClane?"

After a delay—probably as long as they could manage—he found himself once more seated facing the imposing walnut desk, exactly as he had been an hour or so earlier in the day.

"Some technique you have," Quail said sardonically. His disappointment—and resentment—were enormous, by now. "My so-called 'memory' of a trip to Mars as an undercover agent for Interplan is hazy and vague and shot full of contradictions. And I clearly remember my dealings here with you people. I ought to take this to the Better Business Bureau." He was burning angry, at this point; his sense of being cheated had overwhelmed him, had destroyed his customary aversion to participating in a public squabble.

Looking morose, as well as cautious, McClane said, "We capitulate, Quail. We'll refund the balance of your fee. I fully concede the fact that we did absolutely nothing for you." His tone was resigned.

Quail said accusingly, "You didn't even provide me with the various artifacts that you claimed would 'prove' to me I had been on Mars. All that song-and-dance you went into—it hasn't materialized into a damn thing. Not even a ticket stub. Nor postcards. Nor passport. Nor proof of immunization shots. Nor—"

"Listen, Quail," McClane said. "Suppose I told you—" He broke off. "Let it go." He pressed a button on his intercom. "Shirley, will you disburse five hundred and seventy more 'creds in the form of a cashier's check made out to Douglas Quail? Thank you." He released the button, then glared at Quail.

Presently the check appeared: the receptionist placed it before McClane and once more vanished out of sight, leaving the two men alone, still facing each other across the surface of the massive walnut desk.

"Let me give you a word of advice," McClane said as he signed the check and passed it over. "Don't discuss your, ahem, recent trip to Mars with anyone."

"What trip?"

"Well, that's the thing." Doggedly, McClane said, "The trip you partially remember. Act as if you don't remember; pretend it never took place. Don't ask me why; just take my advice: it'll be better for all of us." He had begun to perspire. Freely. "Now, Mr. Quail, I have other business, other clients to see." He rose, showed Quail to the door.

Quail said, as he opened the door, "A firm that turns out such bad work shouldn't have any clients at all." He shut the door behind him.

On the way home in the cab Quail pondered the wording of his letter of complaint to the Better Business Bureau, Terra Division. As soon as he could get to his typewriter, he'd get started; it was clearly his duty to warn other people away from Rekal, Incorporated.

When he got back to his conapt, he seated himself before his Hermes Rocket portable, opened the drawers, and rummaged for carbon paper—and noticed a small, familiar box. A box which he had carefully filled on Mars with Martian fauna and later smuggled through customs.

Opening the box he saw, to his disbelief, six dead maw-worms and several varieties of the unicellular life on which the Martian worms fed. The protozoa were dried-up, dusty, but he recognized them; it had taken him an entire day picking among the vast dark alien boulders to find them. A wonderful, illuminated journey of discovery.

But I didn't go to Mars, he realized.

Yet on the other hand—

Kirsten appeared at the doorway to the room, an armload of pale brown groceries gripped. “Why are you home in the middle of the day?” Her voice, in an eternity of sameness, was accusing.

“*Did I go to Mars?*” he asked her. “You would know.”

“No, of course you didn’t go to Mars; you would know that, I would think. Aren’t you always bleating about going?”

He said, “By God, I think I went.” After a pause he added, “And simultaneously I think I didn’t go.”

“Make up your mind.”

“How can I?” He gestured. “I have both memory-tracks grafted inside my head; one is real and one isn’t, but I can’t tell which is which. Why can’t I rely on you? They haven’t tinkered with you.” She could do this much for him at least—even if she never did anything else.

Kirsten said in a level, controlled voice, “Doug, if you don’t pull yourself together, we’re through. I’m going to leave you.”

“I’m in trouble.” His voice came out husky and coarse. And shaking. “Probably I’m heading into a psychotic episode; I hope not, but—maybe that’s it. It would explain everything, anyhow.”

Setting down the bag of groceries, Kirsten stalked to the closet. “I was not kidding,” she said to him quietly. She brought out a coat, got it on, walked back to the door of the conapt. “I’ll phone you one of these days soon,” she said tonelessly. “This is good-bye, Doug. I hope you pull out of this eventually; I really pray you do. For your sake.”

“Wait,” he said desperately. “Just tell me and make it absolute: I did go or I didn’t—tell me which one.” But they may have altered your memory-track also, he realized.

The door closed. His wife had left. Finally!

A voice behind him said, “Well, that’s that. Now put up your hands, Quail. And also please turn around and face this way.”

He turned, instinctively, without raising his hands.

The man who faced him wore the plum uniform of the Interplan Police Agency, and his gun appeared to be U.N. issue. And, for some odd reason, he seemed familiar to Quail; familiar in a blurred, distorted fashion which he could not pin down. So, jerkily, he raised his hands.

"You remember," the policeman said, "your trip to Mars. We know all your actions today and all your thoughts—in particular your very important thoughts on the trip home from Rekal, Incorporated." He explained, "We have a telep-transmitter wired within your skull; it keeps us constantly informed."

A telepathic transmitter; use of a living plasma that had been discovered on Luna. He shuddered with self-aversion. The thing lived inside him, within his own brain, feeding, listening, feeding. But the Interplan police used them; that had come out even in the homeopapes. So this was probably true, dismal as it was.

"Why me?" Quail said huskily. What had he done—or thought? And what did this have to do with Rekal, Incorporated?

"Fundamentally?" the Interplan cop said, "this has nothing to do with Rekal; it's between you and us." He tapped his right ear. "I'm still picking up your mentational processes by way of your cephalic transmitter." In the man's ear Quail saw a small white-plastic plug. "So I have to warn you: anything you think may be held against you." He smiled. "Not that it matters now; you've already thought and spoken yourself into oblivion. What's annoying is the fact that under narkidrine at Rekal, Incorporated you told them, their technicians and the owner, Mr. McClane, about your trip; where you went, for whom, some of what you did. They're very frightened. They wish they had never laid eyes on you." He added reflectively, "They're right."

Quail said, "I never made any trip. It's a false memory-chain improperly planted in me by McClane's technicians." But then he thought of the box, in his desk drawer, containing the Martian life forms. And the trouble and hardship he had had gathering them. The memory seemed real. And the box of life forms; that certainly was real. Unless McClane had planted it. Perhaps this was one of the "proofs" which McClane had talked glibly about.

The memory of my trip to Mars, he thought, doesn't convince me—but unfortunately it has convinced the Interplan Police Agency. They think I really went to Mars and they think I at least partially realize it.

"We not only know you went to Mars," the Interplan cop agreed, in answer to his thoughts, "but we know that you now remember enough to be difficult for us. And there's no use expunging your conscious memory of all this, because if we do you'll simply show up at Rekal, Incorporated again and start over. And we can't do anything about McClane and his operation because we have no jurisdiction over anyone except our own people. Anyhow, McClane hasn't committed any crime." He eyed Quail. "Nor, technically, have you. You didn't go to Rekal, Incorporated with the idea of regaining your memory; you went, as we realize, for the usual reason people go there—a love by plain, dull people for adventure." He added, "Unfortunately you're not plain, not dull, and you've already had too much excitement; the last thing in the universe you needed was a course from Rekal, Incorporated. Nothing could have been more lethal for you or for us. And, for that matter, for McClane."

Quail said, "Why is it 'difficult' for you if I remember my trip—my alleged trip—and what I did there?"

"Because," the Interplan harness bull said, "what you did is not in accord with our great white all-protecting father public image. You did, for us, what we never do. As you'll presently remember—thanks to narkidrine. That box of dead worms and algae has been sitting in your desk drawer for six months, ever since you got back. And at no time have you shown the slightest curiosity about it. We didn't even know you had it until you remembered it on your way home from Rekal; then we came here on the double to look for it." He added, unnecessarily, "Without any luck; there wasn't enough time."

A second Interplan cop joined the first one; the two conferred briefly. Meanwhile, Quail thought rapidly. He did remember more, now; the cop had been right about narkidrine. They—Interplan—probably used it themselves. Probably? He know darn well they did; he had seen them putting a prisoner on it. Where would *that* be? Somewhere on Terra? More likely Luna, he decided, viewing the image rising from his highly defective—but rapidly less so—memory.

And he remembered something else. Their reason for sending him to Mars; the job he had done.

No wonder they had expunged his memory.

"Oh, God," the first of the two Interplan cops said, breaking off his conversation with his companion. Obviously, he had picked up Quail's thoughts. "Well, this is a far worse problem, now; as bad as it can get." He walked toward Quail, again covering him with his gun. "We've got to kill you," he said. "And right away."

Nervously, his fellow officer said, "Why right away? Can't we simply cart him off to Interplan New York and let them—"

"*He* knows why it has to be right away," the first cop said; he, too, looked nervous, now, but Quail realized that it was for an entirely different reason. His memory had been brought back almost entirely, now. And he fully understood the officer's tension.

"On Mars," Quail said hoarsely, "I killed a man. After getting past fifteen bodyguards. Some armed with sneaky-pete guns, the way you are." He had been trained, by Interplan, over a five-year period to be an assassin. A professional killer. He knew ways to take out armed adversaries . . . such as these two officers; and the one with the ear-receiver knew it, too.

If he moved swiftly enough—

The gun fired. But he had already moved to one side, and at the same time he chopped down the gun-carrying officer. In an instant he had possession of the gun and was covering the other, confused officer.

"Picked my thoughts up," Quail said, panting for breath. "He knew what I was going to do, but I did it anyhow."

Half sitting up, the injured officer grated, "He won't use that gun on you, Sam; I pick that up, too. He knows he's finished, and he knows we know it, too. Come on, Quail." Laboriously, grunting with pain, he got shakily to his feet. He held out his hand. "The gun," he said to Quail. "You can't use it, and if you turn it over to me, I'll guarantee not to kill you; you'll be given a hearing, and someone higher up in Interplan will decide, not me. Maybe they can erase your memory once more; I don't know. But you know the thing I was going to kill you for; I couldn't keep you from remembering it. So my reason for wanting to kill you is, in a sense, past."

Quail, clutching the gun, bolted from the conapt, sprinted for the elevator. If you follow me, he thought, I'll kill you. So don't. He jabbed at the elevator button and, a moment later, the doors slid back.

The police hadn't followed him. Obviously they had picked up his tense, tense thoughts and had decided not to take the chance.

With him inside, the elevator descended. He had gotten away—for a time. But what next? Where could he go?

The elevator reached the ground floor; a moment later Quail had joined the mob of peds hurrying along the runnels. His head ached and he felt sick. But at least he had evaded death; they had come very close to shooting him on the spot, back in his own conapt.

And they probably will again, he decided. When they find me. And with this transmitter inside me, that won't take long.

Ironically, he had gotten exactly what he had asked Rekal, Incorporated for. Adventure, peril, Interplan police at work, a secret and dangerous trip to Mars in which his life was at stake—everything he had wanted as a false memory.

The advantages of it being a memory—and nothing more—could now be appreciated.

On a park bench, alone, he sat dully watching a flock of perts: a semi-bird imported from Mars's two moons, capable of soaring flight, even against Earth's huge gravity.

Maybe I can find my way back to Mars, he pondered. But then what? It would be worse on Mars; the political organization whose leader he had assassinated would spot him the moment he stepped from the ship; he would have Interplan and *them* after him, there.

Can you hear me thinking? he wondered. Easy avenue to paranoia; sitting here alone, he felt them tuning in on him, monitoring, recording, discussing. . . . He shivered, rose to his feet, walked aimlessly, his hands deep in his pockets. No matter where I go, he realized. You'll always be with me. As long as I have this device inside my head.

I'll make a deal with you, he thought to himself—and to them. Can't you imprint a false-memory template on me again, as you did before, that I lived an average, routine life, never went to Mars? Never saw an Interplan uniform up close and never handled a gun?

A voice inside his brain answered, "As has been carefully explained to you: that would not be enough."

Astonished, he halted.

"We formerly communicated with you in this manner," the voice continued. "When you were operating in the field, on Mars. It's been months since we've done it; we assumed, in fact, that we'd never have to do so again. Where are you?"

"Walking," Quail said, "to my death." By your officers' guns, he added as an afterthought. "How can you be sure it wouldn't be enough? He demanded. "Don't the Rekal techniques work?"

"As we said. If you're given a set of standard, average memories, you get—restless. You'd inevitably seek out Rekal or one of its competitors again. We can't go through this a second time."

"Suppose," Quail said, "once my authentic memories have been canceled, something more vital than standard memories are implanted. Something which would act to satisfy my craving," he said. "That's been proved; that's probably why you initially hired me. But you ought to be able to come up with something else—

something equal. I was the richest man on Terra, but I finally gave all my money to educational foundations. Or I was a famous deep-space explorer. Anything of that sort; wouldn't one of those do?"

Silence.

"Try it," he said desperately. "Get some of your top-notch military psychiatrists; explore my mind. Find out what my most expansive daydream is." He tried to think. "Women," he said. "Thousands of them, like Don Juan had. An interplanetary playboy—a mistress in every city on Earth, Luna and Mars. Only I gave that up, out of exhaustion. Please," he begged. "Try it."

"You'd voluntarily surrender, then?" the voice inside his head asked. "If we agreed to arrange such a solution? *If* it's possible?"

After an interval of hesitation, he said, "Yes." I'll take the risk, he said to himself. That you don't simply kill me.

"You make the first move," the voice said presently. "Turn yourself over to us. And we'll investigate that line of possibility. If we can't do it, however, if your authentic memories begin to crop up again as they've done at this time, then—" There was silence, and then the voice finished, "We'll have to destroy you. As you must understand. Well, Quail, you still want to try?"

"Yes," he said. Because the alternative was death now—and for certain. At least this way he had a chance, slim as it was.

"You present yourself at our main barracks in New York," the voice of the Interplan cop resumed. "At 580 Fifth Avenue, floor twelve. Once you've surrendered yourself, we'll have our psychiatrists begin on you; we'll have personality-profile tests made. We'll attempt to determine your absolute, ultimate fantasy wish—and then we'll bring you back to Rekal, Incorporated, here; get them in on it, fulfilling that wish in vicarious surrogate retrospection. And—good luck. We do owe you something; you acted as a capable instrument for us." The voice lacked malice: if anything, they—the organization—felt sympathy towards him.

"Thanks," Quail said. And began searching for a robot cab.

* * *

"Mr. Quail," the stern-faced, elderly Interplan psychiatrist said, "you possess a most interesting wish-fulfilment dream fantasy. Probably nothing such as you consciously entertain or suppose. This is commonly the way; I hope it won't upset you too much to hear about it."

The senior ranking Interplan officer present said briskly, "He better not be too much upset to hear about it, not if he expects not to get shot."

"Unlike the fantasy of wanting to be an Interplan undercover agent," the psychiatrist continued, "which, being relatively speaking a product of maturity, had a certain plausibility to it, this production is a grotesque dream of your childhood; it is no wonder you fail to recall it. Your fantasy is this: You are nine years old, walking alone down a rustic lane. An unfamiliar variety of space vessel from another star system lands directly in front of you. No one on Earth but you, Mr. Quail, sees it. The creatures within are very small and helpless, somewhat on the order of field mice, although they are attempting to invade Earth; tens of thousands of other such ships will soon be on their way, when this advance party gives the go-ahead signal."

"And I suppose I stop them," Quail said, experiencing a mixture of amusement and disgust. "Single-handed I wipe them out. Probably by stepping on them with my foot."

"No," the psychiatrist said patiently. "You halt the invasion, but not by destroying them. Instead, you show them kindness and mercy, even though by telepathy—their mode of communication—you know why they have come. They have never seen such humane traits exhibited by any sentient organism, and to show their appreciation they make a covenant with you."

Quail said, "They won't invade Earth as long as I'm alive."

"Exactly." To the Interplan officer the psychiatrist said, "You can see it does fit his personality, despite his feigned scorn."

"So by merely existing," Quail said, feeling a growing pleasure, "by simply being alive, I keep Earth safe from alien rule. I'm in effect, then, the most important person on Terra. Without lifting a finger."

"Yes indeed, sir," the psychiatrist said. "And this is bedrock in your psyche; this is a lifelong childhood fantasy. Which, without depth and drug therapy, you never would have recalled. But it has always existed in you; it went underneath, but never ceased."

To McClane, who sat intently listening, the senior police official said, "Can you implant an extra-factual memory pattern that extreme in him?"

"We get handed every possible type of wish-fantasy there is," McClane said. Frankly, I've heard a lot worse than this. Certainly we can handle it. Twenty-four hours from now he won't just wish he'd saved Earth; he'll devoutly believe it really happened."

The senior police official said, "You can start the job, then. In preparation we've already once again erased the memory in him of his trip to Mars."

Quail said, "What trip to Mars?"

No one answered him, so, reluctantly, he shelved the question. And anyhow a police vehicle had now put in its appearance; he, McClane and the senior police officer crowded into it, and presently they were on their way to Chicago and Rekal, Incorporated.

"You had better make no errors this time," the police officer said to heavy-set, nervous-looking McClane.

"I can't see what could go wrong," McClane mumbled, perspiring. "This has nothing to do with Mars or Interplan. Single-handedly stopping an invasion of Earth from another star-system." He shook his head at that. "Wow, what a kid dreams up. And by pious virtue, too; not by force. It's sort of quaint." He dabbed at his forehead with a large linen pocket handkerchief.

Nobody said anything.

"In fact," McClane said, "it's touching."

"But arrogant," the police officer said starkly. "Inasmuch as when he dies, the invasion will resume. No wonder he doesn't recall it; it's the most grandiose fantasy I ever ran across." He eyed Quail with disapproval. "And to think we put this man on our payroll."

When they reached Rekal, Incorporated the receptionist, Shirley, met them breathlessly in the outer office. "Welcome back, Mr. Quail," she fluttered, her melon-shaped breasts—today painted an incandescent orange—bobbing with agitation. "I'm sorry everything worked out so badly before; I'm sure this time it'll go better."

Still repeatedly dabbing at his shiny forehead with his neatly folded Irish linen handkerchief, McClane said, "It better." Moving with rapidity he rounded up Lowe and Keeler, escorted them and Douglas Quail to the work area, and then, with Shirley and the senior police officer, returned to his familiar office. To wait.

"Do we have a packet made up for this, Mr. McClane?" Shirley asked, bumping against him in her agitation, then coloring modestly.

"I think we do." He tried to recall; then gave up and consulted the formal chart. "A combination," he decided aloud, "of packets Eighty-one, Twenty, and Six." From the vault section of the chamber behind his desk, he fished out the appropriate packets, carried them to his desk for inspection. "From Eighty-one," he explained, "a magic healing rod given him—the client in question, this time Mr. Quail—by the race of beings from another system. A token of their gratitude."

"Does it work?" the police officer asked curiously.

"It did once," McClane explained. "But he, ahem, you see, used it up years ago, healing right and left. Now it's only a memento. But he remembers it working spectacularly." He chuckled, then opened packet Twenty. "Document from the U.N. Secretary General thanking him for saving Earth; this isn't precisely appropriate, because part of Quail's fantasy is that no one knows of the invasion except himself, but for the sake of verisimilitude we'll throw it in." He inspected packet Six, then. What came from this? He couldn't recall; frowning, he dug into the plastic bag as Shirley and the Interplan police officer watched intently.

"Writing," Shirley said. "In a funny language."

"This tells who they were," McClane said, "and where they came from. Including a detailed star map logging their flight here and the system of origin. Of course it's in *their* script, so he can't read it. But he remembers them reading it to him in his own tongue." He placed the three artifacts in the center of the desk. "These should be taken to Quail's conapt," he said to the police officer. "So that when he gets home he'll find them And it'll confirm his fantasy. SOP—standard operating procedure." He chuckled apprehensively, wondering how matters were going with Lowe and Keeler.

The intercom buzzed. "Mr. McClane, I'm sorry to bother you." It was Lowe's voice; he froze as he recognized it, froze and became mute. "But something's come up. Maybe it would be better if you came in here and supervised. Like before, Quail reacted to the narkidrine; he's unconscious, relaxed and receptive. But—"

McClane sprinted for the work area.

On a hygienic bed Douglas Quail lay breathing slowly and regularly, eyes half-shut, dimly conscious of those around him.

"We started interrogating him," Lowe said, white-faced. "To find out exactly when to place the fantasy-memory of him single-handedly having saved Earth. And strangely enough—"

"They told me not to tell," Douglas Quail mumbled in a dull drug-saturated voice. "That was the agreement. I wasn't even supposed to remember. But how could I forget an event like that?"

I guess it would be hard, McClane reflected. But you did—until now.

"They even gave me a scroll," Quail mumbled, "of gratitude. I have it hidden in my conapt; I'll show it to you."

To the Interplan officer who had followed after him, McClane said, "Well, I offer the suggestion that you better not kill him. If you do they'll return."

"They also gave me a magic invisible destroying rod," Quail

mumbled, eyes totally shut, now. "That's how I killed that man on Mars you sent me to take out. It's in my drawer along with the box of Martian maw-worms and dried-up plant life."

Wordlessly, the Interplan officer turned and stalked from the work area.

I might as well put those packets of proof-artifacts away, McClane said to himself resignedly. He walked, step by step, back to his office. Including the citation from the U.N. Secretary General. After all—

The real one probably would not be long in coming.

Hellas Is Florida

Gordon Eklund and Gregory Benford

After the moon landing in 1969 (as Gardner Dozois points out in his anthology The Good New Stuff*), it was no longer possible to write the same sorts of science-fiction stories as before. Planetary adventures and tales of intergalactic empires were still possible, but they had to be set farther afield . . . and in their wake grew a new set of science-fiction stories based on more accurate knowledge about our neighborhood in the cosmos. We had touched the cold vacuum of space; it was harder to pretend that vacuum brimmed with life.*

One thing that happened in the 1970s is that a new generation of writers—largely influenced by veterans like Arthur C. Clarke, Ben Bova, and Poul Anderson—began to find different sorts of adventure and romance among the stars. The stories used new data from which to extrapolate, and extrapolate they did.

Gordon Eklund and Gregory Benford both started publishing regularly in the 1970s. (Dr. Benford actually started publishing in the 1960s—his third published story, "Flattop," was also about a Mars expedition, as was his 1999 novel The Martian Race.*) Mr. Eklund has gone on to write such novels as* A Trace of Dreams, All Times Possible, *and* A Thunder on Neptune. *Gregory Benford has published several dozen novels, including the classic* Timescape *and most recently* The

Sunborn. *"Hellas Is Florida" is a continuation of the authors' award-winning novelette "If the Stars Are Gods"; these stories were eventually combined with others to form the novel of the same name.*

I

It was a fact, Major Paul Smith reasoned affirmatively, as he gazed at the cratered terrain now sweeping past, that life existed on the planet Mars.

No, not just the present landing party—Kastor, McIntyre, Reynolds, and Morgan—who were surveying the northern reaches of the basin of Hellas, but native Martian life. Up to and most definitely including a number of related varieties of complex spores. The proof was there. For two decades, a succession of robot probes, both American and Russian in origin, had relayed the evidence to a supposedly stunned Earth populace.

It resembled the assassination of a famed political or religious leader: A person never forgot his own first experience. For Smith, the moment chanced upon his final year at the academy. A physics course, the instructor, a former NASA technician, halted the class in midsession, while he scurried to huddle with three beaming colleagues. "Gentlemen, gentlemen," announced the instructor, spinning free to face the class. (His hands actually shook; Smith envisioned them trembling now.) "I have just been informed that apparent evidence has been received at Pasadena which tends to indicate the possible presence of life on Mars."

Fear. He recollected the sweep of emotion like a bitter taste on his tongue. Fear crawled up his spine, held taut and secure in the stiff-backed chair. *We are not alone. Green men. Flying saucers. Slitherly lizardly fiends. Are they watching us?* Smith grinned now (in embarrassment?), remembering the automatic assault of old clichés. In spite of the instructor's carefully placed qualifiers, his soul had quivered fearfully.

The evening headline, with no place for *apparents, tends,* or *possibles,* had screamed bluntly:

LIFE ON MARS!

And, even though Smith by then knew that "life" as yet indicated nothing more frightening than the presence of organic matter in the Martian soil, the icy fingers clutched.

Life on Mars. For the hell of it, Smith uttered the phrase aloud into the tomblike silence of the orbiting command chamber. "Life on Mars." Three such simple little words. Substitute most any other word for that final noun, and the result ranged between banality and silliness.

"Life on Mars," Paul Smith said. A big crater, the circling slopes standing like the spiny ridges on a horntoad's back, drifted past the window. Sure, there was life down there, but the old fear had long ago been eroded. Even the continuing reports from the landing party in Hellas of new and remarkable strains of life failed to stir Smith much. The human mind, he realized, possessed an awe-inspiring talent for converting in remarkable time the most fantastic truths into the most banal facts.

Speaking of time, he guessed he ought to prepare. Smith hung curled in the command chamber nook nearest the window that presently overlooked the passing Martian surface. This vehicle, the *Tempest,* orbited at a mean distance of some two hundred kilometers above Mars. Each successive orbit occupied slightly more than one hour. Except in cases of dire emergency, the landing party below (Nixon Base, Colonel Kastor had named them, supposedly in honor of the man who had served as president during the first manned lunar expeditions, but more likely as a stroking device aimed at soothing the present administration) transmitted every fourth pass. This, as Smith well knew, was number four.

The transmissions, dull and impersonal as Kastor normally made them, served to snap the monotony, but they also forced Smith to move. God, he hated Mars. An incredible truth, not yet banal. Paul Smith, who had given up five years of his life and journeyed through some sixty million kilometers of space only to discover that he passionately loathed the objective of all these efforts. Mars seemed to mock his own world. The mountains climbed higher—he passed the dome of Olympus Mons each orbit and now refused even to glance that way—the canyons plowed deeper, the plains swept wider. And the life—life on Mars!—mocking life. Life that may have once been spawned amid relative beauty (some scientists theorized) but which now certainly existed in infernal ugliness. That's why he hated the damn planet—it was ugly. Through no lack of his own imagination, either—ugly, ugly, ugly! Smith remembered the view of Earth seen from space, a sight familiar to him (but never monotonous) after nearly a full year of preparatory experiments and maneuvers in the orbital lab. The Earth shook the breath right out of your chest. Green and azure blue, brown and puffy white. Not this—not red. He studied the cratered terrain. This was part of the Southern Hemisphere, and the North, more volcanically active, was less tedious. Still, he sometimes guessed that Kastor understood his real attitude, which helped explain why, in an unanticipated, unexplained change of plans, Kastor had elected to take young Reynolds down to the surface instead of the more experienced Smith, who had not disputed the decision at the time. Kastor insisted it was because they needed experience in orbit, when there was already plenty of that below in Morgan and McIntyre. Smith said nothing. Kastor pointed out that Reynolds, as astronomer, already knew more about Martian life-forms than Smith, a military officer. Smith didn't argue. Much later, while the others slept, Smith asked young Reynolds if he'd ever read *A Princess of Mars* by Edgar Rice Burroughs. When Reynolds looked blank, Smith laughed and said, "Then I guess you don't know so damn much about Martian life as Kastor thinks."

Paul Smith forced himself to move. Releasing the straps that bound him, he floated gently up, then kicked out. He drifted across the length of the command chamber, struck a wall softly, then slipped straight on the ricochet into the chair fronting the radio. He checked his altitude and confirmed his location in terms of the Martian surface. Hellas itself would not come into view for another ten minutes. He decided to call now. He spoke softly, but his voice boomed. "Nixon Base, this is *Tempest.* Nixon Base, this is *Tempest.* Nixon Base, this is *Tempest.*"

Silence. Apparently Kastor wasn't quite so eager.

A sudden, angry impatience gripped him. Smith wanted this finished so he could go back to his window. Even in the time so far, he had grown inordinately fond of isolation. During the second week, he had discovered the fragile, spiderlike webs woven by the taut blue veins on the backs of his hands. "Nixon Base, this is *Tempest.*"

Kastor stirred. "Hello, *Tempest,* this is Nixon Base. Paul, is that you?"

No, sir, it's Edgar Rice goddamn Burroughs. "Yes, Jack."

"How about it? Anything especially interesting up there?"

"Nope. Quiet as a little mouse." Smith tried to envision them down there. The plain of Hellas flat as a child's chest. The red dust heaped and piled. The howling, oddly forceless wind. The horizon near enough to be touched. Four figures in matching bulky suits. The mantislike crawlers. Kastor controlled the radio. Once he had permitted McIntyre to speak, but the subject had been a geological matter. After Smith received the party's transmissions, he relayed them to Houston, where the highlights were played—against old images of Mars—on the evening news shows. "There's a light storm brewing at one hundred twenty degrees longitude, thirty degrees latitude south, but that shouldn't affect you."

"It doesn't seem likely—half a planet away."

"I guess not." *You bastard, I'm only trying to do my job up here:* to scan the Martian surface for dust storms. So far—more mockery—Mars had remained uncharacteristically quiescent. The annual Great

Dust Storm was not due to hit till well after their departure, a cautiously predetermined fact: the storm originated in the Noachis region near the edge of Hellas. Still, there was usually some lesser activity.

"We've made some atmospheric samplings, and I want to transmit the preliminary results," Kastor said.

"Sure, go ahead."

While Kastor spoke (repeating no doubt word-for-word only what Morgan had told him), Smith listened with no more than half an ear. He remained vaguely curious, but not obsessed. Spores. Organic compounds. Microbiotic life. He'd heard this all before. Why not, he wondered idly, a silicon giraffe? How about a two-hundred-foot, green-skinned, horn-rimmed Martian worm, with a funny nose?

And he missed Lorna. Horny for his own wife. How little the average citizen knew of an astronaut's agony. With Morgan in the crew, maybe they got the wrong idea. Prolonged nightly orgies. A pornography of the spaceways. They didn't know Loretta Morgan. He grinned at the thought of the old bag stricken with mad lust.

Kastor screamed: "Oh, my God, hold on! Jesus, we're shaking like—!"

Silence.

Paul Smith felt icy fingers of fear creeping along his spine. "Jack!" He spoke softly this time. "Nixon Base!"

And in this emergent moment of crisis, his eyes unfilmed, the padding illusions of the mind fell away, and Paul Smith saw suddenly that this world had now turned on them in some unimaginable way. And that they were unprepared. So many months of stress, boredom—each of them was now tipped at some angle to reality, had made his own private pact with the world and . . . been twisted by it. He, Smith, was now clutched in his Mars-hating neurosis. Below, each member of the ground team was no longer the well-balanced crewman that he'd been Earthside. No, the one thing they'd never been able to check—the effects of isolation and work in new, deep space—had slowly worked some new change in each of them, gnawing away at their personal defenses. And now they were exposed. . . .

Smith grimaced. He needed the others to navigate the return module to Earth. Alone, he would die. Starve or strangle or suck vacuum above the bloated crusted carcass of red, blotchy Marscape, the leering land crushing him to it. . . . "Nixon Base, this is *Tempest.* Nixon Base, this is *Tempest.*"

Smith had to tilt his head to see the ten-inch video screen set at an angle in the hull to his left. The flat pink basin of Hellas crept into view past jagged, towering mountaintops. There was life down there on Mars.

II

Colonel Samuel J. Kastor squirmed in the aluminum frame of his crawler seat and struggled to be content with the worm's-crawl pace Loretta Morgan maintained as she drove across the basin. After all, he reasoned, there was no reason to hurry. Smith wouldn't fly away, the landing module lay safely secured, and the orbits of Earth and Mars remained steady. Hell, he thought, we've already uncovered more firm data in a few weeks down here than fifteen robot flights over a twenty-year period. That $20 billion cost figure for the entire expedition irritated him. Kastor didn't want to have to pay it back out of his own $65,000 salary. We're giving them more than they have any right to ask for, he decided.

Hellas, which from above resembled an elongated pancake, stretched its features around the two crawlers. He saw rocky ridges, smooth bumps, a few boulders, but mostly dust. The wind was a constant factor, but buried inside the hulk of a suit, that was easily discarded. Kastor regretted the necessity of landing here. McIntyre, the geologist, had fought hard against the decision. His reasons were professional; Kastor's were artistic. McIntyre had loudly asserted that it was ridiculous to send a manned expedition to Mars and ignore the volcanic constructs and plains; he favored a landing site somewhere on the volcanic plain between Tharsis Ridge and Olympus Mons. NASA rejected the suggestion. Life-forms, not rocks, had motivated the $20 billion investment, and life-forms happened to be most plentiful in the southern Hellas region. All Kastor had desired were the best, most dramatic videotapes possible. The sight of a volcano twenty-five kilometers high or a canyon seventy-five kilometers wide could have pried open a lot of weary eyes back on Earth. Still, Kastor damn well realized, if the expedition succeeded in solving some of the puzzles of Martian life, then the wildest pictures under creation would mean nothing beside that accomplishment. Maybe that was why he was in such a hurry now. Surrounded by these bleak wastes, he knew it was life or nothing. He had expended five years of his own life on a cosmic gamble. Would it pay off?

McIntyre was driving the second crawler, with Bradley Reynolds strapped to the seat beside him. The two vehicles rode nearly side-by-side. Reynolds, his frail form concealed by the heavy suit, waved an arm high in the air. Understanding the signal, Kastor glanced at his chronometer and then, involuntarily at the clear powder-blue sky.

No, Smith wasn't up there yet. At dawn and dusk the *Tempest* would streak through the sky, a bright yellow star on a frantic course. Except for Morgan, none of them bothered to look anymore.

Reaching lightly across, Kastor waved a hand in front of Morgan's bubble helmet. When she glanced his way, he pointed toward the ground. By common consent, the four of them avoided radio contact whenever possible. Kastor wasn't sure he understood why. Perhaps the reason had to do with their constant mutual proximity these last years. In other words, they were sick to their stomachs with one another.

As soon as Morgan brought the crawler to a smooth halt, Kastor bounded off the side into the piled dust. When the other crawler stopped, he motioned Reynolds to join him. He waited until the other man had approached near enough so that his narrow, angular, bearded face showed distinctly through his helmet, then said, "Brad, would you mind going over with me the data you collected from the last atmospheric sampling?"

"No, sir, not at all." Reynolds began to repeat what he had already told Kastor an hour before. Kastor listened intently, refreshing his own memory. Over the radio he heard Morgan's sour sigh. Screw her. Sure, it would have been easier to permit Reynolds to do his own talking, but Kastor knew full well the value of public exposure. This was his expedition—he was the commander. He didn't intend to allow some bright kid to sneak up and erode that bitterly achieved position.

"Then there's been another quantitative increase?" Kastor said.

Reynolds said, "Yes, sir, that's true."

"Which fits with your previous findings?"

"Perfectly. Would you like to see?"

Kastor said, "Yes, show me." Reynolds trudged back to his crawler and returned shortly with a crude map he and Morgan had drawn of Hellas basin. Various scribblings—lines, circles, dots, and figures—littered the face of the chart. Kastor began to shake his head inside his helmet, but then realized the danger in letting Reynolds guess his confusions. "Where's the focus again?"

Reynolds laid a thick finger on the northeastern corner of the map. "Everything seems to be pointing this way, sir."

"The closer we approach, the greater the quantity of life."

"And the variety and complexity, too."

"I remember that."

"But you still don't think we should tell Houston."

"We've given them all the data."

"But not our own conclusions." Kastor sighed inwardly. Morgan also hounded him constantly on this. "We don't want to look like fools, Brad. We have no explanations for this."

"Maybe, if we told them, they could find one." This argument was also Morgan's favorite.

"There's plenty of time for that later."

"But, sir, don't you—?" Kastor backed off. "I've got to talk to Smith. We can discuss this later."

"But, sir—"

"Later, Reynolds," Kastor said rudely. The communication equipment occupied an aluminum crate in the back of his crawler. Kastor believed he had made a wise choice, selecting Reynolds over Smith for the landing party. Reynolds was damn bright—even Morgan had failed to detect the peculiar patterning of Martian life. Brightness wasn't the reason Kastor had chosen Reynolds. Kastor prided himself on his own ability to see past people's surface maneuverings to their core motivations. For himself, he wanted one thing from life, and that was power. Kastor believed that ninety-five percent of the human race acted for similar aims, but most, ashamed, concealed this fact behind meaningless phrases like "the good of humanity," "the future of the planet," and "the joy in helping others." Kastor didn't give a hoot about humanity, the planet, or any others. Unlike most people, he didn't try to hide his feelings from himself. Twenty-five years ago, he had sought an Air Force commission because he had believed that was where the power lay. A mistake. War, once the primary pursuit of mankind, had dwindled to a vestigial state. He now knew fame was the answer, and that was why he was here. Bradley Reynolds—there was a weird one. Kastor believed Reynolds was part of the five percent—power failed to interest him. But what did? Paul Smith—though, young, ambitious—an obvious rival. But Reynolds was unreadable.

Kastor hauled the communication gear out of the crawler and set up the radio on the Martian sand. Morgan and Reynolds crowded around him, while McIntyre remained seated in his crawler.

Kastor twisted the antenna and twirled a dial. He suddenly heard a hollow disembodied voice: "—this is *Tempest*. Nixon Base, this is *Tempest*."

Adjusting his suit radio so that voice would transmit above, Kastor spoke evenly: "Hello, *Tempest,* this is Nixon Base. Paul, is that you?"

"Yes, Jack."

"How about it? Anything especially interesting up there?"

"Nope. Quiet as a little mouse. There's a light storm brewing at one hundred twenty degrees longitude, thirty degrees latitude south, but that shouldn't affect you."

Kastor spied the opportunity for a lightly sarcastic jeer. "It doesn't seem likely—half a planet away."

"I guess not."

Kastor grinned. Poor Smith, getting bored up there. It took a damn strong man to withstand total isolation; you had to be able to bear your own company. Kastor said, "We've made some atmospheric samplings, and I want to transmit the preliminary results."

"Sure, go ahead," said Smith.

Kastor spoke slowly, repeating as nearly word-for-word as his memory allowed what Reynolds had told him. He tried to envision Smith up there listening, but it was the bigger audience that interested him. The people of the planet Earth. The late-evening news. He tried to add some drama to his voice, but the dry words refused to be manipulated. This was heavy stuff, he knew. It was life. The Martian Garden of Eden. Reduced to facts, the truth sounded not only dull but obvious.

The quake struck without warning, as suddenly as a bolt of pitchfork lightning. The ground trembled and Kastor tottered. He fell flat on his rump and got tossed into the air. Reaching out to grab a secure hold, he realized the whole world was insecure. He screamed, "Oh, my God, hold on! Jesus, we're shaking like—!"

He saw Morgan fall. Reynolds sprawled on top of her. The radio bounced like an energized ball. Kastor threw out his arms and covered it. He hugged the radio. If the world collapsed around him, he wouldn't be alone.

A barrage of voices pounded his ears. Reynolds shouted. Morgan cried. McIntyre screamed. "It's a goddamn quake!" yelled Kastor. "Shut up and hold on." Incredibly, he saw one of the crawlers flop onto its back. A burst of dust and sand covered his helmet. He was blinded, buried. He clawed for the sky and realized he still had hold of the radio. Silence.

The land had stopped shaking. Kastor shoved away the blanket of debris covering him and stood up. Tentatively he tested his limbs. Crouching, he unburied the radio. "Men," he said softly, adjusting his suit to receive.

A woman's voice answered, "Jack."

"Morgan, where are you?"

"Here, behind you."

"Oh." He realized he could see. Turning, he saw Morgan crouched upon the sand. A body—Reynolds—lay sprawled beneath her heavy arms. Deserting the radio, Kastor hurried over. "He's dead."

"I don't think so," said Morgan. "He may have banged his head on his own helmet. Turn up your radio. I think I can hear his breath."

Kastor didn't care about that. His gaze caught hold of the upturned crawler. Much of their gear—food, testing equipment, bundles of paper—covered the ground. A trickle of water from a ruptured vat seeped into the Martian soil. The second crawler remained upright and undamaged.

Morgan's voice spoke into his radio. "Brad, can you stand?"

Reynolds (weakly): "Yeah, but I'm bleeding."

Kastor saw McIntyre and groaned. The poor bastard had been sitting in the crawler. When it turned over, he had flipped out. A sharp heavy strut had cracked his helmet. Kastor looked down at the mangled skull and felt ill. "Jesus Christ!" he cried. "He's dead."

III

Loretta Morgan believed they had underestimated the terrible hostility of this planet. Left undisturbed for eons since creation, Mars lay passive. We're like fleas crawling through the fur of a dog, she thought. And Mars will scratch us off.

She remembered how they'd buried poor McIntyre—the body tightly sealed like their own garbage to avoid any possibility of contamination. Kastor had called her a cold bitch because of her refusal to mourn. Well, to her life was a gift, and crying because it was gone was like a spoiled brat whining because Santa had brought only four presents. We've no right to expect a damn thing from this universe, she thought, and that includes life itself. When she died, anyone who mourned would be later visited by a giggling ghost. (Her own.)
She was damned if she'd shed a single tear for Colonel Kastor, either.

The hard, tight surfaces of a life-support tent encircled her and Reynolds. It was cold Martian night out there, but she'd already completed her evening walk. After sunset, as soon as the cocoonlike webbing of the tent stood upon the sand, she went strolling alone. Kastor had called her walks a sign of feminine sentimentality. She stood poised upon the tip of a dune and peered through her bubble helmet at the steady green orb of the shining Earth glimpsed clearly through the thin Martian atmosphere. For five minutes, she looked away only to blink. Humankind invaded space, she believed, so we could learn once and for all how damn inconsequential we were. That's what that green star told her. So did this: life on Mars. So did McIntyre and Kastor, dead and unmourned seventy million kilometers from what each called home. Who (or what) gave one damn for any of them, dead or alive or indifferent?

She sat naked beside Reynolds. Kastor's death had freed her at night of her own clothes. Not that he would ever have noticed. Sex, Kastor must have believed, was a sign of feminine sentimentality. She would have noticed, though.

"Well, what do you think?" asked Reynolds, who was trying hard to act as though he'd seen a naked woman before. In fact, she believed that he had. Despite the boyish smiles and mere twenty-seven years, Bradley Reynolds was a man whose natural impulses sprang too suddenly to the surface for him ever to know true naïveté; Reynolds might occasionally be artless, but he was never simple. Letting her heavy breasts fall naturally, she leaned over and touched the map with a finger. "I think we're getting damn closer. The source ought to be here."

"The Garden of Eden," he said, peering at the heavily notated northeastern corner of the map.

She drew back. "Don't call it that. That was Kastor's need for dramatics. Life on Mars is drama enough. We don't need PR slogans."

"Maybe we don't, but NASA may." There he was again. Artless, but not simple.

"Then call it what you like."

"How about Agnew Point?"

"Who?"

"The base. Agnew was Nixon's vice-president. He got chased from office for taking a bribe."

"Why? You're not interested in a Senate seat, too, are you?"

His lips formed a boyish smile. "I'm not old enough." Reynolds sat with the radio between his tightly clothed legs. Smith would soon pass. "How long do you estimate it will take for us to reach this source?"

"With only the one crawler and three-quarters of our supplies either consumed or lost, I'd guess three weeks."

"We may go hungry on the way back."

"So?"

He shrugged. "The only solution I can devise that explains the source is that Martian life has evolved so recently that it's still centered on one point." He grinned. "Like a Garden of Eden."

She made a sour face. "It's evolved too far for that to be true."

"But how do we know? Without an ozone layer, in a carbon-dioxide atmosphere, the rate of mutation may be fantastic."

"Not necessarily. The first probes found evidences of life as far from Hellas as Elysium. Maybe the apparent centralization is merely a matter of environmental convenience. On Earth, there's more life in Florida than in Greenland. It's easier to stay alive in Florida. Hellas might be the Florida of Mars." She studied the chronometer strapped to his wrist. "But you better get ready. Try to raise him."

"Smith?" He acted surprised.

"You are going to tell them aren't you?" she said impatiently.

"Take advantage of the fact that Kastor drove his crawler into a twenty-meter chasm? Why should I?"

"You told me you agreed: they could help."

"I don't think so. We're here—they're not."

"But why keep it a secret now? You're not after Kastor's dramatics."

"I'll tell them later. This soon it would make Kastor look like a fool."

She could conceal her irritation no longer. "But he's *dead,* damn it."

Reynolds looked solemn. "All the more reason to protect his reputation."

"But he was a horse's ass."

"I'm sorry, Morgan."

She was realizing how awfully alone this made her. Wasn't there anyone else—man or woman or beast—who truly understood exactly how minute a human being was? This was *Mars,* damn it; native life existed here. Who could worry about the reputation of a dead man?

Smith's high, taut voice came over the radio: "—this is *Tempest.* Nixon Base, this is *Tempest.*"

Reynolds said, "*Tempest,* this is Hellas Base. Paul, I've got some bad news. Colonel Kastor died today."

"Oh, no," said Smith.

You damn hypocrites, thought Morgan.

IV

Bradley Reynolds held his arms around Loretta Morgan as she lay stiffly beside him. Outside the life-support unit, the winds raged, tossing dust and sand in great, huge puffs that obscured the light of day. Reynolds knew that the annual Great Martian Dust Storm normally originated in the northeastern Noachis region where it bordered upon the Hellas basin. That storm, though slow to develop, eventually expanded to the point where it circled the Martian globe. Occasionally, the storm reached clear into the northern hemisphere and covered the entire planetary surface. According to Smith, this particular storm had similarly originated in Noachis as a white cloud perhaps two hundred kilometers in length. The storm was much larger than that now, but it still wasn't the Great Storm. That wasn't due until spring. Morgan said she thought this storm was just Mars scratching for fleas. Her odd wit aside, the storm had kept them pinned down in the tent unable to move for two weeks now. Smith reported that the storm seemed to be dwindling. By crawler, the source point of Martian life (if such a point even existed, Reynolds reminded himself) remained a full week distant.

"I love you," Reynolds told Morgan, but both knew that was not true.

They lay in darkness. An equalizer. Not only were all men and all women no different in the dark, all worlds seemed the same. Except for the howling, raging wind, the noise far in excess of the actual force, this could have been the Earth. A camp high in the Sierras. A man and woman in love. Not extraordinary. "Bradley, let me go. I have to pee."

But this was Mars.

"Sure," Reynolds said, removing his arms.

He couldn't hear her moving across the tent. The wind obscured that, too. Life was precious here, and precarious, too easily ended. McIntyre and Kastor, Morgan's tiny pattering feet. *I am alive,* Reynolds reminded himself. *So are they.* He meant the Martians. The others refused to use such terminology, but the Martians (spores, microbes, bacteria) were alive. Reynolds felt his relative youth caused the difference. By the time he became aware of a physical universe extending beyond the barriers of his own home, the fact of life on Mars had been known. Alien life was thus an integral factor in the fabric of his consciousness—a given quantity. Even Morgan sometimes revealed a careless fear and bitter anger that life, which had seemed one of the few remaining characteristics separating man from the universe, was no longer unique to Earth. Morgan would deny this. She would say that most intelligent people (and many who were not) had accepted for decades the knowledge that life could not be limited to one world. Reynolds knew that theory and fact were never the same. The majority of Earth's population believed that a god existed, but if one appeared tomorrow in the flesh, this belief would in no way lessen the shock of the physical fact. It was the same with alien, Martian life.

But Reynolds, born in a land where God was known, not only accepted but actually expected alien life. These puzzling Martian spores, existing and thriving where they should not, could only be a beginning. There were worlds beyond—Jupiter, Saturn, Titan—and then the stars. When he talked this way, Morgan accused him of idealism, but life was no longer an ideal; life was real.

He pushed aside the blankets that covered him and stood up. He called, "Loretta?" screaming to be heard above the wind. She didn't answer. He was cold. Even in the ultimate privacy of the life-support tent, his own nudity disturbed him. He padded forward and banged his knee against a water vat. "Ouch!"

He searched the floor for a torchlight. "Loretta? Hey, where are you?" A sudden anxious chill touched his heart. She must be eating. His fingers closed around the slick handle of the torch. He flicked a finger, ignited the beam, swung the light.

He saw nothing against the far wall.

She couldn't have gone out. Reynolds turned the light. He recalled how Morgan before the storm had gone out alone every night ritualistically to gaze at the green beacon of the Earth, but both remaining suits and their helmets lay neatly packed in crates on the floor of the tent.

Reynolds completed a full three-hundred-sixty–degree turn. "Loretta!" he screamed, continuing to spin.

She was nowhere in the tent.

As he struggled into the suit—realizing too late that it was her suit and contained the rank residue of her scent—he remembered how she had been: forty years old but still lovely. Her body—squat and too stout, tiny stubby fingers and small delicate feet, wide hips, lines of three children on her belly, loose breasts.

He carefully fitted the bubble helmet over his head.

Sealing the inner airlock door, he waited impatiently for the outer door to cycle open. The shrieking wind would cover the sound of its closing; she could have left unheard.

Inside the suit he could not hear the terrible wind. Dust and sand scoured the face of his helmet. He used his hands as claws to see. Her body lay half-buried no more than a meter from the airlock. Lifting her dead weight easily in his arms, he hurried back inside.

Reynolds hoped that the brief exposure of the body to the open Martian atmosphere had not been sufficient to contaminate the land.

Before leaving the area, he would have to run a careful check to be sure.

Before he thought of any of this, though, he mourned the death of a woman he had loved.

V

The last man on Mars, Bradley Reynolds, cautiously steered the battered crawler across the dunes of northeastern Hellas. He carried with him only sufficient equipment for one man: the radio; a shovel; two picks; concentrated food, primarily cereals; five water vats;

emergency oxygen; a portable life-support bag; and, most importantly, the atmospheric and soil-detention devices. Everything else—including his samples and records—remained behind in the big tent. On his way back, he would stop and retrieve what he needed.

The dust storm had greatly altered the shape and texture of the land. Piles of loose dust and sand lay scattered in great peaks, waves, and swirls. In some places, slabs of hard rock stood exposed to view. The sun directly above shifted subtly in color from powder blue to sable. The horizon loomed so close he thought of touching it. The source—the focus—the Garden—lay nearby. As often as every hour, Reynolds stopped the crawler and collected new samples. He uncovered many new and complex strains of microbiotic life. When he went on, he left the samples behind. There were too many to carry. It was the source of life—not merely life itself—that interested him.

With Morgan dead, Reynolds had not hesitated telling Earth of his own theories. The manned space program had been allowed to atrophy for nearly three decades. Only the presence of life on Mars had sparked this revival. For that reason—because Reynolds believed in the necessity of man in space—he knew he must find something now. A failure—and three deaths would not likely be viewed otherwise—and the program might again shrink. Even Mars, he believed, was no more than a wart on the elephant's snout. The physical universe did exist; humankind had a right to see it.

But Smith, after relaying the data concerning the source, returned in less than a day with a reply. "Mission Control said to tell you this idea about a source for Martian life is nonsense."

Reynolds bristled. The storm groaned outside. "But I gave them the findings. They can't dispute that."

"They said coincidence."

"That's absurd. Coincidence can't—"

Even over the radio, Smith's voice rose shrilly. "I'm telling you what they said."

Reynolds remained calm. "Then they're serious?"

"Totally," said Smith solemnly. "And they want you back here. Three dead out of four is terrible. I can't pilot the *Tempest* to Earth alone. They want you to return at once to the module."

"No," Reynolds said, after a pause. "We came here for a purpose. To study life. Three deaths can't alter that."

"It's an order, Reynolds."

He decided not to disguise his suspicions any longer. "Whose?"

"What?" said Smith.

"I'm asking if you even told them. About the source. Did you keep quiet to get me back?"

Smith appeared to be laughing. "Why would I do something that stupid, Brad?"

"Because you're scared."

"I am not. I like being alone. Isolation is—it's just different."

"Don't lie to me, Paul."

"For Christ's sake, I'm not. It was an order. Houston gave an order."

Reynolds decided that Smith's story had to be treated like God; he would neither believe nor disbelieve. He did disobey. When the storm passed, he went out. The deaths of McIntyre, Kastor, and Morgan would have to provide more meaning, not less, to the search for Martian life. If a source existed out there, Reynolds would find it.

Every fourth pass of the *Tempest,* he spoke with Smith, if only to keep the other man sane. Smith was right: isolation was merely a different, not worse, way of living; Reynolds knew he could bear it. Smith said, "Reynolds, what you're doing is crazy. The others are dead. All of them. Do you want to die, too?"

Reynolds said, "McIntyre died because of a freak of fate, Kastor because he was careless, and Morgan because . . . well, because I think she wanted to. I'm searching for life. I won't die."

"But you've found it. Life is there. We know that."

"But we don't know why."

"Who cares?" Smith cried.

"I guess I do," Reynolds said softly.

VI

The butt of the tiny probe rose out of the sand, a dull gleam that caught his eye and burned his soul.

Reynolds did not have to take a sample to know. Using his hands like the paws of an animal, he uncovered the probe. It was shaped like a crazy wheel on a pole, all struts and nuts and bolts. The message inscribed on one wing, though warped and weathered by the erosion of wind and sand, could be read. There was even a date.

Reynolds read, 1966.

The message itself was written in Russian.

Here lay the source of Martian life. The Garden of Eden shone in the dust. Tottering on his haunches, Reynolds stared at the distant sky, flecked by a single wispy strand of cloud. My God, why didn't they tell us? It was a product of the secrecy of that distant age—the Cold War. And now: contamination. A Russian probe, reeking with Earth bacteria, placed down here in the basin of Hellas.

Reynolds lowered his gaze and peered at the landscape cloistered around him. Life on Mars—yes—but whose? Ours—brought with this probe—or theirs?

He knew this question was one that would never be answered.

His sorrow turned immediately to bitterness and then rage. He leaped to his feet and began kicking at the probe. His boots clanged against it. The Cyrillic script dented. The paint chipped off and the thin metal split.

Reynolds made himself relax. He sat down heavily in the powdery dust. He blinked back tears. So much, so goddamned much, and now this insane, comic, fool's finish.

Smith would arc overhead any moment. He would have to be told.

Reynolds rummaged through the facts. Was *all* the Martian life a contaminant? Or only part? If merely a part, how to explain the Garden of Eden effect?

If, if . . .

Suppose the probe had added a new element to the genetic menu of Mars. New biological information, new survival mechanisms. Something basic, like sexual reproduction itself, on the cellular level. Like adding rabbits to Australia, only symbiotic: The children of the breeding survived better than either the natives or the contaminants. A new breed of Martians, spreading out from the Garden of Eden. Injection of a new trick into the genetic heritage would or could cause such a runaway effect.

Two hypotheses: (a) all Martians were contaminants; (b) this was merely a new breed. Which was right? There was no way to tell. None. Until the next expedition, which could make a careful study of the Garden and its blossoming life.

But this wasn't a simple scientific issue.

Once they heard about this absurd Soviet gadget, they'd leap to the same immediate assumption that he had: hypothesis (b). Only on Earth they wouldn't be able to kick and claw at the probe. They would strike out at whatever seemed handy. And the space program was temptingly handy.

Given two hypotheses, each equally likely in the face of the first facts . . . which do you choose?

The one which leads to more research, a second manned expedition?

Or the idea that closes off discussion? That slits the throat of the inquiry itself?

Reynolds sat in the powder and thought. Silence enclosed him.

Then he went to the battered crawler, fetched the radio, and set it up on the sand.

"*Tempest,*" he said, "this is Morgan Base."

"Roger. Reading you."

"Nothing special to report. Nice landscapes, rusty sand. Microbes everywhere. It's just a good place to live, I guess. Back on Earth, you can tell them . . . tell them Hellas is Florida."

In the Hall of the Martian Kings

John Varley

John Varley, like Gregory Benford and Gordon Eklund, rose to prominence in the 1970s with a host of energetic stories that revisited classic science-fiction themes in new and imaginative ways. In fact, the Encyclopedia of SF *(among others) credits him with shifting science fiction away from its Earth-centric attitudes and instead focusing on "an incessantly humming Solar System." "In the Hall of the Martian Kings" is one of the stories that sparked this claim—it's an adventure that clearly pays homage to the old planetary romances while giving us a picture of Mars that's more in keeping with the planet shown to us by modern science.*

John Varley went on from early stories like this one to publish novels like The Ophiuchi Hotline *and the Gaean trilogy (* Titan, Wizard, *and* Demon *) before getting wooed away to Hollywood. After spending several years writing for Tinseltown, he returned to the sf field with several novels, including* Steel Beach, The Golden Globe, *and, most recently,* Red Thunder. *He lives in Oceano, California these days.*

IT TOOK PERSEVERANCE, alertness, and a willingness to break the rules to watch the sunrise in Tharsis Canyon. Matthew Crawford shivered in the dark, his suit heater turned to emergency setting, his eyes trained toward the east. He knew he had to be watchful. Yesterday he had missed it entirely, snatched away from him in the middle of a long, unavoidable yawn. His jaw muscles stretched, but he controlled it and kept his eyes firmly open.

And there it was. Like the lights in a theater after the show is over: just a quick brightening, a splash of localized bluish-purple over the canyon rim, and he was surrounded by footlights. Day had come, the truncated Martian day that would never touch the blackness over his head.

This day, like the nine before it, illuminated a Tharsis radically changed from what it had been over the last sleepy ten thousand years. Wind erosion of rocks can create an infinity of shapes, but it never gets around to carving out a straight line or a perfect arc. The human encampment below him broke up the jagged lines of the rocks with regular angles and curves.

The camp was anything but orderly. No one would get the impression that any care had been taken in the haphazard arrangement of dome, lander, crawlers, crawler tracks, and scattered equipment. It had grown, as all human base camps seem to grow, without pattern. He was reminded of the footprints around Tranquillity Base, though on a much larger scale.

Tharsis Base sat on a wide ledge about halfway up from the uneven bottom of the Tharsis arm of the Great Rift Valley. The site had been chosen because it was a smooth area, allowing easy access up a gentle slope to the flat plains of the Tharsis Plateau, while at the same time only a kilometer from the valley floor. No one could agree which area was most worthy of study: plains or canyon. So this site had been chosen as a compromise. What it meant was that the exploring parties had to either climb up or go down, because there wasn't a damn thing worth seeing near the camp. Even the exposed layering and its areological records could not be seen without a half-kilometer crawler ride up to the point where Crawford had climbed to watch the sunrise.

He examined the dome as he walked back to camp. There was a figure hazily visible through the plastic. At this distance he would have been unable to tell who it was if it weren't for the black face. He saw her step up to the dome wall and wipe a clear circle to look through. She spotted his bright red suit and pointed at him. She was suited except for her helmet, which contained her radio. He knew he was in trouble. He saw her turn away and bend to the ground to pick up her helmet, so she could tell him what she thought of people who disobeyed her orders, when the dome shuddered like a jellyfish.

An alarm started in his helmet, flat and strangely soothing coming from the tiny speaker. He stood there for a moment as a perfect smoke ring of dust billowed up around the rim of the dome. Then he was running.

He watched the disaster unfold before his eyes, silent except for the rhythmic beat of the alarm bell in his ears. The dome was dancing and straining, trying to fly. The floor heaved up in the center, throwing the black woman to her knees. In another second the interior was a whirling snowstorm. He skidded on the sand and fell forward, got up in time to see the fiberglass ropes on the side nearest him snap free from the steel spikes anchoring the dome to the rock.

The dome now looked like some fantastic Christmas ornament, filled with snowflakes and the flashing red and blue lights of the emergency alarms. The top of the dome heaved over away from him, and the floor raised itself high in the air, held down by the unbroken anchors on the side farthest from him. There was a gush of snow and dust; then the floor settled slowly back to the ground. There was no motion now but the leisurely folding of the depressurized dome roof as it settled over the structures inside.

The crawler skidded to a stop, nearly rolling over, beside the deflated dome. Two pressure-suited figures got out. They started for the dome, hesitantly, in fits and starts. One grabbed the other's arm and pointed to the lander. The two of them changed course and scrambled up the rope ladder hanging over the side.

Crawford was the only one to look up when the lock started cycling. The two people almost tumbled over each other coming out of the lock. They wanted to *do* something, and quickly, but didn't know what. In the end, they just stood there silently twisting their hands and looking at the floor. One of them took off her helmet. She was a large woman, in her thirties, with red hair shorn off close to the scalp.

"Matt, we got here as—" She stopped, realizing how obvious it was. "How's Lou?"

"Lou's not going to make it." He gestured to the bunk where a heavyset man lay breathing raggedly into a clear plastic mask. He was on pure oxygen. There was blood seeping from his ears and nose.

"Brain damage?"

Crawford nodded. He looked around at the other occupants of the room. There was the Surface Mission Commander, Mary Lang, the black woman he had seen inside the dome just before the blowout. She was sitting on the edge of Lou Prager's cot, her head cradled in her hands. In a way, she was a more shocking sight than Lou. No one who knew her would have thought she could be brought to this limp state of apathy. She had not moved for the last hour.

Sitting on the floor huddled in a blanket was Martin Ralston, the chemist. His shirt was bloody, and there was dried blood all over his face and hands from the nosebleed he'd only recently gotten under control, but his eyes were alert. He shivered, looking from Lang, his titular leader, to Crawford, the only one who seemed calm enough to deal with anything. He was a follower, reliable but unimaginative.

Crawford looked back to the newest arrivals. They were Lucy Stone McKillian, the redheaded ecologist, and Song Sue Lee, the exobiologist. They still stood numbly by the airlock, unable as yet to come to grips with the fact of fifteen dead men and women beneath the dome outside.

"What do they say on the *Burroughs?*" McKillian asked, tossing her helmet on the floor and squatting tiredly against the wall. The lander was not the most comfortable place to hold a meeting; all the couches were mounted horizontally since their purpose was cushioning the acceleration of landing and takeoff. With the ship sitting on its tail, this made ninety percent of the space in the lander useless. They were all gathered on the circular bulkhead at the rear of the lifesystem, just forward of the fuel tank.

"We're waiting for a reply," Crawford said. "But I can sum up what they're going to say: not good. Unless one of you two has some experience in Mars-lander handling that you've been concealing from us."

Neither of them bothered to answer that. The radio in the nose sputtered, then clanged for their attention. Crawford looked over at Lang, who made no move to go answer it. He stood up and swarmed up the ladder to sit in the copilot's chair. He switched on the receiver.

"Commander Lang?"

"No, this is Crawford again. Commander Lang is . . . indisposed. She's busy with Lou, trying to do something."

"That's no use. The doctor says it's a miracle he's still breathing. If he wakes up at all, he won't be anything like you knew him. The telemetry shows nothing like the normal brain wave. Now I've got to talk to Commander Lang. Have her come up." The voice of Mission Commander Weinstein was accustomed to command, and about as emotional as a weather report.

"Sir, I'll ask her, but I don't think she'll come. This is still her operation, you know." He didn't give Weinstein time to reply to that. Weinstein had been trapped by his own seniority into commanding the *Edgar Rice Burroughs,* the orbital ship that got them to Mars and had been intended to get them back. Command of the

Podkayne, the disposable lander that would make the lion's share of the headlines, had gone to Lang. There was little friendship between the two, especially when Weinstein fell to brooding about the very real financial benefits Lang stood to reap by being the first woman on Mars, rather than the lowly mission commander. He saw himself as another Michael Collins.

Crawford called down to Lang, who raised her head enough to mumble something.

"What'd she say?"

"She said take a message." McKillian had been crawling up the ladder as she said this. Now she reached him and said in a lower voice, "Matt, she's pretty broken up. You'd better take over for now."

"Right, I know." He turned back to the radio, and McKillian listened over his shoulder as Weinstein briefed them on the situation as he saw it. It pretty much jibed with Crawford's estimation, except at one crucial point. He signed off and they joined the other survivors.

He looked around at the faces of the others and decided it wasn't the time to speak of rescue possibilities. He didn't relish being a leader. He was hoping Lang would recover soon and take the burden from him. In the meantime he had to get them started on something. He touched McKillian gently on the shoulder and motioned her to the lock.

"Let's go get them buried," he said. She squeezed her eyes shut tight, forcing out tears, then nodded.

It wasn't a pretty job. Halfway through it, Song came down the ladder with the body of Lou Prager.

"Let's go over what we've learned. First, now that Lou's dead there's very little chance of ever lifting off. That is, unless Mary thinks she can absorb everything she needs to know about piloting the *Podkayne* from those printouts Weinstein sent down. How about it, Mary?"

Mary Lang was laying sideways across the improvised cot that had recently held the *Podkayne* pilot, Lou Prager. Her head was nodding listlessly against the aluminum hull plate behind her, her chin was on her chest. Her eyes were half-open.

Song had given her a sedative from the dead doctor's supplies on the advice of the medic aboard the *E.R.B.* It had enabled her to stop fighting so hard against the screaming panic she wanted to unleash. It hadn't improved her disposition. She had quit; she wasn't going to do anything for anybody.

When the blowout started, Lang had snapped on her helmet quickly. Then she had struggled against the blizzard and the undulating dome bottom, heading for the roofless framework where the other members of the expedition were sleeping. The blowout was over in ten seconds, and she then had the problem of coping with the collapsing roof, which promptly buried her in folds of clear plastic. It was far too much like one of those nightmares of running knee-deep in quicksand. She had to fight for every meter, but she made it.

She made it in time to see her shipmates of the last six months gasping soundlessly and spouting blood from all over their faces as they fought to get into their pressure suits. It was a hopeless task to choose which two or three to save in the time she had. She might have done better, but for the freakish nature of her struggle to reach them; she was in shock and half-believed it was only a nightmare. So she grabbed the nearest, who happened to be Dr. Ralston. He had nearly finished donning his suit; so she slapped his helmet on him and moved to the next one. It was Luther Nakamura, and he was not moving. Worse, he was only half-suited. Pragmatically, she should have left him and moved on to save the ones who still had a chance. She knew it now, but didn't like it any better than she had liked it then.

While she was stuffing Nakamura into his suit, Crawford arrived. He had walked over the folds of plastic until he reached the dormitory, then sliced through it with his laser normally used to vaporize rock samples.

And he had had time to think about the problem of whom to save. He went straight to Lou Prager and finished suiting him up. But it was already too late. He didn't know if it would have made any difference if Mary Lang had tried to save him first.

Now she lay on the bunk, her feet sprawled carelessly in front of her. She slowly shook her head back and forth.

"You sure?" Crawford prodded her, hoping to get a rise, a show of temper, *anything*.

"I'm sure," she mumbled. "You people know how long they trained Lou to fly this thing? And he almost cracked it up as it was. I . . . ah, nuts. It isn't possible."

"I refuse to accept that as a final answer," he said. "But in the meantime we should explore the possibilities if what Mary says is true."

Ralston laughed. It wasn't a bitter laugh; he sounded genuinely amused. Crawford plowed on.

"Here's what we know for sure. The *E.R.B.* is useless to us. Oh, they'll help us out with plenty of advice, maybe more than we want, but any rescue is out of the question."

"We know that," McKillian said. She was tired and sick from the sight of the faces of her dead friends. "What's the use of all this talk?"

"Wait a moment," Song broke in. "Why can't they . . . I mean, they have plenty of time, don't they? They have to leave in six months, as I understand it, because of the orbital elements, but in that time . . ."

"Don't you know anything about spaceships?" McKillian shouted. Song went on, unperturbed.

"I do know enough to know the *Edgar* is not equipped for an atmosphere entry. My idea was, not to bring down the whole ship but only what's aboard the ship that we need. Which is a pilot. Might that be possible?"

Crawford ran his hands through his hair, wondering what to say. That possibility had been discussed, and was being studied. But it had to be classed as extremely remote.

"You're right," he said. "What we need is a pilot, and that pilot is Commander Weinstein. Which presents problems legally, if nothing else. He's the captain of a ship and should not leave it. That's what kept him on the *Edgar* in the first place. But he did have a lot of training on the lander simulator back when he was so sure he'd be picked for the ground team. You know Winey, always the instinct to be the one-man show. So if he thought he could do it, he'd be down here in a minute to bail us out and grab the publicity. I understand they're trying to work out a heat-shield parachute system from one of the drop capsules that were supposed to ferry down supplies to us during the stay here. But it's very risky. You don't modify an aerodynamic design lightly, not one that's supposed to hit the atmosphere at ten thousand-plus kilometers. So I think we can rule that out. They'll keep working on it, but when it's done, Winey won't step into the damn thing. He wants to be a hero, but he wants to live to enjoy it, too."

There had been a brief lifting of spirits among Song, Ralston, and McKillian at the thought of a possible rescue. The more they thought about it, the less happy they looked. They all seemed to agree with Crawford's assessment.

"So we'll put that one in the Fairy Godmother file and forget about it. If it happens, fine. But we'd better plan on the assumption that it won't. As you may know, the *E.R.B.-Podkayne* are the only ships in existence that can reach Mars and land on it. One other pair is in the congressional funding stage. Winey talked to Earth and thinks there'll be a speedup in the preliminary paperwork and the thing'll start building in a year. The launch was scheduled for five years from now, but it might get as much as a year's boost. It's a rescue mission now, easier to sell. But the design will need modification, if only to include five more seats to bring us all back. You can bet on there being more modifications when we send in our report on the blowout. So we'd better add another six months to the schedule."

McKillian had had enough. "Matt, what the hell are you talking about? Rescue mission? Damn it, you know as well as I that if they find us here, we'll be long dead. We'll probably be dead in another year."

"That's where you're wrong. We'll survive."

"How?"

"I don't have the faintest idea." He looked her straight in the eye as he said this. She almost didn't bother to answer, but curiosity got the best of her.

"Is this just a morale session? Thanks, but I don't need it. I'd rather face the situation as it is. Or do you really have something?"

"Both. I don't have anything concrete except to say that we'll survive the same way humans have always survived: by staying warm, by eating, by drinking. To that list we have to add 'by breathing.' That's a hard one, but other than that we're no different than any other group of survivors in a tough spot. I don't know what we'll have to do, specifically, but I know we'll find the answers."

"Or die trying," Song said.

"Or die trying." He grinned at her. She at least had grasped the essence of the situation. Whether survival was possible or not, it was necessary to maintain the illusion that it was. Otherwise, you might as well cut your throat. You might as well not even be born, because life is an inevitably fatal struggle to survive.

"What about air?" McKillian asked, still unconvinced.

"I don't know," he told her cheerfully. "It's a tough problem, isn't it?"

"What about water?"

"Well, down in that valley, there's a layer of permafrost about twenty meters down."

She laughed. "Wonderful. So that's what you want us to do? Dig down there and warm the ice with our pink little hands? It won't work, I tell you."

Crawford waited until she had run through a long list of reasons why they were doomed. Most of them made a great deal of sense. When she was through, he spoke softly.

"Lucy, listen to yourself."

"I'm just—"

"You're arguing on the side of death. Do you want to die? Are you so determined that you won't listen to someone who says you can live?"

She was quiet for a long time, then shuffled her feet awkwardly. She glanced at him, then at Song and Ralston. They were waiting, and she had to blush and smile slowly at them.

"You're right What do we do first?"

"Just what we were doing. Taking stock of our situation. We need to make a list of what's available to us. We'll write it down on paper, but I can give you a general rundown." He counted off the points on his fingers.

"One, we have food for twenty people for three months. That comes to about a year for the five of us. With rationing, maybe a year and a half. That's assuming all the supply capsules reach us all right. In addition, the *Edgar* is going to clean the pantry to the bone and give us everything they can possibly spare and send it to us in the three spare capsules. That might come to two years or even three.

"Two, we have enough water to last us forever if the recyclers keep going. That'll be a problem because our reactor will run out of power in two years. We'll need another power source, and maybe another water source.

"The oxygen problem is about the same. Two years at the outside. We'll have to find a way to conserve it a lot more than we're doing. Offhand, I don't know how. Song, do you have any ideas?"

She looked thoughtful, which produced two vertical punctuation marks between her slanted eyes.

"Possibly a culture of plants from the *Edgar.* If we could rig some way to grow plants in Martian sunlight and not have them killed by the ultraviolet. . . ."

McKillian looked horrified, as any good ecologist would.

"What about contamination?" she asked. "What do you think that sterilization was for before we landed? Do you want to louse up the entire ecological balance of Mars? No one would ever be sure if samples in the future were real Martian plants or mutated Earth stock."

"What ecological balance?" Song shot back. "You know as well as I do that this trip has been nearly a zero. A few anaerobic bacteria, a patch of lichen, both barely distinguishable from Earth forms—"

"That's just what I mean. You import Earth forms now, and we'll never tell the difference."

"But it could be done, right? With the proper shielding so the plants won't be wiped out before they ever sprout, we could have a hydroponics plant functioning—"

"Oh, yes, it could be done. I can see three or four dodges right now. But you're not addressing the main question, which is—"

"Hold it," Crawford said. "I just wanted to know if you had any ideas." He was secretly pleased at the argument; it got them both thinking along the right lines, moved them from the deadly apathy they must guard against.

"I think this discussion has served its purpose, which was to convince everyone here that survival is possible." He glanced uneasily at Lang, still nodding, her eyes glassy as she saw her teammates die before her eyes.

"I just want to point out that instead of an expedition, we are now a colony. Not in the usual sense of planning to stay here forever, but all our planning will have to be geared to that fiction. What we're faced with is not a simple matter of stretching supplies until rescue comes. Stopgap measures are not likely to do us much good. The answers that will save us are the long-term ones, the sort of answers a colony would be looking for. About two years from now, we're going to have to be in a position to survive with some sort of lifestyle that could support us forever. We'll have to fit into this environment where we can and adapt it to us where we can. For that, we're better off than most of the colonists of the past, at least for the short term. We have a large supply of everything a colony needs: food, water, tools, raw materials, energy, brains, and women. Without these things, no colony has much of a chance. All we lack is a regular resupply from the home country, but a really good group of colonists can get along without that. What do you say? Are you all with me?"

Something had caused Mary Lang's eyes to look up. It was a reflex by now, a survival reflex conditioned by a lifetime of fighting her way to the top. It took root in her again and pulled her erect on the bed, then to her feet. She fought off the effects of the drug and stood there, eyes bleary but aware.

What makes you think that women are a natural resource, Crawford?" she said, slowly and deliberately.

"Why, what I meant was that without the morale uplift provided by members of the opposite sex, a colony will lack the push needed to make it."

"That's what you meant, all right. And you meant women, available to the *real* colonists as a reason to live. I've heard it before. That's a male-oriented way to look at it, Crawford." She was regaining her stature as they watched, seeming to grow until she dominated the group with the intangible power that marks a leader. She took a deep breath and came fully awake for the first time that day.

"We'll stop that sort of thinking right now. I'm the mission commander. I appreciate you taking over while I was . . . how did you say it? Indisposed. But you should pay more attention to the social aspects of our situation. If anyone is a commodity here, it's you and Ralston, by virtue of your scarcity. There will be some thorny questions to resolve there, but for the meantime we will function as a unit, under my command. We'll do all we can to minimize social competition among the women for the men. That's the way it must be. Clear?"

She was answered by quiet assent and nods of the head. She did not acknowledge it but plowed right on.

"I wondered from the start why you were along, Crawford." She was pacing slowly back and forth in the crowded space. The others got out of her way almost without thinking, except for Ralston who still huddled under his blanket. "A historian? Sure, it's a fine idea, but pretty impractical. I have to admit that I've been thinking of you as a luxury, and about as useful as the nipples on a man's chest. But I was wrong. All the NASA people were wrong. The Astronaut Corps fought like crazy to keep you off this trip. Time enough for that on later flights. We were blinded by our loyalty to the test-pilot philosophy of spaceflight. We wanted as few scientists as possible and as many astronauts as we could manage. We don't like to think of ourselves as ferryboat pilots. I think we demonstrated during Apollo that we could handle science jobs as well as anyone. We saw you as a kind of insult, a slap in the face by the scientists in Houston to show us how low our stock has fallen."

"If I might be able to—"

"Shut up. But we were wrong. I read in your résumé that you were quite a student of survival. What's your honest assessment of our chances?"

Crawford shrugged, uneasy at the question. He didn't know if it was the right time to even postulate that they might fail.

"Tell me the truth."

"Pretty slim. Mostly the air problem. The people I've read about never sank so low that they had to worry about where their next breath was coming from."

"Have you ever heard of *Apollo 13?*"

He smiled at her. "Special circumstances. Short-term problems."

"You're right, of course. And in the only two other real space emergencies since that time, all hands were lost." She turned and scowled at each of them in turn.

"But we're *not* going to lose." She dared any of them to disagree, and no one was about to. She relaxed and resumed her stroll around the room. She turned to Crawford again.

"I can see I'll be drawing on your knowledge a lot in the years to come. What do you see as the next order of business?"

Crawford relaxed. The awful burden of responsibility, which he had never wanted, was gone. He was content to follow her lead.

"To tell you the truth, I was wondering what to say next. We have to make a thorough inventory. I guess we should start on that."

"That's fine, but there is an even more important order of business. We have to go out to the dome and find out what the hell caused the blowout. The damn thing should *not* have blown; it's the first of its type to do so. And from the *bottom*. But it did blow, and we should know why, or we're ignoring a fact about Mars that might still kill us. Let's do that first. Ralston, can you walk?"

When he nodded, she sealed her helmet and started into the lock. She turned and looked speculatively at Crawford.

"I swear, man, if you had touched me with a cattle prod you couldn't have got a bigger rise out of me than you did with what you said a few minutes ago. Do I dare ask?"

Crawford was not about to answer. He said, with a perfectly straight face, "Me? Maybe you should just assume I'm a chauvinist."

"We'll see, won't we?"

"What is that stuff?"

Song Sue Lee was on her knees, examining one of the hundreds of short, stiff spikes extruding from the ground. She tried to scratch her head but was frustrated by her helmet.

"It looks like plastic. But I have a strong feeling it's the higher life-form Lucy and I were looking for yesterday."

"And you're telling me those little spikes are what poked holes in the dome bottom? I'm not buying that."

Song straightened up, moving stiffly. They had all worked hard to empty out the collapsed dome and peel back the whole bulky mess to reveal the ground it had covered. She was tired and stepped out of character for a moment to snap at Mary Lang.

"I didn't tell you that. We pulled the dome back and found spikes. It was your inference that they poked holes in the bottom."

"I'm sorry," Lang said, quietly. "Go on with what you were saying."

"Well," Song admitted, "it wasn't a bad inference, at that. But the holes I saw were not punched through. They were eaten away." She waited for Lang to protest that the dome bottom was about as chemically inert as any plastic yet devised. But Lang had learned her lesson. And she had a talent for facing facts.

"So. We have a thing here that eats plastic. And seems to be made of plastic, into the bargain. Any ideas why it picked this particular spot to grow, and no other?"

"I have an idea on that," McKillian said. "I've had it in mind to do some studies around the dome to see if the altered moisture content we've been creating here had any effect on the spores in the soil. See, we've been here nine days, spouting out water vapor, carbon dioxide, and quite a bit of oxygen into the atmosphere. Not much, but maybe more than it seems, considering the low concentrations that are naturally available. We've altered the biome. Does anyone know where the exhaust air from the dome was expelled?"

Lang raised her eyebrows. "Yes, it was under the dome. The air we exhausted was warm, you see, and it was thought it could be put to use one last time before we let it go, to warm the floor of the dome and decrease heat loss."

"And the water vapor collected on the underside of the dome when it hit the cold air. Right. Do you get the picture?"

"I think so," Lang said. "It was so little water, though. You know we didn't want to waste it; we condensed it out until the air we exhausted was dry as a bone."

"For Earth, maybe. Here it was a torrential rainfall. It reached seeds or spores in the ground and triggered them to start growing. We're going to have to watch it when we use anything containing plastic. What does that include?"

Lang groaned. "All the airlock seals, for one thing." There were grimaces from all of them at the thought of that. "For another, a good part of our suits. Song, watch it, don't step on that thing. We don't know how powerful it is or if it'll eat the plastic in your boots, but we'd better play it safe. How about it, Ralston? Think you can find out how bad it is?"

"You mean identify the solvent these things use? Probably, if we can get some sort of work space and I can get to my equipment."

"Mary," McKillian said, "it occurs to me that I'd better start looking for airborne spores. If there are some, it could mean that the airlock on the *Podkayne* is vulnerable. Even thirty meters off the ground."

"Right. Get on that. Since we're sleeping in it until we can find out what we can do on the ground, we'd best be sure it's safe. Meantime, we'll all sleep in our suits." There were helpless groans at this, but no protests. McKillian and Ralston headed for the pile of salvaged equipment, hoping to rescue enough to get started on their analyses. Song knelt again and started digging around one of the ten-centimeter spikes.

Crawford followed Lang back toward the *Podkayne*.

"Mary, I wanted . . . is it all right if I call you Mary?"

"I guess so. I don't think 'Commander Lang' would wear well over five years. But you'd better still *think* commander."

He considered it. "All right, Commander Mary." She punched him playfully. She had barely known him before the disaster. He had been a name on a roster and a sore spot in the estimation of the Astronaut Corps. But she had borne him no personal malice, and now found herself beginning to like him.

"What's on your mind?"

"Ah, several things. But maybe it isn't my place to bring them up now. First, I want to say that if you're . . . ah, concerned, or doubtful of my support or loyalty because I took over command for a while earlier today, well. . . ."

"Well?"

"I just wanted to tell you that I have no ambitions in that direction," he finished lamely.

She patted him on the back. "Sure, I know. You forget, I read your dossier. It mentioned several interesting episodes that I'd like you to tell me about someday, from your 'soldier-of-fortune' days—"

"Hell, those were grossly overblown. I just happened to get into some scrapes and managed to get out of them."

"Still, it got you picked for this mission out of hundreds of applicants. The thinking was that you'd be a wild card, a man of action with proven survivability. Maybe it worked out. But the other thing I remember on your card was that you're not a leader. No, that you're a loner who'll cooperate with a group and be no discipline problem, but you work better alone. Want to strike out on your own?"

He smiled at her. "No, thanks. But what you said is right. I have no hankering to take charge of anything. But I do have some knowledge that might prove useful."

"And we'll use it. You just speak up, I'll be listening." She started to say something, then thought of something else. "Say, what are your ideas on a woman bossing this project? I've had to fight that all the way from my Air Force days. So if you have any objections you might as well tell me up front."

He was genuinely surprised. "You didn't take that crack seriously, did you? I might as well admit it. It was intentional, like that cattle prod you mentioned. You looked like you needed a kick in the ass."

"And thank you. But you didn't answer my question."

"Those who lead, lead," he said simply. "I'll follow you as long as you keep leading."

"As long as it's in the direction you want?" She laughed, and poked him in the ribs. "I see you as my Grand Vizier, the man who holds the arcane knowledge and advises the regent. I think I'll have to watch out for you. I know a little history, myself."

Crawford couldn't tell how serious she was. He shrugged it off.

"What I really wanted to talk to you about is this: You said you couldn't fly this ship. But you were not yourself, you were depressed and feeling hopeless. Does that still stand?"

"It stands. Come on up and I'll show you why."

In the pilot's cabin, Crawford was ready to believe her. Like all flying machines since the days of the windsock and open cockpit, this one was a mad confusion of dials, switches, and lights designed to awe anyone who knew nothing about it. He sat in the copilot's chair and listened to her.

"We had a backup pilot, of course. You may be surprised to learn that it wasn't me. It was Dorothy Cantrell, and she's dead. Now I know what everything does on this board, and I can cope with most of it easily. What I don't know, I could learn. Some of the systems are computer-driven; give it the right program and it'll fly itself, in space." She looked longingly at the controls, and Crawford realized that, like Weinstein, she didn't relish giving up the fun of flying to boss a gang of explorers. She was a former test pilot, and above all things, she loved flying. She patted an array of hand controls on her right side. There were more like them on the left.

"This is what would kill us, Crawford. What's your first name? Matt. Matt, this baby is a flyer for the first forty thousand meters. It doesn't have the juice to orbit on the jets alone. The wings are folded up now. You probably didn't see them on the way in, but you saw the models. They're very light, supercritical, and designed for this atmosphere. Lou said it was like flying a bathtub, but it flew. And it's a *skill,* almost an art. Lou practiced for three years on the best simulators we could build and still had to rely on things you can't learn in a simulator. And he barely got us down in one piece. We didn't noise it around, but it was a *damn* close thing. Lou was young; so was Cantrell. They were both fresh from flying. They flew every day, they had the *feel* for it. They were tops." She slumped back into her chair. "I haven't flown anything but trainers for eight years."

Crawford didn't know if he should let it drop.

"But you were one of the best; everyone knows that. You still don't think you could do it?"

She threw up her hands. "How can I make you understand? This is nothing like anything I've ever flown. You might as well . . ." She groped for a comparison, trying to coax it out with gestures in the air. "Listen. Does the fact that someone can fly a biplane, maybe even be the best goddamn biplane pilot that ever was, does that mean they're qualified to fly a helicopter?"

"I don't know."

"It doesn't. Believe me."

"All right. But the fact remains that you're the closest thing on Mars to a pilot for the *Podkayne.* I think you should consider that when you're deciding what we should do." He shut up, afraid to sound like he was pushing her.

She narrowed her eyes and gazed at nothing.

"I have thought about it." She waited for a long time. "I think the chances are about a thousand to one against us if I try to fly it. But I'll do it, *if* we come to that. And that's *your* job. Showing me some better odds. If you can't, let me know."

Three weeks later, the Tharsis Canyon had been transformed into a child's garden of toys. Crawford had thought of no better way to describe it. Each of the plastic spikes had blossomed into a fanciful windmill, no two of them just alike. There were tiny ones, with the vanes parallel to the ground and no more than ten centimeters tall. There were derricks of spidery plastic struts that would not have looked too out of place on a Kansas farm. Some of them were five meters high. They came in all colors and many configurations, but all had vanes covered with a transparent film like cellophane, and all were spinning into colorful blurs in the stiff Martian breeze.

Crawford thought of an industrial park built by gnomes. He could almost see them trudging through the spinning wheels.

Song had taken one apart as well as she could. She was still shaking her head in disbelief. She had not been able to excavate the long insulated taproot, but she could infer how deep it went. It extended all the way down to the layer of permafrost, twenty meters down.

The ground between the windmills was coated in shimmering plastic. This was the second part of the plants' ingenious solution to survival on Mars. The windmills utilized the energy in the wind, and the plastic coating on the ground was in reality two thin sheets of plastic with a space between for water to circulate. The water was heated by the sun then pumped down to the permafrost, melting a little more of it each time.

"There's still something missing from our picture," Song had told them the night before when she delivered her summary of what she had learned. "Marty hasn't been able to find a mechanism that would permit these things to grow by ingesting sand and rock and turning it into plasticlike materials. So we assume there is a reservoir of something like crude oil down there, maybe frozen in with the water."

"Where would that have come from?" Lang had asked.

"You've heard of the long-period Martian seasonal theories? Well, part of it is more than a theory. The combination of the Martian polar inclination, the precessional cycle, and the eccentricity of the orbit produces seasons that are about twelve thousand years long. We're in the middle of winter, though we landed in the nominal 'summer.' It's been theorized that if there were any Martian life, it would have adapted to these longer cycles. It hibernates in spores during the cold cycle, when the water and carbon dioxide freeze out at the poles, then comes out when enough ice melts to permit biological processes. We seem to have fooled these plants; they thought summer was here when the water-vapor content went up around the camp."

"So what about the crude?" Ralston asked. He didn't completely believe that part of the model they had evolved. He was a laboratory chemist, specializing in inorganic compounds. The way these plants produced plastics without high heat, through purely catalytic interactions, had him confused and defensive. He wished the crazy windmills would go away.

"I think I can answer that," McKillian said. "These organisms barely scrape by in the best of times. The ones that have made it waste nothing. It stands to reason that any really ancient deposits of crude oil would have been exhausted in only a few of these cycles. So it must be that what we're thinking of as crude oil must be something a little different. It has to be the remains of the last generation."

"But how did the remains get so far below ground?" Ralston asked. "You'd expect them to be high up. The winds couldn't bury them that deep in only twelve thousand years."

"You're right," said McKillian "I don't really know. But I have a theory. Since these plants waste nothing, why not conserve their bodies when they die? They sprouted from the ground; isn't it possible they could withdraw when things start to get tough again? They'd leave spores behind them as they retreated, distributing them all through the soil. That way, if the upper ones blew away or were sterilized by the ultraviolet, the ones just below them would still thrive when the right conditions returned. When they reached the permafrost, they'd decompose into this organic slush we've postulated, and . . . well, it does get a little involved, doesn't it?"

"Sounds all right to me," Lang assured her. "It'll do for a working theory. Now what about airborne spores?"

It turned out that they were safe from that imagined danger. There were spores in the air now, but they were not dangerous to the colonists. The plants attacked only certain kinds of plastics, and then only in certain stages of their lives. Since they were still changing, it bore watching, but the airlocks and suits were secure. The crew was enjoying the luxury of sleeping without their suits.

And there was much work to do. Most of the physical sort devolved on Crawford and, to some extent, on Lang. It threw them together a lot. The other three had to be free to pursue their researches, as it had been decided that only in knowing their environment would they stand a chance.

The two of them had managed to salvage most of the dome. Working with patching kits and lasers to cut the tough material, they had constructed a much smaller dome. They erected it on an outcropping of bare rock, rearranged the exhaust to prevent more condensation on the underside, and added more safety features. They now slept in a pressurized building inside the dome, and one of them stayed awake on watch at all times. In drills, they had come from a deep sleep to full pressure-integrity in thirty seconds. They were not going to get caught again.

Crawford looked away from the madly whirling rotors of the windmill farm. He was with the rest of the crew, sitting in the dome with his helmet off. That was as far as Lang would permit anyone to go except in the cramped sleeping quarters. Song Sue Lee was at the radio giving her report to the *Edgar Rice Burroughs*. In her hand was one of the pump modules she had dissected out of one of the plants. It consisted of a half-meter set of eight blades that turned freely on Teflon bearings. Below it were various tiny gears and the pump itself. She twirled it idly as she spoke.

"I don't really get it," Crawford admitted, talking quietly to Lucy McKillian. "What's so revolutionary about little windmills?"

"It's just a whole new area," McKillian whispered back. "Think about it. Back on Earth, nature never got around to inventing the wheel. I've sometimes wondered why not. There are limitations, of course, but it's such a good idea. Just look what *we've* done with it. But all motion in nature is confined to up and down, back and forth, in and out, or squeeze and relax. Nothing on Earth goes round and round, unless we built it. Think about it."

Crawford did, and began to see the novelty of it. He tried in vain to think of some mechanism in an animal or plant of Earthly origin that turned and kept on turning forever. He could not.

Song finished her report and handed the mike to Lang. Before she could start, Weinstein came on the line.

"We've had a change in plan up here," he said, with no preface. "I hope this doesn't come as a shock. If you think about it, you'll see the logic in it. We're going back to Earth in seven days."

It didn't surprise them too much. The *Burroughs* had given them just about everything it could in the form of data and supplies. There was one more capsule load due; after that, its presence would only be a frustration to both groups. There was a great deal of irony in having two such powerful ships so close to each other and being so helpless to do anything concrete. It was telling on the crew of the *Burroughs*.

"We've recalculated everything based on the lower mass without the twenty of you and the six tons of samples we were allowing for. By using the fuel we would have ferried down to you for takeoff, we can make a faster orbit down toward Venus. The departure date for that orbit is seven days away. We'll rendezvous with a drone capsule full of supplies we hadn't counted on." And besides, Lang thought to herself, it's much more dramatic. *Plunging sunward on the chancy cometary orbit, their pantries stripped bare, heading for the fateful rendezvous. . . .*

"I'd like your comments," he went on. "This isn't absolutely final as yet."

They all looked at Lang. They were reassured to find her calm and unshaken.

"I think it's the best idea. One thing; you've given up on any thoughts of me flying the *Podkayne?*"

"No insult intended, Mary," Weinstein said, gently. "But, yes, we have. It's the opinion of the people Earthside that you couldn't do it. They've tried some experiments, coaching some very good pilots and putting them into the simulators. They can't do it, and we don't think you could, either."

"No need to sugarcoat it. I know it as well as anyone. But even a billion-to-one shot is better than nothing. I take it they think Crawford is right, that survival is at least theoretically possible?"

There was a long hesitation. "I guess that's correct. Mary, I'll be frank. I don't think it's possible. I hope I'm wrong, but I don't expect . . ."

"Thank you, Winey, for the encouraging words. You always did know what it takes to buck a person up. By the way, that other mission, the one where you were going to ride a meteorite down here to save our asses, that's scrubbed, too?"

The assembled crew smiled, and Song gave a high-pitched cheer. Weinstein was not the most popular man on Mars.

"Mary, I told you about that already," he complained. It was a gentle complaint, and, even more significant, he had not objected to the use of his nickname. He was being gentle with the condemned. "We worked on it around the clock. I even managed to get permission to turn over command temporarily. But the mock-ups they made Earthside didn't survive the reentry. It was the best we could do. I couldn't risk the entire mission on a configuration the people back on Earth wouldn't certify."

"I know. I'll call you back tomorrow." She switched the set off and sat back on her heels. "I swear, if the Earthside tests on a roll of toilet paper didn't . . . he wouldn't . . ." She cut the air with her hands. "What am I saying? That's petty. I don't like him, but he's right." She stood up, puffing out her cheeks as she exhaled a pent-up breath.

"Come on, crew, we've got a lot of work."

They named their colony New Amsterdam, because of the windmills. The name of whirligig was one that stuck on the Martian plants, though Crawford held out a long time in favor of spinnakers.

They worked all day and tried their best to ignore the *Burroughs* overhead. The messages back and forth were short and to the point. Helpless as the mother ship was to render them more aid, they knew they would miss it when it was gone. So the day of departure was a stiff, determinedly nonchalant affair. They all made a big show of going to bed hours before the scheduled breakaway.

When he was sure the others were asleep, Crawford opened his eyes and looked around the darkened barracks. It wasn't much in the way of a home; they were crowded against each other on rough pads made of insulating material. The toilet facilities were behind a flimsy barrier against one wall, and smelled. But none of them would have wanted to sleep outside in the dome, even if Lang had allowed it.

The only light came from the illuminated dials that the guard was supposed to watch all night. There was no one sitting in front of them. Crawford assumed the guard had gone to sleep. He would have been upset, but there was no time. He had to suit up, and he welcomed the chance to sneak out. He began to furtively don his pressure suit.

As a historian, he felt he could not let such a moment slip by unobserved. Silly, but there it was. He had to be out there, watch it with his own eyes. It didn't matter if he never lived to tell about it, he must record it.

Someone sat up beside him. He froze, but it was too late. She rubbed her eyes and peered into the darkness.

"Matt?" she yawned. "What's . . . what is it? Is something—"

"Shh. I'm going out. Go back to sleep. Song?"

"Um-hmmm." She stretched, dug her knuckles fiercely into her eyes, and smoothed her hair back from her face. She was dressed in the loose-fitting bottoms of a ship suit, a gray piece of dirty cloth that badly needed washing, as did all their clothes. For a moment, as he watched her shadow stretch and stand up, he wasn't interested in the *Burroughs*. He forced his mind away from her.

"I'm going with you," she whispered.

"All right. Don't wake the others."

Standing just outside the airlock was Mary Lang. She turned as they came out, and did not seem surprised.

"Were you the one on duty?" Crawford asked her.

"Yeah. I broke my own rule. But so did you two. Consider yourselves on report." She laughed and beckoned them over to her. They linked arms and stood staring up at the sky.

"How much longer?" Song asked, after some time had passed.

"Just a few minutes. Hold tight." Crawford looked over to Lang and thought he saw tears, but he couldn't be sure in the dark.

There was a tiny new star, brighter than all the rest, brighter than Phobos. It hurt to look at it but none of them looked away. It was the fusion drive of the *Edgar Rice Burroughs,* heading sunward, away from the long winter on Mars. It stayed on for long minutes, then sputtered and was lost. Though it was warm in the dome, Crawford was shivering. It was ten minutes before any of them felt like facing the barracks.

They crowded into the airlock, carefully not looking at each other's faces as they waited for the automatic machinery. The inner door opened and Lang pushed forward—and right back into the airlock. Crawford had a glimpse of Ralston; and Lucy McKillian; then Mary shut the door.

"Some people have no poetry in their souls," Mary said.

"Or too much," Song giggled.

"You people want to take a walk around the dome with me? Maybe we could discuss ways of giving people a little privacy."

The inner lock door was pulled open, and there was McKillian, squinting into the bare bulb that lighted the lock while she held her shirt in front of her with one hand.

"Come on in," she said, stepping back. "We might as well talk about this." They entered, and McKillian turned on the light and sat down on her mattress. Ralston was blinking, nervously tucked into his pile of blankets. Since the day of the blowout he never seemed to be warm enough.

Having called for a discussion, McKillian proceeded to clam up. Song and Crawford sat on their bunks, and eventually as the silence stretched tighter, they all found themselves looking to Lang.

She started stripping out of her suit. "Well, I guess that takes care of that. So glad to hear all your comments. Lucy, if you were expecting some sort of reprimand, forget it. We'll take steps first thing in the morning to provide some sort of privacy for that, but, no matter what, we'll all be pretty close in the years to come. I think we should all relax. Any objections?" She was half out of her suit when she paused to scan them for comments. There were none. She stripped to her skin and reached for the light.

"In a way it's about time," she said, tossing her clothes in a corner. "The only thing to do with these clothes is burn them. We'll all smell better for it. Song, you take the watch." She flicked out the lights and reclined heavily on her mattress.

There was much rustling and squirming for the next few minutes as they got out of their clothes. Song brushed against Crawford in the dark and they murmured apologies. Then they all bedded down in their own bunks. It was several tense, miserable hours before anyone got to sleep.

The week following the departure of the *Burroughs* was one of hysterical overreaction by the New Amsterdamites. The atmosphere was forced and false; an eat-drink-and-be-merry feeling pervaded everything they did.

They built a separate shelter inside the dome, not really talking aloud about what it was for. But it did not lack for use. Productive work suffered as the five of them frantically ran through all the possible permutations of three women and two men. Animosities developed, flourished for a few hours, and dissolved in tearful reconciliations. Three ganged up on two, two on one, one declared war on all the other four. Ralston and Song announced an engagement, which lasted ten hours. Crawford nearly came to blows with Lang, aided by McKillian. McKillian renounced men forever and had a brief, tempestuous affair with Song. Then Song discovered McKillian with Ralston, and Crawford caught her on the rebound, only to be thrown over for Ralston.

Mary Lang let it work itself out, only interfering when it got violent. She herself was not immune to the frenzy but managed to stay aloof from most of it. She went to the shelter with whoever asked her, trying not to play favorites, and gently tried to prod them back to work. As she told McKillian toward the first of the week, "At least we're getting to know one another."

Things did settle down, as Lang had known they would. They entered their second week alone in virtually the same position they had started: no romantic entanglements firmly established. But they knew each other a lot better, were relaxed in the close company of each other, and were supported by a new framework of interlocking friendships. They were much closer to being a team. Rivalries never died out completely, but they no longer dominated the colony. Lang worked them harder than ever, making up for the lost time.

Crawford missed most of the interesting work, being more suited for the semiskilled manual labor that never seemed to be finished. So he and Lang had to learn about the new discoveries at the nightly briefings in the shelter. He remembered nothing about any animal life being discovered, and so when he saw something crawling through the whirligig garden, he dropped everything and started over to it.

At the edge of the garden he stopped, remembering the order from Lang to stay out unless collecting samples. He watched the thing—bug? turtle?—for a moment, satisfied himself that it wouldn't get too far away at its creeping pace, and hurried off to find Song.

"You've got to name it after me," he said as they hurried back to the garden. "That's my right, isn't it, as the discoverer?"

"Sure," Song said, peering along his pointed finger. "Just show me the damn thing and I'll immortalize you."

The thing was twenty centimeters long, almost round, and dome-shaped. It had a hard shell on top.

"I don't know quite what to do with it," Song admitted. "If it's the only one, I don't dare dissect it, and maybe I shouldn't even touch it."

"Don't worry, there's another over behind you." Now that they were looking for them, they quickly spied four of the creatures. Song took a sample bag from her pouch and held it open in front of the beast. It crawled halfway into the bag, then seemed to think something was wrong. It stopped, but Song nudged it in and picked it up. She peered at the underside and laughed in wonder.

"Wheels," she said. "The thing runs on wheels."

"I don't know where it came from," Song told the group that night. "I don't even quite believe in it. It'd make a nice educational toy for a child, though. I took it apart into twenty or thirty pieces, put it back together, and it still runs. It has a high-impact polystyrene carapace, nontoxic paint on the outside—"

"Not really polystyrene," Ralston interjected.

". . . and I guess if you kept changing the batteries it would run forever. And it's *nearly* polystyrene; that's what you said."

"Were you serious about the batteries?" Lang asked.

"I'm not sure. Marty thinks there's a chemical metabolism in the upper part of the shell, which I haven't explored yet. But I can't really say if it's alive in the sense we use. I mean, it runs on *wheels!* It has three wheels, suited for sand, and something that's a cross between a rubber-band drive and a mainspring. Energy is stored in a coiled muscle and released slowly. I don't think it could travel more than a hundred meters. Unless it can re-coil the muscle, and I can't tell how that might be done."

"It sounds very specialized," McKillian said thoughtfully. "Maybe we should be looking for the niche it occupies. The way you describe it, it couldn't function without help from a symbiote. Maybe it fertilizes the plants, like bees, and the plants either donate or are robbed of the power to wind the spring. Did you look for some mechanism the bug could use to steal energy from the rotating gears in the whirligigs?"

"That's what I want to do in the morning," Song said. "Unless Mary will let us take a look tonight?" She said it hopefully, but without real expectation. Mary Lang shook her head decisively.

"It'll keep. It's *cold* out there, baby."

A new exploration of the whirligig garden the next day revealed several new species, including one more thing that might be an animal. It was a flying creature, the size of a fruit fly, that managed to glide from plant to plant when the wind was down by means of a freely rotating set of blades, like an autogiro.

Crawford and Lang hung around as the scientists looked things over. They were not anxious to get back to the task that had occupied them for the last two weeks: that of bringing the *Podkayne* to a horizontal position without wrecking her. The ship had been rigged with stabilizing cables soon after landing, and provision had been made in the plans to lay the ship on its side in the event of a really big windstorm. But the plans had envisioned a work force of twenty, working all day with a maze of pulleys and gears. It was slow work and could not be rushed. If the ship were to tumble and lose pressure, they didn't have a prayer.

So they welcomed an opportunity to tour fairyland. The place was even more bountiful than the last time Crawford had taken a look. There were thick vines that Song assured him were running with water, both hot and cold, and various other fluids. There were more of the tall variety of derrick, making the place look like a pastel oilfield.

They had little trouble finding where the matthews came from. They found dozens of twenty-centimeter lumps on the sides of the large derricks. They evidently grew from them like tumors and were released when they were ripe. What they were for was another matter. As well as they could discover, the matthews simply crawled in a straight line until their power ran out. If they were wound up again, they would crawl farther. There were dozens of them lying motionless in the sand within a hundred-meter radius of the garden.

Two weeks of research left them knowing no more. They had to abandon the matthews for the time, as another enigma had cropped up which demanded their attention.

This time Crawford was the last to know. He was called on the radio and found the group all squatted in a circle around a growth in the graveyard.

The graveyard, where they had buried their fifteen dead crewmates on the first day of the disaster, had sprouted with life during the week after the departure of the *Burroughs*. It was separated from the original site of the dome by three hundred meters of blowing sand. So McKillian assumed this second bloom was caused by the water in the bodies of the dead. What they couldn't figure out was why this patch should differ so radically from the first one.

There were whirligigs in the second patch, but they lacked the variety and disorder of the originals. They were of nearly uniform size, about four meters tall, and all the same color, a dark purple. They had pumped water for two weeks, then stopped. When Song examined them, she reported the bearings were frozen, dried out. They seemed to have lost the plasticizer that kept the structures fluid and living. The water in the pipes was frozen. Though she would not commit herself in the matter, she felt they were dead. In their place was a second network of pipes which wound around the derricks and spread transparent sheets of film to the sunlight, heating the water which circulated through them. The water was being pumped, but not by the now-familiar system of windmills. Spaced along each of the pipes were expansion-contraction pumps with valves very like those in a human heart.

The new marvel was a simple affair in the middle of that living petrochemical complex. It was a short plant that sprouted up half a meter, then extruded two stalks parallel to the ground. At the end of each stalk was a perfect globe, one gray, one blue. The blue one was much larger than the gray one.

Crawford looked at it briefly, then squatted down beside the rest, wondering what all the fuss was about. Everyone looked very solemn, almost scared.

"You called me over to see this?"

Lang looked over at him, and something in her face made him nervous.

"Look at it, Matt. Really look at it." So he did, feeling foolish, wondering what the joke was. He noticed a white patch near the top of the largest globe. It was streaked, like a glass marble with swirls of opaque material in it. It looked *very* familiar, he realized, with the hair on the back of his neck starting to stand up.

"It turns," Lang said quietly. "That's why Song noticed it. She came by here one day, and it was in a different position than it had been."

"Let me guess," he said, much more calmly than he felt. "The little one goes around the big one, right?"

"Right. And the little one keeps one face turned to the big one. The big one rotates once in twenty-four hours. It has an axial tilt of twenty-three degrees."

"It's a . . . what's the word? Orrery. It's an orrery." Crawford had to stand up and shake his head to clear it.

"It's funny," Lang said, quietly. "I always thought it would be something flashy, or at least obvious. An alien artifact mixed in with caveman bones, or a spaceship entering the system. I guess I was thinking in terms of pottery shards and atom bombs."

"Well, that all sounds pretty ho-hum to me up against *this,*" Song said. "Do you . . . do you *realize* . . . what are we talking about here? Evolution, or . . . or engineering? Is it the plants themselves that did this, or were they made to do it by whatever built them? Do you see what I'm talking about? I've felt funny about those wheels for a long time. I just won't believe they'd evolve naturally."

"What do you mean?"

"I mean I think these plants we've been seeing were designed to be the way they are. They're *too* perfectly adapted, *too* ingenious to have just sprung up in response to the environment." Her eyes seemed to wander, and she stood up and gazed into the valley below them. It was as barren as anything that could be imagined: red and yellow and brown rock outcroppings and tumbled boulders. And in the foreground, the twirling colors of the whirligigs.

"But why this thing?" Crawford asked, pointing to the impossible artifact-plant. "Why a model of the Earth and Moon? And why right here, in the graveyard?"

"Because we were expected," Song said, still looking away from them. "They must have watched the Earth, during the last summer season. I don't know; maybe they even went there. If they did, they would have found men and women like us, hunting and living in caves. Building fires, using clubs, chipping arrowheads. You know more about it than I do, Matt."

"Who are *they*?" Ralston asked. "You think we're going to be meeting some Martians? People? I don't see how. I don't believe it."

"I'm afraid I'm skeptical, too," Lang said. "Surely there must be some other way to explain it."

"No! There's no other way. Oh, not people like us, maybe. Maybe we're seeing them right now, spinning like crazy." They all looked uneasily at the whirligigs. "But I think they're not here yet. I think we're going to see, over the next few years, increasing complexity in these plants and animals as they build up a biome here and get ready for the builders. Think about it. When summer comes, the conditions will be very different. The atmosphere will be almost as dense as ours, with about the same partial pressure of oxygen. By then, thousands of years from now, these early forms will have vanished. These things are adapted for low pressure, no oxygen, scarce water. The later ones will be adapted to an environment much like ours. And *that's* when we'll see the makers, when the stage is properly set." She sounded almost religious when she said it.

Lang stood up and shook Song's shoulder. Song came slowly back to them and sat down, still blinded by a private vision. Crawford had a glimpse of it himself, and it scared him. And a glimpse of something else, something that could be important but kept eluding him.

"Don't you see?" she went on, calmer now. "It's too pat, too much of a coincidence. This thing is like a . . . a headstone, a monument. It's growing right here in the graveyard, from the bodies of our friends. Can you believe in that as just a coincidence?"

Evidently no one could. But likewise, Crawford could see no reason why it should have happened the way it did.

It was painful to leave the mystery for later, but there was nothing to be done about it. They could not bring themselves to uproot the thing, even when five more like it sprouted in the graveyard. There was a new consensus among them to leave the Martian plants and animals alone. Like nervous atheists, most of them didn't believe Song's theories but had an uneasy feeling of trespassing when they went through the gardens. They felt subconsciously that it might be better to leave them alone in case they turned out to be private property.

And for six months, nothing really new cropped up among the whirligigs. Song was not surprised. She said it supported her theory that these plants were there only as caretakers to prepare the way for less hardy, air-breathing varieties to come. They would warm the soil and bring the water closer to the surface, then disappear when their function was over.

The three scientists allowed their studies to slide as it became more important to provide for the needs of the moment. The dome material was weakening as the temporary patches lost strength, and so a new home was badly needed. They were dealing daily with slow leaks, any of which could become a major blowout.

The *Podkayne* was lowered to the ground, and sadly decommissioned. It was a bad day for Mary Lang, the worst since the day of the blowout. She saw it as a necessary but infamous thing to do to a proud flying machine. She brooded about it for a week, becoming short-tempered and almost unapproachable. Then she asked Crawford to join her in the private shelter. It was the first time she had asked any of the other four. They lay in each other's arms for an hour, and Lang sobbed quietly on his chest. Crawford was proud that she had chosen him for her companion when she could no longer maintain her tough, competent show of strength. In a way, it was a strong thing to do, to expose weakness to the one person among the four who might possibly be her rival for leadership. He did not betray the trust. In the end, she was comforting him.

After that day Lang was ruthless in gutting the old *Podkayne*. She supervised the ripping out of the motors to provide more living space, and only Crawford saw what it was costing her. They drained the fuel tanks and stored the fuel in every available container they could scrounge. It would be useful later for heating, and for recharging batteries. They managed to convert plastic packing crates into fuel containers by lining them with sheets of the double-walled material the whirligigs used to heat water. They were nervous at this vandalism, but had no other choice. They kept looking nervously at the graveyard as they ripped up meter-square sheets of it.

They ended up with a long cylindrical home, divided into two small sleeping rooms, a community room, and a laboratory-storehouse-workshop in the old fuel tank. Crawford and Lang spent the first night together in the "penthouse," the former cockpit, the only room with windows.

Lying there wide awake on the rough mattress, side by side in the warm air with Mary Lang, whose black leg was a crooked line of shadow laying across his body, looking up through the port at the sharp, unwinking stars—with nothing done yet about the problems of oxygen, food, and water for the years ahead and no assurance he would live out the night on a planet determined to kill him—Crawford realized he had never been happier in his life.

On a day exactly eight months after the disaster, two discoveries were made. One was in the whirligig garden and concerned a new plant that was bearing what might be fruit. They were clusters of grape-sized white balls, very hard and fairly heavy. The second discovery was made by Lucy McKillian and concerned the absence of an event that up to that time had been as regular as the full moon.

"I'm pregnant," she announced to them that night, causing Song to delay her examination of the white fruit.

It was not unexpected; Lang had been waiting for it to happen since the night the *Burroughs* left. But she had not worried about it. Now she must decide what to do.

"I was afraid that might happen," Crawford said. "What do we do, Mary?"

"Why don't you tell me what you think? You're the survival expert. Are babies a plus or a minus in our situation?"

"I'm afraid I have to say they're a liability. Lucy will be needing extra food during her pregnancy and afterward, and it will be extra mouth to feed. We can't afford the strain on our resources." Lang said nothing, waiting to hear from McKillian.

"Now wait a minute. What about all this line about 'colonists' you've been feeding us ever since we got stranded here? *Who ever heard of a colony without babies?* If we don't grow, we stagnate, right? We *have* to have children." She looked back and forth from Lang to Crawford, her face expressing formless doubts.

"We're in special circumstances, Lucy," Crawford explained. "Sure, I'd be all for it if we were better off. But we can't be sure we can even provide for ourselves, much less a child. I say we can't afford children until we're established."

"Do you want the child, Lucy?" Lang asked quietly.

McKillian didn't seem to know what she wanted. "No. I . . . but, yes. Yes, I guess I do." She looked at them, pleading for them to understand.

"Look, I've never had one, and never planned to. I'm thirty-four years old and never, never felt the lack. I've always wanted to go places and you can't with a baby. But I never planned to become a colonist on Mars, either. I . . . things have changed, don't you see? I've been depressed." She looked around, and Song and Ralston were nodding sympathetically. Relieved to see that she was not the only one feeling the oppression, she went on, more strongly. "I think if I go another day like yesterday and the day before—and today—I'll end up screaming. It seems so pointless, collecting all that information, for what?"

"I agree with Lucy," Ralston said, surprisingly. Crawford had thought he would be the only one immune to the inevitable despair of the castaway. Ralston in his laboratory the picture of carefree detachment, existing only to observe.

"So do I," Lang said, ending the discussion. But she explained her reasons to them.

"Look at it this way, Matt. No matter how we stretch our supplies, they won't take us through the next four years. We either find a way of getting what we need from what's around us, or we all die. And if we find a way to do it, then what does it matter how many of us there are? At the most, this will push our deadline a few weeks or a month closer, the day we have to be self-supporting."

"I hadn't thought of it that way," Crawford admitted.

"But that's not important. The important thing is what you said from the first, and I'm surprised you didn't see it. If we're a colony, we expand. By definition. Historian, what happened to colonies that failed to expand?"

"Don't rub it in."

"They died out. I know that much. People, we're not intrepid space explorers anymore. We're not the career men and women we set out to be. Like it or not, and I suggest we start liking it, we're pioneers trying to live in a hostile environment. The odds are very much against us, and we're not going to be here forever, but like Matt said, we'd better plan as if we were. Comment?"

There was none, until Song spoke up, thoughtfully.

"I think a baby around here would be fun. Two should be twice as much fun. I think I'll start. Come on, Marty."

"Hold on, honey," Lang said dryly. "If you conceive now, I'll be forced to order you to abort. We have the chemicals for it, you know."

"That's discrimination."

"Maybe so. But just because we're colonists doesn't mean we have to behave like rabbits. A pregnant woman will have to be removed from the workforce at the end of her term, and we can only afford one at a time. After Lucy has hers, then come ask me again. But watch Lucy carefully, dear. Have you really thought what it's going to take? Have you tried to visualize her getting into her pressure suit in six or seven months?"

From their expressions, it was plain that neither Song nor McKillian had thought of it.

"Right," Lang went on. "It'll be literal confinement for her, right here in the *Poddy.* Unless we can rig something for her, which I seriously doubt. Still want to go through with it, Lucy?"

"Can I have a while to think it over?"

"Sure. You have about two months. After that, the chemicals aren't safe."

"I'd advise you to do it," Crawford said. "I know my opinion means nothing after shooting my mouth off. I know I'm a fine one to talk; I won't be cooped up in here. But the colony needs it. We've all felt it: the lack of a direction or a drive to keep going. I think we'd get it back if you went through with this."

McKillian tapped her teeth thoughtfully with the tip of a finger.

"You're right," she said. "Your opinion *doesn't* mean anything." She slapped his knee delightedly when she saw him blush. "I think it's yours, by the way. And I think I'll go ahead and have it."

The penthouse seemed to have gone to Lang and Crawford as an unasked-for prerogative. It just became a habit, since they seemed to have developed a bond between them and none of the other three complained. Neither of the other women seemed to be suffering in any way. So Lang left it at that. What went on between the three of them was of no concern to her as long as it stayed happy.

Lang was leaning back in Crawford's arms, trying to decide if she wanted to make love again, when a gunshot rang out in the *Podkayne*.

She had given a lot of thought to the last emergency, which she still saw as partly a result of her lag in responding. This time she was through the door almost before the reverberations had died down, leaving Crawford to nurse the leg she had stepped on in her haste.

She was in time to see McKillian and Ralston hurrying into the lab at the back of the ship. There was a red light flashing, but she quickly saw it was not the worst it could be; the pressure light still glowed green. It was the smoke detector. The smoke was coming from the lab.

She took a deep breath and plunged in, only to collide with Ralston as he came out, dragging Song. Except for a dazed expression and a few cuts, Song seemed to be all right. Crawford and McKillian joined them as they lay her on the bunk.

"It was one of the fruit," she said, gasping for breath and coughing. "I was heating it in a beaker, turned away, and it blew. I guess it sort of stunned me. The next thing I knew Marty was carrying me out here. Hey, I have to get back in there! There's another one . . . it could be dangerous, and the damage, I have to check on that—" She struggled to get up, but Lang held her down.

"You take it easy. What's this about another one?"

"I had it clamped down, and the drill—did I turn it on, or not? I can't remember. I was after a core sample. You'd better take a look. If the drill hits whatever made the other one explode, it might go off."

"I'll get it," McKillian said, turning toward the lab.

"You'll stay right here," Lang barked. "We know there's not enough power in them to hurt the ship, but it could kill you if it hit you right. We stay right here until it goes off. The hell with the damage. And shut that door, quick!"

Before they could shut it they heard a whistling, like a teakettle coming to boil, then a rapid series of clangs. A tiny white ball came through the doorway and bounced off three walls. It moved almost faster than they could follow. It hit Crawford on the arm, then fell to the floor where it gradually skittered to a stop. The hissing died away, and Crawford picked it up. It was lighter than it had been. There was a pinhole drilled in one side. The pinhole was cold when he touched it with his fingers. Startled, thinking he was burned, he stuck his finger in his mouth, then sucked on it absently long after he knew the truth.

"These 'fruit' are full of compressed gas," he told them. "We have to open up another, carefully this time. I'm almost afraid to say what gas I think it is, but I have a hunch that our problems are solved."

By the time the rescue expedition arrived, no one was calling it that. There had been the little matter of a long, brutal war with the Palestinian Empire, and a growing conviction that the survivors of the First Expedition had not had any chance in the first place. There had been no time for luxuries like space travel beyond the moon and no billions of dollars to invest while the world's energy policies were being debated in the Arabian desert with tactical nuclear weapons.

When the ship finally did show up, it was no longer a NASA ship. It was sponsored by the fledgling International Space Agency. Its crew came from all over Earth. Its drive was new, too, and a lot better than the old one. As usual, war had given research a kick in the pants. Its mission was to take up the Martian exploration where the first expedition had left off and, incidentally, to recover the remains of the twenty Americans for return to Earth.

The ship came down with an impressive show of flame and billowing sand, three kilometers from Tharsis Base.

The captain, an Indian named Singh, got his crew started on erecting the permanent buildings, then climbed into a crawler with three officers for the trip to Tharsis. It was almost exactly twelve Earth-years since the departure of the *Edgar Rice Burroughs*.

The *Podkayne* was barely visible behind a network of multicolored vines. The vines were tough enough to frustrate their efforts to push through and enter the old ship. But both lock doors were open, and sand had drifted in rippled waves through the opening. The stern of the ship was nearly buried.

Singh told his people to stop, and he stood back admiring the complexity of the life in such a barren place. There were whirligigs twenty meters tall scattered around him, with vanes broad as the wings of a cargo aircraft.

"We'll have to get cutting tools from the ship," he told his crew. "They're probably in there. What a place this is! I can see we're going to be busy." He walked along the edge of the dense growth, which now covered several acres. He came to a section where the predominant color was purple. It was strangely different from the rest of the garden. There were tall whirligig derricks but they were frozen, unmoving. And covering all the derricks was a translucent network of ten-centimeter-wide strips of plastic, which was thick enough to make an impenetrable barrier. It was like a cobweb made of flat, thin material instead of fibrous spider-silk. It bulged outward between all the crossbraces of the whirligigs.

"Hello, can you hear me now?"

Singh jumped, then turned around, looked at the three officers. They were looking as surprised as he was.

"Hello, hello, hello? No good on this one, Mary. Want me to try another channel?"

"Wait a moment. I can hear you. Where are you?"

"Hey, he hears me! Uh, that is, this is Song Sue Lee, and I'm right in front of you. If you look real hard into the webbing, you can just make me out. I'll wave my arms. See?"

Singh thought he saw some movement when he pressed his face to the translucent web. The web resisted his hands, pushing back like an inflated balloon.

"I *think* I see you." The enormity of it was just striking him. He kept his voice under tight control, as his officers rushed up around him, and managed not to stammer. "Are you well? Is there anything we can do?"

There was a pause. "Well, now that you mention it, you might have come on time. But that's water through the pipes, I guess. If you have some toys or something, it might be nice. The stories I've told little Billy of all the nice things you people were going to bring! There's going to be no living with him, let me tell you."

This was getting out of hand for Captain Singh.

"Ms. Song, how can we get in there with you?"

"Sorry. Go to your right about ten meters, where you see the steam coming from the web. There, see it? They did, and as they looked, a section of the webbing was pulled open and a rush of warm air almost blew them over. Water condensed out of it in their faceplates, and suddenly they couldn't see very well.

"Hurry, hurry, step in! We can't keep it open too long." They groped their way in, scraping frost away with their hands. The web closed behind them, and they were standing in the center of a very complicated network made of single strands of the webbing material. Singh's pressure gauge read 30 millibars.

Another section opened up and they stepped through it. After three more gates were passed, the temperature and pressure were nearly Earth-normal. And they were standing beside a small Oriental woman with skin tanned almost black. She had no clothes on, but seemed adequately dressed in a brilliant smile that dimpled her mouth and eyes. Her hair was streaked with gray. She would be—Singh stopped to consider—forty-one years old.

"This way," she said, beckoning them into a tunnel formed from more strips of plastic. They twisted around through a random maze, going through more gates that opened when they neared them, sometimes getting on their knees when the clearance lowered. They heard the sound of children's voices.

They reached what must have been the center of the maze and found the people everyone had given up on. Eighteen of them. The children became very quiet and stared solemnly at the new arrivals, while the other four adults . . .

The adults were standing separately around the space while tiny helicopters flew around them, wrapping them from head to toe in strips of webbing like human maypoles.

"Of course we don't know if we would have made it without the assist from the Martians," Mary Lang was saying, from her perch on an orange thing that might have been a toadstool. "Once we figured out what was happening here in the graveyard, there was no need to explore alternative ways of getting food, water, and oxygen. The need just never arose. We were provided for."

She raised her feet so a group of three gawking women from the ship could get by. They were letting them come through in groups of five every hour. They didn't dare open the outer egress more often than that, and Lang was wondering if it was too often. The place was crowded, and the kids were nervous. But better to have the crew satisfy their curiosity in here where we can watch them, she reasoned, then have them messing things up outside.

The inner nest was free-form. The New Amsterdamites had

allowed it to stay pretty much the way the whirlibirds had built it, only taking down an obstruction here and there to allow humans to move around. It was a maze of gauzy walls and plastic struts, with clear plastic pipes running all over and carrying fluids of pale blue, gold, and wine. Metal spigots from the *Podkayne* had been inserted in some of the pipes. McKillian kept busy refilling glasses for the visitors who wanted to sample the antifreeze solution that was fifty percent ethanol. It was good stuff, Captain Singh reflected as he drained his third glass, and that was what he still couldn't understand.

He was having trouble framing the questions he wanted to ask, and he realized he'd had too much to drink. The spirit of celebration, the rejoicing at finding these people here past any hope; one could hardly stay aloof from it. But he refused a fourth drink regretfully.

"I can understand the drink," he said, carefully. "Ethanol is a simple compound and could fit into many different chemistries. But it's hard to believe that you've survived eating the food these plants produced for you."

"Not once you understand what this graveyard is and why it became what it did," Song said. She was sitting cross-legged on the floor nursing her youngest, Ethan.

"First you have to understand that all this you see," she waved around at the meters of hanging soft-sculpture, causing Ethan to nearly lose the nipple, "was designed to contain beings who are no more adapted to *this* Mars than we are. They need warmth, oxygen at fairly high pressures, and free water. It isn't here now, but it can be created by properly designed plants. They engineered these plants to be triggered by the first signs of free water and to start building places for them to live while they waited for full summer to come. When it does, this whole planet will bloom. Then we can step outside without wearing suits or carrying airberries."

"Yes, I see," Singh said. "And it's all very wonderful, almost too much to believe." He was distracted for a moment, looking up to the ceiling where the airberries—white spheres about the size of bowling balls—hung in clusters from the pipes that supplied them with high-pressure oxygen.

"I'd like to see that process from the start," he said. "Where you suit up for the outside, I mean."

"We were suiting up when you got here. It takes about half an hour; so we couldn't get out in time to meet you."

"How long are those . . . suits good for?"

"About a day," Crawford said. "You have to destroy them to get out of them. The plastic strips don't cut well, but there's another specialized animal that eats that type of plastic. It's recycled into the system. If you want to suit up, you just grab a whirlibird and hold onto its tail and throw it. It starts spinning as it flies, and wraps the end product around you. It takes some practice, but it works. The stuff sticks to itself, but not to us. So you spin several layers, letting each one dry, then hook up an airberry, and you're inflated and insulated."

"Marvelous," Singh said, truly impressed. He had seen the tiny whirlibirds weaving the suits, and the other ones, like small slugs, eating them away when the colonists saw they wouldn't need them. "But without some sort of exhaust, you wouldn't last long. How is that accomplished?"

"We use the breather valves from our old suits," McKillian said. "Either the plants that grow valves haven't come up yet or we haven't been smart enough to recognize them. And the insulation isn't perfect. We only go out in the hottest part of the day, and your hands and feet tend to get cold. But we manage."

Singh realized he had strayed from his original question.

"But what about the food? Surely it's too much to expect for these Martians to eat the same things we do. Wouldn't you think so?"

"We sure did, and we were lucky to have Marty Ralston along. He kept telling us the fruits in the graveyard were edible by humans. Fats, starches, proteins; all identical to the ones we brought along. The clue was in the orrery, of course."

Lang pointed to the twin globes in the middle of the room, still keeping perfect Earth time.

"It was a beacon. We figured that out when we saw they grew only in the graveyard. But what was it telling us? We felt it meant that we were expected. Song felt that from the start, and we all came to agree with her. But we didn't realize just how much they had prepared for us until Marty started analyzing the fruits and nutrients here.

"Listen, these Martians—and I can see from your look that you still don't really believe in them, but you will if you stay here long enough—they know genetics. They really know it. We have a thousand theories about what they may be like, and I won't bore you with them yet, but this is one thing we do know. They can build anything they need, make a blueprint in DNA, encapsulate it in a spore and bury it, knowing exactly what will come up in forty thousand years. When it starts to get cold here and they know the cycle's drawing to an end, they seed the planet with the spores and . . . do something. Maybe they die, or maybe they have some other way of passing the time. But they know they'll return.

"We can't say how long they've been prepared for a visit from us. Maybe only this cycle; maybe twenty cycles ago. Anyway, at the last cycle they buried the kind of spores that would produce these little gizmos." She tapped the blue ball representing the Earth with one foot.

"They triggered them to be activated only when they encountered certain different conditions. Maybe they knew exactly what it would be; maybe they only provided for a likely range of possibilities. Song thinks they've visited us, back in the Stone Age. In some ways it's easier to believe than the alternative. That way they'd know our genetic structure and what kinds of food we'd eat, and could prepare.

" 'Cause if they didn't visit us, they must have prepared other spores. Spores that would analyze new proteins and be able to duplicate them. Further than that, some of the plants might have been able to copy certain genetic material if they encountered any. Take a look at that pipe behind you." Singh turned and saw a pipe about as thick as his arm. It was flexible, and had a swelling in it that continuously pulsed in expansion and contraction.

"Take that bulge apart and you'd be amazed at the resemblance to a human heart. So there's another significant fact; this place started out with whirligigs, but later modified itself to use human heart pumps from the genetic information *taken from the bodies the men and women we buried.*" She paused to let that sink in, then went on with a slightly bemused smile.

"The same thing for what we eat and drink. That liquor you drank, for instance. It's half alcohol, and that's probably what it would have been without the corpses. But the rest of it is very similar to hemoglobin. It's sort of like fermented blood. Human blood."

Singh was glad he had refused the fourth drink. One of his crew members quietly put his glass down.

"I've never eaten human flesh," Lang went on, "but I think I know what it must taste like. Those vines to your right; we strip off the outer part and eat the meat underneath. It tastes good. I wish we could cook it, but we have nothing to burn and couldn't risk it with the high oxygen count, anyway."

Singh and everyone else was silent for a while. He found he really was beginning to believe in the Martians. The theory seemed to cover a lot of otherwise inexplicable facts.

Mary Lang sighed, slapped her thighs, and stood up. Like all the others, she was nude and seemed totally at home with it. None of them had worn anything but a Martian pressure suit for eight years. She ran her hand lovingly over the gossamer wall, the wall that had provided her and her fellow colonists and their children protection from the cold and the thin air for so long. He was struck by her easy familiarity with what seemed to him outlandish surroundings. She looked at home. He couldn't imagine her anywhere else.

He looked at the children. One wide-eyed little girl of eight years was kneeling at his feet. As his eyes fell on her, she smiled tentatively and took his hand.

"Did you bring any bubble gum?" the girl asked.

He smiled at her. "No, honey, but maybe there's some in the ship." She seemed satisfied. She would wait to experience the wonders of Earthly science.

"We were provided for," Mary Lang said quietly. "They knew we were coming, and they altered their plans to fit us in." She looked back to Singh. "It would have happened even without the blowout and the burials. The same sort of thing was happening around the *Podkayne,* too, triggered by our waste; urine and feces and such. I don't know if it would have tasted quite as good in the food department, but it would have sustained life."

Singh stood up. He was moved, but did not trust himself to show it adequately. So he sounded rather abrupt, though polite.

"I suppose you'll be anxious to go to the ship," he said. "You're going to be a tremendous help. You know so much of what we were sent here to find out. And you'll be quite famous when you get back to Earth. Your back pay should add up to quite a sum.

There was a silence, then it was ripped apart by Lang's huge laugh. She was joined by the others, and the children, who didn't know what they were laughing about but enjoyed the break in the tension.

"Sorry, Captain. That was rude. But we're not going back."

Singh looked at each of the adults and saw no trace of doubt. And he was mildly surprised to find that the statement did not startle him.

"I won't take that as your final decision," he said. "As you know, we'll be here six months. If at the end of that time any of you want to go, you're still citizens of Earth."

"We are? You'll have to brief us on the political situation back there. We were United States citizens when we left. But it doesn't matter. You won't get any takers, though we appreciate the fact you came. It's nice to know we weren't forgotten." She said it with total assurance, and the others were nodding. Singh was uncomfortably aware that the idea of a rescue mission had died out only a few years after the initial tragedy. He and his ship were here now only to explore.

Lang sat back down and patted the ground around her, ground that was covered in a multiple layer of the Martian pressure-tight web, the kind of web that would have been made only by warm-blooded, oxygen-breathing, water-economy beings who needed protection for their bodies until the full bloom of summer.

"We *like* it here. It's a good place to raise a family, not like Earth the last time I was there. And it couldn't be much better now, right after another war. And we can't leave, even if we wanted to." She flashed him a dazzling smile and patted the ground again.

"The Martians should be showing up any time now. And we aim to thank them."

The First Mars Mission

✦

Robert F. Young

As Hegel said, first you get a thesis, then you get an antithesis, and ultimately you wind up with a synthesis. Robert F. Young's "The First Mars Mission" is nearly a perfect blend of inner space and outer space in its depiction of how three kids live out the dream of flying to outer space from their backyards.

By the way, do you remember how Edgar Rice Burroughs transported John Carter to Mars? Here's the end of chapter 2 of A Princess of Mars:

> As I stood thus meditating, I turned my gaze from the landscape to the heavens where the myriad stars formed a gorgeous and fitting canopy for the wonders of the earthly scene. My attention was quickly riveted by a large red star close to the distant horizon. As I gazed upon it I felt a spell of overpowering fascination—it was Mars, the god of war, and for me, the fighting man, it had always held the power of irresistible enchantment. As I gazed at it on that far-gone night it seemed to call across the unthinkable void, to lure me to it, to draw me as the lodestone attracts a particle of iron.
>
> My longing was beyond the power of opposition; I closed my eyes, stretched out my arms toward the god of my vocation and felt myself

> drawn with the suddenness of thought through the trackless immensity of space. There was an instant of extreme cold and utter darkness.

And here's the start of chapter 3:

> I opened my eyes upon a strange and weird landscape. I knew that I was on Mars; not once did I question either my sanity or my wakefulness. I was not asleep, no need for pinching here; my inner consciousness told me as plainly that I was upon Mars as your conscious mind tells you that you are upon Earth. You do not question the fact; neither did I.

Robert F. Young was one of F&SF*'s most prolific contributors from the 1950s until his death in 1986. He wrote only a handful of novels (including* The Last Yggdrasil *and* The Vizier's Second Daughter*) and most of his work remains uncollected, although* www.electricstory.com *recently published an e-book collection of a dozen stories and there is likely to be a print-book collection published before too long.*

THEY HAD BUILT the spaceship in Larry's backyard. His backyard was bigger than either Chan's or Al's. This was because his parents' house was on the outskirts of town where the houses were far apart and did not belong to blocks, where in some cases the whole countryside stretched away from your back door.

Larry had had no idea then that someday he would become a real astronaut. Mars had fascinated him as much as it had Al and Chan. But in his heart what he'd really wanted to become was a fireman.

For landing jacks they used a pair of old sawhorses Al found in the loft of his father's garage. Upon them they nailed the deck—a platform constructed of scrap lumber they swiped from behind the new school building. Chan's father, who was a junk dealer, had already told them they could borrow the big conical vented tin smokestack he'd "collected" when the old Larrimore grain-machinery factory was torn down, and one simmering July afternoon they freed it from the debris in the rear of the fenced-in junkyard and rolled it all the way across town to Larry's house. There, panting and perspiring, they jockeyed it onto the deck and braced it with three toenailed two-by-fours.

Scraping and painting the stack took them two days. It didn't cost them anything, though, because there were all kinds of paint cans in Larry's basement, with varying quantities of paint still in them. No two of the colors were the same, but by mixing the brightest ones together they came up with a beautiful greenish blue.

On the third day, after the paint had dried sufficiently, they installed the ion-drive—a 3-HP Briggs & Stratton motor Al's father had saved when he got rid of his old power mower. They'd already sawed out a 2' x 2' section of the deck and constructed a lock that functioned on the same principle as a trapdoor. Lastly they installed the control panel—a 1957 Ford dash donated by Chan's father.

Look out, Mars—here we come!

All this was before *Mariner 4* pulled the plug on Giovanni Schiaparelli's *canali,* Percival Lowell's canals, and Edgar Rice Burroughs's "waterways," and prematurely "proved" that Mars was both geologically and biologically dead.

Weird, their choice of a landing site. Downright weird.

The map they used had all sorts of mysterious shaded areas that designated seas and lakes and swamps and whatnot, and they picked a region that was partially bordered by one of the larger of these areas. They could have picked any one of a half dozen other regions for the same reason. But they hadn't.

The site selected, they began thinking up names for the spaceship, finally agreeing on *The Martian Queen*. Next, they scheduled liftoff for 2200 hours the following night. Mars should be visible at that hour, enabling them to set their course. Since the round trip would probably take at least two hours and they wanted plenty of time to explore, they had to get their parents' permission to stay out all night. Chan and Al had no trouble on this score, but Larry's mother had a fit, and only the intervention of his father had made his participation in the historic Marsflight possible.

They spent the next day loading equipment and supplies on board, painting *The Martian Queen* in big black letters on the ship's prow, and speculating on what they would find when they reached their destination. The equipment consisted of three sleeping bags and Larry's father's flashlight. The supplies comprised three ham-salad sandwiches (courtesy of Chan's mother), three eight-ounce cans of Campbell's Pork & Beans (lifted by Larry from his mother's kitchen cupboard), and three cartons of chocolate milk.

They loaded the supplies on last. "Maybe we ought to take along some kind of weapons," Al suggested. "In case the life-forms turn out to be unfriendly." Chan went home and got a hatchet; Al, a baseball bat; and Larry went up to his room and got the Boy Scout knife that used to be his father's. It had four blades, one of them a can opener that would come in handy opening the Campbell's Pork & Beans.

Nine o'clock arrived. Nine-thirty. The stars began to come out. "I see Mars!" Chan cried. "Right up there!"

It was like a beacon in the night sky, orange and beckoning.

"Let's go," Al said. "We can set our course now."

"But it's not 2200 hours yet," Larry objected.

"What difference does that make?"

"It makes a lot of difference. Space missions are supposed to follow a strict timetable."

"Not when you've got an ion-drive. When you've got an ion-drive, you just say 'Let's go!' and you go."

Larry gave in. "All right. It's almost liftoff time anyway."

They climbed up into the ship, closed the lock and sat down in the darkness. Larry switched on the flashlight, shone the beam on the control panel and set their course.

Al began the countdown. When he reached zero, Larry activated the ion-drive. "We're on our way!" he shouted.

Since there wasn't anything else to do, they ate the ham-salad sandwiches and washed them down with the chocolate milk. After they finished eating, Larry switched off the flashlight to save the batteries. Then they sat in silence for what seemed like hours, but since no one had thought to bring a watch, the hours, for all they knew, may have been minutes. Another thing they'd forgot to do was install a viewport. However, there was a crack in the bulkhead where the two ends of the sheet metal that formed the stack were welded together, and finally Larry got to his feet and peered through the narrow opening.

"What d'you see?" Chan asked.

"Stars," Larry said.

"Gosh, we ought to be there by now," Al said. "Here, let me look."

Larry relinquished the makeshift viewport. "Hey!" Al shouted a moment later. "I see it! Dead ahead!"

"Okay, Al," Larry said. "I'll put her in orbit, and you sing out when you spot the landing site."

"Hey! I see a canal! Two of them! Three!"

"Never mind the canals. Just keep your eye peeled for the landing site."

"I see it now. Right below us. It's a great big plain with a canal running through the middle of it. Hey! I see a city!"

"We're too high up for you to see a city."

"I don't care. I see one anyway. Take her down, Larry. Take her down!"

"I've got to turn her over first so we'll land right side up. Hang on, everybody!"

The maneuver completed, Larry revved up the ion-drive for a soft landing. Minutes went by. Or maybe only seconds. Suddenly there was a faint jar.

There couldn't have been, but there was.

Al in the lead, the three astronauts lowered themselves through the lock and crawled out from under the ship and stood up. In their haste, Al forgot his baseball bat; Chan, his hatchet; and Larry, his father's flashlight.

There *was* a city.

It stood at the confluence of three canals, the nearest of which bisected the broad plain on which the ship had landed. It had two towers as tall as the Empire State Building. Myriad lights gleamed above its lofty wall, and a pair of wide gates provided ingress and egress.

The air was clear and cold. Stars so bright they hurt your eyes to look at them glittered in a stark-black sky. There were two tiny moons. One overhead, the other climbing rapidly above the horizon.

As they stood there staring at the distant city, a sound resembling thunder came from behind them. It crescendoed, separated itself into a swift succession of muffled hoofbeats. Turning, they beheld a huge beast with a great gaping mouth bearing down upon them, a rider on its back. They shrank back against the ship. The beast had eight legs and a long, flat tail. It pounded past them like a flesh-and-blood locomotive, the ground trembling beneath its awesome tread. Larry gasped when he glimpsed the rider's face.

It was the face of a beautiful woman.

If she saw either the three astronauts or *The Martian Queen*—and she could hardly have missed seeing the latter—she gave no sign. The beast continued on across the plain, rapidly diminishing in size. When it reached the wall of the city, the gates swung open long enough for it and its rider to pass between them, then swung to again.

Al took a deep breath. "We must be dreaming."

"We must be," echoed Chan.

Larry didn't say anything. The woman had been tantalizingly familiar. *Where had he encountered her before?*

And that horrid eight-legged beast. It, too, had rung a bell.

"Well," Chan said, a quaver in his voice, "now that we're on Mars, what're we going to do?"

"We're going to explore, of course," Larry said, with far more confidence than he felt.

"The—the city?"

"I—I think we'd better skip the city. Let's take a look at that canal."

"Race you!" Al cried, setting off at a run.

His first step took him halfway to the nearer bank. He landed lightly on his back, bounced to his feet. "Hey, this is *fun!*"

Larry and Chan followed at a more conservative pace, taking little leaps and trying to come down feet-first. Sometimes they succeeded and sometimes they didn't. Al was already standing on the bank gazing down into the water when they got there. The water was so pellucid that the canal bottom seemed pebbled with stars. The opposite bank was perhaps a half-mile away. Funny-looking buildings stood at intervals along it, yellow light showing in their windows.

Numerous flat stones littered their side of the canal and they began shying some of them onto the water, seeing who could skip one the farthest. Al won. He shied one so hard, it skipped almost all the way to the other bank.

"Something's coming!" Chan whispered.

Larry heard the sound then: the *thump-thump-thump* of padded hoofs. It came from the direction of the city.

At first he could see nothing. Then three shapes grew out of the moon and the starlight. The shapes of three gargantuan beasts surmounted by the figures of three riders.

The three astronauts stood there transfixed.

There were other sounds. A rattling, as of weaponry. A creaking, as of leather harnesses.

The beasts were like the one that had thundered past them earlier. The fact that these particular ones were walking instead of running didn't make them one whit less formidable.

Gradually, as the intervening distance continued to shrink, the three riders stood out more and more distinctly. The one on the left was a handsome, dark-haired white man of indeterminate age wearing leatherlike trappings and with a long sword hanging at his side. The one in the middle was the beautiful woman who had zoomed past the three astronauts shortly after their arrival. Possibly the mount she was riding now was the same one she had ridden then: there was no way of telling. Her coiffed black hair was held in place by a golden net; golden breastplates, encrusted with jewels, cupped her breasts, and a skirt comprised of innumerable golden strands alternately concealed and revealed her legs. The darkness of her skin indicated either that it was deeply tanned or that it had a natural reddish tone.

The rider on the right, presumably a male of his species, towered high above the other two and was armed with a ten-foot-long rifle as well as a sword. His trappings were similar to those of the handsome, dark-haired white man, but there all similarity ended. He had white, gleaming tusks, and his eyes were located on the sides of his head. Antenna-like ears sprouted just above them, and in the exact center of his face two vertical crevices took the place of a nose. His size and features would have been enough in themselves to demoralize the three astronauts, but there was more: instead of one pair of arms, he had two; and while the moon- and starlight raining down upon him left much to be desired in the way of reliable illumination, it strongly suggested that his skin was green.

Rocks. Everywhere you looked, rocks.

Mars had come to be associated with rocks. The relatively small ones photographed by *Viking* landers *I* and *II;* the two big ones in the sky called moons.

Standing in the wan sunlight beneath the oddly bright sky, Larry wondered if Hardesty, the astronaut stationed by the landing module training the television camera on him (the one mounted on the module had failed to pass the final series of equipment tests), was as disappointed with the landing site as he was.

NASA's choice of the site had been altruistically motivated, but it did the planet an injustice. *Mariner 9* Mars, as it had come to be called, was a far cry from the romantic Mars postulated by the late-nineteenth– and early-twentieth–century astronomers, but it was fascinating in its own right. East of where Larry stood, well below the horizon, Hecates Tholus, Albor Tholus and Elysium Mons brooded above the broad bulge in the Martian crust known as Elysium. On the opposite hemisphere, just south of the equator, stretched the awesome complex of canyons known as Valles Marineris. Northwest of the complex lay the massive Tharsis Ridge and the shield volcanoes Arsia Mons, Pavonis Mons and Ascraeus Mons, giants in their own right; while farther yet to the north and west the mightiest of them all, Olympus Mons, rose almost fifteen miles into the Martian sky.

But it was the Isidis Region that had got the nod from NASA. Prosaic it might be, but it had posed a minimum of risk and proffered a maximum of safety. NASA had decided as long as a year and a half ago that if man were to walk on Mars, here was where he would walk first.

Only Owens, the third astronaut, orbiting the command module, was seeing the planet as it should be seen; alternately viewing its two "faces"—the young one and the old. In a way, Larry envied him.

MISSION CONTROL: "Everything okay, Commander Reed?"

LARRY: "Everything's fine. Just getting my bearings."

MISSION CONTROL: "You're television's newest star, Larry. The brightest one ever. The eyes of the whole world are on you."

His wife's eyes. His mother's and his father's. The eyes of his twelve-year-old daughter and his ten-year-old son.

Everyone's eyes.

He tried to feel all those eyes, but he couldn't. He felt nothing at all. It was his moment in the sun, and he felt nothing.

Fatigue, that was why. Not physical fatigue, although he knew that too, but emotional. The inevitable result of spending month after month in a cramped environment in the constant company of two other human beings and trying not to become paranoid.

He had paused in the midst of his Marswalk not merely to get his bearings but to try to make sense out of the flight of *The Martian Queen,* out of the Mars he and Chan and Al had seemingly landed on. Now he began moving farther away from the landing module. He had been on camera ever since helping Hardesty plant the metallic flag. The landing site was slightly to the north of the Isidis basin. During the final few minutes of the descent, Larry had had to take over manually in order to bring the craft down in a relatively clear area. It squatted there now on its spindly legs, in grotesque contrast to its surroundings. The rocks and boulders that had spewed forth eons ago during the moment of the immense impact-crater's creation stretched away in all directions: southward to the wind-eroded rim, eastward to lowlands marked with mesas, westward to crater-pocked plains and northward seemingly forever.

He was headed in a northerly direction. He walked slowly, carefully. On Mars, he weighed less than ninety pounds, but the terrain was anything but conducive to giant steps.

Wryly he remembered Al's giant step; recalled once more the canals, the city, and the plain. Had the whole thing been a dream? he wondered. And if so, had he dreamed the dream alone, or had Chan and Al dreamed it, too? He had been afraid to ask them afterwards, afraid of being made fun of. Perhaps for the same reason they had never asked him. Or each other.

After all these years he still didn't know.

* * *

The three riders brought their monstrous mounts to a halt half a dozen yards from where the three mesmerized astronauts were standing on the canal bank.

It dawned on Larry finally who they were. He had met them before.

In books.

So had Al and Chan, although they probably didn't remember.

But knowing who the riders were didn't help. Meeting them in fictive form was one thing; seeing them in the flesh was another. He was no less terrified than Chan and Al when the one on the right shifted his rifle from his lower to his upper pair of hands, and when they turned and fled, he did too.

Two giant steps apiece brought them to *The Martian Queen*. They crawled inside, closed the lock and huddled together in the darkness. No one thought to "activate" the ion-drive, but apparently it "activated" itself. In any event, dawn had found them safely back on Earth.

The rocks had a reddish cast in the enervated sunlight. Larry was about to circumvent one that was considerably larger than the others when a faint gleam near its base caught his eye. Bending down, he saw a small, oblong object. He picked it up.

Straightening, he held it in his gloved hand, staring disbelievingly down at it through the tinted visor of his helmet. He knew that nothing would be the same for him again. Ever.

After Chan and Al went home, carrying their sleeping bags and promising to return the next morning and help dismantle the ship (it had been tacitly taken for granted that there would be no more Marsflights), Larry put the flashlight back in the glove compartment of his father's car and replaced the three unopened cans of Campbell's Pork & Beans in the kitchen cupboard. Then he ate a bowl of cereal and milk and crept upstairs to bed.

He hadn't missed his Boy Scout knife till late that afternoon. He searched the ship for it. He combed the back yard. He looked for it high and low, far and wide. But he had never found it.

MISSION CONTROL: "Commander Reed, a moment ago you bent down and apparently picked something up. Have you found something of scientific interest, by any chance?"

Larry hesitated. If he told the truth, would anyone believe him?

NASA might. They would more or less have to. Before being given the okay to enter the command module, he and Hardesty and Owens had been so exhaustively scanned that they couldn't have sneaked so much as a pin on board.

But whether NASA did or didn't, others would.

Not very many, but a few.

His mother and his father would. His wife.

His twelve-year-old daughter and his ten-year-old son.

They would believe him implicitly.

Did he *want* them to?

Did he want his children, who, like their peers, had been breast-fed on technology, to believe that three kids had traveled to Mars in a tin smokestack in 1/6000th the time it had taken three adult astronauts to make the same journey in the most sophisticated space vehicle that technology had ever devised?

Did he want them to believe that on the cosmic scales *Mariner 9* Mars weighed no more than the Mars postulated by Percival Lowell and populated by Edgar Rice Burroughs?

Did he want them to know that reality was a big joke, and that the joke was on the human race?

Did he want them to doubt—as he was doomed to doubt—the objective existence of everything under the sun and, for that matter, the objective existence of the sun itself?

MISSION CONTROL: "Commander Reed, have you found something of scientific interest? Come in, Reed."

Valles Marineris was worth a thousand silly canals. Olympus Mons dwarfed the tallest tale the romantics had ever told.

Did it really matter that both might be made of air?

LARRY: "So far, all I've found are rocks."

MISSION CONTROL: "So be it. . . . In a few minutes, you and Commander Hardesty will be returning to the module to rest up for your experiments. Before doing so, Larry, would you care to say a few words to commemorate this historic moment?"

LARRY: "I'll try. Today, Commander Hardesty, Captain Owens, and myself have surmounted a pinnacle in man's long and perilous journey to the stars. That we have been able to do so is owing infinitely less to ourselves than to the base camps that technology pitched along the way."

MISSION CONTROL: "That's great, Larry. No one could have said it better. Commander Hardesty, before you and Commander Reed return to the module, would you give the world one more view of the flag?"

Larry waited till he was off camera; then he let the knife fall to the ground. He kicked dust over it. As he turned to walk back to the module, a distant twin-towered city wavered tantalizingly on the periphery of his vision. It faded quickly away.

The Last Mars Trip

Michael Cassutt

There's a simplistic view of science-fiction's history that reads like this: Outer Space ➔ Inner Space ➔ Cyberspace.

Of course, this outline oversimplifies matters, but it helps explain why the field of Martian stories lay fallow in the 1980s. While American efforts in space focused more on the area around Earth (the space shuttle replaced rockets, satellites and the international space station became the focus of most efforts, and remember President Reagan's "Star Wars" initiative?), many writers shifted their attention from "the final frontier" to the wild new world lying inside the computers on our desktops. There's also a definite shift in tone in the stories and novels published in the period as a feeling of "been there, done that" seems to permeate space-travel stories of the period. In fact, my favorite story from this period is Terry Bisson's novel, Voyage to the Red Planet *(1990), suggests that the first trip to Mars will be run by Hollywood, not NASA.*

In the early 1990s, however, something shifted (what? I don't know), and writers began imagining trips to Mars more frequently: novelists like Allen Steele, Kevin J. Anderson, Greg Bear, Paul J. McAuley, Stephen Baxter, and Kim Stanley Robinson began to revisit planet Mars. There was a big shift in tone from the 1970s, however, a new sense of reckoning with the solar system, and I think you'll see some difference in tone between the last two stories and the ones that follow.

Michael Cassutt lives in Hollywood and writes for television, but he frequently turns to prose for stories about the space program. His novels Missing Man *and* Red Moon *are mystery thrillers set within the space program that read like they were written by a NASA insider. His most recent novel,* Tango Midnight, *is a thriller set on the International Space Station.*

SHE HAD NOT had bread in five days, and even then it had been stale. Well, all of it was now. Since the death of her mate, there had been no one left to plant bread, no one left to nurture it, no one—she believed—left to eat it.

Weakly, she wandered southward, moving along the shoulders of the Great One, as much in search of a final resting place as of further nourishment. Her covering, sized when she was neither starved nor pregnant, chafed everywhere, but still she needed its warmth. This did not prevent her from aimlessly grinding it between her greater and greatest claws. Occasionally she regretted the shreds that fluttered away in the wind. But only occasionally.

Near mid-afternoon, she found herself on the bright side of the Great One, on a long slope cluttered with young rocks. She could see no easy way southward; the way she had come seemed equally difficult. For the first time since the death of her mate, she began to weep. The moistness that suddenly seeped from her glands froze where her covering had been chewed off.

She tried to save herself by scooping up clawfuls of the brown salt, packing it on her skin.

It helped only a little, only enough to remind her of the true uselessness of the attempt. Why not surrender to the cold? Join her mate in sleep? But she wasn't quite ready to condemn her kits. She sat, wiggling for comfort in the trench she had made—

—And saw marks on the salt.

The marks were two parallel lines running from downslope up the shoulders of the Great One—interesting in themselves, but mostly because, within each line, tiny clumps of bread had been churned up.

Forgetting the cold, she threw herself on the clumps, every claw worrying at the salt, stuffing herself with pieces of bread. It was stale, of course, but no worse than she expected.

Within minutes, she had eaten all she could. She moved away from the marks, into the rocks, in search of a place to spend the night.

With luck, in the morning she could continue her journey.

Nine Earth days (they amused themselves by making the meaningless distinction between calendars) after becoming the first human to set foot on Mars, Pres Ridley told Giram, "They're already bored with us."

No need to clarify: when Pres said "they," he meant Earth, everyone from the support staff at Korolev to the network vice-president at TBS to the whole Goddamn 8.4 billion population of the blue planet. "This is a feeling you have?" Giram said. He tolerated Pres's attitudes. Sometimes he even found them amusing.

"Feeling, hell. I'm a scientist: they squirted me the overnights. We're down all over North America and Europe. China's still watching, but, shit, they'll watch anything."

"Maybe we need a better time slot." During the uphill phase of the mission, their nightly reports had aired opposite *The Friendly Family,* the most popular sitcom in the Northern Hemisphere. Which, predictably, had killed them in the ratings.

"Nah, it's the war at the South Pole. It's daylight all the time, and so they can shoot the shit out of each other twenty-four hours a day."

Giram had paid relatively little attention: the war at the South Pole was just another in an endless series of annual regional conflicts. He wasn't even sure who was fighting whom this time, and over what great principle.

"Watch that!" Pres said suddenly. Giram was already braking to avoid a slide that had spilled across the trail. "Must have loosened it on our way up."

The rover, loaded with rocks from the upper reaches of Arsia Mons, bounced heavily across what was, in effect, a hole in the road. Three jolts. The rover slewed sideways, its tailfin banging dully against a boulder. Giram killed the forward motion and waited for a warning light.

Pres was at his best in situations like this. "Just like driving on the railroad tracks." He chinned his microphone: "*Eagle, T-Bird.*"

"*Eagle* is here," Tanya's voice came to them. "Is everything all right?" Tanya was monitoring their progress from the lander five miles away, aided by the orbiting *Millennium Falcon* and a *Sputnik* relay satellite.

"No worse than driving to Star City from Moscow," Pres told her. Giram had spent time at the Russian cosmonaut-training center, too, and knew that Pres didn't exaggerate: the roads were still the worst in Europe.

"Very funny."

"Just a little bump in the road. ETA is thirty minutes."

"I'll put dinner on." And that was Tanya's little joke.

"Bitch," Pres said, one microsecond after killing the rover-lander channel.

"She's not so bad."

"That's what I like about you, Giram. You're a peacemaker. You can't drive, but you get along with everybody. Guys like you will be living here someday . . . if anyone does."

Sometimes Giram couldn't tell if Pres was joking. "Do you want to drive?"

"Hell no. I'm gonna take a nap." And he proceeded to tilt his chair back and raise his feet to the instrument panel—quite a trick in a Mars Extravehicular Mobility Suit. Giram grunted and put the *T-Bird* in reverse.

He backed up to the spot where they'd left the trail, pausing a moment. Logic told him that a rock had rolled down the hill, not an impossibility, given the fact that Arsia Mons was a live volcano. (But there were seismic probes all over the area. Tanya hadn't mentioned a quake, and neither had *Falcon* or Korolev.)

Trouble was, Giram couldn't see any rock, just lateral ditches in the brown soil.

Wind? Winds on Mars boiled and blew to frightful speeds. But not at Site Valentine, where they had spent most of the day, just six miles up the mountain. Again, where was the data from Tanya?

He would ask her. He put the rover in forward gear and started off. Then braked, slowly.

Something the size of a letter envelope fluttered in the breeze. Giram drove forward, grabbing his scoop as he did. He snagged the object as he passed, holding it up for Pres's inspection.

But Pres was asleep.

Giram stowed the scoop and continued on toward the *Eagle*. He clutched the fluttering thing in his hand. While keeping an eye on the trail, he examined the object, expecting a page from a manual or a piece of genuine Mars Sortie Demonstration '18 litter. It should be red; Mars was supposed to be the Red Planet, but the dusty sky had the same color as a cloudy day in Europe, and the rocks were closer to chocolate than red.

What Giram saw was a piece of brown cloth. Or a chocolate feather.

When she awoke, the Greater Moon was falling from the sky, and the Great One was gone. Much too late to be starting again: she was amazed that the beast hadn't killed her as she slept. She had to hurry, to be moving.

But she was still too weak, as if the recent meal had only made her feel worse instead of better. It was all she could do to crawl back to the markings, where new bread had been turned up. The churning was not of the wind, which alarmed her, but neither was it caused by beast. She accepted it as a gift from the Moons, perhaps, and managed to claw free several more crumbs, nothing more.

She rested for a while. Then, feeling stronger, she decided to follow the trail. It was already leading generally downslope. Perhaps she would find another field rich in bread. She could not, in any case, stay where she was.

It was Pres's turn to cook, and, as usual, the American made a half-hearted attempt, grabbing whatever packages happened to be on top and tossing them in the microwave, whether they needed heating or not.

As usual, Giram complained about the nutritionists' selections. "Too rich for me tonight," he said.

"Really?" Pres said. "Bastards never get it right for you, do they?"

"It's OK. Why don't you let me fool with it?"

Pres grunted. "No problem." And went below, to "exercise."

"Why do you let him treat you like this?" Tanya asked, the moment Pres cleared the hatch.

"Like what?" Giram examined the packages, replacing the ham with fish ("Let's leave it for our last night here") and adding souvlakia ("For you, Tanya").

"Like a slave."

Giram smiled. "Just because I'm black?"

"You know what I mean."

Well, there were no new arguments at the four-month point in a yearlong mission. Of course, during the Earth-Mars boost, there had been six crew members to share chores; not only had Pres been able to exploit others beside Giram, Tanya had others to whom she could complain. "So he doesn't like cooking. He does other things well."

"Name two."

"He keeps Korolev off our backs." This was true: Pres had four college degrees—he had even been a professor—which gave him substantial weight in any argument with Russian mission control, in addition to what must have been a hereditary (he was Swiss German in spite of the English family name) or regional (from the dismal prairies of North Dakota) orneriness.

"He just doesn't like to be told what to do. It is not beneficial in a situation like this."

"Well, let's just say I owe him."

"For what?" ESA astronaut Giram Tesfaye owed the American Pres Ridley nothing. But as a child, Giram had been saved from kwashiorkor by food from America. His four brothers and sisters had not, nor had any child under the age of six in his whole Tigrean village. Giram knew this wasn't rational, but then, he rarely thought of himself as rational.

"Don't be such a collectivist, Tanya." The oven beeped. "Dinner!"

He had stashed the object—the feather, whatever—in the outer pocket of his MEMS, but had no opportunity to examine it in any privacy. He and Tanya were scheduled to sortie in the morning, and even Pres would insist that they be in bed, asleep, on time. So Giram set his watch to beep him half an hour ahead of schedule.

It wasn't necessary. He found himself sleeping fitfully in his coffin on the mid-deck. Tanya was right above him, zipped up and asleep. On Landing Plus One, Pres had strung a hammock on the flight deck, "in case you and Catherine the Great want to put that first Mars fuck on your résumés." Giram had never considered it—nor, he was sure, had Tanya. Given the noise, the odors and the general decor, it would be like making love inside a Dumpster.

Even though he had no sexual feelings for Tanya, Giram felt a bit of guilt over withholding his discovery from her. Perhaps because sharing it with Tanya would mean automatically sharing it with Takiguchi in the *Falcon,* and, nine minutes later, with every specialist in the back room at Korolev.

Telling himself he wasn't jeopardizing the safety of the mission—all the data were quite clear: there was no life on Mars, certainly no life close enough to allow for, say, the transmission of a plague—Giram unzipped the pocket on his MEMS and took out the Object.

It was a ragged piece of brownish something, more like skin than feather, he now saw. Its shape was roughly triangular, perhaps three inches across at its widest, with torn edges. Holding it up to the light revealed no textures or patterns. He rubbed it between his fingers and found, to his surprise, that it was soft, like a chamois. He took a chance and tried to pull it apart. It didn't even stretch.

Interesting, and perhaps irrelevant. But for the first time since leaving the *Falcon,* Giram wished he were back aboard the mother ship: At least it had a microscope.

This was wrong. She must be dreaming. She must be dead. She had followed the trail, and it had led her into a nightmare.

Here at the end of the trail was something not beast and not like her, a fat tower that reflected the morning sun with such purity that it hurt her to be this close. And where could she hide? Surely it would know—

She backed away quickly, clawing at the salt, trying to burrow beneath a rock. At any moment, she expected to feel an enemy raking her back . . . but nothing came.

She found a shelter, of sorts, a shadowed spot between two rocks. It even held a dusting of ice. As suddenly as it came, the fear left—

another sign of how deteriorated she was—and she began to feel good for the first time in days. Perhaps it was the ice, always welcome. Perhaps it was the escape from certain death. Perhaps it was only her time. She waited. After a while, she slept.

Site Burroughs proved to be a trial. Not the site itself, which was exactly as advertised, but the constant second-guessing from Takiguchi aboard *Falcon,* via *Sputnik*. On his last two sorties, Giram had been teamed with Pres, who managed to have "uplink anomalies" whenever the Japanese mission commander got too corporate for him. Tanya, who was lead for this sortie, merely sucked up the abuse and the litany of changes like a good little soldier. If Giram had balked, it would have looked bad for her, so he went along. And consequently, they got about half of their work done.

They were also late getting back to *Eagle*. "I'm pushing the margin on my consumables," Tanya told Giram as the lander appeared above the rocks. Maybe it was true: She had been revved up for the whole eight hours. More likely, she just wanted to use the head on *Eagle*. Sanitary facilities in a MEMS were downright dangerous when they weren't laughable.

"Go on in. I'll configure *T-Bird* for tomorrow."

She didn't try to change his mind. "You're a saint."

Giram spent the next five minutes—the time it took to reach *Eagle*—looking for marks in the chocolate sand. What kind of marks, he wasn't sure: giant three-toed footprints, maybe. Suddenly, he felt light-headed. Either he was nervous about something, or he was pushing the margin on his consumables, too.

As Tanya bounded up the ladder into *Eagle,* Giram attached the charging cable to *T-Bird* and did the pro forma walk-around.

"*Falcon* goes LOS in three minutes, Giram." Pres was suddenly on the line, sounding, as he always did whenever Big Brother was listening, like Neil Armstrong. Did he wonder what was up? If so, the news that *Falcon* was going out of contact in a few minutes was helpful.

"On my way in."

Giram busied himself for the next 180 seconds doing inventory on *T-Bird*. Time for Plan A. "Pres? I think we dropped a bag somewhere."

"What kind?"

"Core samples, I think."

"Did you leave it at Burroughs?"

"I don't think so. I remember writing a label during the last stop. Shit." Giram rarely cursed; he knew it would shake Pres up a little.

"Come on in. We can get it tomorrow."

"I think it probably fell off between here and the ridge. Why don't I just go look? Otherwise, you guys'll be all screwed up tomorrow."

Giram counted to six before Pres answered. "How are your consumables?"

"Fifteen minutes before redline." He started walking up the trail.

"The light's in the window."

He found the sack of core samples easily enough, considering that he'd let it slip off *T-Bird* halfway between the ridgeline and *Eagle*. He snapped it to his belt and turned around. *Eagle*'s stub nose loomed above the rocks less than three hundred yards to the east. Giram knew he was effectively invisible to Pres or Tanya: the cameras on *T-Bird* were too low to see him, and the two real-time monitors on *Eagle* were pointed north and south. Only the store-dump cameras would even show him at all, and then no one would know for weeks or months.

If he did this right.

"You OK out there?" Pres again, breaking up a bit.

"Just fine." The machinations you had to go through to get five minutes of free time . . . no wonder robots were better suited for spaceflight.

Giram looked first to the south of the *T-Bird* trail, scuffling along in the cold chocolate dust, and finding no marks that could not have been caused by wind. Forty yards of that, and he crossed over, ranging to the south.

He glanced at his consumables. Twelve minutes to redline.

He was closer to *Eagle* here, but in a blind spot. No chance of Tanya looking out the window and asking him where he was going. (No doubt she and Pres were keeping watch.) The soil seemed looser and dustier. Giram found himself sinking in . . . like snow, he realized. Like the snow he'd seen around Nordvik one winter.

That's when he saw the marks, a cluster of scrapings that gave way to two groups of parallel scrapings marching their way into the rocks. Go ahead, be anthropomorphic: the Martian came this way, saw the ship, turned, and ran. Ran this way.

Oops, don't say Martian. Takiguchi wants only the new nomenclature. Emboss. MBOS. Mars-Based Organic Structure.

He was being stupid, he knew. Someday he would laugh at the memory of his futile search for life on Mars—

Then, of course, he found it: a lump the size of a small dog covered in the same fabric as the sample in his MEMS pocket. A lump with at least three arms that he could see. A lump that was visibly crouching away from him.

"Did you say something, Giram?" Pres's voice, through static.

"Sorry. Did I?" He held out his hand, just like in the movies. The MBOS didn't react.

"Sounded like you were laughing."

"It's an Ethiopian thing." Wait . . . the thing clawed at the dirt, as if backing away from him. He spread his arms and stepped back himself, as if to say, *Don't worry about me.*

"Time to come back in."

"In five." He knew he was ready to redline his consumables. No point in killing himself today when he could come back tomorrow. If the MBOS were still here. He fumbled in his pocket for the Object, unfolding it and presenting it to the MBOS. "I think this is yours," he whispered. He set the Object down in front of the MBOS, then turned and headed back to *Eagle*.

Paralyzed with fear, weak with hunger, she did not move until the Great and Greater Moons rose. Even then, her only desire was for escape. But her route was blocked by the very rocks that had given her shelter: she had to go the same way the beast had, to use its tracks. It was terrifying, but she did it, one claw at a time.

She quickly reached the spot where the beast had dropped something and saw that it was a piece of her garment.

She clutched it, and found it so rich in scent that she almost fainted again. *The beast smelled like bread.* She wept as she rolled the fabric in her claw, and moved on.

"So you found gold."

Two hours later, Pres cornered Giram in the mid-deck near the MEMS. Tanya was on the flight deck, out of earshot, cleaning up dinner. Giram had been doing a suit check, recharging the canisters.

"Excuse me?"

"You found something out there, didn't you?"

"Why do you say that?"

"Because ever since you got back, you've been acting like a guy who just won the lottery. So I'm guessing it's gold."

Giram was too tired to play games. Besides, he needed someone to trust. "Better than gold."

He had the pleasure of seeing Pres, probably for the first time in years, react with surprise. "No shit? I was kidding. You really found . . . what? Frozen oil? A poppy field? Martian crack: there's a concept. *What?*" he hissed.

"Better."

Pres blinked. "Better. A skull, maybe? Wait till Takiguchi hears about this. Our ratings will go—"

"Pres, I found an MBOS."

"Speak in English, Goddammit—"

"A Mars-Based Organic Structure. A Martian."

Just like that, Pres was no longer excited. His eyes narrowed. "You know, oxygen narcosis is a funny thing—"

"I'm a doctor, too, Pres. I know what I saw."

"What exactly are we talking about here? Somebody looking over the same real estate?"

"No. A native MBOS."

"Come *on*—"

"It's the same color as the rocks. From a distance, it looks just like them—"

"Giram!" That was Tanya calling from the flight deck. "Takiguchi wants his debrief."

As Giram reached for the ladder, Pres grabbed his shoulder. "I want to believe you."

"Nothing's stopping you."

Pres grunted. "Are you going to tell Takiguchi?"

"I don't know."

Giram hated the debrief procedure: he sat in front of a camera and spoke to a real-time image of Takiguchi that was split-screened with the operator and support staff at Korolev—which was nine minutes behind. Ever since the landing, Giram had tried to finish his statement in eighteen minutes, before the assholes on Earth had a chance to start firing questions at him out of sequence. This never quite worked, because Takiguchi always had one more question . . . and Korolev saved up questions from the previous day.

The first seventeen minutes went well, with Giram giving his second thoughts on the efficiency of various experiments and assignments. He thought he had gotten away cleanly when Takiguchi suddenly said, "Channel B, Giram," theoretically cutting Korolev out of the conversation. Then: "Why did you stay out late?"

"I dropped a sample bag—"

"I know what you *said*. I just don't believe it."

Giram knew his physical parameters were monitored during the sorties—his MEMS was wired for it. It hadn't occurred to him until this moment that the same monitoring system could double as a lie detector. "You're right. I deliberately dropped the bag."

"I'm listening."

"I think I just wanted some free time. We're so programmed we can't even take a walk."

Giram listened to the hiss of the carrier for ten seconds, long enough to wonder if there had been a loss of signal. Finally Takiguchi said, "I understand. This is Mars, after all. But remember that Korolev holds me responsible for everything you do."

"Sorry."

"You're not a free agent. Thousands of people put their lives and souls into this mission. It's tough to remember, but you work for them. We can't have any black zones: Record every step." Another pause. "You can edit when we go downhill, you know."

"I guess I didn't think of that."

"Just get through the next two days."

Falcon went LOS, leaving Giram with his face burning, like a schoolboy sent to a corner. It was atypical Takiguchi performance—Pres called it the No-Yes-No Play. He's on your side; he's on their side; you don't mind being spied on, do you? It's all for the good of the mission. If you complained about him, people thought you were a crank.

Giram knew there was nothing Takiguchi could do about his "lapse" right now. Two days from now, when *Eagle* docked with *Falcon,* it would be different.

Takiguchi hadn't wanted Giram on the mission, anyway. Giram was qualified, of course, through the European Agency, but so were hundreds of people. His background was too unstructured, too unfocused. Giram had not dreamed of going into space all his life, the way Takiguchi (who was both a test pilot and a Ph.D. astronomer) and Tanya and even Pres had. It had merely been an opportunity that presented itself, the same way a chance to go to medical school in France had suddenly appeared to an eighteen-year-old Ethiopian refugee. The same way a job with ESA designing medical equipment had happened to open up seven years later. Giram could just as easily have become a United Nations doctor—the U.N. had been behind the original medical scholarship—or even gone into business.

His selection had been a bone thrown to the Third World, nothing more. Consequently, he had always felt like an unwanted guest in the crew . . . when he didn't feel like a traitor to the great god of the mission itself.

But then, as a child, Giram had never looked at the stars. He had never had the strength.

She regretted having touched the fragment given her by the beast. Not because it hadn't refreshed her; it had. But because it had awakened things within her, things she had thought dead. Memories of her dead mate, physical stirrings of the kits she carried. Now they might be born . . . and now they would surely die.

Knowing she was condemning herself and her young . . . unable to do anything but crawl, she barely moved that night. Morning found her within sight of the silver rock that held the beast. She waited for it to come to her.

The Day Eleven sortie took Pres and Tanya to Site Weinbaum, which Giram could only monitor. Every few minutes, it seemed, during the eight hours they were gone, he would slip from one window to the other, various cameras in hand, hoping for a sign of the MBOS. Nothing showed up visually or thermally, which was not surprising:

neither system was able to see through rock. Imaging radar would have helped, but the nearest one was overhead in *Falcon.*

He wasn't that desperate.

And when Pres and Tanya returned right on the timeline, Giram wanted to scream with frustration. Obviously, Pres hadn't been able to find the creature, meaning there was only tomorrow's sortie remaining, and that one was half-duration. To pick up the garbage.

They didn't even have a chance to talk before dinner because Pres—for the first time since leaving Earth orbit—insisted on taking his turn as cook. That left Giram to recharge the suits with Tanya on the mid-deck. All she offered was a tired smile. "One more day."

"Sick of Mars?"

"Just tired."

He began to think he should tell Tanya about the MBOS. She wouldn't necessarily run right to Takiguchi, not if he begged—

"Giram, did you see anything funny out there yesterday"

"Funny in what way?"

"Geologically." She popped a disk from her helmet cam into the player. The picture panned across the *T-Bird* trail looking back toward *Eagle* from the east. It had been taken on the trip out to Site Weinbaum, because shadows fell away from the camera. Giram felt his heart go into arrhythmia: in the upper left of the screen was a reddish lump that had to be the MBOS. "See that?" Tanya said.

Giram could only grunt as Tanya tapped the screen in the lower right. "Look at the edges on this wash. Doesn't that look eolian to you?" Eolian. It took a moment for his geological training to come back: wind-formed.

"Uh, no."

"I don't think so, either. It looks like a new cut, maybe from a quake. Best one I've seen so far. Pres pointed it out." A bit stunned, Giram watched her use the board to give the image the appropriate keywords—SORTIE/DAY 11/SOIL—then stash the disk in the case with fifty others. She scampered up the ladder. Then Pres slid down, a shit-eating smile on his face.

"Now you know where your MBOS is," he said quietly. "Best I could do today, given the situation." He glanced upward, meaning either Tanya or Takiguchi, or both.

"And she never saw it?"

"Sure she saw it. But she was interested in something else. It's called *The Purloined Letter* method. Hide something in plain sight."

"I'll remember that."

Pres looked his age for a moment. "What do you want to do with your MBOS, anyway? Since you aren't gonna stick it in a bag and take it back to Earth."

"I don't know yet."

"Well, whatever you do, don't tell."

"It's the reason we came here—"

"Bullshit. We came here to keep people on Earth employed. Which is fine by me, since I'm one of those people. But if they knew about your . . . discovery, this whole fucking planet would be crawling with humanity in about five years. If we can't keep that from happening, this should be the first and last Mars trip."

He grinned. "I got a good look at it, you know. Threw down a scope when Tanya was busy rediscovering chocolate rocks. It was moving. Waving a claw." He was silent. "Reminded me of something . . . it looks sick, listless. Almost like it was starved. Of course, that may be how it's supposed to look."

Tanya appeared in the access. "Are you two coming up or not?"

The Day Twelve sortie was the most structured of all, beginning with the last sweep by *T-Bird* to the northeast, the region of Arsia Base that had been surveyed least. There was to be a live-to-Earth farewell-to-Mars broadcast three hours in, which gave Giram and Pres barely enough time to learn their speeches.

" 'So we say, good-bye, Red Planet, until we meet again.' " Pres laughed. "Who wrote this, Takiguchi?"

"The fax said it came from headquarters. Probably one of the usual speechwriters."

"Sounds like a translation from a foreign language."

"Well, it'll be subtitled for most of the planet."

"The nine people who aren't watching the war."

In spite of Pres's cynicism, the ceremony went well. Korolev surprised them by closing with a live song from schoolchildren, one from each global time zone. Giram found himself longing to be home again, in any of those time zones. Tanya did her part as TV commentator, too.

Then it was time to configure the site, as the timeline put it. The midday winds had kicked up a bit, making it difficult to tie down the Mylar flaps on *T-Bird,* in case some future visitors from Earth might want to use it again. They were almost through, when Giram heard, "Shit," from Pres.

The U.N. flag had come loose and gone flapping away over the rocks. Air pressure on Mars was pretty low, but pure velocity made up for it.

"Giram," Pres said, "Why don't you go get that? I'll finish up here."

It took Giram at least a second to realize that Pres had deliberately sliced the line holding the flag. Giram had to act quickly. He had already put together a bag with scraps—food, water, even a blanket—and had been filling it with likely or unlikely objects from the landing site, not knowing, of course, whether any of it would be of use. Wondering if, in fact, it would kill the creature. But he had to do something.

He found MBOS cowering right where Pres had left it, less than a hundred yards downwind and east of *Eagle.* It hadn't moved for a while: there was already a thin sprinkling of brown dust on its coat. He had no time for the pseudo-traditional first-contact niceties; all he could do was dump the "gifts" out and push them toward the

MBOS. The creature was still alive: It actually shook as Giram came close, as if it needed calming or comfort. "You're on your own," Giram told it. "Stay the hell away from us." Then he gathered up the U.N. flag and hustled back to *Eagle*.

Giram's helmet cam recorded it all. He left it filed under the keywords SORTIE/DAY 12/CLEANUP. With a little luck, he'd never need to edit it.

Many things happened quickly, all of them surprising. She was not surprised when the beast loomed out of the rocks—she had expected that for days. What was unusual was the way it spilled itself, then went away without killing her.

She wanted to get away from the beast's spoor, but that, too, was unexpected, unlike that of any beast in her experience. The moment she sensed that it had left her bread, she could not control herself. She tore into the spoor with all her strength . . . spitting out and discarding the contents, and feasting on the containers.

She had barely begun to eat, when the silver mountain to the west exploded and disappeared. She had been warned of such things by her mate, and was surprised to survive.

She ate what she needed, and stored the rest in what would serve as a good nest.

That night, she gave birth to three kits: one male, two female.

The next morning, she died.

But the young ones fed on the beast's spoor. It kept them alive until they were able to continue on their mother's journey south.

Twenty-two years later, Carter Figueroa, a graduate assistant in planetary sciences at the University of Arizona in Tucson, noted the presence of what appeared to be a living Aresian (that being the preferred terminology, circa 2040) creature in videotapes of the Day Twelve Sortie.

For several hours, Figueroa was in a state of delirium, until his natural excitement gave way to suspicion: he couldn't believe that a discovery like this had been overlooked. He suspected it might even be a hoax—a little prank played on graduate students. Given that the diversion of resources to the Asteroid Capture Demonstration meant that the Mars Sortie Demonstration would not be followed up within his professional lifetime, Figueroa elected not to disclose his discovery to anyone.

On the same day that Carter Figueroa put the Day Twelve tape back in its storage box, Giram Tesfaye worked, as usual, at a clinic in a village in Tigre district, Ethiopia.

Unknown to either of them, the MBOS population of Mars stood at eleven—and growing.

The Great Martian Pyramid Hoax

Jerry Oltion

Okay, so the pictures came back from Mars and those canals weren't what we thought they were. Actually, there's no sign at all to indicate anyone ever lived on our nearest neighbor. But wait, what if there is? This picture, doesn't it look a little like a face to you. . . ?

It's easy to see how the so-called "Face on Mars" arose as a modern myth intended to imbue the Red Planet with a new sense of mystery. We humans like—no, need—to have some mystery in our lives. We need to have our dreams. (If we didn't, The Magazine of Fantasy & Science Fiction *would not have lasted fifty minutes, let alone fifty years.)*

Jerry Oltion's story takes the question of whether intelligent life ever preceded us on Mars, and has a bit of fun with it.

Jerry is the author of Abandon in Place, The Getaway Special, Frame of Reference, *and several other novels. His most recent books are a story collection titled* Twenty Questions *and a novel,* Paradise Passed. *He and his wife Kathy live in Eugene, Oregon.*

"AT LEAST IF they recover the film, they'll find out how we died." David Nelson struggled to keep his voice from quavering as he gripped the Jesus bar bolted to the instrument panel before him, and he tried not to look at the kilometer-high pyramid rushing toward the bridge of his nose.

Beside him in the scout plane, his companion, Muriel Mondou, seemed frozen in place, her right hand steady on the control stick, her left poised on the throttle. The instrument lights illuminated her form-fitting spacesuit with a soft glow that accentuated all her curves, and even now as she flew the plane into the yawning brink of disaster, David felt his hormones respond to the sight. He was not unique in that. The news media back on Earth ran her photos whenever they could, usually with captions like "Mon Dieu Muriel!" and they wrote articles describing her as "a broad interpretation of the term, 'space spectacular.' "

David, whose life depended more on her skills as an astronaut than on her measurements, was just glad she could fly.

She had brought their airspeed down as slow as possible, but in Mars's thin atmosphere, that wasn't very slow. "If they recover the film, we're dead anyway," she said without looking away from the windshield.

David didn't bother asking why they were taking pictures, then. He'd already argued that with her. Posterity, she'd said. They owed it to posterity to expose the fraud once it'd served its purpose.

The proximity alarm went off with a bone-tingling wail, and David slapped the quiet switch. His spacesuit wasn't nearly as form-fitting as hers, but after weeks of operating the navigation and science controls while wearing it, he hardly noticed the extra thickness of his gloves. "Two kilometers and closing," he said, but in the time it took him to say it, that distance had diminished by half.

Deimos and a sky full of stars provided the only light. Without amplifier goggles over their helmets, they would have been flying nearly blind. Even with the goggles, the pyramid was just a gray triangle against a black sky. Its leading edge loomed like an assassin's knife, then slashed past only ten meters beyond their left wing.

David jabbed at the fire button for the port-side laser spectrometer, and a beam of intense blue light lanced out from the wingtip. Where it struck, the pyramid's rock face erupted in a line of lava.

An instant later they were clear. Muriel pulled the plane up and around in a crop-duster turn, then leveled out for another run. The building of the great pyramid of Cydonia had begun.

The pyramid had always been there, of course. Building one of the kilometer-high mountains that littered the Cydonia plain would have taken the entire Army Corps of Engineers a couple of centuries. Muriel and David were the only two people on Mars, and they had struggled for over a week just to erect their living bubble, an inflated plastic dome covered with Martian soil for radiation shielding. What they were doing now was simply turning a natural feature into an alien artifact by drawing lines so it would look like something constructed.

This was the last week of a long and ultimately disappointing expedition. They'd been a year just in transit from Earth, a beefcake hunk of a man and a blond goddess of a woman packed into a cylinder smaller than most studio apartments, driving each other crazy even though they'd been selected for compatibility just as much as for audience appeal or exploring ability. Arriving in Mars orbit and setting up their expedition base had broken the monotony, but the surveying flights had quickly become as dull as drifting in space. Their plane was even smaller than their spaceship, and it was almost all wing; after six weeks in the tiny cockpit, radar- and photo-mapping half the planet, they could count the rivets in their sleep.

And to top it off, they hadn't made any Earth-shaking discoveries. Oh, they'd learned all sorts of interesting things about the geological makeup of the surface, and uncovered plenty of evidence that the streambeds seen in satellite photos had indeed carried water millions of years ago, but they hadn't discovered anything useful in selling Mars to the taxpaying public, and that was the real catastrophe. As Al Shepard had once said about the Mercury program, "No bucks, no Buck Rogers." You had to have public support if you wanted money enough to fly; the near-death of the space program after the lunar landings had proved that. Muriel and David had provided as much inspiring footage as possible, both in flight and at home in their dome shelter, which they kept at about 75 degrees so they could lounge around in front of the cameras with very little clothing, but the *planet* hadn't produced anything spectacular, and that was the problem. Unless they could come up with something about Mars that would inspire the masses back home, theirs would likely be the only mission there in the twenty-first century.

"There's always the Face," Muriel had said when the subject had first come up. Ever since a *Viking* photo had shown what looked to be a face staring up out of the Martian landscape, tabloid newspapers had been milking the story to death. They'd printed photos of the Face and the mysterious pyramids surrounding it, photos retouched to make it look like the Face was changing expression, speaking, even crying when the Pope died. The Martian Face was such a popular symbol that when NASA had announced its intention to send an expedition to Mars, the tabloid-reading public had naturally assumed the whole reason was to check out the Face.

NASA had stubbornly scheduled the flyby for last, holding out for a legitimate scientific discovery, but time was running short. A few planners had secretly hoped the survey plane would malfunction before the end of the mission and the public would have to make do with more pictures from orbit, but for once the machinery had performed as designed. They would be able to do the flyby after all, and as the time drew nearer, more and more of their hopes rested on it.

And fear that it, too, would be a bust began to weigh heavily on the crew. Nobody who knew anything about Mars seriously expected the Face to amount to anything more than a chance arrangement of impact craters on a hillside, and the "pyramids" around it were almost certainly just mountains that had eroded with unusual symmetry. So when Muriel had said, "There's always the Face," David had responded with, "Oh sure. That ought to be good for about fifteen seconds of drama."

They'd already done their usual getting-ready-for-bed show with the lace nightie and the spandex bikini briefs, and had turned off the cameras for the night. They'd been enjoying their precious few moments of privacy by scratching and belching and trimming their nose hair like normal people, but Muriel had turned away from the mirror where she was flossing her teeth and said, "Maybe longer, if we do it right."

David had blown his nose, then said, "Oh? And what do you think we can do to make the Face more exciting than a mountain with old craters on it?"

"I don't know," she'd replied, beginning to pace the narrow confines of the dome. Ten steps took her from the glitzy chrome bathroom/kitchen on the north wall past the lab/dining table in the center of the room to the bed on the opposite side. "We'll have to see it up close first. But once we know what's actually there, we could choose our approach angle to enhance the illusion, or maybe even use the exhaust from the emergency takeoff boosters to carve out the features a little better."

"With the cameras running all the time, documenting everything we do. Uh-huh."

She'd paced back into the kitchen. "We can shut off the real-time cameras in the plane and just use the still cameras with our personal film reserve. Mission Control doesn't ever have to know we were there, but we'll have documentation if we need it."

"You don't think they'll notice when our signal suddenly stops?" he'd asked sarcastically.

"That's why we go at night." She'd walked back over to the bed, picked up his pile of discarded clothing, and tossed it to him. "Mission

Control thinks we're about to hit the sack; we can rig the computer to keep sending fake heartbeat and respiration telemetry while we go check it out."

"Tonight?"

"Tonight and tomorrow night are all we've got before we make the daytime flyby, and we may need both nights to do the touchup work."

So off they'd gone, overjoyed to have slipped their reins for the first time since they'd begun training for the mission, but when they arrived after a three-hour flight, they'd found the Face to be even less than they'd hoped for. If it had been built to resemble a human visage, then it had been intended to be seen only from orbit. Up close it was little more than an enormous sand dune with blowout hollows in the right places to suggest eyes and a mouth. In anything but oblique light, and from any view but directly overhead, it wouldn't look like anything at all. And it was far too big for Muriel and David to modify in any significant way, even with the fusion engine on their landing craft.

But the pyramids had looked promising. Straight-edged, flat-sided, all they lacked was some sign of an intelligent hand in their construction. As the two explorers circled the biggest of them, David had fired the laser spectrometer at the side of it, letting it vaporize some of the rock surface so he could read an emission spectrum from it and see what it was made of. Just ordinary Martian dirt, it turned out, but when they'd made another pass and saw the spidery line the laser had traced, Muriel had whooped with delight and said, "Hey, that's it! We can carve it into blocks!"

After half a dozen passes, they backed off to study their handiwork. With the exception of a minor squiggle in one line from turbulence, the laser burns were arrow-straight and perfectly spaced.

"God, that looks great," David said. "They're just thin enough they won't show up from orbit, so it'll look perfectly legit when we take close-ups the day after tomorrow."

"I don't know, though," Muriel said. "They're fifty meters apart. Who's going to believe Martians could lift fifty-meter blocks into place?"

David laughed. "You're kidding, right? We're talking about the kind of people who thought the face was trying to speak."

"Ah. Good point."

"What worries me," said David, "is how we're going to cut the uprights. If we want it to look like blockwork, we have to cut vertical joints, too, and they're going to be a lot tougher. They have to connect with the horizontal lines, and if we overshoot by more than a few centimeters, it'll blow the whole effect."

"Hmm." Muriel banked around for another look. She studied the lines for a minute more, then said, "We could rig the uplink antenna motor to aim the forward laser, and program the pattern we want into the navigation computer. If I flew us straight toward the middle of the pyramid, it could draw the vertical lines for us."

David winced. "Straight at it? You know how close we'd have to get before the navcom could get a fix on the pattern?"

Muriel tipped the plane over in a slow barrel roll. "Hey, you forget who's flying this thing. We can do it."

David looked out at the pyramid doing its pirouette around them. Shaking his head, he said, "The things I do for the space program."

The next night came far too quickly. They arrived back at base from their first night just in time to take off for the next day's mapping flight over Xanthe, so they were pumping stimulants most of the day just to stay awake. On top of that, David had to spend most of his time in the cramped equipment bays in the wings to either side of the cabin, hooking the uplink motor to the spectrometer laser and patching the navigation computer into the system.

They landed at their base camp just before nightfall and made a show of getting ready early for bed, then as soon as they'd shut off the lights they jumped up and snuck out of the dome like teenagers heading to a party. Muriel flew at top speed toward Cydonia while David recalled the photos of the lines they'd drawn the night before and fed them into the navcom's pattern-recognition buffer.

"All right," Muriel said when the first triangular peak slid up over the horizon. "Lock onto the west side of number one; we might as well make our first run count."

"Ready here," David replied.

Muriel slowed the plane to just above stall speed—still almost the speed of sound—and lined it up so they were flying directly toward the pyramid. They watched it grow larger and larger, waiting nervously for the navcom to recognize it and lock on.

"Come on," David pleaded. "Find the son of a bitch!"

The wall eclipsed nearly half the sky before Muriel banked hard to the left and pulled back on the stick, shoving the throttles forward at the same time to keep them from stalling out. The pyramid slid past only meters below.

"Why didn't it lock on?" she asked.

David was still staring straight ahead. "Because there weren't any lines there for it to lock onto," he replied softly.

"What? There had to be. We marked every side of every damned pyramid in Cydonia last night."

He looked over at her. "Well we must have missed this one, because I guarantee you, I'd have seen a paper cut if there'd been one."

Muriel looped and banked the plane through an Immelmann turn, taking them back alongside the face they'd nearly smacked into. Sure enough, it was smooth as a stretch of beach at low tide.

She banked the plane tight around the edge, but the next face was just as smooth. Once more with the same result, then she continued around until she was aimed at the next pyramid.

It, too, was smooth.

"I *know* we etched this one," she said. "I remember that little crater down there at the base of it."

"Yeah?" David asked. "Then what happened to the lines? Did little Martians come out and patch them up today?"

"Maybe," she said. "Do me a favor and aim the penetration radar at it when I swing us around."

"What, you think it's *hollow*?"

"I don't know what it is, but something funny's going on, and that's one thing we can check pretty easily."

"True enough," said David. He turned on the radar unit, and while he set it for maximum penetration he said, "We should have thought of doing this last night."

She laughed. "Are you kidding? We were so intent on setting up a big find, we forgot to look for a real one."

David laughed with her. "God, who'd have believed it? The tabloid writers were right. This *is* where all the action's at on Mars."

"Maybe. Get ready, we're coming up on it."

The plane swept past a few hundred meters from the pyramid, but David didn't look up from the radar screen. Sure enough, the cone-shaped image was darkest at the edges, and nearly transparent in the middle.

"Jesus, it's only a few meters thick," he said. "There's no way that thing's built out of rock. It's got to be something else, with a layer of rock and dirt over the top."

"Just like our dome," Muriel said. She banked the plane and began circling.

David looked out at the sharp triangles against the night sky. "What, like a radiation shield?" he asked. "Why would Martians need a radiation shield? They evolved here, didn't they?"

Muriel shrugged. "There used to be water here, and more atmosphere. Maybe they evolved under that, and when it got thinner they had to go underground."

"Jesus," David said again. "Why did we have to find this *now*? We've only got two more days before our launch window!"

"Hey, look at the bright side," Muriel said. "All we've got to do tomorrow is shoot one radar image like that one and we'll be coming back for sure."

David shook his head. "*Somebody* will, but it won't be us."

"Why not?"

"Did Armstrong and Aldrin ever go back to the moon? Hell, no. Once they got home, they were national heroes; NASA wasn't about to risk them on another flight. They even tried to take away their jet privileges."

"You're kidding."

"I wish I was. Trust me; we may have made the find, but we'll be watching on TV along with the rest of the great unwashed when the first people walk inside it."

Muriel banked the plane lazily left, then right. "Not if we beat them to the punch," she said. "I bet that little crater I saw is actually the doorway."

David looked at it as they flew past again. "Why would there be just one?" he asked. "If it's a door, wouldn't every pyramid have one?"

"Maybe they're all connected underground," Muriel said. "Maybe the Martians don't go out much anymore. Or maybe they don't go out at all, and that's there just for us."

David looked over at her, but it was impossible to read expressions in the darkness. He said sarcastically, "And I suppose the Face really was made to draw us here after all."

"Could be. We won't know unless we investigate closer."

He laughed a high-pitched, nervous laugh. "Mission Control would never let us go inside, not on our last day."

"What if we don't ask? We're here right now; I say let's land and check it out."

"In the *dark?*"

"Sure. We've got the emergency retros. I can skid this thing to a stop in less than half a klick. The sand is flat all around the base of the pyramids; it'll be a piece of cake."

David looked down at the radar screen. The image confirmed Muriel's statement; there was plenty of flat ground down there. No sign of life, but . . .

"Do you think it's smart to just waltz in there? I mean, we were firing lasers at them last night."

Muriel was already banking for her approach. "They haven't fired back yet. Besides, this'll give us a chance to apologize before we leave."

"Oh sure, like they're going to understand anything we say."

"Who knows? They could have been listening to our radio and TV broadcasts for years."

"Now, *that's* a scary thought."

Muriel laughed. "That's what I love about you; you're so positive." Before he could reply, she said, "Hang on, this could get bumpy," and she lowered the nose of the plane.

She brought them in near the base of the pyramid with the crater at the bottom of it. The wall was a flat mountainside to their left, and the ground rushed past only a few meters below as she killed velocity by tilting the plane higher and higher toward a stall. At the last moment, just as the warning buzzer sounded, she leveled it out again and lit the retro rockets, which braked the plane to a near-stop in the air. It fell like a rock the last couple of meters, bounced and slid a little ways on the sand, then came to rest less than a hundred meters from the crater.

Muriel let out the breath she'd been holding. Turning to David, she said, "Well, let's go see if the natives are friendly."

Muriel had been right; the doorway was obvious enough once they hiked to the edge of the crater and looked inside. The pit hadn't been formed by meteoric impact; it was merely a depression carved like a strip mine next to the pyramid. A depression whose angled sides matched the pyramid's slant perfectly, and from the bottom of which a tunnel led underneath the wall.

"Why the basement access?" David wondered aloud, shining his helmet spotlight around as he took it all in.

"Maybe the Martians are built like beavers, and this was a pond before the planet dried up."

"Hah. Right. More likely it's a trap; we get to the middle of it and the bottom falls out or something." All the same, he walked down the crater's steep slope, carrying the suitcase-sized portable EVA kit in his left hand. It held sample containers, air and soil test equipment, spare power packs for the pressure suits, and an emergency radio transmitter that would be useless under all that dirt. David snorted at the thought of using it anyway. Who would they call? They were going to have to rely on their own resources here; nobody at mission control could help them now.

Muriel was right beside him, her form-fitting spacesuit making her look almost unclothed in the dim starlight and the reflected glow of their helmet beams.

"I hope Martians have the same standards of beauty we do," David murmured.

"I hope they don't," Muriel said. "I've already got half of Earth ogling my body; I don't need a planet full of Martians staring at me, too."

"They're staring at us anyway," David said. "I can feel it."

"Hah. They've probably been dead for millennia." Muriel stepped out ahead of him, but at the mouth of the tunnel she leaped back in surprise, nearly crashing into him.

A meter or so in front of her, a spider the size of an outstretched hand stood motionless on the ground.

David backed up a pace. "Whoa, what the heck is that?"

"I don't know," Muriel said, "but whatever it is, we're outnumbered. Look." She tilted her head back to illuminate the side of the pyramid, which was littered with them.

None of the spiders moved, so after a minute they bent down to examine the one by their feet. Its resemblance to a spider was only superficial; it had four legs instead of eight, and its hollow body held a tiny mound of dirt that made it look more like a toy dump truck than an arachnid. In front of the hopper was a flat plate a few centimeters on a side that looked for all the world like a solar collector.

Sure enough, under the glare of their spotlights, the creature began to move. One leg at a time, it crept forward with its minuscule load of soil.

"Hah!" Muriel said, straightening up. "I bet they're repair robots. Solar powered and slow as hell, but they're probably fast enough to keep ahead of weathering. All they have to do is haul a teaspoonful of dirt at a time up the side of the mountain for the rest of eternity, and the pyramid's radiation shield will stay good as new."

"Or maybe they're the local equivalent of scorpions," David said.

Muriel snorted. "I don't see anything they could bite or sting with." She stepped over it contemptuously and continued on into the tunnel, David following nervously behind.

The roof was smooth as poured concrete, and way out of reach overhead. The tunnel was wide enough for both of them to walk abreast to the far end, which sloped upward again after a few dozen steps and terminated at a closed door. An L-shaped handle stuck out from about head high.

"I don't see a doorbell," Muriel said. "Think we should knock?"

"If aliens came to my place in the middle of the night, I think I'd appreciate it," David said. "Give me time to get into my underwear, at least."

"Right. The great American phobia: getting caught by aliens without your underwear." Muriel reached up and banged her spacesuited hand flat against the door a few times.

While they waited for something to respond, she said, "So do we go with the traditional 'We come in peace,' or do we make something up?" Despite her nonchalant attitude, her voice was fast and nearly breathless.

David wasn't doing much better. His laugh sounded forced and his voice cracked when he said, "How about the even more traditional 'Take me to your leader?' "

"Sounds good. You want to say it or should I?"

"How 'bout we say it together. In a monotone, of course."

"Right. As soon as the door opens."

But after five more minutes and another couple rounds of knocking, it became apparent that they weren't going to be greeted at the door.

"Okay," David said as he reached for the handle. "Plan B." It took both of them tugging on the lever before it would budge, but when they pulled it downward they felt a latch click and they were able to pull the door outward.

As in a refrigerator, a light came on inside when the door cleared the jamb. It could have *been* a refrigerator light for all the illumination it provided, but it was enough to let them see what lay beyond the door: another five meters or so of smooth-sided tunnel and another door.

"Hah, an airlock." David hauled the EVA kit inside and the two of them pulled the door closed behind them. The pressure in the lock began to rise almost immediately.

David opened the EVA kit and switched on the spectrometer. He read off the list of gases as they appeared on its screen. "Nitrogen, methane, ethane, propane, hydrogen cyanide—What the hell is this? Mars never had hydrocarbons in its atmosphere. And where's the carbon dioxide?"

"My ears just popped," Muriel said. "The pressure must be higher than ours, too."

"One-and-a-half times Earth normal. That's crazy. Mars couldn't hold that kind of pressure for a day. It'd all blow off into space."

Their spacesuits had gone from shaped balloons around their bodies to tight, wrinkled, constricting clothing. Only the rigid helmets retained their original shape.

"I hope these things hold against pressure from the other side," David said. "There's enough cyanide out there to knock us flat in no time."

"Let's make this a short visit, then," Muriel said. She went to the other door and repeated her knocking.

Nobody answered her that time, either, so they pulled open the inner door as well. Beyond it they found a dimly lit locker room, obviously a suiting-up area. Thick orange dust covered the floor and the benches—which were high enough to be tables for a human.

"Doesn't look like anybody's been here for a while," Muriel said. "Like maybe a couple thousand years."

In the larger chamber, they could see a distinct orange haze to the air as well. "This isn't right," David insisted. "This is more like Jupiter's air, or Saturn's."

Muriel shook her head. "No, they're mostly hydrogen. It's more like one of their big moons."

"It's cold enough to be." He looked at his suit thermometer. "Uh-oh. It's over a hundred below in here. Our heaters aren't going to be able to keep up with that, not with this much air to suck the heat away."

"Let's grab what we can, then, and get out of here." Muriel opened one of the lockers. It was nearly twice her height, and so was the spacesuit it contained. She and David pulled it out and dragged it into the airlock.

"Tripod legs," she pointed out immediately. "Four arms. And it's tall and thin as a light pole."

"That fits, at least," David said. "Mars's gravity is low enough to make tall an option."

"So's just about every Jovian and Saturnian moon."

They made another run, grabbing an armful each of what little portable equipment they could find, then they slammed the airlock door behind them, their fingers and toes already numb with cold, and waited impatiently for the cyanide-laced air to bleed away.

When their pressure suits had ballooned back to normal, they opened the outer door and carried their treasures to the plane. Muriel went back for the spider and stowed it in a heavy metal sample canister, just in case it decided to wake up again in flight.

Inside the plane, David called up the astronomy database on their reference screen. It only took a minute to find a perfect match for atmospheric composition. "Titan," he said. "These guys were from Saturn's moon, Titan."

Muriel strapped herself in and started the engines. "Then this was their outpost when they explored Mars." She looked over at the pyramid. "God, I'd love to come back with the right kind of equipment and go deeper inside there."

"Dream on," David said. "I'll bet you Mission Control won't even let us come back tomorrow. They won't want to risk losing us in there, not now that we've already got a few artifacts. And when the public catches wind of this, there won't be a nickel for another Mars expedition."

Muriel paused with her hand on the throttle. "Huh? Why not? This place could be a gold mine. Think what we can learn about the beings who built it."

David sighed. "You're thinking like a scientist again. Try thinking like the average voter. We've discovered evidence of life on Titan; where do you think the next space shot is going to go?"

"Even with these pyramids just sitting here waiting for us?"

"Even so. Planetary missions are expensive; people are going to spend their money on the ones with the shiny new package."

Muriel powered up the engines, and the plane began to slide across the sand. As it lifted into the air, David said, "Forget coming back here; from this moment on, Mars is a dead issue."

At the base of the pyramid, two thin, leathery Martians peered out of the tunnel at the departing airplane. One of them turned a talking stalk toward the other one and blinked its biolight in speech. "I think they fell for it," it said.

The other one blinked back: "Good. I was beginning to worry that the Face wouldn't draw them here after all."

The first Martian blinked in staccato laughter. "No, humans will always succumb to curiosity. Now, if the Titans are ready with their fake Pluto outpost by the time the Earthlings get there, I bet we can keep them from bothering either of us for another century at least."

Pictures from an Expedition

✦

Alex Irvine

It was this story, not the recent space probes, that made me think a collection of Mars stories was in order. "Pictures from an Expedition" does not seem to be a radical reimagining of the trip to Mars, but it strikes me as being so different from "A Rose for Ecclesiastes" or from "In the Hall of the Martian Kings" that I thought it would be great to bring these stories together in one book. After we published "Pictures," several readers commented in online message boards that "Y'know, I think that story is really how it'll be when we go to Mars."

What are the odds that they're right?

Alex Irvine is a relatively young writer who seems to be having the sort of impact in the 2000s that John Varley had in the 1970s. His work fuses the "inner space" imaginings of writers like Philip K. Dick (on whom Alex wrote his doctoral dissertation) and the more realistic tradition of John W. Campbell and Astounding/Analog. *Alex's first novel,* A Scattering of Jades, *won several awards and his second novel,* One King, One Soldier, *was published last summer. His short fiction has been collected in* Unintended Consequences. *He lives with his family in Portland, Maine.*

Who are they kidding, man? Sure, she wanted to stay behind. And sure, she destroyed her VR rig. Ooooookay. I believe it.

—sockpuppet446, in Rod Shaver's Forum, 17 March 2012

There were those who had argued caution. Wait until 2014, they said, when there will be unpowered return trajectories available. Wait until 2018, when the fast-transit trajectories are the best. Remember what happened to *Apollo 13.*

But it was 2009, and humans were going to Mars.

Fidelis Emuwa was one of them. His grandfather had been a miner killed in the Biafran War. His father survived to become a doctor in Waltham, Massachusetts. And now he was going to step onto another planet.

When he looked at *Argos I,* Fidelis Emuwa saw progress.

"And *Argos I* has separated from the International Space Station. You'll see now that it's rotating its thruster cones away from the station—a little astronaut's courtesy—before touching off the jets that will take David Fontenot, Jami Salter, Edgar Villareal, Katherine Yi, Fidelis Emuwa, and Deborah Green on humankind's first voyage to another planet. Wait—there's a transmission coming through from the pilot, David Fontenot."

"This is for my old professor Chapman: 'Happy he who like Ulysses has made a glorious voyage.' "

"Is that Homer there, David?"

"No, that's some sixteenth-century French poet, I think. Ask Dr. C. He—"

"Well, stirring words to begin mankind's journey into the uncharted paths of our solar system. Ladies and gentlemen, on November 17, 2009, humankind began our glorious voyage to the stars."

ROD SHAVER'S FORUM:

What does the Martian expedition mean to you?

LUVJAMIXOX>It m33nz Jami Salter's going 2 bring « the sporz, & I want her 2 assiml8 me 1st.

SOCKPUPPET446>It means that even when we go to Mars, we have to look like the cast of *Sesame Street.* I mean, come on. You've got your black guy, your Asian, your Hispanic. Three men and three women. And Deborah Green's Jewish, isn't she? Where are the Hindus and Eskimos? Jesus.

LUVJAMIXOX>*Sesame Street?*

THEBEAMINYROWN>It means that a hundred million people will starve to death who might otherwise have been fed.

SOCKPUPPET446>Look it up.

CHARIOT>It means, when you look in the face, the face looks back.

Eileen Aufdemberge looked up at the sky. I wish it was night, she thought. If it was night, I might be able to see their ship when they fire the engines. It would be like a star coming to life. Or like a last wave from the deck of the ship as it pulls away from the pier. She resisted the impulse to lift her hand.

"Mom?" Jared was there, looking where she was looking. "What do you see?" His ten-year-old face was puzzled. No face, thought Eileen, looks so puzzled as a puzzled little boy's.

"I was looking for your Aunt Debbie," she said, and his frown deepened.

"Come on, Mom," he said. "Aunt Debbie's over the Indian Ocean right now. You can't see her from here."

Thank God she hadn't waved, Eileen thought.

HotVegas betting lines on *Argos I*, 16 November 2009:

Odds on *Argos I* reaching Mars: 1 to 4
Odds on *Argos I* landing successfully: 7 to 5
Odds that the fuel plant and supplies will have survived their landing: 11 to 7
Odds that all six *Argos* crew members survive the mission: 3 to 1

"Three men, three women. What do you bet there's some serious space hubba-hubba?"

"Except they say it's almost impossible to, you know, get a grip without gravity. I'm serious. NASA did studies and shit."

"Where there's a will, there's a way, man. I'm thinking, let's see, they'll pair off about the time they get past the Moon."

"If they haven't already. I heard there's an astronaut ritual, they pick someone to welcome the space virgin to orbit. So they must have figured something out."

"Fontenot's the pilot, he'll get first pick."

"Jami Salter."

[reverent pause]

"Damn."

"Then we have our minority representatives. Villareal goes with who, the Chinese girl or Debbie Green?"

"I'm thinking the Chinese girl. Yi."

"So that leaves the black guy with Green. Black and Green. What color will the kids be?"

[laughter]

[pause]

"No way he's going to be able to keep his hands off Jami Salter."

"Shit, man, that's why they brought the," [sound of knuckles on table] "NASA Nigger-Knocker!"

[louder laughter]

* * *

From the *New York Times,* December 30, 2009:

> "Given the fact that the crew was going to be together for two years, we thought it best that they come from a similar national background," explained Gates Aerospace spokesman Roland Threlkeld. "But, to avoid too much homogeneity, we deliberately sifted our candidate pool for potential Marsnauts who would represent America as a nation."
>
> Threlkeld went on to deny accusations made by NASA and the Cato Institute that Gates Aerospace was more interested in a photogenic crew than a competent one. "Well, that's absurd. I can only guess that this kind of mudslinging is a result of sour grapes on NASA's part. They've said from the beginning that a Mars mission couldn't be mounted sooner than their timetable, and here we are five years earlier. And the Cato Institute would blame affirmative action for the African origin of mankind."

Zero gravity made Jami Salter's bladder feel like it was about the size of a thimble. This wasn't a standard astronaut reaction, and she had done her best to conceal it from the years-long gauntlet of clipboards and lab coats she'd had to run to get here.

Some interplanetary sex symbol, she kidded herself. Running to the john every hour. But she was due to make the crew's daily media dispatch today, and she didn't want to be drumming her feet on the deck in front of the time-delayed pupils of Earth. The PR hacks at Gates had told her that her dispatches drew ratings fifty percent better than any other crew member's, and even though she knew this was just a temporary skewing of the audience composition toward young, male, and horny, she had come to feel an odd sort of duty to live up to the standard that had been set for her. So she washed her hair when it was her day to dispatch, and touched a little makeup here and there. Katherine and Debbie kidded her about it, but they knew the score, and Jami thought they were a little grateful that she was taking the pressure off them.

Said gratitude did not prevent them from nicknaming her Barbarella, though.

All in a day's work, when the day was spent working for the largest private space venture in the history of humankind. They were seventy-five million kilometers from Earth, and the time delay was now almost four minutes each way. The lag hung between *Argos I* and Earth as much as the distance itself. Every time they spoke to friends or family or (more often) media, it felt more and more like they were speaking to the silence and less like any real human beings existed on the other side of the commlink.

She had written those words down in a leather-bound journal she was keeping: speaking to the silence. It had been hard not to write them again. And again.

Barbarella is not coping, she said to herself.

EBONY FREYTAG, MSNBCNN: Jami, how do you like interplanetary space?

JAMI SALTER: Well, I haven't been outside in it, so all I can tell you is that it looks pretty much like space looks like from the Moon. (laughs)

EF: How big is Earth from where you are now?

JS: Tiny. About one-fiftieth the apparent size of the Moon from Earth, and shrinking all the time. And we're starting to be able to resolve Mars as a disk.

EF: Is the crew having any problems?

JS: It's surprising how little friction there has been. We're all getting along great. After all, it doesn't do any good to get angry out here; it's not like you can take a walk to cool off. All of us are very careful to talk out differences, make sure we know where the points of disagreement are and what can be done to resolve problems.

EF: One last question. How do you manage to look so great when you're seventy-five million kilometers from a beauty salon?

JS: Can't answer that one, Ebony. Us astro-girls have to have some secrets.

"How do I manage to look so great?" she asked Edgar and Katherine who, as usual, were sitting just out of camera range, commenting on the interview. They made an interesting pair, Edgar stocky and Mayan-looking next to Katherine, the tallest of the group and rail-thin except for a roundness in her cheeks. Jami kept thinking they looked like cousins, with their epicanthic folds and their identical spiky haircuts.

"I say genes. Katherine's got her money on plastic surgery and good lighting." Edgar pushed back from the table and jumped toward the stairwell that led up to the crew berths. He loved the low gravity. It brought out the monkey in him.

"Good lighting, in this can?" Jami looked at Katherine and they both laughed.

The commlink pinged. "Your adoring public," Katherine said, and winked.

"A Martian's work is never done." Jami tapped the screen to open the link.

[a split screen: Jami Salter on one side, Filomena Huxtable on the other. Running footers identify Jami as *ARGOS* / ELECTRONICS SPECIALIST;

Filomena Huxtable is tagged as KTCM SCIENCE/CULTURE REPORTER. Behind Jami, the *Argos* common area: polished lockers, a microwave oven, a live camera feed of the Sierra Nevada. A studio audience is visible behind Filomena.]

F: So you're the mission electronics specialist.

J: That's right.

F: What does that involve, exactly?

[animated schematics of various missions systems pop up as Jami speaks]

J: Well, the success of our mission depends on our ability to communicate with each other and with Gates mission control back in Houston. My job is to make sure that the communications gear keeps working, and the navigational and laboratory computers, and basically anything else that uses electricity.

F: So when your hair dryer goes on the fritz, you'll be able to fix it.

[laughter from audience; Jami's smile tilts]

J: Well, we've all gotten our Mars cuts here, so nobody brought a hair dryer. But if anything goes on the fritz, it'll be my job to get it shipshape again.

F: Including the space suits? We hear you have all kinds of camera gear in those suits.

[as Jami speaks, various areas of the suit light up. Camera zooms in for close-ups]

J: That's right. And monitors, and transmitters, and temperature-control systems, and everything else needed to keep one of us warm and happy for three days.

F: Three days? I hope they're self-cleaning, too. [louder laughs from audience] Seriously, those suits look great. Do you know who designed them?

J: I don't. That's not really my department.

[vid of Jami, with longer hair and a deep tan, modeling space suit without helmet; crowd erupts]

F: Well, honey, wearing them is definitely your department!

David Fontenot didn't want the Great White Hero label, any more than he sensed Jami was comfortable with the Mission Babe tag. But there it was, and he wasn't about to take a knife to his face or stop working out just so people would stop taking his picture.

Especially not now, when in less than six hours he and Jami would be the first human beings to set foot on Mars. They'd drawn straws, and when he and Jami had won, the reaction from the PR folks at Gates had been decidedly mixed. A photogenic first step was good, but a multiculturally photogenic first step was better. Would the crew reconsider, in light of their standard-bearing situation, representing all nations and races, et cetera?

All of them remembered the lesson of *Apollo 11:* Everybody remembers Armstrong. All of them wanted to be first onto the ground.

When the answer came back to Gates, it was negative. Fair was fair.

From David Fontenot's testimony before the Bexar County grand jury, July 11, 2012:

We all of us felt that the farther we got from Earth, the farther we got from any kind of connection with human civilization. Not that we were turning into barbarians or resorting to cannibalism; just that everything on Earth had stopped applying about the time we cleared the orbit of the Moon. The word alone doesn't even begin to describe it.

I read once the diary of a sailor who was marooned in the eighteenth century for killing one of his shipmates. He records his slow starvation, his efforts to find food and ration water. And he spends a lot of time thinking about his sins. The more he gets resigned to the fact that he's going to die, the more he starts trying to come to terms with what he's done wrong. He never admits that he was wrong for killing his shipmate, but he does think about all kinds of other things that he should repent.

I forget his name, but his diary was found next to his skeleton a long time after he died. All of us, during the time we spent on Mars, I think felt like we were writing a diary like that in our heads.

The odd thing was that nothing had gone catastrophically wrong. Every detail of the mission had come off more or less as planned, from separation from the International Space Station right on up to injection into Mars orbit and the exhilarating, exalted space of time when they had fallen out of the sky to a planet no human had ever touched. The ERV was where it was supposed to be, the power plant was churning out water and oxygen, the rocks cried out to be chipped and sampled and mined for new discoveries. Plants were already growing in the greenhouse next to the main station building. No group of explorers had ever been so well prepared.

So why, wondered Katherine, were they all so damned morose?

The commlink pinged. For Jami, most likely. It almost always was.

"They were supposed to encrypt us," she grumbled.

Fidelis shrugged and stroked his mustache. "I always figured someone would find their way through."

"I mean, we're on Mars, here. It's dangerous. Would help if the goddamn commlink didn't ping every two minutes with someone wanting to know Jami's goddamn cup size."

Katherine sighed. They had all just seen too much of each other during the transit. Gates had done the best it could to give them adequate living space and recreational facilities, but no matter how you sliced it, going to Mars still meant nine months in a tin can with five other people every bit as driven and opinionated and sure of themselves as she was.

"You think now that we're here, everyone will relax a little?" Edgar stood next to her looking out at the Valles Marineris. They had landed and set up at the head of the great canyon system, where its stupendous channel broadened out of the chaos of the Noctis Labyrinthus. One theory had it that sublimation of liquid water caused the landslides that pocked the canyon system's walls, and satellite observations predicted large amounts of water locked up in the crust. *Argos I* had come to find it, and to find out if Gates could make money exploiting it.

Eight hundred miles to the west-northwest, the giant shield volcanoes reared up: Arsia Mons, Pavonis Mons, Ascraeus Mons. A thousand miles beyond them, Olympus Mons. All of them, even Jami and David, dropped their voices a notch when saying those words: Olympus Mons. As if they all half-believed that the gods really did live there.

Which was foolish, of course. None of them were really religious. But *Olympus Mons* . . .

"I don't know, Ed," Katherine said. "I hope so. I hope everyone straightens out so we can really get some work done."

The strange Martian light caught the planes of Edgar's face. A mechanical engineer by training, he'd taken doctoral coursework in geology during preparation for the expedition, intending to use this unprecedented fieldwork as material for his dissertation. He always complained about being the guy everyone looked to when wrenches needed turning; when they got back to Earth, he said, he'd finish his Ph.D. and never touch a tool other than a rock hammer as long as he lived.

Argos's primary geologist was Deborah Green. She and Edgar and Katherine had been assigned a series of expeditions into the canyons to look for water and life. In that order. The Gates people realized the stir that life would make back home, but shareholders cared more about the commercial potential of water. In the words of Roland Threlkeld, Gates mission liaison: "Look for water. If you find life, great, but look for water."

Katherine, as the resident life scientist, tried to stifle her aggravation at the skewing of the expedition's priorities. They had fifteen months on Mars, until October of next year; plenty of time to indulge some personal hunches without the Gates people having to know and still get back to Earth for the New York Olympics in 2012.

Fidelis joined them at the window. The light did something odd to his face, too; something about the texture of his skin that Katherine couldn't identify. He looked out at the landscape of Mars, and she could see the want in his eyes. "When are you going out?"

"Scheduled for tomorrow."

She watched him track the side canyon they would take the next morning down into the head of Valles Marineris. "I know you want to go, Fidelis," she said.

He nodded. "I wanted to go tomorrow. Way things are around here, I'm in all kinds of a hurry to get out."

This was a lot of emotion, coming from him. Katherine paused. He was the mission physician, but she was an M.D., too, and both of them had undergone training in psychology and psychiatry. "Are you okay?"

Fidelis cocked his head to the side when he looked at her. "None of us are okay, Katherine," he said. After another long look out the window, he headed for the door. "Good luck tomorrow."

From HotVegas, April 7, 2010:

> Odds that the crew will find commercial quantities of water: 8 to 5
>
> Odds that the crew will find evidence of vanished civilizations: 150 to 1

Odds that the crew will find microbial life: 3 to 1
Odds that the crew will find multicellular life: 25 to 1
Odds that the crew will be killed by Martians: 175 to 1

"Killed by Martians?" Deborah said incredulously. "Killed by Martians!?"

"I think it's a wonder the odds are only 175 to 1," Edgar said. "I figured every nutcase with twenty bucks to blow would push it down to 10 to 1 or so. Score one for rationality."

Deborah was never sure whether she should be taking him seriously. Quoting odds on the *Argos* crew being killed by Martians was rational? Well, yes. It was. But betting . . . !

She scrolled through some of the other odds. "Well, now. This is interesting."

Odds that violence will break out among the crew: 1 to 3
Odds that violence will break out as a result of sexual jealousy: 2 to 1
Odds that a crew member will be murdered: 12 to 1
Odds that the murdered crew member will be Jami Salter: 6 to 5
Odds that the murdered crew member will be Edgar Villareal: 3 to 1
Odds that the murdered crew member will be Fidelis Emuwa: 7 to 4
Odds that the murdered crew member will be David Fontenot: 8 to 1
Odds that the murdered crew member will be Katherine Yi: 5 to 1
Odds that the murdered crew member will be Deborah Green: 2 to 1
Odds that more than one crew member will be murdered: 22 to 1
Odds that the *Argos* mission will fail due to the murder of one or more crew members: 35 to 1
Odds that all six *Argos* crew members survive the mission: 9 to 4

Edgar came to look over her shoulder. "So you're more likely to get it than I am. What did you do?"

"You haven't heard?" She popped a new browser window and played a short video clip.

EBONY FREYTAG: So you've slept with Deborah Green.

STATUESQUE BLONDE: On numerous occasions.

EF: And we're not talking about a pajama party here.

SB: [with a wink] Well, it never stayed that way.

EF: She doesn't seem like your type, does she?

SB: Deb? Honey, she's everybody's type.

"Yikes!" Edgar said. "She looks a lot like Jami."

"For God's sake, Edgar, she's six inches taller than Jami, and her eyes are brown." Deborah closed the window, cutting off a titillated, exultant roar from Ebony's studio audience. "I'm not only a dyke, I'm a slutty dyke. Who better to kill if there's going to be killing?"

Edgar was looking over the HotVegas odds again. "Well, you're not as bad off as Jami and Fidelis." The commlink pinged.

"Half of the people on Earth who are in love with Jami would love to see her killed," Deborah said. "And a lot of the rest of them are figuring that Fidelis won't be able to keep his pants zipped."

Edgar laughed. "Fidelis? Our doctor-monk? Wonder what they'd say if they knew about us."

She laughed. "Well, when Ebony Freytag interviews you, make sure you tell her how happy I was to get out of *Argos* and back on the ground." Her hand found his, brought it to her mouth. "I sure am glad to have gravity all going in one direction again."

Rod Shaver's Forum, July 30, 2010:
Is Deborah Green a lesbian? Is she having an affair with Katherine Yi? Where does Edgar Villareal come into it?

COSMO0OMSOC>All of you people are ignoring the most important thing.

GODSAVENGER>Wait and see. Not all of them will return. God will exact his justice.

LUVJAMIXOX>Justice?

GODSAVENGER>They knowingly brought a sodomite with them. Who knows how many of the crew she's corrupted by now? Do you think God will stand by and allow this to happen?

THEBEAMINYROWN>No real Christian takes this kind of crap seriously.

CHARIOT>When they come back, it won't matter whether they're gay or straight or what color or anything. What they bring back will destroy all of our petty disagreements, destroy religion.

GODSAVENGER>You've all had your chances.

After all the time they'd spent looking for water, it was almost an anticlimax when they found the lichens in crevices on the sunny sides of Valles Marineris channels. Edgar and Deborah were conducting a hydrological assessment of a series of collapses in a canyon wall, and right before they were due to wrap everything up, she leaned over and said, "Well, I'll be damned."

"What?"

"I think this is lichen."

He went over to look, and it looked like lichen to him, too, worked into the seams of individual rocks that had broken away from the canyon wall. They took a number of samples and went back to the rover, wondering when it would hit them that they were the first people to discover life outside Earth.

Back in the lab, Katherine took the samples and ran some quick tests. "Sure enough," she said. "Lichen. I'm going to sequence the algae and pipe it back on the hotline."

That night, they were a little more boisterous then usual around the dinner table. David cracked a bottle of Laphroaig he'd been saving for a special occasion, and they toasted each other. "But did we find any water?" Jami cracked, and laughed a little too loudly at her own joke. Of course they all knew there was water—they could see traces of it wherever they looked—but their evidence of life was quite a bit more convincing than their evidence of water. Gates would be happy for the good PR, but their expectations were more geared toward long-term financial viability. And everyone at the table knew how expectations were beginning to oppress Jami.

InkStainedWretch.Com's Headline Search, August 30, 2010:

LIFE ON MARS!
Life on Mars
Life on Mars Questioned
Critics Question ET Claims
Wait And See on Life Claims, Experts Say
Mars Life Could Be Native to Earth, Scientist Says
Biotech Stocks Volatile on Mars Life Claims

EBONY FREYTAG, MSNBCNN: So you've discovered life on another planet.

JAMI SALTER: Well, I haven't personally. It was Edgar and Deborah.

EDGAR VILLAREAL: It was Deborah.

EF: Deborah Green, you're the first person to set eyes on alien life. How's it feel?

DEBORAH GREEN: Exciting. It's humbling. I'm not sure any of us have really gotten our minds around it yet.

EF: Jami, tell us how it happened.

JS: I wasn't there. You should really ask Ed and Deborah.

EF: We'll get the science from them later, don't you worry. But our viewers want to know what it was like.

JS: I can tell you it wasn't like I thought it might be. There we were, on Mars, with Martian life in our lab, and it was wondrous, but . . . well, we had a drink, toasted ourselves, danced around the campfire a bit and went to bed.

EF: There's a lot to do tomorrow, isn't there?

JS: Always. Always a lot to do tomorrow. So I should sign off here and let you talk to Deborah and Ed.

EF: I think we've about used our bandwidth, unfortunately. We'll get the science from the nets; I'm sure Deborah Green and Edgar Villareal will be only too happy to tell us their stories. Talk to you next time.

"Well, I guess we shouldn't be surprised, should we?" Edgar said when they'd broken the link.

Don't get angry, Deb told herself. You knew this would happen.

She kept her temper, but only just. Eileen, she thought. My little sister, tuning in to hear about her big sister who discovered life on another planet.

And getting Jami Salter.

"Sorry, Deborah," Jami said, and that was the worst of it; she was such a fundamentally decent person, and had the grace at least to be screwed up by the relentless attention focused on her. Still . . .

Ping.

"Fuck it, never mind. Why don't you get that? It's for you," Deborah said, and didn't think she'd snapped. "I discover life on Mars, they want to talk to you about it. That's how it works. We've known that for a while."

"That's just Ebony," Jami said. "You'll have all the tech nets after you." She laughed, short and bitter. "God knows they're not interested in anything I'm doing."

Ping.

Deborah exchanged a quick glance with Edgar, saw that they were thinking the same thing. Jami upset because she wasn't being recognized? She was an engineer; nobody ever recognized engineers unless the bridge fell down. And she was a pilot, and nobody ever recognized the pilot until the crash.

"Public figuring's a bitch," Edgar said. Deborah was startled. She could see Jami was too. Edgar, saying bitch?

They laughed, Edgar at his joke and the two women at him. Public figuring.

Ping.

HotVegas, August 29, 2010:

Odds that lichen is most sophisticated life on Mars: 175 to 1

Odds that the "discovery" is a hoax: 1 to 1

Odds that Mars lichen descended from Earth species: 4 to 1

Odds that Earth lichen descended from Mars species: 5 to 8
Odds that human beings are descended from Mars lichen: 7 to 5
Odds that all six *Argos* crew members survive the mission: 7 to 1

Rod Shaver's Forum, August 29, 2010: Is it real? Does it matter?

CHARIOT>Of course they discovered life. Does anybody out there seriously think they weren't going to?

THEBEAMINYROWN>Does anybody out there seriously think they'd let us believe they hadn't? Come on. Gates needs this trip to pay off. Water's one way; ETBOs are another. And let's not forget that Gates has a piece of all vids, interviews, even books on all the crew. When D. Green talks to *Scientific American,* creds flow into Gates accounts. No way they were going to let an opportunity like that go by.

COSMO0OMSOC>So you don't think they found anything?

CHARIOT>Of course they found something.

THEBEAMINYROWN>I don't know whether they did or not. It's possible. I'm just saying that we were going to be told they'd found something whether they did or not.

COSMO0OMSOC>But it's lichen, man. Not like little green men or a big monolith or something.

THEBEAMINYROWN>The ways of Gates are devious and subtle, amigos. Just keep your eyes open, is all I'm saying.

The sequence came back from the Gates database with three beautiful words: NO SPECIES MATCH.

"Life on Mars," Edgar breathed. For a while all of them stood around the sample containers watching the brown lichen.

Ping.

Ping.

Ping ping ping.

"We're watching brown lichen, people," David said presently.

InkStainedWretch.Com's Headline Search, August 31, 2010:

> ARE WE ALL MARTIANS?
> Panspermia Gets New Lease on Media Life
> Humankind Not Descended from Martians, Pope Says
> Society for Christian Medicine Floats *Argos* Crew Quarantine
> Results Still Not Definitive About Mars Life
> Lichen: Symbiotic Explorer

They spent the next two months absorbed in the problem of the lichen: where it grew, what could kill it, what made it grow, whether it performed the same ecological function on Mars that it did on Earth. Gates, of course, made sure that they spent most of their time looking for water, but hell, they'd found the original lichen while looking for water; it wasn't that hard to make one activity look like the other.

And they found water, too.

Again, Deborah was the lucky party. Late on a surveying mission, irascible from the grit of Martian dust in her underwear and her eyes and her teeth and her socks, she'd said to herself: Fine. One more sweep. Fill out one more grid. Then back to base and I'm not going out for a week. A fucking week. No more peroxide taste, no more dust in the crack of my ass. Seven days.

Something rumbled below her feet.

She was forty meters from the lip of a canyon wall that dropped something like three hundred meters to a titanic jumble of fallen rock. Edgar was about a hundred meters away from her. Both of them dropped their instruments and ran toward the edge.

Deborah threw herself on her stomach and scooted forward until her head was hanging over the sheer drop. Below her, mist swirled above the rockfall at the bottom of the canyon. Carbon dioxide; they saw that all the time. They'd even seen water mist once in a while. Never water in commercially useful quantities, though. Never until this huge beautiful plume that came exploding out of the canyon wall two hundred meters below her pounding heart, eclipsing the carbon-dioxide mist in a thick fog of sublimating water.

She was screaming into her mike, and she screamed louder when the vapor cloud rose up to envelop her. The world went white, and Deborah opened her mouth and let the frustration of the past two months chase the joy, the never-to-be-repeated joy of this moment, out of her mouth and through her mask and into the thin wet Martian air.

"Deborah! Deb, Jesus! Deb! You there? Come in, Deb!"

"Toggle your cams to me!" she shouted. "God, look at this!"

She heard their exclamations as they saw through her cam. Water beaded on her mask, held for a moment by her body heat before it sublimated away. Something gripped her hand, and Deborah started before she realized it was Edgar, talking to her on their private channel: "You again, Miz Green. Lucky I have you around."

She squeezed his hand through their bulky gloves, and in that moment a ridiculous thought flashed through her mind: *Oh, God, I'd better be sure to shower before tonight or we're going to scrape each other raw.* She laughed out loud, and Edgar joined in. Over their mikes they heard the rest of the crew shouting, clapping each other on the back, calling them to come back in and start the celebration.

HotVegas, November 9, 2010:

Odds that *Argos I* crew will suffer infection from Martian life: 1 to 4
Odds that Martian infection will kill *Argos I* crew member: 7 to 2

Odds that *Argos I* crew will carry dangerous microbes back to Earth: 2 to 5

Odds that all six *Argos* crew members survive the mission: 8 to 1

Late in the night, Edgar asleep beside her, Deborah remembered stepping out of the airlock into Bohlen Station and thinking as she did that she would really have to find out why Jami had suggested they call the station that. A character in a book, Jami had said.

Katherine had been there inside the airlock door with a puzzled expression on her round face. "Again," she said. "You, again."

Yes, Deborah had wanted to say. Me again. But the look on Katherine's face was so pained; she had wanted very badly to discover life on Mars herself, or at least to pronounce life absent, and then her grand moment was usurped by a geologist. Who then found water, too. It was all a little much, Deborah thought.

"It's your work they're going to remember," she'd said to Katherine. "You're the one who did the sequence and all that. I was just in the right place."

"Thank you," Katherine had said. "Thank you for believing that."

Rod Shaver's Forum, November 8, 2010:
Ghoulies and Ghosties and. . . ?

SOCKPUPPET446>You heard it here first: one of them's already sick. They're going to cover it up, but watch and see if they all come back. They won't.

THEBEAMINYROWN>Hooray, Shaver's paranoids are alive and well.

SOCKPUPPET446>Whatever, beam. You wait until they come back and spread it to you.

CHARIOT>Whatever it is, it couldn't be worse than the shit we've already got. I'll challenge any Martian microbe to ten rounds with HIV3.

LUVJAMIXOX>Funny sh!t coming from u, chariot.

CHARIOT>What they're going to bring back is much much stranger than we can imagine.

InkStainedWretch.Com's Headline Search, November 9, 2010:

> WET MARS
> Mars Crew 2 for 2
> Gates Stock Up 37 Percent on Water News
> GM, Airbus, Vishnu Ready Mars Plans
> "Life Is Interesting, Water Makes Money," Says Chair of NSF
> Ebony Freytag Sued Over Naked Jami Vid—Fake?

Ping.

It was never so good again. Once they'd found life, found water, basked in their accolades, there was still nearly a year to spend on Mars and seven months of sandpapering each other's nerves on the voyage home. The Gates scientific crew thought up more than enough experiments and missions to keep them busy, but their real work was done. They had established that Mars held both life and enough water to justify colonization. Already a dozen Mars colonies were moving from pencil-sketch imagining to nuts-and-bolts reality. In ten years, Mars would be utterly changed.

"We'd better enjoy it while we can," said David. "Who knows if we'll get to come back?"

"Would you want to?"

Jami's question surprised him. They were running the latest in an endless series of inspections of joints, hoses, bearings, and seals—anything that could be eroded by peroxides or clogged by dust. Which was to say, everything. They'd taken to doing it in pairs, and when it had become apparent that the pairs were rubber-stamping each other (after Katherine and Fidelis had both missed a badly corroded seal that then blew, freezing the station's water supply), they'd taken to sending out pairs who weren't getting along with each other. This meant that Fidelis hardly ever got inspection duty, since everyone liked him.

It also meant that David and Jami were at last going to have to get out into the open whatever it was that had been hanging between them since they'd been anointed *Argos I* media darlings. Or so, they both knew, Fidelis was hoping.

So here we go, David thought. "Yeah," he said. "I think I would."

Jami looked at him for a long time. The Sun was setting, the Martian landscape settling from golds and reds back into evening browns. There was enough dust on her faceplate that David couldn't see her expression.

"I bet you would," she said eventually.

Ebony Freytag's show became the crew's guilty pleasure. On a Tuesday in December, they watched as she devoted an entire show to random things her audience wanted to know about the *Argos* crew. Did they lose a lot of weight in space? Were they more religious than when they'd left? What were they really doing?

And why, someone asked, was everyone so heated up about David Fontenot when Fidelis Emuwa was so gorgeous?

"I guess Fidelis is a pretty good-looking guy," David said.

Katherine snorted. "Why do we watch this garbage? Just because they want us to be a sideshow. Why do we let them?"

The two of them were sitting in the common room. Fidelis came down from the dorm level. "Are we a sideshow?"

"When was the last time we got a call from someone other than Gates about either exobiology or water?"

David got up for a cup of tea. He wanted to stay to the side of this discussion. After his exchange with Jami a few days before, he'd tried to be more sensitive to the mood of the crew, and what he'd seen thus far wasn't encouraging. Holiday blues, he thought; all of us get a little crabby around the New Year. He hoped that was all it was.

Deborah came in from the direction of the lab. "Another day, another goddamn revolutionary discovery about Martian geological history. I'm sick of it."

"Maybe we should take a couple of days off," David said, and then wished he hadn't spoken. Where were Jami and Edgar? Edgar was probably tinkering with something, cleaning out a ball joint somewhere or changing the rover's battery terminals. Jami, who knew? Jami was doing her Martian Bedouin-mystic thing somewhere nearby. She had enough to do keeping station computer equipment up and communicative, but recently she'd developed a tendency to wander off once things had reached a bare minimum functionality. Katherine and Deborah were getting sharp about it.

HotVegas, February 11, 2011:

> Odds that one or more *Argos* crew members has attempted suicide: 4 to 1
> Odds that one or more *Argos* crew members will attempt suicide: 2 to 3
> Odds that all six *Argos* crew members survive the mission: 6 to 1

David gathered the *Argos* crew in the station greenhouse. All of them liked it there. It was warm, it smelled good, it wasn't brown. "I think we ought to have a chat. All of us."

Everyone settled into a rough circle. David looked around the group, saw that Deborah wasn't next to Edgar and Jami was between Fidelis and Katherine. So they hadn't arranged themselves according to cliques. That was good. "Katherine," he said, "I know this is more your territory—"

"Fidelis is more of a psych guy than I am," she said. "I was a surgeon."

He let the interruption pass, then plunged ahead. "I'm concerned about our collective well-being here."

The wind kicked up, rattling dust and gravel against the greenhouse walls.

"So am I," said Fidelis. David was looking at him just before he spoke, and he saw Fidelis look quickly at Jami and then away. Worried about Jami? he wondered. Or is Fidelis worried about himself, and Jami's the reason?

"I think we're all worried," Katherine said. "We're on another planet, halfway through a three-year mission. It's lethal and ugly outside, and we're all sick of looking at each other, so inside isn't much better. All of this was in the mission prep. We knew it would happen."

Edgar cut in. "That's not the same as dealing with it when it does."

"But anticipating the problem at least gives us a basis for dealing with it," Fidelis said calmly.

"So let's deal," David said. "What do we need? I'll start. I need to play some euchre."

"What's euchre?" everyone else said more-or-less at once.

"Card game. It's simple. I used to play with my dad and my uncles up in Petoskey. I've been playing on the computer, but it's not the same. I miss it." He looked to his right, where Deborah was picking dead leaves from a grapevine. She kept picking, but he could see her thinking.

"I need Edgar to leave me alone for a while," she said.

From the *Washington Post,* March 13, 2011:

The Fading Fad of Mars
by Allen Holley

During the six weeks before *Argos I* left the International Space Station, the bandwidth of the developed world crackled with nothing but Marsnauts. During their voyage to the Red Planet, we worried how they would get along, if they would fall in love; we bet on the possibility of their failure; we spent our free time pouring information about Jami, David, Deborah, Edgar, Katherine, and Fidelis into our heads.

I thought it would peter out before they got there. Interest would spike again once they landed, of course, but apart from that and another flurry of information if they discovered something exciting—little green men or underground rivers or veins of iridium—but beyond that, I figured that the obsessive persistence of American consumerate was of fairly short duration.

I was wrong.

We have been gaga over the Marsnauts for much longer than I ever would have guessed. Chatthreads devoted to Deborah Green's sexual orientation unspooled posts in the millions; viewership of talk shows that took Jami Salter as their subject exceeded the number of eyeballs trained on last summer's World Cup in South Africa; applications to *Argos* Marsnauts' alma maters are up more than one hundred percent since the selection of the crew.

So yes, I was wrong.

I can admit this because we are, at last, beginning to forget. Bandwidth consumption at all the newsnets is down, or at least redirected to the pipes carrying the Chinese incursion into India; Ebony Freytag is stinging from the lawsuit; the various chat forums, if not exactly quiet, are no longer as riotous as they were in the halcyon early days of Mars-mania. This despite the fact that the crew of *Argos I* has in fact discovered extraterrestrial life, throwing biology (and religion) on its collective ear, and begun to map huge quantities of water under the planet's surface, meaning that colonization has abruptly become a question not of if but of when.

They have been amazingly successful. And we are starting to ignore them. Part of me can't help but think it's a relief.

"Deborah," Edgar said. She snapped a tendril from the vine.

"David asked what we need. I'm telling you. I tried to think of something else, but that's it. I need you to leave me alone for a while."

Edgar stood very still for several seconds before picking up his tool belt.

"Edgar," David said before Edgar could leave. "Please stay."

After a pause, Edgar put the tool belt back on the worktable in the center of the greenhouse. "Thank you," David said, trying to keep the real gratitude out of his voice. Things were getting very deep very fast, and he had to make sure the gathering didn't fly apart. "Katherine?"

"I would like you to ask Gates to give us more leeway in running experiments. The schedule is still predicated on searching for life that we've already found, and I'm wasting valuable time running useless experiments because people back in the Gates labs have already arranged to publish the results."

David nodded. "Okay. Let's do it this way: You start reporting to me, and I'll send abstracts of your results to Gates. *I'll* take the heat."

"Thank you," Katherine said. "Also, I would like to learn how to play euchre." She smiled at him, and in that moment he could have kissed her. Whatever she said about Fidelis being the psych guy, Katherine knew the thin line David was treading, and she was doing her best to help.

"That's two things," he said, "but we are a resilient enough crew to handle them both, I think. Jami."

"I need everyone to stop looking at me like I'm going crazy."

There was a long pause.

"And I need people to please stop getting so quiet when I talk," Jami added. "Please."

Dear Ms. Salter,

I am a sixth-grader at Fred P. Hall Elementary School in Portland, Maine. I want to go to Mars some day. Can you tell me what college

I should go to? I want to be a pilot and make sure aliens don't take over Mars or come to Earth. Will they let me do that even though I still have to wear glasses because my mom won't pay to burn my corneas?

Sincerely,
Megan Machado

"Noted," David said. "We got it. You aren't crazy, and we'll start interrupting you. Fidelis?"

"We're all too alone," Fidelis said. "I need everyone to start talking to each other again . . . no. I need everyone to start *listening* to each other again."

Leave it to Fidelis to be levelheaded and precise, David thought. Carrying around his own self-assurance, a banked coal hidden from the winds that tore through the rest of them.

Or he was just deep, deep water, with all the turbulence down there in the dark.

"You heard the doc," David said. "Everybody start listening. We're all talking—hell, I talk all the time—but we're talking to ourselves." Greenhouse spring, he found himself thinking. A little island in the midst of so much cold and dark. A little spring, like the one they were all missing on Earth. "I think we need to get control of this," he went on. "As of tomorrow, we resume burst transmissions back to Earth. No more recording and storing; we send everything live."

"Gates won't run it," Deborah said.

"I don't care if Gates runs it or not. We all need to know that someone knows we're out here. When we just record and store for the backup pipe, we're talking to ourselves. Starting tomorrow, we talk to Earth again."

"And I guess we'll find out if Earth wants to talk to us," Jami said. Her voice was barely above a whisper.

"Oh, for Christ's sake!" snapped Katherine. "You're the last person around here who should worry about that."

Jami was nodding before Katherine finished her sentence. "Right, you're right. It really helps knowing that they all care so much about me. How can I be lonely knowing that so many people care?" Her voice throughout was soft, and when she finished speaking, she got up and pushed through the door that led back to Bohlen Station.

David watched her go. When the door had settled shut behind her, he surveyed the four people left in front of him.

Only Deborah was looking back at him. "She's cracking up, David. You need to do something. She named the station after a schizophrenic mechanic in an old science-fiction novel, for Christ's sake. Doesn't that worry you?"

"Katherine?" David said. "Fidelis?"

The two doctors looked at each other. David couldn't tell if some kind of secret physician's exchange was passing between them. After a moment, both shrugged. "She's been under a lot of pressure from the beginning," Fidelis said. "It's a good sign that she's still performing all of her work."

"But barely," Katherine interjected.

"That's true of all of us," said Fidelis. "None of us is working anything like we did our first few months here."

David stepped back in. "If Jami, or anyone else, starts leaving critical work unfinished, someone tell me right away. I'll keep an eye out, but the water separator's a full-time job lately. I need people looking out for each other. None of us can afford to crack. Stay together, people."

It was the moment to end the gathering, mission mostly accomplished, crew refocused and given a little momentum to get through the day. Right then David realized he'd forgotten to ask Edgar what he wanted.

* * *

Edgar Villareal, interview with Bruce Pandolfo of 700MHz, June 9, 2065:

> It's odd to be the last one alive. When we went to Mars, I think we all figured we were immortal. Along the way we figured out that we weren't, and realized how awful it would be if we were. Jami couldn't handle it. David could—he was always better at that kind of thing. I know I was glad to have both of them sopping up most of the attention before it got to me. Remember, I was only 3-1 to be the murdered crew member. Jami, Fidelis, and Deborah were all way ahead of me. People paid more attention to them. And David.
>
> Anyway, I figured half of us would live to be a hundred. Now here I am, ninety next weekend, and I'm the last. And it's sad that three of us . . . Fidelis's accident was almost a relief after hearing about David and Katherine and Deborah.

For three days the wind did not blow. Sand and dust settled in gentle drifts around the camp. Fidelis spent each of those three days immersed in his work, keeping himself away from the windows. He wanted to go outside, but he didn't want to see what he knew would be there.

Blow, wind, he said to himself, and felt creeping unease. Madmen on a dead red heath, that was all of them. Blow, wind. He steeled himself to resist Mars. If the wind would not blow, neither would Fidelis Emuwa go outside. He could outwait the planet. It could not break him.

You're personifying, he told himself. You're seeing agency in randomness. That's what they call paranoia.

Finally he couldn't stand it anymore. He suited up and went outside into the absurd stillness. The sky was bright and clear. His footsteps crunched as he walked around to the back of the greenhouse, where he'd seen Jami writing in the sand three days before, after David's meeting in the greenhouse. Writing, brushing it away, writing again.

Between his feet, the words: *speaking to the silence.*

Fidelis knelt and brushed them away.

The first day nobody called was hard on all of them. Except Jami.

"Twenty-four hours and no ping," she announced with a broad smile. "It only took a year and a half. Longer attention span than we thought they had, I bet."

"By about a year," grumbled Katherine, who Edgar figured was grouchy because Gates hadn't gotten back to her about her proposal to go into the lava tunnels looking for life other than the scrawny lichen that survived in cracks in canyon walls. He wanted to do it, too, but until today he hadn't figured Gates would let them. Too much to lose. Now that the data flow from Earth had slowed to a trickle, though, he thought Gates might change its mind. They'd be looking for something to rejuvenate news coverage. Katherine wanted to go, but she also welcomed the relative peace and quiet.

Far as Edgar was concerned, anything that got him out of Bohlen Station and away from Deborah (for weeks now he'd been thinking of her as that bitch Deborah, but he was beginning to get over that) more than justified whatever risks arose. And away from Jami, who had suddenly begun to act like she was on the vid all the time. Of course, all of them were on the vid all the time; they'd agreed to sell "uncut" VR of the voyage as part of their contract with Gates. The feeling Edgar got, though, was that she had started playing a part. She was playing Barbarella the Mission Babe again, only now it was for her colleagues instead of Earthside media.

He wondered if she'd forgotten how to be herself. If somehow the intensity of the news coverage had overwhelmed whatever natural person had existed before they'd all become Marsnauts. Edgar thought back to training and their early publicity junkets. He'd liked Jami. She'd been at ease with everyone, able to joke about herself without seeming to make a point of it. The cameras found her, and the rest of them were grateful—even Edgar, who had once wanted to be an actor. He quickly found that they needed Jami to take the pressure off them. They would all have imploded long ago if she hadn't done that.

"Now we can go back to being the anonymous discoverers of life beyond Earth," he said.

Jami flashed him a grin. "Thank God. You doing anything today?"

"Not unless Katherine gets the go-ahead to check out the tunnels."

"Then come with me. Reactor sensors are due for inspection."

"Let's do it." Anything to get out of here, Edgar thought again.

The Quiet Day, as it became known around the station, turned out to be an anomaly. Apparently people on Earth were still interested. But where before they'd struggled to answer the flood of scientific and media inquiries, now they found that most of their incoming volume was kids looking for help on science projects and lonely postgrads wishing they were on Mars instead of in Ann Arbor or Heidelberg or Jakarta. "It's official," Deborah said. "We're a niche."

On Jami's birthday, August 22, she took off on a long solo hike. David almost didn't let her, but there was only so much he could do, and he settled for making sure that she had twenty-four hours of oxygen and a tested distress beacon. She's an adult, he said, and if she's going to kill herself, I can't do much about it.

The more he watched her, the more convinced he was that she would be better once they'd all gotten on their way home. Surrounded by the empty red immensity of Mars, David thought, memories of Earth started to get a little abstract, like something he'd done once and might someday do again.

Deborah, Katherine, and Edgar were shouting at Fidelis when

David came back in from doing the final check on Jami's suit. He got in among the four of them and calmed things down enough to get a sense of what was going on. It was cold in the station—something wrong with the thermostat—and he could see his breath.

"She's up to something," Edgar said. "And he knows what it is."

"Up to what?" David asked. He caught Fidelis's eye and tried out his telepathy: Is Edgar okay? Do we have a problem here?

Fidelis looked away from him and said, "She's having a hard time. This is true. And we have talked about it. She's entitled to some privacy, though, and I'm not going to just repeat what was said for all of you."

"If she's cracking up, it endangers the mission, Fidelis," Deborah said. Edgar was nodding along with her. "I could give a shit about her privacy."

"You know she's been skating on the edge of pathological for months, Fidelis," Katherine said. "If she's fallen over, you're the one who will know, and you can't keep it from us." Edgar and Deborah started to join in.

"Let me be clear about something," Fidelis snapped. The rest of them fell silent; they'd never heard him raise his voice except to laugh. "If I thought Jami was putting the mission in danger, I would of course tell David. I would not just tell whoever wanted to know, and I will not be bullied because you are all anxious. Do not insult me by turning me into a snitch, and do not insult me by suggesting I will not carry out my responsibilities." He glared at each of them in turn. When nobody said anything, he walked between Katherine and Edgar and went upstairs.

"He's not telling us everything he knows," Deborah said.

David waited to see if Edgar or Katherine had something to add. After a pause, he said, "He doesn't have to. You heard what he said. Do any of us really think that Fidelis Emuwa, of all people, is going to let personal feelings get in the way of his job? Come on."

Again he waited, and again none of them contradicted him, but David could tell they weren't convinced.

* * *

Gates Corporation communications records, August 22, 2011 (subpoenaed as evidence in the trial of Fidelis Liber Emuwa, David Louis Fontenot, Deborah Ruth Green, Edgar Carlos Villareal, and Katherine Alexandra Yi):

Date: 22 Aug 2011, 14:35:06 GMT
To: *Argos* PM Roland Threlkeld
From: Tammy Gulyas, *Argos* Mission Liaison
Re: *Argos* trouble?

Rol,
David was in touch today. He's worried about Jami (still, or again) and Edgar (again). Doesn't think there's an immediate crisis, but wants to know how much pressure he can put on Fidelis. Jami's been talking to F. and the rest of the crew thinks he's holding out on them. D. worried that E. might get violent. Ethical issues are your dept., so I'm shuffling this one off. Vid of David's call attached.

Next time we need to send an actor along. Fuck brains, fuck weight restrictions. J. might look good, but she's an engineer. We need someone who can handle celebrity.

TG

Date: 22 Aug 2011, 16:11:53 GMT
To: Tammy Gulyas, *Argos* Mission Liaison
From: *Argos* PM Roland Threlkeld
Re: *Argos* trouble?

Tammy—58 days to Earth-return liftoff. Sit tight. David's strung out like the rest of them. Jami's going to be fine, so is Edgar. Fidelis is a rock. ~R

* * *

They all took Labor Day off. It was a gesture, really, since they could take all the days off they wanted. Their scientific objectives were long ago accomplished, and with the launch back to Earth less than six weeks away, Gates had clamped down on discretionary travel and exploration. So they played lots of euchre and went over preliminary checks and tried not to get on each other's nerves.

Fidelis spent the morning in the common room reading *Don Quixote* on the table screen. He had been keeping a careful eye on Jami for weeks now, since he'd seen her writing in the sand. She was holding herself together, but he could tell it wouldn't take much to unravel her. Everyone else in the crew had come to him wondering about her bright brittle smile, the metronomic way she did her work, ate her meals, slept and bathed and spoke. David in particular was worried, and seemed to be carrying some kind of guilt. "First I thought that when the attention went away, she'd settle down. And she did, kind of, but it wasn't real. Then I started to figure that as launch got closer and the nets started talking about engineering obstacles, she'd perk back up because they'd ask her technical questions, you know? Questions about her area of expertise. Things that make her sound good."

David scratched at his ear, something he did when he wasn't sure how to proceed.

"Then this goddamn latest Ebony Freytag," he said after a pause. "Getting my idiot cousin and Jami's twenty-year-old sister together. I can shake my head and forget about that kind of shit, you know? But I think that was some kind of last straw for her. The way she walks around now I keep thinking she's just going to fly apart. Like every wrinkle in her skin is a crack."

"We're still getting lots of questions," Fidelis pointed out.

"I know," David said. Edgar came in, and he lowered his voice. "But they're from twelve-year-olds and nutcases. It doesn't mean anything to her."

"Where's Deborah?" Edgar said. He had shaved his beard.

Fidelis looked at David. They both shrugged. "Haven't seen her."

"Maybe she's in the lab." Edgar turned to go.

"Edgar," Fidelis called. "Are you all right?"

"Fine fine fine, Doc," Edgar said. "Just time to talk, is all. She wanted me to leave her alone, I left her alone. Now she's got to do something for me, and that's tell me what the hell is going on. Don't worry—I'm not mad, and she could kick my ass anyway, I think." It was probably true; Edgar and Deborah were about the same size, but when it came right down to it, she had a mean streak and he didn't.

Edgar wasn't the one Fidelis was worried about, anyway. "You know I have to ask," he said. Edgar waved a hand and left in the direction of the lab.

"You really think there's no problem?"

Fidelis shook his head. "They're not going to be back in bed, but I don't expect any real trouble, either. They were always together more out of some kind of rockhound solidarity than because they liked each other."

David was looking at the doorway. "I wondered about that."

Jami walked in. "Fidelis!" she said with that bright and hopeless smile. "Just the man I wanted to see. Let's go for a hike."

From: Blaine Taggart
To: *Argos I* crew
Subject: 15 minutes

Dear Marsnauts: How does it feel to know that your moment in the spotlight has already passed you by? My dad was a comedian, had three minutes on Johnny Carson one night in 1981, and never got over it. Just curious. By the way, I hear the fungus in your Mars lichen has a common ancestor with some terrestrial fungus. So three cheers for panspermia, right?

* * *

"I'm not going back."

He had known she would say this sooner or later, and he had lost much sleep over the previous six or seven nights rehearsing possible responses. None of them seemed appropriate now. What could he tell her? That she would die? Of course she would die. That her family would miss her? She knew that. That she was going to be rich and famous, feted in castles and capitals?

"Jami," he said. "Do you know what will happen to us if you don't come back?"

She glanced at him. "No. Come on, Fidelis. Appeal to my sense of responsibility to science, my desire for fame. Something. Just don't make me worry about you anymore."

"I don't think you have those things anymore. Once you did. All of this has fallen away from you."

Jami laughed. A little static sparked in Fidelis's mike. "Wasn't nirvana supposed to be the relinquishing of all desire? I forget. Can't remember religious things anymore. Here's your bodhisattva wisdom, Fidelis: you don't want me with you on the way back." She started walking away from him, gliding easily between boulders in the direction of the trail that led to the bottom of the canyon. "And I don't mean that personally, like people on the mission would rather see me stay. What I mean is, if you make me come with you, none of us will survive the trip home."

Look at me, he thought. I have to see what's in your face.

She did not speak, and he could not, and after a while she reached the trailhead and began her descent into the canyon.

HotVegas, September 5, 2011:

> LABOR DAY SPECIAL—PLACE A $100 BET ON *ARGOS I*'S SAFE RETURN AND GET A FREE $50 BET ON THE WORLD SERIES! UNTIL THE 15TH ONLY!

* * *

Never in her life had Katherine come closer to violence than when she saw Jami chiseling circuitry out of the VR corder built into her suit helmet.

"What the hell are you doing?" she said.

Jami didn't look up. "I think I've had it with being a spectacle."

"Well, I haven't had it with fulfilling our contract. Stop that."

"Okay." Jami put down the small hammer and chisel she'd been using. "All done anyway."

Katherine punched the wall intercom mounted next to the interior airlock door.

"David," she said. "Come here, please."

His voice popped through the speaker. "Problem?"

Katherine stabbed the button again. "Just come here, please."

Jami mounted the plate over the corder and started screwing it back into place. "Don't," Katherine said.

"Cleaning up, Katherine," Jami said. "Not hiding." But she put the plate back down.

David arrived. "What?"

Katherine was about to speak when Fidelis came into the lock, too. It was crowded with the four of them and the eight suits hanging on wall racks. "I didn't ask him to come," Katherine said, pointing at Fidelis.

"Is this a private dispute?" David asked.

Briefly, Katherine considered pushing the point. She and David both knew that Fidelis would defend whatever Jami was doing. To a certain extent, that canceled out the benefit of the defense. "Never mind," she said. "I walked in here and Jami was sabotaging the recording equipment in her suit."

"Jami?" David asked.

"Guilty," she said immediately. With the toe of one shoe she scuffed at the bits of broken circuitry on the floor.

David sighed. "All right. Look. Jami—"

"How much money did she just cost us?" Katherine asked. She could already see David preparing to go easy on Jami. Well and good for him. He was one of the stars of the mission. She was just a member of the chorus, though, and nobody would be clamoring for her memoirs or her face on their screens. She'd have a good job when she got back, but she'd had a good job before leaving. The only reason she'd wanted to go to Mars in the first place was to cash in on whatever fame might come her way. The science she could have done at home, and Mars itself was so much empty, rock-strewn wilderness. She wouldn't miss it.

"I don't know," David said. After a pause he added, "Station vids are still going. Gates can piece something together. Unless—"

"Speaking of which," Jami said. She stood up and went to the intercom. "Everyone please come to the lock," she said. "No hurry." Then she woke up the terminal next to the intercom.

"What are you doing?" Katherine said.

"Shutting down the autofeed from the station vid." Katherine started to object, but David held up a hand.

"It's okay," he said. "Everything will still record. We can pipe it later."

The four of them stood there looking at each other until Edgar and Deborah arrived. They had obviously been making love, the smell of it preceded them into the lock, and Katherine thought to herself, Jesus Christ.

"Okay," Jami said. "First, I want to apologize. I haven't done anything to station recorders or the suit recorders except for mine. Gates will be pissed, but to be frank, what I'm about to do is worth a lot more money than what otherwise would have been on my corder."

"Jami," Fidelis said quietly.

"Shut up, Fidelis," Katherine said. "Let her take her own weight for once."

A ghost of a smile crossed Jami's face. "Thank you, Katherine. The short version is this: I'm not going back to Earth." The smile grew broader. Something about it made Katherine a little sick. "There. You're all rich."

"You're not staying here," David said.

"You can't make me go back. You could jump me and tie me down, but if you do that, I'll kill myself. Can you keep me too doped up to do it for the next seven months?" She shook her head. "I don't think so. Katherine? You're the doctor. Fidelis? What kind of star material will I be after seven months of minimal-g drooling into my collar?"

The only sound in the room was the rattle of a loose valve cover on the outside of the lock. After some time, Fidelis spoke.

"I think Katherine will agree with me that there would be serious long-term consequences."

"There will be serious long-term consequences if she stays here," Katherine answered. "Since we're all being honest here, I'll admit that I'm sick and tired of the way we've all catered to Miss Jami Salter, but I don't want to see her dead. If she stays here, she'll die."

"I don't know about that," Edgar said. Deborah looked startled.

Jami was nodding. "The station is staying behind. The greenhouse will be here. The reactor will still be working long after all of us are dead. What else do I need?"

"This is ridiculous," Katherine said.

"I'm not going back to Earth," Jami said. "One way or another, I'm not going back."

InkStainedWretch.Com Headline Search, October 18, 2011:

> COMING HOME!
>
> Marsnauts Come Home!
>
> On Their Way
>
> Gates, ISS Ready Decontamination Procedures
>
> Demonstrators Demand *Argos* Quarantine
>
> Mars Lichen Called "Threat to Humanity"

* * *

Early in the morning of their last day on Mars, while Jami was running a last preflight check on the rendezvous vehicle, David gathered the rest of the *Argos I* crew in the common room. "We have a decision to make here," he said. "We're in a communications blackout for the next hour, so we vote right now. Leave Jami or force her to come along? Edgar: go."

"It's on her," Edgar said. "David and I can do her job on the way back. Let her stay."

"Fidelis."

"If she stays, she might survive. If we take her, she won't."

"Deborah."

"Bring her. We'll all be in jail if we don't."

"Katherine."

"Fidelis is wrong. And Edgar. She'll die here, and we don't have enough crew redundancy to be safe without her. Bring her."

David sighed. "Okay. Tiebreaker's on me." He paused. "She stays."

"You're fucking kidding," Deborah said.

"I'm fucking not." David looked around at all of them.

"This is Mars, David," Deborah said. "Not a desert island. Mars. She'll die."

"She'll have all the stuff that's kept us alive for the past fifteen months."

"And she'll die if she comes," Fidelis said. "If not on the voyage, soon after."

"You are endangering the mission," Katherine said. "Not to mention all of our lives. You can't do this."

"If we force her and something goes wrong, she could take all of us with her," David said. "I don't think we can risk it. There will be colonizing missions in four years. Six at the most. She'll be fine until then."

"Fine?" Katherine said incredulously. "Fine?"

They all heard the inner airlock start to compress. Nothing was left to say.

"It really is beautiful here," Jami said. She was spending more and more time outside now, and since she'd wrecked her VR corder, her mood had grown lighter. Some of the old genuine Jami Salter effervescence had returned, although tinctured by a sort of maturity that made Fidelis think of the stately poets he'd read in college English classes. Wordsworth, maybe.

He turned off his VR and lay back. Earth was one hundred days away, and Jami Salter was beyond human help.

During their last day on Mars, Fidelis had personally recorded everything after the meeting. He had been unable to take his eyes from her face, from the somehow-beatific gaze she cast on him, on the rest of the crew, on the Martian landscape. He watched her as she helped them run the flight checks on the orbiter, as she brought the ERV back up from its hibernation, as she ran Edgar through all of the things she worried he might have forgotten. All of them had drilled in protocols for returning with a partial crew, and none of them was really afraid of what Jami's absence would mean for mission success. She had repaired and jerry-rigged electronics, yes, and piloted when shift scheduling called for it, and it was certainly possible that something would go wrong on the return voyage that only she would be able to correct. That worry was distant somehow, like the abstract concern of being holed by a meteor. Nothing that could usefully be worried about.

It hit him then: Jami, who had been their movie star, was now their guide. She would make sure they got home.

Fidelis had not cried since the birth of his daughter Emily. He found tears again on that last day he spent on the surface of Mars, and now on every day since when he gave himself over to the enormity of what they had done in leaving her behind.

* * *

From Fidelis Emuwa's personal multimedia record, October 17, 2011 (submitted as evidence in Bexar County Court, September 14, 2012):

> Can you imagine? It's already over. They're already moving on. Tomorrow *Argos I* lifts off, returns to Earth, and everyone on it commits to being forgotten. And I'm not such a drama queen that that's the most important thing. We commit to forgetting, too, or to becoming the kind of person who does nothing but remember. That's the hell we've made for ourselves, Fidelis. For the rest of our lives, we'll either be answering questions about this mission or wishing people would ask. When they stop asking, we'll get louder, and then what happens?
>
> No. Not me. Barbarella has left the building, Fidelis. I'm just Jami, and I'm just staying here. Nothing for me to go back to.

They made the ERV rendezvous without a hitch, and had already done the first acceleration burn when the commlink pinged with the Gates security code.

"What in the living fuck did you just do?" screamed Roland Threlkeld when David opened the connection.

David had to stifle a grin, imagining Rol boiling over while the rendezvous vehicle was incommunicado, and then while the ERV came out of Mars's communication shadow. It was a wonder he hadn't stroked out.

Are you laughing? he asked himself. You left a crewmember behind on Mars. How can you laugh?

The smile wouldn't go away.

Another burst from Roland: "Are you out of your fucking mind!? Jesus Christ on a goddamn Popsicle stick, you fucking left Jami fucking Salter on fucking *Mars!!?*"

The connection went dead.

"What are you going to tell him?" Deborah asked.

David thought about it. "Nothing until we've tweaked the accel burn and set the rotation. Once that's all settled, I'll figure something out."

Thirty-five minutes later, another profane tirade from Roland crackled out of the monitor. Thirty-five minutes after that, another. And another. Eventually, when they had the ERV moving like it was supposed to and rotating to give them Martian gee, David called everyone together. "Now we've done it," he said. "So we have to defend it. We can't lie, and we can't just say that we did what Jami wanted. We have to convince people that it was the only thing we could do. So. I'm listening."

"We're all going to go to jail," Katherine said.

"I don't think so," countered Edgar. "If we argue that she was a danger to the mission, then all we were doing was saving ourselves."

"Do you believe that?" Fidelis asked.

Edgar lifted his chin. "Yes, I do."

"I think we endangered the mission by leaving her," Katherine said. "And not just our mission; have any of you thought about what this is going to do to the possibility of other Mars missions? What kind of harm have we done here?"

"None," David said. "Mars is bigger than us; people latched onto our faces, but the guys who put up the money are figuring that the consumerate will do the same for any group of Marsnauts. If nothing else, we've proved that sending six people hundreds of millions of miles to a hostile planet is like a license to print money. We won't be the last."

The commlink pinged. "That'll be Roland again," said Fidelis.

"Guess I should start putting together some kind of response. Unless one of you wants to do it?" They all just looked at him. Deborah and Fidelis at least had the grace to grin. "I didn't think so."

Roland Threlkeld's message started to unspool. All of them

started to laugh. Even Edgar, who hated profanity, couldn't help but chuckle.

"One thing more," David said. "And this is not funny. Nobody in this crew is going to duck what we've done. We all stand up and we admit it, we take the heat for it. No excuses. We did what we did."

"Fair," Edgar said. "No hiding. We did this. We stand by it."

Article from the *Houston Chronicle,* August 18, 2012:

Charges Against *Argos I* Crew Dismissed

Bexar County District Judge Fulgencio Salazar has thrown out charges against David Fontenot in the marooning of Jami Salter on Mars.

Citing the prosecution's inability to produce any evidence either that Salter would in fact be harmed by remaining on Mars or that the crew had conspired against Salter's well-being, Judge Salazar dismissed felony charges against Fontenot and left little doubt that conspiracy and accessory charges against Fidelis Emuwa, Deborah Green, Edgar Villareal, and Katherine Yi would be dismissed as well.

"I have as yet seen no persuasive evidence that a crime was committed by any of those charged," Judge Salazar said in the courtroom this morning, as Salter family members sat shocked and relatives and supporters of the other crew members exchanged broad smiles.

Outside the courtroom, Salter family attorney Michelle Braunschweig said that the family would consider its options. Attorneys for Emuwa, Green, Villareal, and Yi refused comment. David Fontenot's attorney, Britt Kirschner, told reporters that he considered his client's actions completely vindicated. "No one who was not on Mars with David Fontenot and the crew of *Argos I* should be sitting in judgment of what they did there. None of us has ever experienced anything like what they have. I have total confidence that David acted in the crew's best interests, the mission's best interests, and Jami Salter's best interests."

Kirschner, as he has done throughout the case, laid the blame for the situation on the voracious celebrity culture fostered by the commercial newsnets. "It is my fervent hope, and David's," he said, "that future Mars crews and colonists will not be turned into grist for the celebrity mill."

Planned future Mars missions at this time include hydrological surveys sponsored by Merck, JohnsonCo, and Werner GmbH. Each of these missions has been asked to determine the whereabouts and health of Jami Salter. A planned rescue/forensic-investigation mission financed by Gates appears to be on hold for now.

Eileen Aufdemberge looked at her sister Deb. Looked hard. They hadn't seen much of each other since Deb had returned from Mars, and today, out in the backyard where three years ago she'd tried to see *Argos I* when it was on the other side of the world, Eileen wanted to try to get to know her sister again.

Jared came out of the house. He'd slouched his way into adolescence since the last time Deb had visited. The ten-year-old who knew everything about his Aunt Deb had given way to a thirteen-year-old who pretended not to care. Now he walked up to Deb and presented her with a bottle. MARTIAN HAIR, it said.

"They say it's got Martian chemicals in it, that it'll bleach your hair but not dry it out. Girls at school can't get enough of it."

"Are you serious?" Deb said. Eileen watched her turn the bottle and read its ingredients. She handed it back to Jared. "Tell them that peroxides are peroxides. If this stuff bleaches without drying, it's got nothing to do with Mars."

"Thanks, Aunt Deb," Jared said. He flipped the bottle up in the air and caught it behind his back. "You just made me ten bucks."

The screen door slid shut behind him. Eileen sat on the deck behind the house outside Knoxville she'd bought with Derek and kept when Derek left her for the woman who sold him his new car.

She'd kept Jared too, but was happy to see the car go; it was one of those low-slung ostentatiously sporty models that Deb had always called "penis extenders."

Labor Day was the next Monday, and Deb had taken a long weekend away from her round of conferences and public appearances to lie on the grass in her sister's back yard and catch up on the previous three—almost four now, counting all the pre-launch buildup—years.

Where to start?

"So tell me all about it," she said.

"All about what?" Deb said, and they both smiled. Deb laced her fingers behind her head and looked up into the bright blue Tennessee sky. "I'm not sure I know how to talk about it yet," she said.

"Seems like that's all you do."

"I'm not sure I'm doing it right, though, really getting at it the way it was." Deb turned her head toward Eileen, who was sitting on the deck stairs with a glass of iced tea. "I wonder if Erik the Red had this problem.

"People made bets on whether we'd survive. People I didn't know got on international media outlets and said they'd had sex with me. I'm the first human being to discover life somewhere other than Earth, and when we piped the result back, everyone wanted to talk to Jami about it."

"What was that like? Discovering life, I mean." Eileen amended herself quickly, not wanting Deb to get into a Jami Salter rant. She still hadn't sorted out how she felt about the abandonment of Jami. The crew knew best, she supposed, but her sister had wanted to bring Jami back, and Eileen had always trusted Deb's judgment. Except once: Deb hadn't liked Derek Aufdemberge.

"It was, it was, it was," Deb said, rolling back to look up at the sky, "so mundane. Picking through rocks at the bottom of a giant rockslide, at the bottom of a canyon that makes the Grand Canyon look like a drainage ditch. Turn a rock over, hey look, there's some lichen. It's dead—obviously it lived in more-protected circumstances—but it's lichen. You want to know something interesting? I can't tell the story like that when someone asks in public. I have this urge to embellish, or I'm afraid they won't be interested. I discovered life on Mars, and I'm afraid people will be bored because I'm not Jami Salter telling them. Jesus!"

Neither of them spoke for a while. Music started up in Jared's room.

"What about Jami, Deb?"

"What about her?"

"You know what I mean."

Another pause.

"I have a little secret about that, too," Deb said eventually. "As much as I got sick of everyone loving her and everyone wanting to talk to her and everyone ignoring me because I wasn't her, I have to admit that she took the heat for all of us. People wanted a mission babe, and they decided—for obvious reasons—that it was going to be Jami, and she hated it. But she did it."

"Did she want to stay on Mars, do you think?"

"Yeah, I think she did. I still don't think we should have let her, but, as usual, the men got their way."

This had been pointed out repeatedly in the media, with a variety of spins. Eileen wondered how to pursue it. "Didn't they like her? Were they afraid of her?"

Deb was shaking her head. "None of that. I think everyone there voted exactly what they thought was best. But still, all the men voted to leave her."

The music in Jared's room changed to an amped-up version of a song Eileen vaguely remembered from her own adolescence.

"It's still not fair," Deb said. "It's still not fair that they recognized her so much more than the rest of us. Sometimes I still think she stayed behind as one last gesture, so she had the last trump card over the rest of us. We'll never measure up to that. How can we?"

Eileen got up and went to lie in the grass next to her sister. "Who wants to measure up? What's to measure up to? You discovered life and water on Mars. She cracked up and couldn't go home. You want to measure up to *that?*"

Deb was shaking her head, but she reached over to clasp Eileen's hand. "Not that simple. She didn't just crack, she was broken. I don't think anybody could have just sailed through what happened to her."

"You just said that you went through the same kind of thing."

"Not the same."

"Yes, it is the same," Eileen insisted. "People seized on what was obvious about you, and they blew it up into something monstrous. They did the same thing with her. And with the rest of you, except David."

"David doesn't make much of an impression," Deb said. "A good guy, a smart guy, but not exactly memorable. Edgar asked me to marry him."

"What? Oh my God!"

"I know. I'm terrified."

"What are you going to do?"

Deb was shaking her head. Eileen saw how much gray Mars had threaded into her hair. "Pick the petals off a daisy. Get my palm read. Consult a Magic 8-Ball. I don't know. God, I want to, Eileen. I think about him every second of the day, I want him next to me. If not closer." She grinned at Eileen. "He sure is fine between the sheets."

Eileen's first instinct was to say Derek wasn't bad, either, but she bit it back. This was no time to mention Derek. So instead she said, "Do you think you can get along when you're not in the sack?"

"That's the thing," Deborah said. Now she looked sad and tired. "He voted to leave Jami. That's the thing."

Hearing before the Senate Subcommittee on Space and Colonization, September 7, 2012:

Senator Joshua Lindvahl: Jami Salter had everything to come back for. She was famous, she was going to be rich, she had made a professional name for herself in her field. She was a hero to the people of Minnesota, whom I am privileged to represent, and to the country, and to the world. Why in God's name, Dr. Emuwa, would she just decide not to come back?

Fidelis Emuwa: Because seventy-three million people placed a bet with HotVegas on whether or not she would be killed in a fit of sexual jealousy.

The talk at Boston University had gone well, Fidelis thought, and it was good to be back in Massachusetts. He'd spoken all over the country, and in Switzerland and Italy and Japan, about the psychological stresses of deep-space missions. Everywhere people responded to his low-key authority, and in optimistic moments he felt that he might be doing his small part to effect some kind of change. There would be no avoiding commercial sponsorship of space exploration; given that, he felt it critical that the astronauts were protected better than the *Argos I* crew had been. He had his critics, but with Katherine saying much the same thing—in her more confrontational way—Fidelis was guardedly sure that future crews would not be quite the commodities that he and Jami and the rest of them had become.

He was standing in front of the business school watching the traffic on Commonwealth Avenue. Earth gravity still felt heavy in the muscles of his thighs. Maybe he would walk down Comm Ave., pick up a book and a burrito in Kenmore Square, walk the bridge over the Mass Pike to Fenway Park. The Sox, as usual, were out of it, but this looked to be Nomar Garciaparra's last year at short, and Fidelis wanted to see him play there one more time.

"Excuse me, Dr. Emuwa?"

Fidelis looked at the young man who had spoken, his dealing-with-the-public smile already falling into place. "Yes?"

"I'm Brad Reynolds, Dr. Emuwa. I'm a student here, and I wanted to tell you that I'm sorry."

"Sorry for what?" Fidelis looked more closely at this Brad Reynolds. An unexceptional young man. Spots of red in his cheeks, a fraternity ring his only jewelry. He had the khaki-and-razor-cut look that business students had chosen since World War II.

"I bet four hundred bucks that you'd be killed during the mission." Brad Reynolds looked down, then back up into Fidelis's face. Gathering his courage, Fidelis thought. "I thought you'd all get into some kind of fight over Jami Salter, and I figured David and Edgar were tougher than you."

"You were right about that," Fidelis said.

"I shouldn't have done it," Reynolds went on. "It was a joke, you know, the whole thing." Reynolds squinted at Fidelis. "None of you were real."

"That's right," Fidelis said. "None of us were."

The wedding of Deborah Green and Edgar Villareal took place on September 24, 2012, in the Garden of the Gods outside Colorado Springs. It was attended by forty-seven people and half a dozen hovering video drones sent by the more gossipy newsnets. The bride wore white. Her veil was beaded with pearls. The groom wore a morning suit, and was proud of having tied his cravat himself.

They had written their own vows, and the ceremony was quick. The only commotion occurred when Edgar's cousin Gerardo "accidentally" scattered the news drones by blasting through them in an old F-4 borrowed from the Air Force Academy, where both Edgar and Deborah had graduated too many years before. Afterward the newlyweds presided over their reception at the Broadmoor Hotel before hopping into Edgar's restored 1959 Bel Air and heading off on a driving honeymoon through the Rocky Mountain West.

No members of the *Argos I* crew were invited.

* * *

Hearing before the Senate Subcommittee on Space and Colonization, January 14, 2013:

David Fontenot: We found seventeen species of extraterrestrial life. We found enough water to ensure that colonization of Mars could be beneficial and productive in the long term. But mostly people were interested in a faked pornographic video of our engineer and backup pilot, and I think Jami couldn't come back to that. I think it got the better of her, and I think the only reason the rest of us survived is because she took the pressure of all that voyeurism onto herself.

That's all I have to say, Senators.

Permissions

About the Editor

Gordon Van Gelder published his first short story while in high school and says his writing career went downhill from there. He worked as an editor for St. Martin's Press for more than twelve years, during which time he helped publish such writers as George P. Pelecanos, Kate Wilhelm, Christopher Priest, and William Browning Spencer. In 1996 he became the eighth person to edit *The Magazine of Fantasy & Science Fiction* over its fifty-plus–year history. In 2000 he left St. Martin's Press in order to become the magazine's publisher. He lives in Hoboken, New Jersey, with his wife, Barbara.